THE ACCIDENT

THE ACCIDENT

Hans Heinrich Ziemann

ST. MARTIN'S PRESS • NEW YORK

Library of Congress Cataloging in Publication Data

Ziemann, Hans Heinrich, 1944–
  The accident.

  Revised translation of Die Explosion.
  I. Title.
PZ4.Z666Ac 1979   [PT2688.I367]   833'.9'14   78-19387
ISBN 0-312-00219-X

Like the lemming, man too sees only the other side of the river. He is not suicidal by nature. But is he wise enough to turn back?

Gordon Rattray Taylor

PART ONE

A single major accident in an atomic reactor could cause extraordinary damage, not because of the explosive force, but because of the radioactive contamination. Until today we have been very fortunate in this respect. But with the spread of industrialization, with the growing number of fools who tinker around with things they cannot control, sooner or later some fool will prove to be stronger than a foolproof system.

> Edward Teller
> Co-constructor of the
> atom bomb

The night was hot. The lights of villas set back from the road shimmered through the trees. A sonata wafted out through an open terrace door. The bearded man, who was walking home, stopped and tried to decide whether it was late Mozart or early Beethoven. He couldn't make up his mind. This annoyed him. He was a technician, and unsolved problems caused him anxiety.

When the roar of a jet plane drowned out the sonata, the man started walking again. He looked up to where the navigation lights were moving across the starry plains. The first blow from the lead rod struck him in the neck. The man wanted to touch the pain with his right hand, but his arm was paralyzed. He wanted to turn around, but his left leg buckled under his weight. He sank to his knee. The second blow struck his cranium, and the man fell on his side. He whispered something incomprehensible. He could feel that his scalp was torn open. It was very painful. The man felt the blood on his neck, and he sensed that a hand was searching him. He saw a shadow bending over him.

The hand reached into his right hip pocket, pulled back, reached into the left pocket and tugged out the billfold. A small flashlight glowed. The man heard paper money crackling, then a curse. The billfold dropped to the ground.

The pencil-thin ray of the flashlight blinded the man. He had to concentrate all his energy just to shut his unfeeling eyelids. Then he passed out.

Seven minutes later, the man had enough strength to call for help. Eleven minutes later, he was found by a moving man, who came running out of his house, wearing a bathrobe and clutching a shotgun and a hurricane lamp.

1

Martin Born threw the brochure describing the biggest atomic reactor in the world into the wastepaper basket. He buzzed his secretary. She brought in a tray of mineral water and a bowl of ice cubes, which she deposited on his desk.

"Thanks, Kitty Katz," said Martin Born. "Did you read what the PR men turned us into?"

Gerlinde Katz smiled brightly. "I think it's terrific. I just don't like your photo. It makes you look gloomy. Not like you at all."

"Well," said Born, "as long as you like the brochure, it must be good. It makes us all look like supermen. Could we run through my appointments again?"

Gerlinde Katz had known Dr. Martin Born for ten years, and had worked with him for eight of those years, from the time he was fresh out of college and starting at the West German Electricity Company, West-Elektra. His career could be traced along her pay checks. Eight years ago, as secretary to junior executive Martin Born, she had been earning 1,700 marks. A year later, 1,900 marks—as secretary to Born, the assistant manager of the development department. Then 2,000, when Born became head of the department of reactor technology. And now, for three years, she had been secretary to the director of the nuclear power plant, Helios, and with all the bonuses and perquisites, she was earning over 3,000 marks a month.

Money could only confirm but not strengthen her loyalty to Born. She would have stayed with him for half her salary. Gerlinde Katz was forty-nine, thickset, robust. She had thin hair, and her tough face terrified people without appointments and even shook up members of the board. Her hands were powerful and the thick fingers sprang accurately over the typewriter keys. And she had an unflattering weakness for flowery silk dresses. Gerlinde Katz was attached to Martin Born with a silent love dimmed only by her regrets that she wasn't twenty years younger—and three grades more beautiful. Or at least six years older, so that she could have called Born her son.

She opened the appointment book.

"This afternoon you're free. Do you want to talk to Larsen? I didn't make any definite appointment."

Martin Born took a swig of ice water. He was annoyed about the air conditioning, which wasn't working. Some relay was out of order—in the largest atomic power producer in the world and on one of the hottest days of the decade.

He said, "I'll drop in on Larsen."

"At eight P.M. you've got that discussion with the citizens of Grenzheim at the Black Eagle restaurant.

Born groaned.

"You did promise," asserted Gerlinde Katz. "It *is* the last time, you know. After the opening day ceremonies, everyone will calm down."

"Hopefully," said Born. "I'm fed up with all these discussions. They're interminable."

"Okay then. Eight P.M.: discussion," his secretary repeated. "And now about the dedication tomorrow, Friday, July 31. Ten A.M.: meeting with the Governor's PR officer. Eleven A.M.: arrival of the Governor, research minister, and other invited guests—foreign delegates, state parliament members, and federal parliament members, scientists, industrialists, and so forth. The opening address and the first toast will last until 11:30. Next come the speeches, and then at 12:30, a guided tour of the plant."

"If it's this hot tomorrow," said Born, "I think I'll call in sick."

"Nothing doing," commanded Katz. "You are needed. At

around one P.M., the Governor will switch on the plant to full capacity. 1:30 P.M.: press conference and cold buffet lunch. 2:30 P.M.: the guests leave. That's it."

Born stretched and pulled at his shirt, which was sticking to his back. "I wish you could take my place, Kitty Katz. I hate this whole bedlam."

"You can't avoid it, said Gerlinde Katz soberly. "You're an important man, Herr Doktor."

At home, she had a file containing every newspaper article that had appeared during the last three years about Helios— and its director.

The telephone jingled. The secretary picked up the receiver. She put her hand over the mouthpiece. "It's for you. He doesn't want to give his name. I think it's that same. . . ."

Born took the receiver. "Hello," said an adolescent voice. "Are you the director?"

"Yes," said Born.

"The director of Helios?"

"Speaking."

The resonance of a phone booth. Muted engine noises. Not much traffic. Born jotted down on a slip of paper: "Police. Phone booths at Grenzheim-Garding." His secretary nodded and hurried out of the office.

"I have something important to tell you," said the child-like voice.

"Please, not another bomb," said Born. "Why don't you cut the bullshit. If the police get you, you'll end up in the jug."

"No tricks! Don't try to gain time. You won't get us."

Born smiled, though he was raging. "Okay. What's up?"

"My brother and I hid a bomb in your plant. You'd better get out of the place right away." The boy tried to make his high voice sound like an adult's.

"Fine," said Born. "Where's the bomb?"

"That's for me to know and you to find out," said the boy. "But I'll give you a hint. It's near the chimney. Watch out. The fuse is sharp."

The boy hung up. Born went out into the front office, where Gerlinde Katz handed him the receiver. The policeman on the line said, "He didn't talk long enough for us to trace it. But we sent out four cars. Maybe they'll get him. I'll call you again."

"Get me Larsen on the phone," said Born to his secretary.

Twenty minutes later, the head of the surveillance department rang.

"Have four men search the area around the exhaust chimney," said Born. "We have another bomb threat."

Larsen snuffed. "I need those guys to load the waste. The bomb's another hoax, isn't it?"

"Four men," said Born. "On the double. I want to know the result in half an hour."

"Okay," grunted Larsen. "If that's the way it's gotta be."

Born banged down the receiver. Gerlinde Katz gave him a worried look. "The usual?" she asked.

"The usual bomb," said Born. "The third one. And the usual Larsen."

2

The man on the hill lowered his binoculars. It was 4:30 P.M.; the sun in the southwest was still fairly high. His head was surrounded by a swarm of buzzing mosquitoes, apparently not bothered by the cigarette smoke. The man was young, twenty-five, tall and slender. He wore sneakers, blue jeans, a T-shirt, and an expensive leather jacket that chafed at the seams. His face was narrow, bony, and drops of sweat glittered in his beard. He took soft steps to the bench under the fir trees. There, he opened a dark leather attaché case and unwrapped two porkchops out of silver foil. He unscrewed a jar and, using his forefinger, spread mustard over the chops. He ate up the meat, chewing it thoroughly. He washed it down with lemon-flavored tea from a thermos bottle. He lit a cigarette. He unfolded an 8½-by-11 inch sheet of paper covered with dense writing. He reread what he already knew by heart:

10:00 P.M.: Marcks gets off work
10:15: Marcks leaves
10:25: Meeting place

The man folded the sheet. He still had a lot of time. He lifted the binoculars. What he saw wasn't good for tourist advertising: Along the western bank of the Rhine, where the man was standing, there were rocky vineyards, more gray than green even now in the middle of summer. The eastern bank was flat, covered with brownish-green soil and strewn with a few rye fields. A couple of factories were smoking. To the right of the hill, there were three piers of a defunct railway bridge. The damp layer of moss and mold on the pedestals could be clearly made out—a sign that there wasn't much water in the Rhine.

The Helios plant flickered directly across. The man hated it. He was happy that it was worthy of his hatred: beautiful, perfect, inviolable. He could watch it for hours, like a woman too beautiful to be desired.

The giant dome, the center of the plant, loomed out of the plain like a cream-colored egg. The egg shone in the sunlight, but to the man it seemed to be glowing from within, heated by the enormous fire at its core. The exhaust chimney, slender and narrowing towards the top, looked as if it were being driven by the dome right into the sky, trembling with energy. Without the two cooling towers to the right and the left, the plant would have been aesthetically perfect, a Taj Mahal of the atomic era. The cooling towers were gross, fat, and ugly, cylindrical monsters, over five hundred feet high, some hundred and fifty feet higher than Freiburg Cathedral, and very dirty. They were watch-towers, bulwarks, superdimensional bastions, planted in the landscape by a giant. They were a reminder that forces were brooding under the eggshell, forces that could annihilate everything within a radius of hundreds of miles. A reminder that the peace and perfection radiating from the power station were mere camouflage: the belly of Helios was filled with a burning atomic fire—though not yet at full strength. Tomorrow, when Helios would be officially opened and switched on to top capacity, the fire would blaze up brightly.

The man, still looking through his binoculars, followed a group of plant workers walking from the dome to an adjacent building. They wore yellow suits and yellow helmets. They paced across the terrain surrounding the exhaust chimney. They were bent over, and pulled along a white metal cube on rubber wheels.

"The radiation protection squad," murmured the man. He kept peering. After ten minutes, the yellow figures had vanished behind the low building adjacent to the chimney.

The man was nervous. He carefully studied every section of the plant grounds, but he didn't detect anything peculiar. Nobody was running, there were no other people on the plant roads. And when he lowered his binoculars and listened, he could hear only birds, mosquitoes, and the screeching of the power shovels in the gravel pits. No alarm sirens.

"A drill," thought the man. For an instant, he imagined he saw the figure of Werner Marcks, wearing a white smock. But he saw the blond shock of hair, and knew he was mistaken. "Keep calm," thought the man. "Keep calm." When he lit the next cigarette, his hand was trembling.

3

The moment he stepped out of the administration building, Born felt the heat like a punch. He shaded his eyes with his hand and walked through the heat waves between the concrete walls, towards the dome. In front of the huge entrance, under the four powerful pillars, stood three trucks with steel bodies. Overhead, a crane with a lifting capacity of five hundred tons, was moving along the cross girths of the pillars, one hundred and fifty feet above the ground. The sides of the trucks bore the barely visible symbol of radioactive danger—an airplane propellor with three blades and a hub in the middle. Underneath, in tiny red letters, were the words, "CAUTION. RADIOACTIVE MATERIAL."

Born shook his head. Probably only one percent of the population knew the meaning of this warning sign, and only people with eagle eyes could decipher the lettering. The sign and the script had missed their goal, namely to call the attention of laymen to the hazardous contents of the trucks, and to make them especially cautious in the event of an accident. But the people who earned their livings with atomic energy—the constructors of power stations, electricity plants, and transporting and processing businesses—they were only concerned with their good image. They were afraid that large warning signs and legends would arouse more fear than respect. They were probably right, thought Born.

The crane roped down a yellow steel drum—one of three dozen in which the radioactive waste had been stored during the last few weeks. The less radioactive waste. The waste coming straight out of the atomic oven—pipes, cables, screws, filters—had to lie in the isolation chamber of the plant for a few months, radiating off its deadly energy before it could be transported.

Workers in frog suits were stowing the drum in the trucks. Born greeted the man supervising the loading with a list in his hand. He was fat, and his head was sweating and dripping in the sun. "Shitty job," he said. "And no beer in the canteen."

Alcohol was prohibited throughout the Helios grounds.

Born pulled a 20-mark bill from his wallet and pinned it under the windshield wiper of the truck. "For the beer, when you've delivered the stuff," he said. "But only because of the dedication tomorrow. Don't get used to it. The foreman grinned and raised his hand. Then he started yelling because a drum had been badly placed.

Born passed through the two controls—I D card and identity verification by a TV camera. He rode up to the fourth level of the dome. He slipped into his white anti-radiation frog suit. Yellow denoted the more resistant uniform of the radiation squad. Next he took care of the measuring and registering formalities with the guard, went through the hydraulic lock (there was sub-atmospheric pressure inside the dome) and entered the hall where Peter Larsen oversaw the lugging and roping of the waste drums. When he heard Larsen's loud laughter, Born stopped behind a concrete pillar. His mouth became thin and his eyes darkened.

Peter Larsen, head of anti-radiation and plant safety, was standing in a light-colored summer suit, next to a waste drum, and he was laughing. The workers were laughing with him.

The scene reminded Born of photographs in Boy Scout books of the twenties. That was because of Peter Larsen, who created a Boy Scout atmosphere. He was the type who goes on twelve-hour hikes with adolescent boys in *lederhosen* and then gathers them around a campfire to twang guitars, croon patriotic songs, and eat pea soup with sausage.

The workers weren't laughing because Larsen was their boss. They were laughing because Larsen knew how to make the situation look funny with a gesture and just a few words.

18

Larsen could make people enthusiastic—his personnel file described him as having "an excellent faculty for motivating his fellow workers"—probably because he was so enthusiastic himself. But: "Tends to become arrogant in regard to jobs that do not require his full abilities."

Larsen was short, about five foot-seven, with a delicate physique. Now that he was laughing, the most conspicuous feature in his long, bony face were his healthy, yellow teeth. Otherwise, his face was dominated by a birdlike nose, which was always slightly red around the nostrils, as though he had a permanent cold. The flaxen hair, thinning at the temples, was carefully parted and shaved over the ears, with just a hint of sideburns. Larsen's mouth looked crooked, for immediately next to the right corner of the lips, slanted a deep, white scar. In his student days, Larsen had belonged to a dueling fraternity —the same one, Born knew, that counted among its alumni the president of the board of directors of West-Elektra.

Born now saw what they were laughing about. A man was creeping along the floor in between the drums, looking for something. He called out to his colleagues: "Cut the bullshit! Give them back to me. Otherwise, I'm splitting."

More laughter, then Larsen's metallically clear voice: "You'd better get hosed down right away, Massmann. You may be radiating like three pounds of radium. You never can tell."

The workers howled. Massmann stood up. He was the only one in the group who was dressed according to the regulations for working in a room with a high radiation danger. His white, radiation-proof suit was zipped up to his throat, his feet encased in white overshoes, his head covered with a hood. Only the gloves were missing.

Because of the heat, the other workers had their suit zippers open down to their hips, and most of them were wearing street shoes. Two of them, like Larsen, had even taken off their frog suits and rolled up their sleeves.

"Oh, Massmann," said Larsen, "you're really something. Do you think the gloves could help you if something ever did happen? All you could do then is pray, and for that you ought to take your gloves off."

"It's the regulation," said Massmann, short, fat, and red with embarrassment, anger, and heat.

"Oh, all right," sighed Larsen, pretending to be struck to the quick, "you win. The show's over. Give him back his gloves so we can finish up."

Two workers each pulled one glove from his trouser pockets and threw them to Massmann. The short fat man pulled them on.

Born walked over to the group. The workers, who were rolling the crane cables around one of the drums, froze. Larsen smiled and took a step towards Born. "Hi there, Herr Doktor Born. We'll be done right away. Then I'll be at your disposal."

Born did not smile. He said, "I would like you to make a list of all the men in this room who are ignoring the regulations for radiation protection. I expect to find your name on the list, too."

Larsen's eyebrows shot up. His eyes were reddish, with light blue irises. He caught himself quickly. "I think my name is enough," said Larsen. "Any sin against the thousand commandments I'll take on my shoulders."

The irony in his voice was unmistakable. The workers waited nervously for Born's mood to change. It didn't. "I want all the names," said Born. "And any man not dressed according to regulations within two minutes will be fired today." The workers reluctantly complied. The voice of the crane driver roared from the loudspeaker: "Hey, you jerk-offs, are you asleep?"

Born called, "One second, please."

Then he said to the fat man with the gloves, "I have to talk to Mr. Larsen for a moment. Can you take over?" The fat man nodded. Born asked, "When's your next shift?" The fat man said, "Monday. I'm off tomorrow and the weekend."

"Call me on Monday when you have a break," said Born. Born took Larsen to the opposite end of the hall. Larsen said, "I don't understand why you're taking the matter so seriously, Herr Doktor Born. The men aren't deliberately ignoring the regulations. It's just awfully hot, and it won't kill anyone to forget about the uniform occasionally. You know the radiation in this room is practically zero."

Born looked at Larsen, shaking his head. "I don't understand *you*, Larsen. I don't understand why you don't take your duties seriously. The suits are required by regulations no matter what the temperature. They're not meant to harass, they're to protect the health of the workers. And *you* are paid to hammer that into their heads and make them see that the protective regulations are a matter of life and death. You know what happens when a drum leaks!"

Larsen ran his hand through his hair. "I've never seen that happen. The probability is. . . ."

"I *have* seen it happen. Your probability computations might be interesting for a term paper. But they're worthless here. How long have you been head of safety?"

"Eleven months."

"That's really long enough," said Born, "for you to grasp the importance of your position. You are responsible for the lives and health of two hundred people, Larsen. You cannot forget that for even an instant."

"I know. But in my opinion. . . ."

"As head of safety, you are not entitled to opinions. It makes no difference whether *you* personally consider the regulations overly stringent. You have to abide by every single paragraph like an article of faith. If that goes against your grain, then you're in the wrong job."

"Yessir," said Larsen.

Born was groping for a nasty concluding remark, but a man from the anti-radiation squad came up with a cigar box and handed it to Born. "This thing was lying near the exhaust chimney, Herr Doktor, right by the auxiliary works building. You can open it. It's a very special kind of bomb."

Born opened the cigar box. Inside, there was a small

21

plastic rocket and underneath that a note in capital letters: NEXT TIME IT WILL BE REAL.

The writing was smudged, the box soggy.

"The thing's been out there a long time already," observed Born.

The anti-radiation man nodded. "At least four or five weeks, just like the tin can we found last week after the second phone call."

"A dumb prank," said Larsen. "I'd like to get my hands on those brats."

"If the Grenzheim police weren't so lazy, we'd have them by now," said Born. "They must have hidden the thing during some guided tour, and now they're playing the Easter bunny and want us to go hunting eggs. We ought to be glad the kids are harmless. At least till now."

As if by way of apology, Larsen said, "There are a lot more guards now during plant tours. It won't happen again."

The anti-radiation man vanished with the cigar box. A police car was waiting below to take it to the laboratory in Frankfurt.

"Are you on night shift today, Larsen?" asked Born.

"Yes."

"How many security men are detailed?"

"Eight."

"I think it would be good to have eight more."

"The normal number is enough," said Larsen.

"All the same, I'd feel better if there were extra men. Can you take care of it?"

"Okay," said Larsen. "Now I'll put on my frog suit. According to regulations."

Born looked after him and thought: "He'll never learn."

4

Date of birth: 10/22/1950
Place of Birth: Munich
Height: 5'7"
Hair: Blonde
Eyes: Green
Special marks: Appendectomy scar.
Profession: Teacher
Marital status: Divorced
Children: One daughter, Michaela, age 4.
Address: 5 Buchenweg, Grenzheim

A.W. was observed from 1/2/73 to 5/4/73. Reasons: Activity
in the Socialist German Student Alliance at the University of
Frankfurt. Founded the Women's Group (information on addresses of abortionists, loans for abortion fees). Took part in
Vietnam demonstrations (9/20/72) and sit-in (12/7/72).
    During the entire observation period, A.W. did not take
part in any political events. She apparently concentrated totally on finishing her degree. Left the S.G.S.A. on 4/1/73.
According to information from friends (verbal statements, see
subjoined): crisis because of deteriorating marriage with Jürgen Bachler. Bachler, member of Communist Party, known
to G.F.A.P.C., allegedly "motivated A.W. to political work."
According to a female friend: "She did it mainly because
of Jürgen." On 2/1/73, Bachler, with five adherents,

23

visited Cuba; returned 6/17/74. (See file on J.B.)

A.W. graduated with honors (see records subjoined). Teaching assistant at the Schönberg High School, Frankfurt. No apparent connections with radical groups.

Conclusion: Once a fellow traveler; no activity now.

Addendum: On 12/20/74, A.W. applied for the position of English and German teacher at the Grenzheim High School. Upon inquiry by the Ministry of Education, her employment was declared to be safe.

Addendum: In January of this year, A.W. joined the Civic Initiative against the Helios Atomic Power Station. In February, she was voted spokesman. Since then, increased activity for the Civic Initiative (archive material subjoined). On 3/4, illegal sit-in at the plant grounds. Ten ringleaders apprehended, including A.W. No arrest, no charges. Question: Should she be observed again?

Recommendation: No observation.

5

The three most active members of the "Civic Initiative of the Town and Community of Grenzheim against the Helios Atomic Power Station" met at five P.M. in the physics room of the Grenzheim High School. The meeting place was unauthorized since the school administration had not granted permission. But it was comfortable. Two of the three Initiative people taught there—Anne Weiss, the spokeswoman, and her vice-spokesman, Achim Berger. The third member was Thomas Müller, auto mechanic and member of the German Communist Party, Maoist/Leninist group (GCP/ML).

The spokeswoman of the Civic Initiative read the leaflet for the third time, hissing furiously every so often. Achim

24

Berger leafed in his manila file and played with his reddish moustache. Müller's athletic figure was sprawled over two chairs, and he was grinning. He grinned a bit more every time Anne Weiss hissed.

Anne Weiss looked up. "Tommy, this is a filthy trick. We decided collectively on a text. Now all that's left of it is one paragraph, and you've changed even that."

"The first text was unclear, timid, and cowardly," said Thomas Müller. "Liberal crap. I summed it up very neatly. What's wrong with that?"

"Just get a load of this," said Anne Weiss to Berger. " 'The murderous atomic plant, Helios, the greatest civil annihilation machine in the world is a product of the laws inherent in the late capitalist system. Multinational concerns and an imperialistic government clique have collaborated . . .' and so on and so on. It's terrible. Ninety percent of the people we represent are vintners, farmers, craftsmen, and office workers. They won't understand a word of this nonsense."

"You cannot articulate the truth with sentences from a tabloid," said Müller.

"This says nothing," retorted Anne Weiss, waving the leaflet in the stifling air. "Absolutely nothing. It doesn't even explain how an atomic station operates, it doesn't explain why it's dangerous. All it says essentially is that if Mao becomes Federal Chancellor, then everything will be fine and dandy."

"That's overdoing it," said Müller, "but it's in the right direction. What about you, Achim, cat got your tongue?"

"I'm trying to figure out how to punch you without having you beat the shit out of me afterwards."

"You wanna try?"

"Stop it, both of you!" said Anne sharply. "You're in a schoolroom doesn't mean you have to act like kids."

The two men looked at her, Achim Berger with obvious affection, almost veneration, Thomas Müller, amused, with a match between his teeth and a Marlon Brando smirk on his lips. Anne Weiss stood before them in her teaching posture, one hand on her hip, the other holding the leaflet. Her jeans and thin sweater emphasized her height and her slender figure. Her arms were darkly tanned, slim, yet solid and muscular.

At first glance, her face seemed ordinary. At a second glance, it was striking. At a third glance, older men fiddled with their ties and drew in their bellies, while younger man began rapping smartly. Anne's face was not beautiful, but it was intense—a face that was never boring, whose expression was always changing. At this moment, Anne's face was full of scorn.

"You may think you're clever, Tommy, but it's really a filthy trick. You've turned our information leaflet into a propaganda pamphlet for your own party, and you've used our money to print it. I could scream when I think of how long it took us to scrape together the five hundred marks."

"C'mon, honey," said Thomas Müller, with a mollifying gesture, "get it all out."

Anne's eyes sparkled. She fought back her tears. "You've abused our trust, Thomas, and you've put us in an ugly situation with the other members. What are we going to tell the people who've contributed money for the leaflet?"

"They got good merchandise for their good money," said Thomas Müller.

"You're a bastard," said Anne Weiss. "You're no longer one of us. Get out of here."

"Oh, c'mon," protested Müller.

"Get the hell out of here," said Berger. "Anne's right. You're out. And we'll get the money back!"

Müller leaped up and punched. His fist glanced along Berger's chin and struck his shoulder. The force of the blow knocked Berger off his chair. He wordlessly groped about for his glasses. Müller was about to kick him. Anne stood at the door and said: "I've got my hand on the janitor's bell. If you don't get out of here, you'll be under arrest tomorrow. Someone who's already been convicted of a crime once won't get off so easily."

Müller gasped. He grabbed his briefcase and strode to the door. "You petty bourgeois assholes. Dirty pack of philistines. You'll hear from me! Especially you, Anne. My comrades are looking forward to getting you. The atomic rebel of Grenzheim! What a laugh! A middle-class broad with a big mouth. You belong on a piano stool. In a lace dress."

He slammed the door behind him.

Berger warded off Anne's attempt to help him to his feet. "What are we going to do now?" he asked.

"He's going to show up with his friends tonight and hand out the leaflets," said Anne. "We can't let them do it."

"They're the worst gorillas between here and Frankfurt. What can you do to stop them?"

"I've got an idea. But I don't think you can help me. Thomas is going to get the surprise of his life."

"Police?"

Anne smiled. "Something better. Just wait and see. Now the question is: How do we get the discussion going tonight?"

"The stupid thing is," said Berger, "that it's their evening. Helios invited *us,* we're the guests. They're going to play the old question-and-answer game—one second for a question, one hour for an answer from the podium."

"But there will be television coverage, too," said Anne. "That'll weaken the position of the officials. In front of cameras, they won't have such an easy time muzzling suggestions made by the majority of citizens in the hall."

"What suggestions?"

"How about, on behalf of the Civic Initiative, I ask to read a few resolutions prior to the discussion. By the third resolution, they'll be getting very fidgety up there. After that, we'll move that a limit be set to any speaker. Three minutes. Exceptions to be voted on."

"I can't think of anything better myself. Who asks questions during the discussions? Do you have a list?"

Anne shook her head. "That's useless. There'll be lots of people that we've never seen at a meeting. We can't organize them. Naturally, we have to try to get the floor as often as possible. We're better informed than anyone else, so it won't be too difficult. We have to make sure we don't become too aggressive. We can't take anything personally. We're speaking for the citizens of Grenzheim. We have to talk and act in such a way that the citizens can identify with us and our arguments."

Berger nodded. "Is there anyone on the podium we can focus on? Rapp's a good target, isn't he?"

Anne smiled. "Of course. The mayor isn't too popular nowadays. You absolutely have to repeat the story about how he fooled Grenzheim seven years ago with the approval to construct the atomic plant."

"Right. And the others?"

Anne studied her notebook. "The Minister of Economy, Hühnle. He's a tough nut. We can't shoot at him. The best thing would be not to ask him any questions, so that he won't talk too much. As for those two experts, those scientists—no one's going to listen to them anyway. And then there's Born."

Berger said: "At the last meeting, three weeks ago, he did pretty well for himself. The people liked him."

Anne didn't say anything. She drew a rectangle around Born's name with her felt pen. Then she painted an arrow, its point touching the top of the rectangle.

"He's arrogant," she said. "But he knows how to sell himself, and he's up on his profession. We shouldn't get into any confrontation with him."

Berger leaned back in his chair. "In theory, it all looks very good. I hope it works in practice, too."

"We won't accomplish that much," said Anne. "Tomorrow they turn the plant on and officially open it. There's nothing more we can do. We can only show them that we're not giving up." She stood up. "That's all, I guess. The demonstration as scheduled, tomorrow morning at ten. I'll bring it up again at the meeting."

"May I see you home?"

Anne smiled. "The last time I was asked that question was in dance class. I think I can make it on my own." She saw his disappointment. "Don't take it so hard, Achim. Or rather, if you prefer, don't make it so hard on me."

"Still no hope?"

"No hope. You're such a tragedian."

She waved and left. Achim Berger studied the formula on the blackboard. Three parts nitric acid, one part hydrochloric acid. That was the formula for aqua regia—the only solution that can dissolve gold.

6

Inspector Kramer (Federal Criminal Agency, Department T4, investigation of terrorism) was dissatisfied. He brooded over the three xeroxed pages on his desk. They listed sixteen names and addresses. Kramer had jotted a tiny checkmark in front of each number. It was missing only in front of number 7.

The telephone rang. Kramer let it sound three times, then he lifted the receiver, exchanged greetings, and said: "We've located all the people who might take part in a plot. Three are under arrest; they've been awaiting trial for months already. Four are in prison, none for less than two years. The rest are being watched. There's only one we don't have. . . . No, I don't think he's dangerous. A loner. Doesn't belong to any gang. Ivory tower type. Three years ago he planted a dummy bomb in a general's jeep, and so they kicked him out of the army. But he's had training in explosives. Two years ago he was stopped for speeding by a highway patrol. They found some fuses in his car. He said he had taken them with him inadvertently. We couldn't prove the contrary, but we put him under loose surveillance. . . . Disappeared six months ago. Without a trace.

He's still registered at the university in Frankfurt, but he hasn't been to classes since last semester. I'll try his father tonight. He's a surgeon in Hamburg, and he's coming back from a congress in America in two hours. . . . No, if he doesn't know anything, then the chances are slim. . . . Of course. I'll call if there's any news."

Kramer sipped the lukewarm orange juice. He was annoyed at his own annoyance. After all, he'd done a good job of tracking down 15 out of 16 potential bombers in just ten days. The list, naturally, was only pseudo-complete. The Federal Criminal Agency had data only on people who had been suspicious in the past. The list did not include the new lunatics who might this very minute be hitting on the idea of blowing up the atomic plant on dedication day.

But Kramer was a pedant. The missing checkmark for name number 7 bothered him. And he knew that the man he just had talked to, Commissioner Herlin was thinking the same way. Next year he would need Herlin's recommendation for his promotion, which was already long due.

He put a slip of paper with a Hamburg phone number next to his telephone and stood up. Although he had no appetite, he thought he ought to have a sausage on reserve. He might be getting home very late that night.

7

"Herr Marcks," Gerlinde Katz announced over the intercom.

"Ask him to come in," replied Born, "and fix him some coffee. A cup for me too, please."

They had come to terms about the coffee. Gerlinde Katz saw the job of making it as a distinction, not a menial task. Of course, they could have ordered coffee from the canteen. But anyone who had savored the hot black coffee brewed by Born's secretary never touched the watery, tea-colored liquid (30 pfennigs a cup) from the kitchen. Born did not have the choice: His secretary would have been insulted.

Werner Marcks, head of the maintenance department dropped wearily into an armchair. Born said, "You look like you just spent a month in the trenches."

Marcks groaned, "That's how I feel."

Marcks was the same age as Born. Normally, the most noticeable thing about him was his beard. For four days now, however, the beard had been outdone by a white bandage covering his head like a helmet. His eyes were bloodshot, and bags hung below his black horn-rimmed glasses. Marcks hadn't slept for twenty-four hours.

He gulped down the coffee. Born waited. "Erna's all right," Marcks said. "But we can't ask too much of her. Otherwise, she'll start dancing again."

Erna was not a woman. Erna was the 230-foot-long, three-part turbine of the power plant. Erna was capricious. She was causing trouble for the third time in three months. Whenever she approached her rated power (1,500 revolutions per minute), she would start vibrating beyond the tolerance limit.

"If you think we have to, we'll switch off the reactor," said Born.

Marcks pulled his smoking paraphernalia out of the side pocket of his white smock and filled his pipe.

"It's not necessary. She'll hold until the next fuel change."

Born was relieved. Switch off. That sounded so simple. But a reactor can't be flipped on and off like an electric bulb. Even if computers oversaw every move, there were still a dozen chances of making a mistake. Mistakes that weren't necessarily hazardous (these were prevented by the automatic protection system of the reactor), but that could wreck parts and prevent the reactor from running for days, even weeks. And every day the atomic pile didn't burn meant a waste of hundreds of thousands of marks. The nightmare of every atomic plant director was the Würgassen reactor, which had stood idle for a total of two years out of its first three of existence, creating a loss of two hundred million marks.

Helios, in contrast, had proved to be a downright wonder of technology. In the twelve months of the test run, during which a reactor is supposed to show its childhood diseases and get over them, Helios had broken down only three times and been out of commission for 174 hours and 24 minutes. Born knew that he owed this record not just to good luck and to the manufacturer, but also to Werner Marcks, who had spent sixteen hours a day at the plant since the reactor had started. He had watched over it as keenly and attentively as a mother over a teething child.

Born said, "I can't help thinking you've been waiting hand and foot on Erna just to impress the Governor."

Marcks belonged to the party that the Governor referred to as the "gravedigger of western civilization." Marcks smiled. "I was wondering whether I shouldn't prescribe total rest for Erna, and try that Bavarian trick. But I wouldn't want to lose you. You're a pretty decent boss."

Born laughed. A few years earlier, a Bavarian nuclear plant had broken down on the dedication day because of a defective valve. Scared of bad publicity, the management, freely emulating Prince Potemkin and his phony village fronts, had staged a magnificent show. Under the admiring eyes of ministers, state secretaries, industrialists, and newspaper men, the plant employees feigned full capacity, although not a gear was turning and the reactor was producing less current than a pocket battery. The operations staff played on the multicolored buttons like Artur Rubinstein on his Steinway, as they made the lights glow. The Governor had told the representatives of the press that he had felt an awesome shudder at the measureless forces of Nature. The lines, however, were dead.

The truth came out six months later when a dismissed employee wanted to get even. The newspapers made the most of it. The anti-nuclear plant people immediately launched a new campaign, and the Governor wrote nasty letters. A few weeks later, the director of the plant retired.

Marcks stood up. "I'm staying for another two or three hours in case Erna suffers a setback. I have to check once more to see how the people in the annular space are getting on with the emergency diesel."

"I thought everything was back in order?" asked Born, worried.

The four diesel units in the reactor dome, each attached to a generator, were the vital energy reserves of the power station. The complicated Helios machinery—pumps, condensers, filters, compressors—needed a great deal of electricity. When Helios was running and producing its own current, the supply was no problem. Two transformers siphoned off the power for Helios. But when the plant was not running, then the indispensable machines, like the cooling pumps, kept going. Helios used the power network of West-Elektra. But in case of an emergency, if, for example, the long-distance network stopped while Helios was not producing its own electricity, then the plant needed an independent supply of its own. This was taken care of by four emergency diesels, which were tested every two weeks to see if they were working. When tested the day before, one diesel had been on strike.

"It ran for ten minutes," said Marcks. "I think it's a faulty piston rod. We probably won't get replacement parts before tomorrow. But in a pinch, the other three diesels would be enough."

"I'd rather have all four functioning," said Born.

"They will be."

Marcks walked to the door.

"Stay at home tomorrow," said Born. "Get a good night's sleep. You can be glad you'll miss all the ruckus. I have a bad conscience about making you work since your injury."

33

Marcks felt the bandage on his head. "It's nothing. I don't even notice it any more."

"Have you heard anything from the police?"

"No. You can call me anytime tomorrow if you need me."

"I hope I won't," Born said.

8

The clanging of the church-tower clocks, striking seven, came from all sides. The sun floated big and rusty through the dirty mist over the skyline. The man on the hill trained his binoculars on the plant across the river. He readjusted the focus. For more than an hour now, the parking lot in front of the gates had been emptying, and windshields were sparkling on the light-gray asphalt ribbon as the cars drove to the entrance of Federal Highway 44—all of them much faster than the speed limit. At the crossing, most of them turned off towards Grenzheim and Darmstadt. Only a few turned right, towards Garding and Worms.

The man caught a dark-blue Mercedes. "Just look at that," he murmured, "the director in person." He followed the automobile until it vanished among the trees. He stowed the binoculars in his small leather attaché case and climbed down the hill between the fir trees, his left arm stretched out in front of him so that his face wouldn't run into a cobweb. A white BMW 1502, with a Frankfurt license plate, was parked among the bushes at the foot of the hill. The man put his case in the back seat and switched on the headlights. Then he steered the car cautiously around the potholes and sand furrows in the dirt track until he reached a red clinker road. He wanted to eat something in Worms.

9

Eberhard Hühnle, Minister of Economy, was on his way to the Black Eagle restaurant. He enjoyed the drive through his state. The Rhine, the vineyards, and the picturesque market squares of villages didn't interest him. He was on the lookout for new factories—ones that weren't over six years old, the time he had been in office. They passed a collection of light brown concrete blocks. A neon sign glimmered on the biggest one.

"That's Wilm," said Hühnle to his chauffeur. "That cost me a few sleepless nights. Did I have to talk! First I had to convince old Wilm that this was the ideal spot for his branch, and I only brought him round by agreeing to conditions that would cost me my neck if they ever came out. Investment facilities, guarantees, tax abatements, and more and more. But the local board was even worse. The moment I came to terms with Wilm, they started in on me. A chemical plant would pollute the air. It would hamper tourism. They hit upon something new every day. You know what I did? I got hold of the records from the tourist office and counted up. And do you know how many tourists had been to that nest the previous year?"

The minister didn't expect an answer from his chauffeur, and the chauffeur would never have dreamed of giving him one. For six years now he had been a mute audience for soliloquies, and Hühnle needed him in this role the way a tennis buff needs the stone wall on which he practices his routine strokes.

"Fifteen hundred. Fifteen hundred tourists spent the night there in one year! I calculated it all for those people. And I showed them the results. I was very generous, I even assumed that the tourists had eaten an average of three meals—very

35

unlikely considering the junk in that greasy spoon. All in all, the town got about one hundred thousand marks a year from their so-called tourism. That was just enough to pay the mayor and the teachers. Whereas the new factory branch would probably bring in four million marks in taxes annually. Four million against one hundred thousand! Well, of course, that convinced them. Now they're in seventh heaven."

They drove past other plants and factories, and Hühnle kept commenting—the shoe factory that wasn't doing so well, the gravel pit, the cement works, the brickyard, the steel-kettle and pharmaceutical manufacturers. Once all of them had been nothing but a piece of paper on Hühnle's desk. Now they stood there in the countryside, providing work for the people and money to previously poor towns for building schools, hospitals, and roads. Hühnle took personal credit for everything—the results of energy, tenacity, and pragmatism. Hardly a soul doubted it—the opposition didn't, and certainly not the population.

Minister Hühnle was the most popular politician in the state. Ninety-two percent of the people knew who he was, and in the last state elections, he'd captured 68 percent of the actual vote—against the leader of the opposition.

Hühnle owed his popularity not just to his accomplishments; he realized that better than anyone. He knew of enough able men who would never get anywhere in politics because they simply couldn't make it with people.

Hühnle was convinced that his success was due to his presenting himself as what he was: A farmer's son who had managed to get through high school and work his way up in his shirtsleeves. A man for whom talking was a waste of time and whose favorite phrase was "tackle it!"

Now they were driving along the Rhine. To the left lay miles of fields and meadows. Hühnle leaned back in the cushions. Despite the air conditioner, despite the antiglare effect of the tinted windows, through which the landscape seemed twilit, his shirt stuck to his body. Hühnle was thirty pounds overweight. The excess weight didn't show as padding on the belly or neck. It was spread over the entire body and made the muscles even more massive, the legs even more powerful. Hühnle had been a trained construction worker. He looked like a well-fed bull, and his round skull, with its stubbly hair, and his jutting, blue-black chin, didn't help to soften the impression.

Women liked him.

He asked his chauffeur, "How far still?"

"Half an hour."

Hühnle dug around in his crumpled case, which was more like a shopping bag than a minister's briefcase. He glanced through some facts and data on Helios, which his personal consultant had put together.

Two minutes later Hühnle closed his eyes. His healthy snore joined the purring of the engine.

10

Sibylle's car wasn't there. Born parked the Mercedes in the driveway. He ambled through the garden. The lawn needed mowing. He'd take care of it over the weekend. Born placed the two sprinklers by the rose beds and rhododendron bushes and turned on the water. The blossoms and the ground became more fragrant.

Born entered the house through the basement. It was empty and still. He walked through the two large living rooms into the kitchen. The refrigerator contained a little milk, which he drank up, and two slices of salami, which he put on crackers and quickly ate after glancing at his watch. He went up the stairs, took off his jacket, and unbuckled his belt.

Dresses, slacks, blouses, stockings, hairpins, shoes, and kerchiefs were scattered over the bedroom. Born threw his shirt, underwear, and socks into the hamper, placed his suit on a hanger, and stepped into the shower. Born didn't care for cold-water shocks. He started with hot water, gradually toned it down to warm, and then let ice-cold water splash over his body for the last fifteen seconds only. As soon as he turned off the shower, he noticed there was only a hand towel in the bathroom. Cursing, he rubbed off a good deal of the wetness, scurried to the bedroom on tiptoe, and wrapped a bath towel around himself. His foot caught in a pair of sky blue silk panties.

The room vibrated with the sound of an Alfa Romeo engine. Then a triple-tone horn beeped through.

"Martin?" called Sibylle from the front door. He didn't answer. His wife came up the stairs humming. She stopped when she saw him.

Sibylle was dressed in a tennis outfit—a short skirt and snug blouse, which revealed two inches of her brown abdomen and slid up to her breasts when she served a ball. Her dark hair was tied with a red ribbon and fell to her shoulders.

She was in her typical posture: the right leg slightly in front of the left and her hand touching the hair at the back of her neck. Her small face—high cheekbones, full lips—was radiant. Her eyes looked past Born into the gold-framed baroque mirror on the wall behind him.

"Darling! If I'd known you were coming home, I'd have gone shopping or told the maid to make you some sandwiches."

Sibylle pronounced "sandwiches" as though conversing with an Englishman who set great store by an Oxford accent.

"Was your meeting cancelled?"

"No," said Born. "I have to leave right away."

"Too bad." Sibylle made a sad face. "It would be nice if we could have an evening to ourselves again."

Born rubbed his hair dry. He eyed Sibylle and then said resolutely, "Okay, I'll stay. They can get along without me."

Sibylle was unable to hide her disappointment. "I'm delighted you're staying, but won't there be important people there . . . ?"

"Forget it," said Born. "I was kidding."

He took a blue silk shirt from the closet.

"You're still built like a twenty-year-old. But an attractive man at home is not the same thing as an attractive man in bed."

She pulled off her tennis blouse while Born tried to manipulate his cufflinks. Her breasts were full, solid, almost too heavy for her delicate frame, and as brown as her whole body.

"You know what it's been like these past few weeks," said Born. That was an understatement; he really meant months. "There's nothing we can reproach one another for. Sometimes I'm too tired, sometimes you are. Sometimes both of us."

Born slipped on the trousers of his navy blue suit. Sibylle undid her skirt and let it drop to the floor. All she had on now were white socks and sneakers. That made her seem very naked, fleshy, and sensuous. She stepped up to the mirror and switched on the two Tiffany wall lamps. She said: "I'm not too tired now."

"And I don't have the time."

Sibylle slipped out of her sneakers without untying the laces. Martin stood behind her, knotting his tie.

"How was tennis?"

"The usual."

"Did you play, or were you just playing around in athletic gear?"

"I was taking a lesson," said Sibylle, pouting and eyeing Born in the mirror.

"From that Yugoslav?"

"We were practicing. Lobs and half volleys."

Born combed his hair and donned the lightweight cotton jacket. Sibylle sat down on the bed and rolled her sweaty socks off her feet.

"You look posh," she said. "You know, I first got interested in you because you reminded me of Cary Grant in *Notorious.*"

"Never saw it," said Born. "Can't you at least throw your socks in the hamper? I don't feel like sleeping in foot sweat, even if it's yours."

"Okay, okay," said Sibylle. "I'll clean up afterwards."

"Too much of a mess makes me nervous," said Born.

Sibylle said, "Do you know the joke about the lunatic with the ruler, who——"

"No. Tell it to me tomorrow."

"I always forget jokes so quickly," Sibylle stood up and kissed Born on the cheek. He kissed her on the forehead and asked: "Do you have a tissue?"

He wiped off the lipstick. "What are you doing tonight?"

"Don't know. Maybe I'll eat out. I really shouldn't, though, because of my diet. But if Brigitte calls up. . . . Maybe I'll even go to bed early. But first into the bath."

"I'll probably be home late," said Born at the door. "Don't wait up for me."

"Okay," said Sibylle. "Have fun."

Born hesitated. "If you don't have anything planned, why don't you come along?"

"But Martin! By the time I get dressed! And my hair's a catastrophe. Besides, I don't understand anything about all those atomic things." Born left.

"Cheerio!" Sibylle called after him. She waited till she heard the engine of Born's Mercedes. She smiled mischievously because Born had to switch gears and put on the brakes several times to get around her Alfa. When it was quiet again, she reached for the telephone. She waited a minute, then hung up. She pushed the brass table with the small television set in front of the bathroom so that she could see the screen from the bath. She turned on the water. The room smelled of bath oil. The melody of a Pepsi commercial came out of the tube. Sibylle sang along with it.

11

The Black Eagle restaurant was in the center of Grenzheim, on Kilian Square, opposite the church and flanked by a savings bank on the left and a supermarket on the right. It was shaded by three linden trees, which had been slated for chopping down thirteen years earlier. But the citizens of Grenzheim had prevented it, driving out the forestry workers with dogs and tractors.

The restaurant was a former farmhouse. The renovators had masoned up and whitewashed the bricks around the old skeleton. The former barn was now a banquet hall, which could hold six hundred people.

The hall filled. The proprietor, his wife, and their two daughters served the first carafes of wine.

Anne Weiss and Achim Berger were standing out in the square, twenty yards from the door to the banquet hall. They were watching the crowds coming from Grenzheim and Garding, coming in response to the invitation for the discussion on the Helios atomic power station. There were many people Anne didn't know. But, as she contentedly noted, the members of the Civil Initiative were almost all present. They constantly greeted Anne Weiss or stopped to speak with her. At least most of the men did.

A Grenzheim shoemaker complained to Achim Berger about the F his son had gotten on his last French test. Berger assured him that his son was in no danger. A few parents brought their children, who were now playing hide-and-seek at the war memorial. It wasn't dark yet, but the gaudy chains of lanterns, swinging over Kilian Square since last week's shooting festival, were already switched on. They bathed the people, the houses, and the trees, in a soft light.

For a minute, Anne Weiss lost her sense of place and time, as she enjoyed the blend of velvety air, mild light, confused voices, loud laughter, remote music, and jingling glasses.

Achim Berger touched her shoulder lightly. She looked up. A rusty Volkswagen van, banging and backfiring, drove into the square, where it stopped near Anne. Out of the cab jumped three young men while another five got out of the back. Two of them wore jeans and T-shirts, the others, greasy overalls. Thomas Müller stood squarely before Anne and said: "You sure dolled yourself up, my bourgie girl. You'll get rid of your leaflets like hotcakes."

Anne was wearing a cream-colored silk blouse and a navy skirt.

She said: "The leaflets were printed with money belonging to the Civic Initiative. The Civic Initiative has decided to throw them out."

Müller laughed. "Did you get that, guys? The leaflets were printed with our money and we decided to throw them out. Can you imagine?"

Müller's comrades whistled. One of them straightened the red flag on the antenna.

"Annie," said Müller. "We are the Civic Initiative. We are the legitimate representatives of the proletariat. If you come along with us, okay. If you resort to terrorism, there'll be trouble.

He nodded to his comrades, who had meanwhile loaded up with packets of leaflets. They began handing them out to people walking into the banquet hall. Anne shook off Berger, who tried to hold her back. She knocked the leaflets out of one young man's arm. The packet crashed to the ground. Anne kicked the leaflets about with her foot. Müller knocked over Berger, who tried to get in his way. He pulled Anne up and slapped her. Anne whistled. Footsteps sounded all around them. Müller had raised his arm to punch Anne, but then he slowly let her go and stepped back.

They were surrounded. A chain of twenty seventeen- and eighteen-year-old boys encircled them. Some of them wore thin white sweaters that said: "Rowing Team—Grenzheim High School." Anne felt her cheek. One of the boys said, "It would be better if you moved away, Frau Weiss." The circle grew tighter. Around the circle, a second one formed, a circle of citizens anxious to see the fight. They got what they wanted. It was ten minutes before someone called the police. When the two officers showed up, Müller was crouching on the back wheel of the VW, holding his broken hand. A comrade was throwing up at the trunk of a linden tree. A third one was trying to stem his bleeding nose with his crumpled-up shirt. The five other Maoists had vanished, like the high-school boys. A student who had twisted his ankle and couldn't walk had sought refuge behind the broad shoulders of the town slaughterer, who kept turning around and patting him on the back.

The policemen took down the names of witnesses, who unanimously stated that Thomas Müller and his crew had started the fight. The officers apprehended the three Maoists. One policeman started off to the hospital with Müller. The other waited until Müller's comrades had gathered up the leaflets and loaded them in the VW. He wrote out a ticket because the VW was standing in a no-parking zone. Upon finding brass knuckles and a blank-cartridge pistol under the front seat, the policeman confiscated the vehicle, to the applause of the spectators. He made the two Maoists get in, and they drove off to the police station.

Berger eyed Anne: "Are you all right?"

She laughed. "He didn't quite get me, and besides, he was afraid to really let go. Well, what do you think of my idea?"

"It was great," said Berger. "But did it ever occur to you that they might try to get even with you when your guys aren't around?"

Anne shrugged. "They didn't hand out their leaflets. That's the main thing."

"Here comes the mayor," said Berger. "And Hühnle.

Look at the way Rapp's hanging on his every word. His master's voice."

Eberhard Hühnle and Mayor Josef Rapp were flanked by four younger men with ready-made suits and faces. Anne Weiss and Achim Berger waited until clapping and whistling came from the banquet hall. Then they followed the bodyguard escort. The wings of the door stood open, and as they entered, a black-haired man in a navy blue suit caught up with them.

"Good evening, Herr Doktor Born," said Anne, pronouncing each syllable strongly.

The man turned. "Oh, good evening, Frau . . . uh. . . ."

"Weiss," said Anne. "As in *vice* squad."

Born reddened. "My memory for names. . . ."

"One should know one's opponents," said Anne.

12

The man in the white BMW sweated. The car stood in a dirt road by Federal Highway 44. He had rolled down the windows. There was no wind. The weather forecast on the eight-o'clock news had indicated a temperature of 80 degrees Fahrenheit in the Rhein/Main area and threatened 97 degrees for tomorrow. It was sticky out. He would have liked to remove the tight jacket of his uniform. A costume rental was no custom tailor. A white police cap lay next to him on the front seat. The moon was rising over the mountain chain in the east, while the western sky was still glowing from the setting sun. The vineyards on the other side of the Rhine were turning into shadows with hazy contours. In front, on this side of the Rhine, two miles up, the gigantic dome of the Helios Nuclear Plant was covered with radiant gold. The man looked at his watch. It was 8:28 P.M. The traffic on the road to the plant had waned. A car appeared at the crossing only every ten minutes, and turned off into the highway. But 44 was livelier than usual. The man in the BMW wanted it to get dark soon.

13

"I'm sorry to bother you, chief," said Inspector Kramer. "Something's come up. I've talked to the father of our vanished number seven. A very reasonable fellow. Worried about his son. Thinks he's got into bad company. Can't understand why. The usual story. Good background, money, first car at sixteen. Went to study in Frankfurt. All he did was mouth political speeches when he came home on vacation. Dad sends him a check made out to cash every month, to a PO box in Frankfurt. The last time was a week ago. The postal clerk's description of the recipient fits the boy's description to a T. But it won't help us. The check was already picked up. I've got another trail. The father says his wife got a card from Sylt four weeks ago, on her birthday. She doesn't have it anymore, but she believes the boy was there with a woman and living in an expensive hotel. At least, she thinks she read that between the lines. I'll fly over with Henning within the hour and go through the resorts. I'll talk to all the night clerks. Maybe we can do something with the woman's name, in case we find the hotel and in case he did have someone with him."

14

In the banquet hall of the Black Eagle, the TV crew had put
up four spotlights. The glare was irritating and made the
stifling air even warmer. Two spotlights stood on the podium,
shining on Hühnle, Mayor Rapp, and the two scientific experts
who had just arrived, Dr. Genzmer, a Munich radiobiologist,
and Professor Schubert, former director of the Institute for
Reactor Safety, Cologne. He was a consultant there now. The
spotlights also shone upon a young smiling man with prominent teeth, an aquiline nose, and flaxen hair. Martin Born
couldn't believe his eyes: Peter Larsen. Born threaded his way
between the tightly-packed tables and chairs. He side vaulted
up to the podium, bringing whistles and applause from the
room. He greeted Hühnle, Rapp, and the scientists and sat
down next to Larsen. Larsen grinned, friendly but uncertain.

"You're on night shift," said Born.

"I traded with Zander," Larsen said. Zander was Larsen's
deputy in the supervision department. "He's got precise instructions. He's very reliable."

The mayor gave the introductory speech. Born whispered
sharply: "We've always got along well up till now, Larsen. That
was my mistake. I was too generous. When you started your
job, I told you I didn't like authoritarian leadership, I prefer
teamwork. That's still true. But as of today you're the exception. As of now you can regard my suggestions as instructions.
How come you're here? To wave to the cameras?"

Larsen didn't react. He said, "I find such discussions
informative and interesting, and I believe I can contribute to
making anti-nuclear people more sympathetic to Helios and
West-Elektra."

46

"Herr Larsen," said Born. "Only one man in this room is responsible for the prestige of the plant, and *I'm* that man. With people like you, of course, I'm going to have a helluva time defending the prestige of the plant in the future. This is the second time I'm telling you today: You have a responsibility, Larsen, and that responsibility is so great that nothing else can compete with it. Not even vanity. I hope you realize that I am informing the president of the board about your behavior, including that blatant negligence this afternoon."

Larsen pushed his chair back. "If my presence disturbs you that much, I'll leave—for the plant, of course."

Born hissed, "Stay where you are. It's too late now."

Mayor Rapp was saying: ". . . . welcome the director, Dr. Born, and department head, Herr Larsen, who in his capacity as director of safety will certainly give us information to put our minds at ease about the protective facilities at the Helios Nuclear Power Station."

Larsen hoisted up about eight inches in his chair and took a bow.

Mayor Rapp, a prototypically frail-looking official with glasses, and with only half an ear (the other half had been ripped off by a grenade splinter in the war), concluded: "The feelings on opposing sides could not be more conflicting. In the words of one of our greatest poets: 'Things strike each other hard in space.' But the very fact that everyone here has his own opinion, and that not everyone has the same opinion, is what democracy is all about. Democracy means that we have to fight it out. And that is what I would like to recommend warmly to the younger people especially: In the thick of battle, do not forget how fortunate you are to be able to wage this battle— and in a face-to-face discussion between citizens and the responsible people who will not avoid answering questions in public. And do not forget, my fellow citizens: Though trenches may lie between us, they are not insuperable abysses. Never forget: All of us who have gathered together here can be proud to call ourselves citizens of Grenzheim. And I am sure that all

47

of us want the very best for our Grenzheim. In view of this. . . ."

Before anyone could start with a question, Anne Weiss stepped up to the microphone in the narrow path between the tables. She asked permission to read a resolution by the Civic Initiative of Grenzheim. Mayor Rapp adjusted his glasses and hesitantly turned his head to Hühnle. The minister shrugged his shoulders. The TV cameras hummed. Rapp said, "Very well . . . if it doesn't last too long." This remark provoked a few hisses from Civic Initiative members. Anne started reading quietly and in a clear voice. It was not so much an appeal as a report on activities: When, why, and how the Civic Initiative had been launched, what it had done, and what it intended to do.

After ten minutes, Anne's voice sounded weaker, not because she was speaking more softly, but because people in the hall were beginning to talk to one another. The members of the Initiative knew the text, and the non-members weren't interested. Still, no one protested, for it was obvious that Hühnle and Rapp were growing more fidgety the longer Anne Weiss was reading. Everyone was delighted to see the massive Minister of the Economy, overcome by the smoke and steam of the packed room, mop at drops of water on his forehead and cheeks.

Martin Born was getting sleepy. He counted the tips of the antlers on the walls. He squinted through the glare of the TV spotlights to detect a few faces. He wondered whether one of these six hundred people was the threatening kind—or were there several? Were they only kids? Playing mad bomber instead of cops and robbers. Anne Weiss paused. Born thought he saw the corners of her mouth quivering. At his right, Mayor Rapp was tapping a pencil on the table. Born said to himself: "The vixen! She's very clever. Any minute now, Rapp's——"

The mayor took the microphone standing in front of him and pulled it close to his mouth. In a stentorian tone, he said:

"Could you please finish up, Frau Weiss. This is a discussion, not an oratory contest. You should have enough tact and respect to consider the presence of Herr Minister of the Economy——"

The hall awoke. A bearded man sprang up and yelled: "Democracy, Herr Rapp! Democracy! That means giving other people a chance to speak their minds."

Applause. In the back of the hall, some people were chorusing: "Rapp, Rapp, Rapp! He's got the cash on tap!" an allusion to Rapp's career. During his nine years in office, he had used a convenient marriage and even more convenient business dealings to make his way from a minor revenue official to the richest man in Grenzheim.

Anne Weiss said: "Why don't we vote on it? Who is in favor of my reading the rest of the resolution?"

Hardly a hand did not leap into the air.

"All against?"

Hühnle, Rapp, Born, and Larsen raised their hands. The scientists remained neutral—as was proper for specialists. In the hall, only a dozen hands stretched up.

Rapp hacked away at the tabletop with his pencil point. The point broke. Hühnle took off his jacket, hung it over the back of his chair, and folded his arms over his powerful chest. He whistled softly to himself.

Larsen whispered to Born: "What impudence! Something should be done about this!"

Born gazed at Anne Weiss. When she leaned her head to the side, the light fell on a slender, beautifully curving throat, which reminded him of the bust of Queen Nefertete. Born started drawing wavy lines on his pad.

15

The murderer dumped the witness to his first murder into the silvery, moonlit lake in front of his hunting lodge. Little did he know that the lieutenant of the homicide squad was standing on the shore, training his nightglass on him. At that very moment, Sibylle Born, for the fourth time, dialed the number she had known by heart for three months. Normally, she could never retain phone numbers. She let the telephone ring for two minutes, then she pressed the cradle with the edge of her hand before replacing the receiver. On the TV screen, the lieutenant's Plymouth was chasing the murderer's Ford.

She walked over to the bar in the middle of the room. This was a legacy of the previous owner, a used-car dealer. And Sibylle had held on to it despite her husband's objections. She opened the liquor cabinet and hunted for the 150-proof white Jamaica rum. Finding it, she poured herself half a glass. She walked over to the grand piano, sipping the rum, and struck a few keys. She couldn't play. She gazed at her image in the mirror over the antique desk. A note in her husband's handwriting was attached to the mirror. Sibylle plucked it out of the frame: "Don't forget your mother's birthday on August 2."

Typical of Martin, she thought. What a pedant. She really had forgotten, though he had probably reminded her at least twice that week.

Sibylle sighed and sat down at the desk. She took out one of the dull-yellow sheets of handmade paper, which bore her name in a finely engraved British script in the upper right-hand corner. She put the sheet upon the mahogany desk, lit a cigarette, and picked up the gold fountain pen.

"Dear, darling mother.

50

"Here is your faithless daughter writing to you once again on your birthday. I hope you're as healthy and cheerful as ever and that you'll remain our beloved and joyous Mom for many more years. If you're wondering about me, I'm so-so.

"We've gradually become used to our new house, even though six rooms, two baths, and three thousand square yards of garden space are pretty large for two people, and I'm often lonely when that rush-about manager Martin leaves me here all by myself.

"It's hard getting a circle of friends here. Martin is so busy he never has time to go to a dinner or a party. I've met a few nice people at the tennis club and horseback riding, and I see them every now and then. But sometimes I wish we had stayed in Frankfurt and Martin were doing what he did during his first year as a director—I mean, staying at the plant during the week and coming home on weekends. I know it's not exactly what people expect of an ideal marriage. But Martin actually only comes here on weekends, and then he's summoned back to the plant right away. Tomorrow is the big opening ceremony. Maybe you'll get to see your son-in-law on the news, though you're already proud enough of him. Well, now I have to sign off, my hand's already stiff. Once again, the very best of everything. Give my best to Father and come and visit us soon. Let me know so I can send you the plane tickets."

Sibylle smiled at herself in the mirror. She found she was very attractive. A little like Claudia Cardinale. During her tennis lesson, more onlookers had stood by the instructor's court than at court 6, where the best players in the club were competing. Her smile increased as she wondered what her mother would say if she knew her daughter was cheating on Martin.

How happy her mother had been when Sibylle brought Martin home for the first time. He was exactly the man she had always dreamed of for her daughter: able, reliable, ambitious, well bred.

Back then, thought Sibylle, he was exactly the man I had

always dreamed of: young, good-looking, successful, on the way up, the prince who carried off the little secretary out of a bleak office existence into an exciting life. She was very much in love with him when she had married him five years ago, and for two years everything had gone smoothly—exactly as Sibylle wanted it. They took four vacations a year. Martin would call in sick, especially during the first few months of their marriage, in order to spend whole days with her. They frequently had sex in the afternoon, and there was always something on at night —a party, a dance, a dinner. Then Martin learned that he was being considered for the position of director of the new nuclear station. Sibylle could still remember how radiant he had been when he came home that evening. They had gone out to celebrate the honor. It was the first time he had spoken about his work—and he had told her that her life would change too if they really made him director. It was a full-time job, and his personal life would have to take second place for a while. A vacation was possible only if nothing came up. Naturally, something always did. And then he started talking about a baby again, as though he wanted to say, "You'd at least have something to do while I'm away."

Soon after that night, Martin, charming Martin, became more and more irritable and impatient. Sibylle saw his mouth get hard when he came through the door and found her lying on the couch in front of the TV. Their sex life dwindled to once a week, then once a month, and now it was so infrequent that Sibylle couldn't remember her last orgasm with Martin. April? May?

She thought of the day when they had had their first big fight. That was a year back, maybe longer. Her husband had come home pretty late. He was pale and tired, and Sibylle had proudly shown him the English grandfather clock she had bought that afternoon at an antique store in Frankfurt.

Martin had merely grumped, asked the price, and then said, "Collecting antiques is something for frustrated old widows. You could really do something better with your time, maybe something that's not so expensive. I'm no millionaire, Sibylle. You know English and French. You can take dictation and type. Do something with all that. I can get you a job tomorrow. It doesn't have to be an export company again. Join a newspaper. That's sure to be interesting."

Sibylle had laughed, first in surprise, then in rage. "No, Martin. That's past history for me. It's over and done with. No one's getting me back into an office. No one. I'll never fool around with an office coffee machine again. I'll never listen again to those ugly cows talking about their weekend adventures. I'll never be felt up by fat bosses again. And when I think of the canteen, the table talk, and those floury sauces—it makes my gorge rise, do you hear? And then at 3:45, the run on the toilets. Compacts and lipstick out, all the boasting about boyfriends—it turns my stomach. I'd rather walk the streets. That way, I'd at least get enough money for my nausea."

Martin had merely shrugged and never brought the subject up again, merely hinted at it indirectly. "Zander's wife, she's working as a bookkeeper. . . . X's sister just became head of a department. . . ."

Sibylle ignored these hints.

She closed the envelope. The rum glass was empty. She was tired. She reached for the phone, pulled her hand back again, stretched out on the couch, wept a bit, and fell asleep.

16

Shortly after ten o'clock, the head of the maintenance department, Werner Marcks, left the Helios Nuclear Station, half-satisfied with the latest vibrations of the turbine on the oscillograph. A man was sitting in the bullet-proof watchhouse.

Marcks asked: "All alone, Rogolski? How are you going to defend us?"

Rogolski, eager for a conversation with the engineer, limped out of the glass room, against all rules. "The patrol's been increased," he said. "The others are out there."

"Because of that bomb this morning?"

"And because of the ceremony tomorrow, in case a few lunatics start getting ideas tonight. So c'mon and show me how much plutonium you're sneaking out today."

Even Marcks, polite as he was, didn't laugh at this ancient joke anymore. He handed his briefcase to Rogolski. All plant employees had to have their belongings checked on the way out. Marcks took back the briefcase. "Okay then—have a good night's watch."

Rogolski looked disappointed. He would like to have chatted a bit. Luckily he remembered Marck's wound. He was so used to the bandaged head that he didn't even notice it anymore. As Marcks stood by the door, Rogolski threw his question after him. "Anything new from the police?"

Marcks halted impatiently. "No."

"Is the injury healing well?" asked Rogolski.

"Thank goodness. I'll be rid of the bandage by Monday."

"Imagine," said Rogolski. "Right in the middle of town. And now they want to reform the prisons so that the bastards can live it up. They even want to let women in to see them. It's time I committed my first murder."

Marcks laughed. "No woman's worth it."

"If I ever get a creep like that in front of my gun," Rogolski patted his revolver, which dangled on his hip like a sheriff's pistol, "then there'll be one bastard less in the world. Get him in the head, and then afterwards I'll say I was aiming at his legs. Bang-bang! The police are too easygoing."

Marcks climbed into his Volvo. He had a headache. On normal days, he enjoyed driving the six miles to Garding, where he had a small bachelor's apartment. Today he would have preferred to stop and lie down on the back seat.

At the Highway 44 crossing, he turned right. He switched on the radio. A pop singer was crooning: "Let's do what the swallows do."

When Marcks saw two spotlights approaching in the rear-view mirror, he stepped off the gas and pulled right. A white BMW caught up, swung in front of the Volvo, and slowed down. "Asshole," said Marcks and touched the brake. A blinking, red stop-sign loomed out of the BMW window. Marcks halted. His heart was beating as it always did when he was stopped by the police.

An officer climbed out of the BMW. Marcks rolled down the window. He was surprised that the policeman was alone. Even in plainclothes vehicles, the police always traveled in pairs. He was surprised at the Frankfurt license plate. Were the big city colleagues helping out the village constables?

"May I see your license and your registration card, please?" asked the policeman. He was young and had a carefully trimmed beard much like Marcks's own. Marcks became less nervous. Among bearded men there was a kind of solidarity. He handed over his papers. "Fine," said the policeman. "Now I'd like to see your trunk."

Marcks got out. As he opened the trunk, he felt the policeman's breath on the back of his neck. His stomach convulsed. He knew he was in danger. The crickets chirped in his head. He wanted to say: You can have my money. He wanted to say: Don't hit me. My head still hasn't healed. He wanted to talk to the man. He turned his head. Behind him, to the right, the power plant was shimmering. He moved his lips.

The policeman rammed his pistol against Marcks's spine and squeezed the trigger. Marcks's upper half toppled into the trunk. The policeman picked up the slack legs of the dead man, pushed the body in, and closed the trunk.

The murderer climbed into the BMW and steered it a hundred yards farther through a gate into the cover of a few willow trees. Taking his attaché case, he walked back to the Volvo, stuffed his cap and uniform jacket under the passenger seat, turned the car, and drove back. The gearshift was trouble-some at first. After five hundred yards he stopped at a phone booth. The number he dialed was more familiar to him than his own. He said, "Marcks speaking. I forgot some blueprints, Rogolski. I'm coming back." He drove on, steering the car into the dirt road at the crossing, where he had waited for Marcks.

He was happy that his first assault on Marcks nearly a week ago had failed. He'd done it because he had wanted Marcks's ID card. But Marcks hadn't carried it on him that night—maybe because it had been his day off. When he saw Marcks return to work two days later with a bandaged head he knew that his chances of getting into Helios were much better now. If he was clever enough. If the others were stupid enough. And if he was lucky.

Now he undressed down to his shorts. He opened the trunk and pulled the clothes off the corpse. Sweat burned his eyes. He pulled on the corpse's shirt. The collar was too tight. He couldn't close the top button. The pants fit. The jacket was narrow. He left it open. He knotted the tie very tight so it would hide the open collar. He checked the contents of the wallet in the jacket. He wanted to close the trunk, hesitated, removed the corpse's shoes, and put them on.

He shifted over to the passenger seat and pulled down the sunshade. There was a make-up mirror on the other side. He opened his attaché case, took out a white roll of gauze and deftly wrapped a bandage around his head. He fastened the end with two clips and stuck two strips of adhesive on the bandage over the temples. He wiped his hands on the bandage, making it dirty. He inspected himself in the mirror. He saw a bandage, bright eyes, an average nose, and a beard. He put on horn-rimmed glasses with clear glass and grinned.

He dumped out the contents of his victim's briefcase and packed three flat metal boxes inside. He put the briefcase in front of the passenger seat and slid behind the wheel. He drove out to the highway and turned after fifty yards, following the sign that had a flower and, in small letters, the name: Helios.

He knew the flower was no flower. It was the symbol of the atom: a nuclear dot elliptically orbited by three electrons. The three elliptical orbits intersected. The symbol looked like a six-petaled daisy.

He steered with only one finger. He could have driven the stretch blindfolded. The white dome in front pulled him like a powerful magnet.

He parked the Volvo in the employees' parking lot. From there he could see the main part of the plant building. A hundred yards ahead of him, behind the administration building, was the dome of steel and concrete, 250 feet high, 150 feet in diameter, larger at close range, but not nearly so imposing as at a distance of two miles. Behind the dome, attached to it, stood the machine building, reaching east and west, towards the Rhine. It was 400 feet long, 180 feet high. The brains of the nuclear plant, the central switching station, was adjoined to the machine building. It was comparatively low, 150 feet.

Farther on, near the river, he saw a part of the concrete block containing the giant pumps that drew 250,000 cubic meters of water from the Rhine every hour, spewing the water through conduits several yards wide, into the heart of the plant, the reactor core, inside the dome, where the atomic fire glowed. To the left lay the transformer area. That was where the current, created by turbine and generator, was tamed and sent into cities by way of high-tension lines. Four men, electricians on night shift, walked through the jumble of cables, masts, and isolators, and then they vanished in the transformer block.

Flat concrete cubes surrounded the main building like a village around a medieval church. The cubes were the boiler houses, workshops, garages, and water purification stations, the diesel building, the administration building, the storehouses, and the pump houses.

He knew the geography of Helios by heart. He had been on ten guided tours. West-Elektra was delighted to have people spend their Sundays at Helios and rave about the atomic egg to their friends on Monday.

He also knew the parts of Helios that were not shown on tours.

He took his briefcase and walked across the brightly lit parking lot to the glass cabin at the entrance to the administration building. Two watchmen with a sheepdog came toward him. He waved a greeting at them. One smiled back. The sheepdog growled and tugged on the short leash.

He inserted an image into his brain as into a projector. The image of how he had seen Marcks walking a hundred times. He pulled his head into his shoulders and dragged his heels.

The old man in the watch house seemed to be glad that he came. The door hummed, and he opened it. Rogolski was about to stand up. He waved him to stay seated and kept walking. He took the ID card from his wallet and pushed it into the crack of the control computer. It was scanned by a laser beam. The computer registered the number, compared it with the stored personal numbers, set off a second mechanism that noted the name and the arrival time, gave its okay, and pushed the card out again.

The door to the entrance hall opened. He walked over to the staircase and went up. Rogolski was now on the phone, laughing.

Room 107 was locked. He tried four of the keys on Marcks's keyring, until he had the right one. He took a white smock out of the locker and pulled it on. He withdrew two flat plates from the metal box in the briefcase. They were gray and soft, as large as a magazine and about one inch thick.

A blueprint of the turbine lay on the desk. He folded it around the two gray plates. In the pockets of the smock, he stowed two miniature clocks and small capsules rolled in a thin blue wire.

He left the administration building through the back entrance and walked along a tiled path to the reactor dome. Once again he inserted his ID card into a control slit, once again the door glided open. He walked over to the elevator. The elevator had no floor indicator; it only showed the height by meters. He pressed the +15 button. When the elevator stopped, it showed a small white room, six feet square, closed off by a steel door. A round disc of bullet-proof glass was inserted in the wall over the door. The lights of two TV cameras were flickering between the glass. He stationed himself in the red circle on the floor.

The TV cameras projected his image to a monitor in the central control room.

Don't sleep up there, he thought. He was now sure they would mistake him for Marcks just as Rogolski had.

The steel door slid open. "Don't fall into the oven, Werner," squawked a voice from the loudspeaker. He entered a dressing room. All around the walls were rows of hooks on which white suits were hanging, mostly by their hoods. Benches were built into the walls at knee level. The entire room was plastered with ventilator signs, the signal for radioactive danger. A watchman sitting at a table wore the same green uniform as Rogolski. The watchman's legs were propped up on the table, and he had a copy of *Playboy* open on his knees, the centerspread showing the Playmate of the Month. The watchman was asleep.

The murderer looked for the white frog suit with the nametag "Marcks" on the left side of the chest. He twisted into it. The anti-radiation suit was like a mechanic's suit—made out of one piece. It reminded him of a costume party he had attended fifteen or sixteen years ago. He had gone against his will as the Easter bunny, because his mother wanted him to. Disgustedly he had let himself be locked up in the costume. First the legs, then the arms, then the zipper from navel to neck. He pulled on the hood. The frog suit was made of a thin synthetic material. Unlike the heavy, multi-isolated, yellow asbestos suits worn by the anti-radiation squad at Helios, this suit couldn't keep out penetrating radiation. It was only designed to prevent radioactive dust from clinging to the clothes. He slipped on white cloth overshoes with rubbery bottoms, the kind distributed to visitors on castle tours, for the sliding contest across the baroque parquet. He walked over to the table.

He let the watchman sleep. He checked the book in which arrivals and departures were registered, till he found Werner Marcks's signature. He signed, registering a number next to his name. The number was constant under the headings "radiation-in" and "radiation-out"—an eight. This referred to mini-roentgens—the measure of radioactive radiation. He softly opened the white round steel door facing the elevator.

17

FROM THE BROCHURE NUCLEAR ENERGY FOR A BETTER TOMORROW

Opponents of nuclear power stations maintain that every station driven by atomic energy is an "atomic bomb ticking in our neighborhood." In truth, atomic reactors and atomic bombs are two totally different ways of using nuclear energy. The difference was clearly pointed out by the Russian atomic scientist Pyotr Patpitsa thirty years ago: "If we always talk about atomic energy and atomic bombs in one breath, it is as senseless as associating electricity mainly with its use in an electric chair."

18

The Minister of Economy stood up and took his jacket from the back of his chair. Instantly, his four bodyguards leaped from their seats along the back wall of the podium, on which the backdrop of a sunset in a German spruce forest was still adhering from the last shooting festival. Without a microphone, Hühnle's powerful voice boomed out: "C'mon, people. This is bullshit. I'm not sittin' my ass off for this. Goodnight. I'm leaving."

Mayor Rapp turned pale. Anne Weiss fell silent at the microphone. Then came the first whistles and heckles: "Go to hell. . . . let him go. . . . All the better. . . ."

Born was waiting for Rapp to do something. But the mayor patted his white forehead with a checkered handkerchief and breathed heavily. Born clutched the microphone.

"I am certain the minister will remain if we finally start the discussion. The ladies and gentlemen of the Civic Initiative certainly don't have any questions. After all, they already know everything and have formed their biases. But tonight, there are fellow citizens in the room who do not know the material as well as they do. It is to you that I say, ladies and gentlemen, make the most of this chance and ask us questions."

The Civic Initiative people booed.

"Let's vote," yelled Minister Hühnle, who, with a nod to Born, had sat down again.

Most hands went up for Born's proposal.

Anne Weiss said, "I move that there be a three-minute limit to all speakers."

Born answered. "That's not practical. A few answers about particular problems will be longer. Besides, after your

61

half-hour lecture, you don't have the right to demand restrictions. Let's agree that all the participants make an effort to be as succint as possible."

"Let's vote," yelled Hühnle.

No limit on speaking time was passed by the majority.

Hühnle leaned behind Rapp's back and said to Born: "The girl's not bad. She's got more than balls!"

The microphone was still in front of Born on the table. It sent Hühnle's comment out into the hall. The bearded young man next to Anne Weiss clenched his fists. Now Born remembered his name—Berger. Anne stepped back to the microphone. "So do you, Herr Hühnle, but I'm not sure where."

"Hoho," laughed Hühnle. "One to nothing. And now let's get going."

A farmer's wife, wearing a spotted kerchief, raised her hand. She pushed her broad hips between the rows of tables up to the microphone, assisted by the eager hands of the older men, who were gradually getting into a good mood after four ryes and beers or a bottle of Grenzheim wine.

"How can we live and work in peace, if there's a bomb here that can explode any minute?" She clutched the mike holder and, encouraged by the applause, added: "I can't sleep anymore since they've built that thing, but those high and mighty gentlemen up there, they've got their houses in Switzerland."

The farmer's wife waddled back to her seat.

Martin Born replied. "That is a good question. It can be answered very simply. An atomic reactor like Helios and an atomic bomb have nothing to do with one another. It is the tragedy of atomic energy that its first practical use was in the form of a bomb.

A heckle from the middle of the hall. "Fuck tragedy! That was mass murder."

Born raised his hand. "Let's leave that aside for now. The fact remains: The fear of atomic energy and Helios is really the

62

fear of the atom bomb, the fear of a new Hiroshima or Nagasaki. This fear is groundless. An atomic bomb is meant to explode. That's how it's built. But a reactor cannot explode even if someone wants it to.

"You know that a reactor produces heat from the fission of uranium atoms. More precisely one ought to say, the fission of the atomic nuclei of different sorts of uranium, which make up the reactor fuel. Scientists call these various forms uranium isotopes. And they supply numbers for them. An isotope that's hard to split is uranium-238. One that's easy to split is uranium-235. So if you want to construct an A-bomb, you need large amounts of uranium-235, the easy-to-split isotope. But it flies apart so fast that it releases an enormous quantity of energy. In other words, it explodes. Uranium-238 is totally useless for such a purpose.

"You might best compare the two isotopes to dry wood and damp wood. Uranium-235, the A-bomb material, is like absolutely dry wood. If you light it, it burns lightning-fast, developing a huge amount of heat. Uranium-238, on the other hand, is like wet, green wood. You can use up ten boxes of matches, and it won't burn. Do you see? That's the effect we utilize in an atomic reactor. We store a huge mountain of wet wood—uranium-238. Of the 180 tons of uranium fuel in the Helios reactor, about 174.6 tons are of that isotope. And with this damp wood, we mix in a little dry wood—at Helios, 5.4 tons of uranium-235. Then we light the dry wood. It burns instantly. But since it's distributed among damp wood, it can't burn up all at once. It's held up, and all it can do is make the damp wood smolder, the uranium-238. That's all there is to it. But this controlled heat suffices to turn the water into steam. The scientists call the whole process controlled chain reaction."

Born noticed that Dr. Genzmer and Professor Schubert, the two scientists, were eyeing him dubiously. His comparison of uranium and wood was no doubt a questionable analogy for them.

Berger stood up. "A typical example of the manipulation that we have been experiencing for years, ladies and gentlemen. They turn uranium simply into wood, and that's how they can hide the fact that the fission of uranium creates inconceivable amounts of radioactive radiation. Today, after only twelve months of operations, the Helios reactor contains as much deadly radiation as a few thousand Hiroshima bombs. Do you deny that?"

Born pushed the microphone over to Professor Schubert, an ascetic type with hollow cheeks, a narrow mouth, and large, dreamy eyes.

Schubert looked up from his pad. "I do not know the exact scope of the radiation. But even if you are right, this radiation is only dangerous when free. However, in the seven years of planning and constructing the Helios reactor, every, but simply every, possibility of having the radiation leak from the reactor was totally abolished. The approval procedures are more rigorous for a nuclear plant than for any other construction work. The manufacturers and applicants had to deal with over fifty government agencies—from the hamlet of Grenzheim to the Federal Ministry of the Economy—before and during the construction. Every agency went even further than the existing regulations in demanding security measures for the protection of the staff and the neighboring population. Before the first spadeful of soil was scooped up, some fifty boring operations and thirty pressure soundings were undertaken on the construction grounds in order to test the constitution of the soil. The foundations of Helios are so powerful that they could even survive a strong earthquake. The concrete steel dome could not even be destroyed by a crashing Boeing. And the reactor was put on such high ground that the Rhine would have to undergo a deluge to endanger it in any way."

Anne Weiss interrupted, "Would you stop all that self-adulation, Herr Schubert. "Tell us about the GPA factor. Talk about the five thousand, ten thousand, fifty thousand people killed or crippled because they had the bad luck to live near an atomic reactor."

Berger shouted, "Do you know what Enrico Fermi, one of the founders of atomic research, replied to his colleagues when they reminded him of the dangers of nuclear fission? He said: 'Don't bother me with your remorse. It's such beautiful physics.' We could revise the statement slightly for the gentlemen on the podium: 'Don't bother me with your remorse. It's such a beautiful nuclear station.' "

The people in the hall applauded.

"Nonsense," shouted Professor Schubert above the roar in the hall. And then once again, louder: "Nonsense!" He banged his hand on the table. "We won't get anywhere with panic. The 'greatest possible incident' factor, which we call the GPI factor, is by definition an incident, not a catastrophe. It takes place only in the reactor and has no impact on the surrounding world. This is what happens. One or more pipes that bring the coolant to the reactor start leaking. The water shoots out of the leaks with seventy atmospheres of pressure. The water level drops in the reactor. The chain reaction is instantly stopped in the core by control rods that automatically enter the fuel cells and absorb the neutrons. They are assisted by a special physical law. Nevertheless, the uranium remains hot, just as ashes keep smoldering long after the flames have gone out. Without cooling water, the uranium fuel rods inflame one another with the heat generated. Their temperature rises—from 1,800 degrees Celsius to, 2,-000 degrees and finally to 2,800 degrees, the melting point of uranium—always assuming, of course, that the core is bone dry. Once the uranium melts, it can no longer be held back. It eats through the bottom of the fuel container, through the safety sphere, through the foundation, deep into the ground, all the while releasing considerable quantities of radioactive radiation."

The people in the hall were silent. Very clever of Schubert, thought Born. The catastrophe gimmick always works, and the people listen. But he shouldn't lay it on too thick. Born gazed at Anne Weiss. She was talking to Berger. The damp heat creeping through the open windows, the bad air, and the fatigue weakened him. He figured that was why, as he watched the girl, her upswept hair, her delicate neck, he felt like touching her. It had nothing to do with sex, he thought. He knew Anne Weiss from a few similar discussions, but he had never found her particularly attractive. She was too cool and matter-of-fact. Born wondered why she had greeted him so blatantly at the door. Irony? Did she want to show him that she and the Civic Initiative didn't take him seriously, merely considering him—as the leaflet put it—"a marionette of big business?"

Born liked the way she moved. Her movements were spare and sensible. When she brushed the hair off her forehead, it was because there was really a blond strand hanging over her eyebrows, not because she had practiced the gesture in order to seem more feminine. He liked the way she spoke, her precision and aggressiveness contrasted with her dark, soft voice. And somehow, Born couldn't account for it, Anne Weiss made him unsure of himself. Her husband probably had no easy time of it—if she had a husband. She certainly had a suitor. Berger worshiped her. Anne Weiss seemed to ignore his enthusiasm. Born's wife would have blossomed under such gazes.

But Sibylle was totally different, a sex bomb in comparison to Anne Weiss. Her sexiness had overwhelmed him when they first met. He had been just over thirty, had slept with fourteen women, not counting two visits to a brothel. But none of them had had such an enthusiastic and spontaneous joy in sex: a desire to get pleasure and a readiness to give pleasure. Sibylle loved bodies—her own, his, probably a lot of others. Born wasn't sure whether she had had enough of his during their marriage. She lived only through her body. Born had grown up in a strict atmosphere, learning that you earn the right to pleasure only through hard work. Most people allowed their senses to enjoy themselves each in its own time, by itself, restricted. But Sibylle's lust tasted, heard, saw, smelled, touched, and felt with a whole concern of senses. The result was an intensity of enjoyment that Born had never previously suspected existed. He often recalled the early days of their marriage. Sibylle loved eating in bed, and every meal became a long, exhausting feast, in which the taste of lobster and skin, meat and sex, sweat and wine blended into an aroma that Born could often still taste when he awoke.

Odd, thought Born, that it was actually Sibylle's honest, giving body that separated them now. No, not the body alone —the dictatorial, usurping sensuousness that ruled her life.

Two years ago—or was it longer?—Born had started defending himself against it. Not consciously, but by an instinct that he didn't comprehend. Sibylle still turned him on, but suddenly he had forced his own body not to give in anymore. He withdrew from her. He tried to hurt her, and that was easy, for at first she didn't notice the change in him, and she was still tender, without restraint. When she came to him at night, a comment like "I'm not a sex robot" was enough to really upset her. Today they were both experts in these pistol cracks, each of which destroyed a bit of their togetherness.

Naturally, there were reconcilations—superficial compromises he went along with, always aware that every concession he made to Sibylle cost him a part of his personality.

Not normal, thought Born. I'm not normal. I've got everything that the men I know merely fantasize about lying next to their curler-wearing wives.

But in contrast, there was that evening they had been invited to the home of a colleague, now working somewhere in America. A nice guy. Sibylle had flirted with him in her way. Every conventional flirtation evolved with her—unintentionally—into an open offer of sex. The colleague had played along, more out of politeness, thought Born, than interest. His wife was bony, ugly, and smart. She followed the game calmly as she told Born about her trip to Africa. While bringing filled glasses from the kitchen, she very lightly touched her husband's hair, and he put his head into her hand for a second. There was so much trust, so much strength, in the gesture that Born was ashamed and told Sibylle they had to leave. Sibylle hadn't noticed anything. She assumed Born was jealous.

Born jumped.

Professor Schubert was saying loudly: "I repeat. The horror story about melting uranium is totally beyond acceptance by any serious scientist. In practice, the 'greatest possible incident' factor stops at the latest when the fuel rods heat up by a few degrees because of lack of water. Anything else, and you can protest as loudly as you like, is nothing but an invention by sensationalist reporters. Only useful for a disaster movie. The facts give me the right to advocate this opinion with all sincerity.

"First of all, ladies and gentlemen, a break in a pipe carrying water to the reactor is highly improbable. The pipes are manufactured under the most rigorous supervision, they are made of the best material, and during operations they are constantly scanned by TV cameras and measuring instruments. Second, if by some chance a pipe were to start leaking, then in fractions of a second two mutually independent emergency cooling systems switch on. One pumps water from below into the reactor. The other floods it from above. Furthermore, there is a substitute system for each of these emergency cooling systems. That is to say, the uranium is recooled instantly, before it can reach anything near the melting point. The probability of a pipe breaking and all auxiliary equipment stalling is, by even the most pessimistic estimates, one in seventeen thousand. It means that in seventeen thousand years, an atomic reactor can—*can,* not must—be struck by such a serious accident."

Heckle: "Not the reactor—us!"

Professor Schubert shrugged his shoulders. "I personally hold the accident risk to be much smaller. A possible reactor accident would result from a simultaneous accumulation of so many flukes that—seen in the light of everyday life—it would be about as probable as being attacked in Grenzheim by a polar bear, by a crashing airplane, by a cannibal, and by a meteor— all in one minute."

The people laughed, especially the older ones. Minister Hühnle laughed. Mayor Rapp did not. Peter Larsen murmured: "Very true."

Anne Weiss took the floor. "Herr Schubert is playing with statistics and calls it factual proof. There is more telling proof that doesn't fit in with Herr Schubert's version. In the United States, someone noticed a two-inch crack in a pipe at the Dresden atomic station, and that was only at the last minute. Immediately, twenty other nuclear plants were closed for several months in order to check for similar defects. That's how certain the experts were of their perfect supervision. The scandal moved one of the greatest advocates of atomic energy to resign his position with the atomic agency and rescind his positive attitude. He stated, 'Despite the lulling assurances given to the uninformed and misled public, the unresolved questions of security in atomic energy are so crucial that the United States ought to think about fully terminating the construction of nuclear power stations.'

"That's what I call character, Herr Schubert. But we're not even asking you to come over to our side. We would be delighted if you and your colleagues merely admitted to your ignorance—and gave up your arrogance. Why do we never hear an honest word from your side. For instance, 'Yes, something might happen, it's possible, but we're doing our best to prevent it.' But no! You bask in your infallibility as though you were the Lord God in person."

Professor Schubert did not consider this unscientific assault worthy of a scientific answer.

19

He closed the round, steel door. Now he was inside the sluice
leading into the reactor dome.

The room behind the other steel door was described as the
"middle annular room" in the Helios diagram. The annular
rooms (there was also an "upper" and a "lower" one) lay
between the thick concrete walls that screened off the hydraulic accumulator with the core and the steel walls of the dome.
Unlike the inside of the reactor, they could be entered during
operations since they contained equipment that gave off little
or no radioactivity.

The middle annular room consisted of yellow pipes and
narrow corridors. Most of the pipes were a yard high and ran
horizontally. Thinner pipes pushed into them from above.

For half a minute, he observed the flaring and snuffing of
the control lights. Then he turned right. He was able to carry
out his plan because of the meticulousness of the Nuclear
Power Station Construction Company, the NPSCC, which
had built the Helios atomic reactor for West-Elektra.

The NPSCC experts had been training the West-Elektra
personnel for Helios over the past eighteen months, and they
had supervised the test runs going on for the past twelve
months. To help the maintenance squads get their bearings in
the chaos of pipes, the NPSCC people had labeled the pipes.
Black script in a red frame indicated the function of each pipe:
condensation, fresh steam, emergency feeding (small), emergency feeding (large).

Through the yard-thick steel arteries, forged out of the
most resistant alloys, the vital circulation pulsated and made
the heart of the reactor beat with it. That's what it said in the

brochure, NUCLEAR ENERGY FOR A BETTER TOMORROW. West-Elektra had printed 500,000 copies of that brochure, distributing it gratis, especially in the Grenzheim area.

But the brochure left something out. The reactor heart does not react like the human heart when the circulation stops. The human heart comes to a halt if no blood reaches it, and the body then dies. The reactor heart, on the other hand, 180 tons of uranium, is not dead when the cooling water no longer gurgles around it. It falls into a raging, feverish agony, burns itself up, expands to white heat, and bursts. It spews poison.

He followed the pipe that said FEEDWATER (1). Six feet away from the place where it fed into the concrete shield en route to the core, he knelt down. He took a clock, a capsule, and one of the gray, soft plates from the briefcase. He twisted eight inches of wire from the capsule and wedged the ends into the back of the clock. He squeezed the clock and the capsule into the white mass. Then he crawled under the pipe and attached the plate, which conformed easily to the curve, on the bottom of the pipe.

He scuttled back to the corridor and prepared a second plate in the same way. He walked along a concrete wall, hissing, gurgling pipes over and near him, until he discovered the FEEDWATER (2) pipe on the opposite side.

When he crept out from under the pipe, a pair of cloth overshoes was standing in front of his eyes. He stood up slowly. It was crazy of him not to have taken the pistol. The man in front of him was a head taller, and his powerful body seemed too large for the roomy anti-radiation suit. He was young and he had a blond crewcut. The man grabbed his right wrist and turned the arm against his back. It was over.

20

Born was mistaken. Professor Schuber's graphic depiction of the improbability of a reactor accident did not bring any change of mood in the banquet hall. On the contrary. The more wine and beer they drank, the more aggressive the people became. Animated by the liquor, people who in a sober state would never have dared to speak in front of several hundred spectators, took the floor.

In every question, Born could sense the almost tangible fear and hatred that the sinister atomic egg at their doorstep inspired in most of Grenzheim's inhabitants. Fear, because they sniffed the danger they were helplessly exposed to. Hatred, because for the small farmers in this region—who barely managed to scrape their way along the verge of bankruptcy year after year, just scarcely saving their mortgaged farms—Helios was the symbol of industrialization, rationalization, brutal progress. The powers that had driven them from the fields their forebears had tilled. The powers that carried away their vineyards in order to build highways leading to new factories, whose exhaust fumes poisoned the once limpid sky.

Minister Hühnle had drawn some nasty heckles with some of his typically deft comments about "eco-fetishists" who "wanted to turn the highly industrialized nations back into agricultural countries and banana republics," if possible with "the barter system and the "three-class voting rights," just so that they "could wash their dirty laundry in spic-and-span rivers."

Peter Larsen had supported Hühnle and thundered enthusiastic statements about progress, like a moral rearmament man. He saw "the world only at the beginning of its technological upswing." And he asserted that "if the technologists with their logic and reason would rule the world, then the world would be put in order overnight."

Untouched by the boos, he had praised the safety system of Helios, for which he, as he distinctly pointed out, was responsible—that was a guarantee for its perfection. And then, when Born had put the brakes on him, he had gloried in technological dreams of the future—nuclear fusion, the fusion of hydrogen atoms with which men would soon be imitating the sun's energy production on earth.

Now a pregnant woman spoke. She was wearing a flowered dress, a pearl necklace, a sportsman's cap. "But what if I give birth to a freak? And what if my child dies because of those damn rays?"

Dr. Genzmer, the radiobiologist from Munich, answered. "Those are old wives' tales, Madam. American legends. Nothing more. Someone in California claimed that a nuclear station had tripled the number of deformed births. But how did it turn out? The tripling had occurred a whole year before the station had begun operating—when there could not have been any radioactivity in the area.

"Equally questionable are the allegations concerning the rise of leukemia cases in the vicinity of nuclear plants. I might even say that such assertions are ridiculous. Every single accusation was convincingly disproved. The realization, a sad realization for me as a scientists, in all this senseless fighting was that the anti-nuclear people will not scorn any means to turn the ignorance of laymen into fear—with the help of false data. Truly," (Born noticed that Dr. Genzmer lisped when he got excited), "truly, a shameful method."

"And what about Gofman and Tamplin," asked a man from the floor, "the two American professors who proved the connection between atomic radiation and leukemia? And Professor Sternglass, who investigated the infant mortality near atomic reactors and came up with some awful results? And here in Germany, Professor Walter Bechert, who's been warning us about the consequences of atomic energy. Are you trying to say that they're lying?"

Dr. Genzmer cleared his throat. "Perhaps not consciously. But the ultimate effect. . . ."

The Civic Initiators at the tables in the front rows protested with trampling feet and hisses.

"Just listen to the genuine, the irrefutable figures," said Dr. Genzmer. "Do you realize how much natural radiation you absorb every year, radiation from outer space and from the earth? In the measuring units that we use for the biologically effective radiation dose absorbed by the body, that would amount to eighty-thousandths of a rem, that is, a roentgen equivalent man. Do you know how much radiation you take in every year through X-ray machines and cobalt bombs, and so forth? Thirty-thousandths of a rem per annum. And can you imagine how much radiation all the big nuclear stations together give off into the environment? One-thousandth of a rem per annum, ladies and gentlemen—a barely measurable, totally harmless dose.

"A committee of prominent scientists, the International Commission for Protection against Radiation, came to the conclusion that a technologically produced radiation load of one hundred and seventy-thousandths of a rem per annum is quite unproblematic for the population—along with the natural radioactivity. Thus, nuclear stations do not even achieve one percent of the permitted dose. And this one percent is so thinned down by water and air that the radiation is practically zero."

Berger shouted, "Do you know what the first man said when he pissed into the Baltic Sea? 'A little piss won't hurt in all this water.' And just look at the Baltic Sea today!"

21

The blond man who had grabbed him laughed and let go. "Bad reaction," he laughed. "Jesus, Werner! Ever since you got your turban, you haven't been up to scratch."

He gasped and kept his head down. The blond was no senile brownnoser like the watchman at the entrance. And he was a friend of Marcks's. He would realize he wasn't Marcks. He wondered how he could kill the blond. He couldn't do it with his bare hands, even if he managed to catch him offguard.

He put on a coughing fit to gain time. There was a metal locker thirty feet away. The door was open. Inside hung wire, a pair of pliers and a dipstick, probably for oil, about five feet long. With his head down, he walked around the blond over to the locker.

"Hey," exclaimed the man, "are you pissed off?"

Three more paces. Now he had the stick in his hand. Now he could talk.

"No," he said. "I thought I heard something hissing by a tube."

"There's hissing everywhere here," said the blond. And then, "Werner, what's with you, anyway?"

Only the blond's head was free, the body was stuck in the white frog suit. He struck the head from the side with all his strength. The thin stick was like a whip. It tore open the skin and ripped up the side of the nose. The man instinctively held his hands over his face and lowered his head. Now the killer rammed the stick obliquely from above against the blond's neck. The stick slid off the spine and bored inches down into the flesh between bones and muscles. He pulled out the stick. The blond sank to his knees. He sighed—a sigh so full of pain that the killer was paralyzed for two seconds. The left shoulder of the white suit was already drenched with blood. He staggered blindly back to his feet, but he had lost his sense of direction. He reeled past the killer and was only stopped by a pipe wall. The label said CONDENSER. As the blond stood there with his back to him, the killer ran with the stick towards the red-splashed back like a clumsy toreador and stabbed the stick into the back hip high. The stick barely bent; it cut through the suit, slid through skin, nerves, tissue, and cracked against the pipe after emerging from the body. The blond fell like a sack. He breathed short and loud like a man having a heart attack. The gasping wouldn't stop. The other man bent over him, whispering, "Keep quiet—keep quiet—keep quiet!" And rattled the stick in the wound.

When the blond stopped breathing, the murderer pulled the stick out of his body and dropped it on the corpse. He tried to shove the corpse under the pipe. He couldn't do it. He crawled under the pipe and, creeping backwards, pulled the body along by the feet, in brief tugs. After ten minutes, he had covered ten yards. He crawled back to the corridor.

His white overshoes were full of blood. He took them off carefully so as not to stain the sleeves of his suit. The shoe cloth didn't soak up very well. Red spots remained. The murderer threw the shoes under the pipe. He trembled. His testicles hurt. He followed the exit sign.

The man at the table in the dressing room was still sleeping. The murderer signed Marcks's name in the departure column of the control book. The man he had killed was named Zander. His signature was over that of the murderer, who copied it with an unsteady hand. The murdered man had thus officially left the room.

In Marcks's room, the murderer hung the smock up in the closet. He spread the blueprint of the turbine over the desk.

The watchman, Rogolski, was drowsing. He waved the murderer off when he raised the briefcase and tapped his fingers on it questioningly.

76

The murderer walked over and leaned on the car. He felt drained. He had a lot to learn if he was going to do similar jobs in the future. Especially cold-bloodedness. Killing hadn't bothered him. But the fear of getting killed. He was no Kamikaze type, no crazy Palestinian. He had to learn, for he was needed. Everyone needed him, even though they didn't know that he existed. They would never find out.

He imagined an army of invisible men, men without names or faces, who would never be mentioned in any history book, any news report, never receive a medal, a title. These men were the custodians of mankind. They tried to stop wrong developments, to silence false prophets. They prevented and committed murders. They were not all-powerful. They often failed. But they kept fighting. It was these men, he imagined, who had given the American journalists the information that had ultimately forced a dishonest president to resign. A late revenge for Dallas, when the invisible men had been unable to prevent Kennedy's assassination.

He, the murderer, the custodian, was a soldier in this army. He didn't know his comrades. But he knew he wasn't fighting alone. He didn't want gratitude. He hoped that some day, when mankind no longer obeyed the principle of destruction but the principle of life, when mankind was ruled by thinking and feeling men and not by cold technologists—he hoped that then one of the new men would know how to read the signs of the bloody past, that he would perceive where doom had been averted without visible grounds and where a turn for the better had been inaugurated. He hoped that this happy descendant of unhappy forebears would sense that he owed his unthreatened, peaceful life to the sufferings and efforts of anonymous heroes.

Halfway between the plant and the highway, the murderer halted. He prepared the third bomb. To the left, near the road, stood one of the powerful pylons through whose isolator forests the lines ran, connecting the plant to the electricity grid.

With the bomb in his hand, he leaped over the dried-out roadside ditch and walked towards the pylon. He attached the bomb to a steel girder three feet above the ground. Then he walked back to the car.

He drove the Volvo to the dirt road, where he had waited for Marcks more than two hours ago. After three hundred feet, he steered the car over a potato field into an unused hay shed. He loaded the metal boxes from Marcks's briefcase into his own. He wiped all the areas he had touched. He opened the car trunk, undressed, and threw the clothes and the bandage over the corpse. He put on his own clothes. He struck off for the BMW standing about a mile farther on the road. His momentary ennervation had left him and now he was happy.

22

"I'm sorry to call you at a time like this, Commissioner," said Inspector Kramer of the Federal Criminal Agency at Wiesbaden. He was in Sylt. "Yessir, I won't excuse myself any more. We began with the hotels and the better rooming houses in Kampen, but we haven't found anything yet. If we don't have any success here, Henning will drive to the South Tip and I'll go through the North around List. What? This fucking telephone line! Hello? I didn't understand the question. Okay, I can hear you now. . . . No, the bomb threat this afternoon had nothing to do with it. I'll stake my pension on that. Those were kids or teenagers putting on a big act. The danger is with people who don't say anything, or else call up when it's all over and say 'The credit for the assassination belongs to the December 24 commando or the April First' or whatever. . . . I'm sorry I can't report anything better from here. Maybe we're wearing out shoe leather for nothing. Maybe number seven is a harm-

less figure. But Commissioner, I have a weird feeling. . . .
What? I always do! But my hunches turn out right three times
out of four. Much too high for my peace of mind. . . . Okay,
I'll call back. Yes, no matter what time it is. My pleasure.
. . . What? . . . We already did. . . . Two colleagues from
Kampen are helping us. We couldn't get more. Everyone's on
vacation. That reminds me——It's okay. Good night."

23

FROM THE OPEN LETTER OF THE ASSOCIATION OF VINTNERS'
ORGANIZATIONS GARDING AND GRENZHEIM, TO GOVERNOR
BERTRAM KLINGER. JULY 22 .

The state and the federal governments, by pursuing the construction of the Helios nuclear power plant, are endangering
the existence of hundreds of vintners and their families. The
famous and respected wine from our farming areas is already
being condemned as the "atomic wine." And that is not the
worst of it. The cooling towers, which are supposedly meant
to protect the Rhine from overly hot waste waters, will impov-
erish the quality of our wine and will some day destroy our
entire viniculture. The huge amounts of steam expelled by
those towers have increased the formation of fogs and mists.
We have engaged the meteorologist Dr. Klaus Ganske, to
prepare a report on this situation and he has established the
following: Even without cooling towers, the area around
Grenzheim and Garding has two hundred sunless days per
year. The billows of fog caused by the cooling towers have
raised this number to two hundred and fifty days. Furthermore,
Governor Klinger, you have lied to the citizens. In order to
break the resistance against the nuclear power station, you

claimed that Helios would be indispensable for providing electricity to hundreds of thousands of households from Worms to Frankfurt.

The truth is that the current supplied by conventional power plants is more than enough for these households. The atomic power plant is chiefly intended for heavy industry. It has been announced at the state capital that within three years, an aluminum plant, a steelworks, and a chemical factory are to be built in Grenzheim and neighboring hamlets. These plants will seriously endanger the future of viniculture.

The state elections are about to be held. We appeal to our fellow citizens that they teach you, Governor, and your consorts, a sharp lesson by voting for the men who do not intend to annihilate our life's work, and the existence of ourselves and our children with sanctimonious arguments about "infrastructure" and similar meretricious rhetoric. . . .

24

At about midnight, the discussion had reached deadlock. The tables in the back rows were emptying. Most of the Grenzheim people had to be at work early in the morning, in the fields, the vineyards, the factories. And in school, thought Born, gazing at Anne Weiss. As usual after a debate, not only such public ones, but also private confrontations, he felt he had wasted valuable time. For him, this talk battle, with its old, long-familiar information, was as boring as a debate between believers and atheists on the topic: Does God exist? Always the same arguments.

The opponents in the hall had been bombarding one another with figures. All figures were correct. But figures alone meant nothing. They had to be interpreted, and so much for sober statistics. Each person interpreted them according to his faith. For some, atomic energy was a deadly hazard, which would some day extinguish all life, and even the slightest possibility was enough to confirm their pessimism. For others, atomic energy was one of the greatest achievements of human inventiveness, which could be used without harm for the good of humanity.

The general mood perked up again when the Minister of Economy frankly described all the critics of Helios as "goddamn kittens," as "goody-goody products of a society that wants to have every luxury but not face any risk—insured in every phase of life from womb to tomb. If Robert Koch had been afraid of tubercular infection, where would medicine be today?"

Berger had attacked the "wheelings and dealings of the mayor during the approval procedures."

Mayor Rapp had pointed out that the construction companies and the tradespeople in town had for the past few years virtually lived from the employment connected with building the nuclear plant. And the Helios reactor and the new industrial plants would be pouring ten million marks a year into the town treasury. Money that Grenzheim needed for a hospital, a kindergarten, for long overdue roads.

Those Grenzheim citizens still present were not of the same opinion.

Now Anne Weiss asked to make a concluding statement. For four hours, she had been sitting in the same hot, foul air as Born. His shirt and trousers stuck to his body, sweat trickled from his forehead, and his eyes burnt. Anne Weiss looked as though she had just entered the place after sleeping twelve hours and spending one hour in front of a mirror. Her skin was matte and dry, her blouse had no creases.

She said, "We ought to stop the dismal performance of the amateur actors up there. None of us expected very much from this discussion on the eve of the so-called dedication. Only the old assertions, the old ignorance, the old high-handedness of the officials and the neutral experts, with 'neutral' in quotes.

"I thank all of you for coming tonight in support of the Civic Initiative. I ask you to keep supporting us. We shall keep fighting until this nuclear plant is gone. Or until it kills us all.

"We are against the Helios atomic power station because it pollutes the environment with radioactive rays. Even if this radiation is small, it is still dangerous. There is no such thing as a harmless dose of rays. Everything exceeding natural radiation, to which the human body has adapted over thousands of years, can cause sickness and death. The consequences may only become apparent decades from now, when this country will be teeming with atomic cretins and hundreds of thousands of people die of leukemia. To maintain that radiation is harmless because we do not see the consequences immediately is as logical as denying that smoking is hazardous just because you don't drop dead at the first puff.

"We are against the Helios nuclear station because even a minor accident can release a fatal amount of radioactivity that will pollute us all.

"We are against the Helios nuclear station because an accident that gets out of control would wipe out all life within a radius of ten, twenty, miles or more. We do not believe in the reliability of the safety system.

"A concatenation of neglect and unfortunate circumstances can lead to a catastrophe far outdoing any gloomy fantasies.

"The fact that the atomic advocates do not believe in the infallibility of their protective systems can be shown by the prohibition issued by the then Minister of Research for a nuclear plant near Ludwigshafen. The reason for the prohibition was clear to everyone involved. The planned reactor would have stood in the middle of an area of high urban concentration, and any accident would have affected millions of people. Are we, who live in Grenzheim and Garding, less valuable than the people of Ludwigshafen or Mannheim? What kind of lunatics are these who icily calculate: Ludwigshafen is too great a risk. But Grenzheim is expendable. Only six thousand people live there."

Anne Weiss received applause, and even the weary minister listened again.

"Our struggle against the Helios nuclear station has a special significance. Helios is the nineteenth atomic plant poisoning the inhabitants of West Germany. It is the greatest reactor in the world. It is a symbol of new German megalomania. Whereas the Western industrial nations with the longest experience in building reactors, England and the United States, limit their atomic energy programs (Great Britain has canceled more than sixty percent of its projected nuclear stations), whereas those nations constantly tighten their safety regulations, Germany is experiencing an atomic mania. Although German scientists have nowhere near the same experience as their American colleagues, although there is no research institute in this country where one might try out reactor accidents on realistic models, although the Germans are still apprentices in the practical use of atomic energy, they stick giants like Helios into our densely populated land and congratulate themselves as though they were geniuses.

"Do you really believe, Herr Hühnle, Herr Born, that the Americans could not have built a plant the size of Helios ten years ago? But they didn't. For they say: That's too dangerous for us. We still know too little. We might lose control of such a monster. The Germans don't have such scruples. In their old, familiar way, they march at the forefront of scorn for human life. An English newspaper has written: 'It looks as if the Germans, with their atomic reactor fanaticism, are trying to get a belated revenge for not having managed to construct the first atomic bomb back then.' And that's exactly what's happening. Go ahead and laugh, Herr Hühnle, go ahead and laugh. We know the types of men who show their teeth at the word 'humanity.'

"We are struggling against Helios so that megalomania

will not push us into a catastrophe. The courts have thrown out our cases. Herr Hühnle and his Prime Minister call us nitpickers, enemies of civilization, Communists, a tiny radical fringe, sentimental romantics, dangerous agitators, panic makers. Certain newspapers describe us as hysterics. But we will keep fighting, and we will not give up until murder weapons like Helios have vanished.

"We are not alone. We have support in Germany, in France, England, America, Japan. Some of our friends are present today. In a few hours, they will be at the demonstration, which I hope you will all take part in. Even if it means losing sleep. We are meeting at ten A.M. in front of the nuclear plant. We will prove that there are still people in this country who have something on their minds besides profit, rates of growth, and delusions of progress."

Huge applause, and with that the meeting broke up. The Civic Initative people surrounded Anne Weiss, shaking her hand. The Grenzheimers left the Black Eagle, some of them reeling. Most of them would sleep well despite the heat. The Minister of Economy stretched and groped unsteadily down the left-hand steps into the hall. The mayor was talking with the police chief of Grenzheim. He was probably worried about the announcement of the demonstration, even though the Governor would be arriving with a whole squadron of bodyguards and policemen. Born had heard that they had even asked for a hundred national guardsmen. Just in case.

Born paid Professor Schubert and Dr. Genzmer the appropriate compliments and thanked them for their lucid contributions. Schubert and Genzmer assured him the pleasure was all theirs. Born knew that each man had received two thousand marks for this evening. And rightly so. He accompanied them to the stairway at the front, leading to the guest rooms. Both were spending the night in the Eagle, as was the Minister of Economy. Both were taking part in the ceremony, as guests of honor. Born promised them a plentiful cold buffet.

The TV crew was taking down the spotlights and winding

up the cables. Born heard Larsen's clear voice. He was arguing with an older man. The man was saying that capitalists were putting up atomic reactors merely to produce plutonium for atomic bombs, Larsen answered that reactor plutonium is not suitable for atomic bombs. The man said that any child could make an A-bomb with plutonium, and in America every year twelve pounds of plutonium vanished without a trace from reactors and processing plants. Besides, with a ball of plutonium the size of a grapefruit one could contaminate all mankind. Larsen asked the man why he didn't go to East Germany and agitate against nuclear stations there. The Russians were tacking together reactors that scared the daylights out of Western safety experts. Born shook his head.

"Are you Herr Larsen?"

Born turned around. It was a woman of about forty, darkly tanned, her face glowing, with a touch of age, silver jewelry, an expensive outfit, her sunglasses pushed high into the tightly combed hair, which had a broad silvery streak to the right. The woman introduced herself with a double last name that Born forgot instantly. She said, "From the magazine *Yvonne*. We spoke on the phone yesterday.

Born tilted his head towards Larsen, who was surrounded by a group of people vainly trying to interrupt Larsen's sonorous, penetrating lecture on the blessings of the atom. "You'll find him over there. The blond guy who's speaking."

"But I know you," said the woman. "Of course! You must be the director. You look a lot younger than your photos."

Born didn't know what to reply.

"You see we're running a series on young men on the way up," said the newspaper woman. "That's why I made an appointment to interview Herr Larsen. Too bad you won't be in the series. But you must be over thirty-two, right? That's our absolute limit."

"Herr Larsen would be just the man for you," said Born. "If I were you, I'd go over to him right now. Otherwise he'll talk himself hoarse before you get a chance to speak to him."

Born was amused to see Larsen break off his sermon the moment he spotted the newspaperwoman. As the two of them walked towards the hall door, Born saw Larsen's eager smile, and it made him feel malicious.

"Herr Larsen!"

Larsen turned his head and halted reluctantly. Since Born didn't stir, he finally had to come over to him—after a gesture of excuse to the woman.

"Larsen, I forgot something," said Born. "The maintenance people are supposed to be examined for radiation, but the doctor only has time early tomorrow——" he looked at his watch, "early *this* morning. I would have called you about it if you'd been at work as planned. It would be best if you drove out there and told the men on night shift not to dash home at six but to wait for the doctor. They'll be paid overtime."

Larsen wanted to object, but Born left him there. He thought to himself, "It's not fair, but he deserves it."

Anne Weiss was leaning against one of the oak beams in the middle of the room. Berger was sitting at a table a few yards away from her. Hühnle was swaying in front of Anne Weiss on the balls of his feet. His jacket hung loosely over his shoulders, his tie was loosened, revealing a forest of reddish hair on his chest.

Born heard him saying, "Too bad you're on the wrong side. I can always use capable people. We could agree on a trial period, say one month. A responsible job in the campaign office. For a fee. How's that for an offer?"

"You're drunk," replied Anne Weiss.

"But, my girl," laughed Hühnle, "that's no answer."

Anne Weiss tried to get past him and go back to her table. Hühnle stood in her path. She bounced off him, and Hühnle put his arm around her waist. Berger leaped up and pulled Hühnle back. Anne Weiss stumbled against Born.

"Don't, Achim," she called to Berger. But Berger was already on the floor, two bodyguards holding down his arms, one kneeling on his back.

"Dumb broad," said Hühnle. "Let him go, boys." Hühnle noticed Born, grinned, walked over to him, took his arm, and said, "We don't have any friends here, director. Let's go have a drink."

Mayor Rapp scurried up and pushed over to the minister. "Excuse what happened, please," he stammered and then hissed, "You'll hear from me, Frau Weiss." Born drew away from Hühnle's arm and left him to the mayor, who together with his guest (a Hühnle did not honor Grenzheim every day) was marching off to the back room, followed by the bodyguards.

Anne Weiss and Born helped Berger to his feet.

"Thank you," said Anne.

Born asked Berger, "Everything okay?"

Berger nodded hostilely.

"That wasn't very smart, Achim," said Anne. It sounded like a bad mark for a term paper.

Berger looked at her.

The poor guy, thought Born, he's got it bad.

Berger took a briefcase from the table and left without saying goodbye.

Born then turned to Anne and said, "Minister Hühnle is an earthy type. You shouldn't hold it against him."

Anne said, "You don't have to apologize, or are you in the same party? I think he's a pig, whether he calls me a dumb broad or not. He probably doesn't have a woman for the night."

Born knew she was wrong. Mayor Rapp had spoken briefly with the proprietor before, and not about drinks.

"You made an impression on him," said Born.

The room was nearly empty. Glasses were clinking. The proprietor's wife and their two daughters were clearing up. Anne packed manuscripts, leaflets, and newspaper clippings from her table into a leather briefcase. The full briefcase tumbled to the floor, and they knelt down together to gather up the papers.

"Are you satisfied?" asked Anne.

"About what?"

"About the opening of your station tomorrow, despite our protests, which you don't take seriously anyway."

"That's not true," said Born. "I do take them seriously. But I don't agree with you."

He walked alongside her towards the door. She pointed at the bodyguards in front of the back room, in which Hühnle and Rapp had disappeared. "Aren't you needed inside?"

Born said, "I would only be in the way."

He took her arm. As they came out into the street, the proprietor was walking towards them with a fat girl at his side. Poor Hühnle, thought Born.

25

"Why are you actually in favor of the atomic plant, Rapp?" asked Hühnle. "Two-thirds of the population are against you, and you're having elections in another year. They'll kick you right out of the town hall."

Rapp said, "For me, the interest of the community stands above any concern about my personal success. . . ."

"All right," said Hühnle. "You have a lot of land here in the area, according to the register."

"Oh well," Rapp cleared his throat. He felt queasy. "What do you mean a lot? A few fields, some meadows, nothing special."

Hühnle guffawed. "C'mon, Herr Mayor. We're among friends."

Rapp smiled with relief.

"For the three plants projected in this area," said Hühnle, "there are only five suitable lots in the development plan. Four of them belong to you."

"The offers were advantageous," said Rapp. "And some of them belonged to me before I ever knew that——"

"Bullshit!" said Hühnle. "Don't piss in your pants. You did some clever speculating. You were smart. That's fine. We don't want any slowpokes in our party. But there's one catch."

"What?"

"It was wise of you to transfer the property to your wife's sister and her husband. But that'll only work as long as no one investigates. If you aren't reelected, your successor is going to start sniffing around in the records. And when they find out how much you've skimmed off, there'll be a scandal. We can't use it. It'll hurt our image."

"What should I do?" asked Rapp.

"The party has four real estate companies. We'll buy your lots. The sale will be back-dated to the dates you bought the property yourself. You won't be in the picture anymore, and no one can step in your shit."

Rapp was surprised. "But the prices are at rock bottom now! It's not even certain that there'll be any factories. I'll lose——"

"Bullshit!" said Hühnle. "You won't lose anything. You bought for two marks. You would sell to the factories for ten marks per square meter. We're offering you eight marks today. That's way over the market value. Are you in?"

Rapp nodded. He had no choice.

"Rapp," said Hühnle. "If you're not back in town hall next year, call me. I'll find something for you."

Rapp thought, Yes, if *you're* reelected in four weeks.

"Thank you, Herr Minister," he said.

"That teacher broad," asked Hühnle, "is she from around here?"

"Frau Weiss? She's from Frankfurt. But she acts like she was born here."

"Nice-looking broad. She popular?"

"With the students. Not so much with the parents. Pretty left wing. Actually the whole business started with her. Previously, the Civic Initiative was very peaceful."

"There's a rule against radicals in public service," said Hühnle. "If it helps you, I'll be glad to give a tip to my colleagues in the cultural department."

"You'd be doing me a big favor, And the town too, of course," added Rapp.

The minister downed his beer and walked to the open door to the terrace. He pulled down his pants zipper and pissed noisily into the darkness.

"What do you think about the plant, Rapp, about Helios?"

"As you explained, Herr Minister, the infrastructure of the community——"

"Cut the bullshit. I mean, are you scared of that atomic stuff, the rays and so on?"

Rapp stood up straight. "Certainly not."

The minister pulled up his zipper. "You're an asshole, Rapp. I'm scared."

Someone knocked. The proprietor entered bowing, a tray full of foamy beer glasses in his left hand. He put down the tray, placed the glasses on the table, and took along the empty ones. He scurried to the door. He murmured: "She's here, if you. . . ."

"Let her wait," said Rapp.

"I always feel queasy about these atomic eggs," said Hühnle, "even though three of them are right here because I went all out for them. I'm not so sure the damn things won't blow up in our faces some day. But do you know what I tell myself, Rapp?" "I tell myself: We're the third biggest industrial nation in the world. Our greatness is dependent on getting raw materials. And we're so poor in raw material ourselves. The oil crisis proved it. I wouldn't want to go through that again. A couple of hook-nosed camel drivers fucked up our whole economy. A syphilitic sheik can destroy in one year what we've built up in decades of work since the war. That's why we have to become independent of the oil robbers. We owe it to our pride and our honor.

90

"We need atomic energy. Even if it's dangerous. Live dangerously, said Nietzsche. Prosperity isn't a gift. It requires sacrifices. We sacrifice eighteen thousand people a year, not counting cripples, to our auto industry. Thank God it's running again. If we suddenly prohibited cars out of humanitarianism, what would be the consequences? Misery, unemployment, reduction of the gross national product. We'd be up shit's creek. And we're also up shit's creek if we don't build nuclear stations. That's what *I* say, I, Eberhard Hühnle. And when someone tells me: The nuclear plants cost fifty thousand lives a year, then I ask: Is that too much to supply work and bread to sixty-one million nine hundred and fifty thousand people? No. That's not too much."

Hühnle stood up. "What've you brought me out there?"

"Iris," said Rapp. "She's only seventeen. But. . . ."

"Jesus!" said the minister. "You're getting me into a real mess."

26

The midnight chimes of the clock aroused Sibylle Born. She had bought it in London for a thousand pounds because of the aristocratic striking and the painted dial face, which showed the position of the constellations. Sibylle could barely breathe, she was so thirsty. She drank up half a bottle of mineral water. Her head ached. She went to the telephone and dialed. No answer. She threw a light linen coat over her shoulders, stumbled down the entrance steps, and groped her way to the red Alfa Romeo, which had its top up. She pressed the radio button and hunted for Radio Luxemburg. George McCrae was singing "Rock Your Baby." Sibylle hummed along and drove past the castle park, through the quiet streets, across the square with the slender statue of Archduke Ludwig, along the gray building with the sign that read ELECTRICITY—THE ENERGY OF THE FUTURE, then through narrow streets. At some point she realized she hadn't switched her headlights on.

She stopped in front of a house squeezed between a car park and an office building. No light anywhere. She accidentally pressed a buzzer instead of a light switch. She unlocked the door and climbed the steps. One flight up stood an old man, wearing a night cap.

He was furious at the disturbance, but excited, "If you have to carry on at this time of night, don't bother decent people."

Sibylle said, "Oh, please excuse me, Herr Birnbaum."

Herr Birnbaum was a widower. He had probably been born a widower. Sibylle suspected him of having attached microphones to the ceiling to gather as much information as possible from the overhead bedroom. She didn't mind. She stepped towards him and had to smile at the way he timidly stepped back. She pulled up her skirt, not too high, and said, "We've got mosquitoes again this year. What a plague!" She scratched her thigh. Herr Birnbaum slammed his door.

Sibylle climbed up another flight—the stairwell smelled of floor wax—and listened at the door. A dirty scrap of paper on it said FUCHS. The apartment was still. She unlocked the door. Alexander Fuchs, lying on his bed fully dressed, blinked into the light. Sibylle asked him, "Were you asleep?"

"No."

"I was thinking about you. Where were you?"

"Out."

"A woman?"

"No."

"You don't want to talk to me?"

"No."

Sibylle didn't ask any more questions. During the first few weeks of their relationship, she had interrogated him whenever he vanished for a couple of days. He had told her nothing and had even—he, the quiet, gentle Alexander—become annoyed. He acted as though he led a double life. Yet Sibylle reasoned that his secrets were harmless. She had entered his second life twice by accident. Once, she had seen him on a lake in the woods. She was on an outing with Martin and a few friends. They had rowed out into the lake, and there sat Alexander in a boat. He wasn't rowing, he wasn't fishing, he wasn't swimming, he just sat there staring at the water. He didn't notice her.

And once she had followed him through Frankfurt for half a day. She had seen him while she was shopping, and had then started trailing him. After four hours, she gave up. He was running about the streets and stopped only once, to eat a sausage. Sibylle was embarrassed and wanted to go over to him, but she didn't dare because he would think that she had been spying on him—which she was.

She undressed. Skirt, panties, blouse, all in one swoop. She gazed in satisfaction at her brown body in the mirror. She bent over him and rubbed her swinging breasts in his face. She put his right hand between her thighs. "What's wrong?" she asked. "Don't you feel like it?"

"I'm tired."

"Sasha, you have to do something for your money."

She knew he was indifferent to remarks about her paying his rent.

"I'm tired," he said.

"You're talking like my husband."

She pulled off his pants. He moaned. She examined him cautiously. His left testicle was burning red and thickly swollen. Sympathetically she sucked air in through her teeth. She then moistened a cloth and cooled the swelling. He closed his eyes. She whispered sweet nothings as though lulling a child to sleep. When she saw that her touch aroused him, she carefully sat down upon him. After her orgasm, he fell asleep. Sibylle put her head close to his mouth so that his breath caressed her skin.

27

It had begun on an ice cold afternoon early last April. Martin hadn't been home for three days. He had been sleeping at the plant. Problems with something, as usual, a valve or a pipe, she wasn't listening. Nor did she feel any desire to see him. For two months she had been sleeping with an architect who had built a supermarket on the outskirts of town. A pleasant diversion, they met three times a week. On weekends he drove to his family in Munich. He was pretty good in bed, simpleminded, but thorough, energetic, no frills. She had met him at one of the few parties for which Martin had had time. The man brought her presents—a lighter, a bracelet, expensive things. She took them because he'd have been disappointed if she refused. He viewed their relationship as a business transaction although he wasn't a cold sort. He was really warm, human, interested in her marriage and why she was deceiving Martin. He regarded their relationship, as he put it, realistically—a pleasure clause in his supermarket contract, which would terminate with the close of construction.

And it had. He had gone back to Munich, and she had no new man. A few days earlier, she had almost succeeded in seducing Peter Larsen, the safety head at the plant. Not because she desired him. He was too smooth, too emphatically boyish, a type who almost drove her to love Martin again— Martin, who was a totally different kind of man, superior, honest, unerring.

She didn't realize it till later but she really wanted to get back at Born by flirting with Larsen. Larsen, however—that's the kind of guy he was—backed out at the last minute. She had offered herself to him, first inconspicuously, then more clearly,

94

and he had put on a show like a bull with the most beautiful heifers charging into his stable. Naturally, he was also fascinated at the idea of the boss's wife.

But it quickly turned out that he was scared shitless of actually entering the boss's territory, even if the boss wasn't in such high form anymore. Born had power. And his power could hurt Larsen's career if Born found out that his safety expert and anti-radiation man had made it with his wife. Larsen decided not to savor his triumph except for a little petting once when he brought Sibylle home. Since then, he had never seen Sibylle without Born's being present.

On that cold April afternoon, she had hurried through town, smirking at what the Darmstadt boutiques were vending as the latest Paris fashion. Then she had crossed the Rhine to the Taubenschlag.

The Taubenschlag was a hill facing Grenzheim. Its name meant "dovecote." She had never seen a dove there. The vineyards in the surrounding area were bare. Fir trees grew on the hill. The peak (actually, only 500 feet high) offered a wide view of the Rhine plain.

Straight across from it stood a radiant domed building. Not a puff of smoke came from the chimney: The Helios nuclear station.

Sibylle didn't know why she occasionally stood here, gazing at the building that she hated. Martin was down there, telephoning, conferring, basking in responsibility, enclosed by white, hygienic walls.

Some detachment, Martin, she thought. Detachment from yourself, from your damned Calvinist work mania, and your plant. Why is that so hard for you? With a gesture and the right word, you could have me. . . .

The underbrush crackled. The man walking towards her looked like a teenager. He couldn't have been more than twenty-five. He wore jeans, soaked sneakers, and an expensive leather jacket, which the light rain had darkened on the sleeves and shoulders. He was tall, his hair was black or brown, it was dripping, and his long, bony chin was shadowed with stubble. His left hand held a rifle. He tried to hide the gun behind his back. "I'm sorry," he said. "If I'd known there was somebody here. . . ."

"This is a public hill," Sibylle retorted.

He turned around. "Are you alone?"

"All alone," said Sibylle.

"Are you afraid?"

"No," said Sibylle. "As long as you don't kill me."

The boy sat down on the wooden bench that encircled a tree trunk. He asked, "Do you come here a lot?"

"Seldom," said Sibylle.

"Otherwise I would have run into you here," said the boy.

"Do you come for the view?" asked Sibylle.

The boy nodded. "I believe the countryside used to be very beautiful. But today? Factories, dirt, stench. Do you see that black cloud to the left there in the Rhine? That's oil. And detergents and mercury and shit."

The boy didn't say anything for a long time. The hair at the back of his neck was so long that it was curling.

"And the nuclear station," he finally said. "Beautiful, white, and clean. Do you know that . . ." he broke off. "What's the difference. I don't want to bother you any more."

"Do you go hunting?"

"What?"

"Do you go hunting up here? With the rifle?"

"Yes. I do some shooting around here."

"What kind of game is around now?

The boy shrugged. "I don't know. Rabbits, partridges."

"But you didn't shoot today?"

"No."

"What kind of a gun is it?"

"A Winchester," said the boy. "An imitation of the 1890's model. A present from my father."

"Is he a hunter?"

"He has a hunting ground."

"Around here?"

"In the Eifel."

"I'm getting on your nerves," said Sibylle.

"No," said the boy.

"Where do you come from?"

"Frankfurt."

"What do you do?"

"I study."

"What?"

"I don't know."

Sibylle gazed at his earnest profile. She said, "May I shoot it."

"Do you know anything about guns?"

"I once shot paper flowers at the county fair."

The boy stood up. He released the safety catch and said, "I'll show you how."

Sibylle took the gun and aimed.

"Not like that." He stepped behind her. "Aim at the fir tree to the right there."

He had his head against her hair and shifted her hand to the right place. "There. Then the barrel's calm. And now notch, bead, and trunk."

She pressed the trigger. The kick pulled up the gun. The bullet splintered the white trunk. She leaned against him.

"Thank you," she said. "See? I learn fast."

He sat down again on the wet bench. He asked, "When you saw me, were you afraid I'd rape you?"

Sibylle shook her head. "You don't look like the type."

They were silent. A cold April rain dripped from the fir trees.

"I'm cold," said Sibylle. "And I'm hungry too. There's a restaurant nearby."

"Okay, then. . . ." The boy was about to shake hands.

Sibylle said, "Where's your car?"

"Down below, on the slope."

"Then drive after me."

28

Sibylle propped her head on her arm and gazed at Alexander Fuchs in the dim reflection of the neon light that fell into the room from the street. Fuchs slept the way he spoke, moved, or loved—gently and softly. He could lie there for hours, forgetting Sibylle's presence and "thinking," as Sibylle called it, although she didn't know whether he was simply staring into space, empty and lost in dream worlds, in which he never let her cast a glance.

He had never hurt her. He wouldn't have been capable of making bitter and sharp comments like Martin. At first she had mistaken his gentleness for helplessness. She had started her relationship with motherly feelings. But soon Sibylle had sensed strength and purpose (though she didn't know the goal) behind his gentleness.

A quiet energy to which she yielded, in which she wanted to participate, to which she ultimately became addicted. He had taken her offer as a matter of course. She would rent a small apartment for him in Darmstadt so that they could be together as often as possible. He had dropped out of school. His father sent him a check for eight hundred marks every month. He was writing a book, but he didn't let on very much about the contents. It was about the future of mankind, the dangers of technological development, the decline of the West.

For the chapter on nuclear stations, Sibylle had given him books and designs from Born's rich library, without Martin's noticing it.

Sibylle stroked Alexander's beard and the dry soft skin on his chest. He kept sleeping. She stood up and dressed quietly.

She wrote a note: "Thank you, chéri." And sealed it with a lipstick imprint.

She stood in front of the mirror. Her hair was chaotic and twisted about her head like an Afro. Her blouse was crumpled. She felt infinitely fine.

29

Peter Larsen had no intention of following Born's order and driving to the plant. He had more important things to do. He had to make the newspaperwoman with the double name realize that industry in general and West Germany in particular needed men like Larsen, men who did pioneering research, men of action, men who kept progress going. Despite the late hour, he invited her to his home, two miles from Grenzheim. It was a two-room apartment, of which he was very proud. One room was filled with a water bed. The other room was sparely but expensively furnished: a white Italian leather couch, a Charles Eames chair, a silvery white desk set by Miller, and the accompanying bookcases, which were filled with technical books, arranged by subject matter. An engraving of a Picasso faun hung in the bedroom, a Steinberg lithograph in the living room. A small atomic model stood on a glass table in the living room. It was a miniature edition of the logo at the Brussels World Fair.

He filled two glasses with whiskey and called the Helios plant, Zander's extension. Zander didn't answer. He dialed the guard station and gave Rogolski Born's instructions. The night shift people were to wait for the radiation doctor in the morning. Rogolski said he would leave a note on Zander's desk.

"Did something happen?" asked the newspaperwoman.

"What do you mean?"

"Radiation doctor. Sounds dangerous."

Larsen guffawed. "Routine. All Helios employees have to be examined regularly. They can only absorb a certain amount of radiation every year, just like X-ray personnel. The examination shows what percent of the permissible radiation quota the workers have taken in. If a worker's helped to load the uranium fuel cells, he's probably gotten more than the average amount. In absolute terms, it's practically nothing, totally harmless. But the law's the law. For the rest of the year, the man can only work on jobs that won't expose him to radiation above his limit."

"So your job is to supervise that?"

"Among other things," said Larsen casually. "Aside from controlling the fulfillment of all anti-radiation measures, supervising the alarm facilities, and the loading and transporting of atomic waste, and then of course the safety of the plant. My department includes the plant police."

"That's some responsibility," said the newspaperwoman. Larsen nodded.

"For a lay person like myself, that all sounds terribly bureaucratic and thoroughly organized, almost inhumanly so."

Larsen sighed. "I'm telling you! All the rules certainly don't make the work any easier for us. But I just look upon them as psychological. The rules are meant to put people's minds at ease, especially the overly anxious critical souls you saw at the discussion tonight. My employees and workers have a sound sense of whether a law is reasonable or not. If we stuck to the letter of each regulation, we'd never get anywhere. It would be like an overly meticulous air traffic controller—total chaos. We watch out for the general structure, and sometimes we close our eyes to a detail here and there. Naturally, we have to know the tolerance limits."

"Do you like your work?"

Larsen kept silent for a long time to show he was thinking. The tape cassette was whirring softly. Since agreeing to this interview, Larsen had been carefully preparing himself for such questions. He said, "It's an organizational and administrative job of utmost importance. But I do not believe that it can satisfy a scientist in the long run—although every scientist ought to get such experience *in situ.*"

"And you're a scientist?"

"With all my heart. The exciting, the new and crucial, things in atomic physics are happening on the research front, and not—I am not implying any value judgment with the term —and not behind the lines.

"Haven't the most important discoveries been made already?" asked the newspaperwoman.

"Certainly. The pioneer days are past. Göttingen, Cambridge, Copenhagen, Rome, Rutherford, Curie, Bohr, Hahn. They've all become history. But there's still virgin soil in front of us, and we don't know how vast it is. It's waiting for us to open it up. For the good of mankind. Nuclear fusion, for instance, is a gigantic field with many unsolved questions. The man who will someday tame hydrogen fusion will rightfully stand next to the great figures of science. Let me explain it to you. Deuterium is. . . ."

Larsen talked, the cassettes filled up, the newspaperwoman dozed. She had left her girlfried in Hamburg, a pretty thing, just twenty. At the airport, she had sworn she'd be faithful. The newspaperwoman felt the fatigue digging craters and cracks into her skin. She didn't believe her girlfriend.

30

"A beautiful night," said Born. The moon was misty, the air soft and dense like water. Swarms of mosquitoes flitted around the neon lamps. Mayor Rapp had promised that the taxes from the atomic plant would first go for new street lighting.

"It's the most beautiful summer since my childhood," said Anne.

"Just smell."

They stopped. Born inhaled deeply. The air was redolent of blossoms. Anne put her hand on his arm and gazed at him. "I would like to ask you something because I believe that you will answer me honestly. I promise I will keep your answer to myself, no matter what it is."

Born stood motionless so as not to frighten away her hand. The scent of her hair mixed with the scent of the blossoms. Anne asked, "Would you guarantee with your life that atomic reactors will never trigger a catastophe?"

Born thought: She's not married. Rapp said so at some point or other. Does she live with someone. He answered, "Yes."

"You're very certain."

"I would make one qualification."

"Namely?"

"Reactors are safe as long as they're run by human beings who are aware of their enormous responsibility."

Anne said, "You're taking back your 'yes.' No human being can concentrate on his responsibility every second. Everyone makes a mistake some time."

"We can deal with those mistakes," said Born. "We've got electronics for that. It blocks off wrong decisions. If, for instance, the reactor is running at full capacity and some idiot presses the button that usually increases operations, nothing will happen. The electronic system won't react. On the other hand, it can act faster than a man if something is not in order —say a loose valve. The reactor will automatically be halted."

"If the system is foolproof," asked Anne, "why are you worried?"

"A fool can always find a loophole for his folly. You can give him the most perfect computer in the world, and he'll be so sloppy that he'll pull out the plug. Our security system at Helios is not immune to fools. It's designed for people for whom mistakes are exceptional, for whom reliability and responsibility are the rule. If this principle were upset and frivolity and sloppiness shuffled in. . . ."

They turned into a narrow road lined on both sides with rhododendron bushes.

"We have huge checklists for every job at the plant," said Born. "They cover every movement so that no one will be exposed to radioactivity because of carelessless. There is no way of preventing a certain routine from settling in. And it's only a step from there to bungling. A container clasp is supposed to be checked regularly. You check it carefully fifty times, and because it's always okay, you get sloppy the fifty-first time and you may not even bother to look. You simply check off the entry on the list. That can be fatal. That's why we constantly hammer it into our people's heads: The regulations are not for harrassment. They're an indispensable protection of their health."

They had just left the bright circle of one street light and reentered darkness. They almost ran into the four shadows barring their way.

"Best wishes from Thomas," said one of the figures. "He wants to see you. He'd like to tell you how things were at the station house."

"He can talk to me tomorrow," said Anne. Born heard fear in her voice.

The four young men looked familiar to Born, but he couldn't place them. One of them stepped up to him. "Get lost. This is private."

Born asked Anne, "What would you like?"

"It's all right. Please go."

"Get going, man. Didn't you hear the lady? Get lost!"

Anne's face turned white. Born said quietly, "Let us through."

Anne touched him and shook her head.

The spokesman of the four took two steps and pushed Born aside. Anne's briefcase was under Born's arm. He threw it in the man's face. He reeled against the other three. The group formed and came slowly towards Anne and Born. Born saw the brass knuckles glittering on one man's fist. The man Born had attacked was swinging a bicycle chain. Born said to Anne, "Run quick. Run!"

Anne didn't stir.

Born had a scar on his left shoulder, from a razor blade wielded by a member of the Black Devils during a Rocker battle twenty years ago. The blade had ripped through the skin down to the bone. The man with the bicycle chain struck first. He wasn't practiced. He struck from above and first swept out his arm. Born bent his arm. The chain wrapped around it. Born pulled the man up to himself on the chain and kicked him in the knee. The man dropped. But two were already behind Born, grabbing his arms. One of them hauled off and smashed his fist into Born's stomach.

The scream he heard didn't come from him or from Anne. He felt the weight of his attacker falling away on his left side. He banged his elbows into the other man's kidneys and sprang back. Achim Berger was fighting with two of the attackers. Born raised the bicycle chain and gave one of them a powerful blow from the back. The man groaned and held his hand over his right eyebrow, which had burst open. Blood was pouring down the right half of his face. Berger, who had lost his glasses, was hammering blindly and furiously into the second attacker until the man spun around and dashed off. The others followed. The man Born had kicked in the knee limped away in pain.

"Are you hurt?" asked Anne.

"I'm not. But Herr Berger. . . ."

Berger put on his glasses. "I'm all right."

Berger had vanished in the shadow of the bushes.

"He followed us," said Anne. "He lives on the other side of the village."

"He's in love with you," said Born. "Luckily. Otherwise those guys would have done me in. Who are they anyway?"

Anne told him about Thomas Muller and the Maoists.

After five minutes, they stopped in front of a red brick two-family house. Roses were blooming in the garden.

"This is where we live."

"We," thought Born. So there *is* a man. He had a bitter taste in his mouth. He sweated but his hands were cold. Anne's face was olive-colored in the dim light of a faraway lamp. A dark-green shimmer, like verdigris on a copper roof, surrounded her hair. For the first time he saw that she was naked under her blouse.

Born handed her the papers, which he had gathered up after the fight.

Anne left her hand down and said, "Let's talk a little more. Inside. If you like."

"I'd really like to," said Born, relieved. "I'd really like to."

Then he thought of the other tenant in the house, who was probably asleep or perhaps not even at home. Both possibilities dampened his enthusiasm. But he couldn't turn back now, so he followed her like a racing car driver who's been lapped and is doing his compulsory circles, undaunted, far behind the field.

31

Shortly before 12:30, Baumann, the head of plant protection, came to Rogolski in the watch house. He walked with a four-square gait, his Colt on his hip, and he sprawled into a chair, propping his feet on the table. "I'll keep you company for the rest of the shift," he said. There are supposed to be two men in this room according to regulations."

"Is something going on outside?"

"Niente." Baumann drew a cigarette from his breast

pocket without pulling out the pack. He lit it. "Not a bird peeping."

"How many men are still on patrol?"

"Fourteen. More than enough."

"For a 500,000-cubic-meter power station?" Rogolski had this figure from the Helios PR brochure: 500,000 cubic meters of built-in space, 160,000 cubic meters of concrete, 18,000 cubic meters of steel—nothing but records in the history of atomic reactors.

"If it's as easy to keep an eye on as Helios, then all we need is two men and two dogs," said Baumann. "The bigwigs are overcautious. By the way." Baumann reached for the telephone. He dialed a plant extension, waited, hung up. He dozed for ten minutes. Rogolski munched his second cheese sandwich of the night. Baumann dialed again. No answer.

"Zander's here tonight, isn't he?" he asked Rogolski.

"Sure. He's the boss tonight. Larsen went to that hippie evening."

"I'll bet the Reds are behind it," said Baumann. "And we have all the work. The VIP's are scared shitless. The Governor's coming tomorrow with an army of cops and national guardsmen. Practically all of us'll be there."

"Not me," said Rogolski and drank some cold tea from the thermos bottle. To smell the rum, Baumann would have had to hold his nose four inches in front of his mouth.

Baumann laughed. "Just between you, me, and the lamp-post, Tony. Let a whole company of parachutists guard a Governor. Give me an A-1 rifle with a first-class telescope—my Remington—and I'll wipe the guy out and disappear before they even know what's happened."

He dialed. "Listen. You sure he's not absent?"

"Impossible. I left a note for him from Larsen. I put it on his desk. All his things were in the office—briefcase, jacket, and so on. Something important?"

"Just something about the plant protection squad tomorrow. Oh well. We'll hear from him."

Baumann dozed off. Rogolski took a worn magazine from the drawer. He cursed when he saw that his wife had already done the crossword puzzle.

32

Anne led Born into a large room with old mahogany furnishings. They were used, scratched, with burns in several places. A brown piano stood in the corner. Anne opened the terrace door. "We can sit outside," she said. Born waited in the room while she clinked ice cubes in the kitchen. He discovered four photos on the bookcase—her parents probably, and two pictures of a child that looked like Anne. It was probably her, although the photographs looked new.

Anne handed him a glass. "I didn't ask you what you'd like because I only have vodka. With orange juice."

They walked out to the terrace. The cane chair crackled. In the dim moonlight, Born recognized the contours of massive trees. An animal rustled in the bushes.

"We were lucky to get this apartment."

That "we" again, thought Born.

Anne had put one leg over the arm of her chair and balanced her glass on one knee. Her face was dark, her hair shone. "Tell me more about your reactor. If you think I'm trying to pump you, you're right."

Idiocy, thought Born. Alone with a girl on a night like this and talking about reactors. But what else could they talk about? For years now, he had had nothing but the plant on his mind. He hadn't read a book, seen a movie. Sometimes a game on

TV if he came home on a Saturday before ten. He hadn't had any chance to practice conversation. And he didn't even want to talk now. He wanted to take hold of her. Impossible, he thought. Especially if there was someone in the house.

"Aren't you ever afraid?" asked Anne.

"Of what?"

"When I see the reactor, I'm afraid. I can't help it. It's like when I see a spider or a snake. Primeval fear, that's what psychologists call it, I think."

"There are two things I'm afraid of at Helios," said Born. "The thing I fear most is the current. I know it sounds funny, but I'm in great awe of electricity. The tensions running through our lines are as high as thirty thousand volts. If you don't watch out, you don't even have time to notice you've made a mistake. I get stomach pains whenever I'm in the transformer building."

"And what's the second thing?"

"I'm afraid of perfection. I know that sounds paradoxical, too. After all, perfection *is* the goal of my work. But it's dangerous for inexperienced people to deal with radioactivity. Most of our 250 employees are not physicians or chemists. They're power-station technicians, bookkeepers, laborers, who know something about electric accounts, turbines, and pipes.

"But they've never had any experience with radiation. Before starting to work for us, they take a course on radiation protection and learn how dangerous radioactivity is behind the concrete walls of the core. At first, they behave cautiously, almost reverently in the plant. But the reverence quickly vanishes because our radiation shielding system is perfect. The people can measure anywhere they like in the place. The radiation is always zero. Little by little, they become bored with measuring. I once heard an employee say, 'I feel like a car driver who gets out at every crossing and checks via telescope to see whether the street is really free. ' At some point, they stop measuring altogether. They rely on a feeling: If the radiation ever comes out, they'll notice it soon enough."

"Can people feel radiation?" asked Anne.

"No. That's the damn thing about radioactivity. It can't be seen, felt, smelled, or heard. The body has no organ for it. We require artificial organs to detect radiation—dosimeters, Geiger counters, film strips that turn black. But we tend to believe the body more than any instruments. If you live near a tiger's cage, you keep making sure it's locked, because you see the fangs and you hear the roaring. But when you enter a radioactive room, you don't notice anything. And by the time the body reacts, minutes, hours, days, maybe even months later, it's much too late."

"Actually, said Anne, "you ought to deliberately cause a minor radiation accident every so often, so that no one forgets the danger. Excuse me, that's a stupid remark."

"Not at all," said Born. "I've already thought of it. But it's impossible. We can't be like the volunteer firemen who light up an old barn to try out their hoses. Radiation is unpredictable once it's gotten past the shield."

They were silent. Something stirred in the apartment. The half-open terrace door swung wide open. Born got up to greet the man of the house. In the door stood a little girl, blond, wearing a long nightgown. She looked up at Born with huge eyes while making for Anne.

"Did we wake you up?" asked Anne. She lifted the girl to her lap and buried her face tenderly in the child's hair.

"It's so hot," murmured the girl, staring distrustfully and curiously through the strands of hair at Born. "And his voice is so loud."

"This is Dr. Born," said Anne. "This is Michaela. Okay, you can have some orange juice and then it's off to bed." She carried Michaela towards the door. Born stood up. Anne turned. "I'll get you another vodka." Born sat down and waved at Michaela. Embarrassed, she hid her head on Anne's shoulder.

"How old is she?" he asked when Anne came back.

"Four. She seems older. But that's usually true of only children. And try living with a teacher."

"Doesn't she have anyone else?"

"You mean a father? No. He couldn't stand living with a teacher. We're divorced."

"Isn't it pretty hard for you, working and bringing up a child?"

"Compared to the last year of my marriage, it's heaven. I take Michaela to the nursery every morning, and we have the afternoons for ourselves."

"Does she miss her father?"

"She's quite independent already. She takes things as they come. She's never tugged at my apron and said, 'Mommy, we need a new daddy.' Do you have children?"

Born shook his head.

"It's about time isn't it? How old are you? Thirty-five, thirty-six? It's not good to have children when you're old."

"My wife wants to wait a bit," said Born.

"Is she that young?"

"Thirty."

"Aha!"

"She's not the maternal type, really."

"Ahh," said Anne. "Am I? What's a maternal type anyway? A special breed? External characteristic: large breasts?"

Born laughed. "No, no. I'm just afraid she can't do anything with kids. Not yet, anyway."

"What does your wife say when you come home so late?"

"She's usually got something on herself. Parties, friends, and so forth. I'm often not around anyway."

Born had fallen into a self-pitying tone and noticed it only when Anne softly laughed.

"That's not like you, this practiced barstool misery of an unhappy husband."

Born said, "I think it's time to go. I've already been here too long——"

"Now you're acting silly," said Anne. "Don't be so quick to take offense. You're sitting here because I enjoy talking to you and because I like you and because I'm interested in the man who rules the monster that I'm fighting.

110

It doesn't bother me that you're married. You don't have to tell me anything about your marriage petering out, your bad sex life, and your being on the verge of divorce. On the contrary, I'd much prefer your being happily married. Your conversing with me even though an attractive wife is expecting you home is a much bigger compliment for me than when I have to be the comforting balance for some snarling battle-axe."

After a pause she asked: "What does your wife think about the nuclear plant? Doesn't she find your work sinister somehow? *I* would in her place."

"She doesn't like the plant," said Born, "because she believes I worry more about Helios than her."

"And isn't that so?"

"Yes, it's true."

"Then I can understand your wife."

"So can I," said Born. "But I wish she would learn to deal with it—well like an adult. There are things that are so important, at least for a while, that a private life has to take second place."

"The plant?"

"The monster, as you call it," said Born. "For three years now, it's been the most important thing in my life. A man gets a task like that only once. It requires all my knowledge and ability and all my concentration. For an outsider, it seems like an *idée fixe*, and it probably is. But that's the only way to perform good work. The plant is my last thought in the evening and my first thought in the morning, and things like vacations or private life come at the very end."

"Pretty inhuman," said Anne.

"Maybe. But necessary. I think it would be much more inhuman to let lovable amateurs with a ditty on their lips take on tasks on which thousands of lives depend—good husbands who come home punctually, play with the kids, love their wives, and never hurt anyone—and, in a decisive moment, wipe out five people because they're so good-natured and so human."

"I don't like this absolutism," said Anne. "It causes unhappiness."

Born was silent. He thought: I didn't say I like it. Maybe we could find a compromise. But not with Sibylle. She flares up the moment she hears the word Helios. Not with Sibylle. Anything that doesn't have to do with her, she puts down and calls boring. The last thing she called boring was me.

Somewhere in the darkness a premature bird sang. A white mist floated up from the lawn to the treetops. In the distance, milk cans were clattering, and nearby, a brook was gurgling. Probably a sewer, but its gurgling sounded fresh.

"Nights like this," said Anne, "are the reason I'm your enemy. No, let me make a distinction, why I oppose the plant that you direct."

Born was weary, not exhausted. The same weariness he had felt a few hours earlier in the smoky ballroom of the Black Eagle. A weariness of yielding. It flooded over all barriers, exposed the nerves, sharpened the senses, and paralyzed the brain. He no longer understood what Anne was saying. He perceived her, her appearance, her fragrance, her words like a landscape that was too far away for the eyes to focus on a definite point.

Anne continued, "The earliest things I can recollect are summer days: brooks, dusty roads, sheaves of rye, horses with flies in their faces, green shadows, and long storms in the evening. We moved to town when I was eight. But I'll never forget all these summer things. I muse about them whenever anyone says 'life.' I know perfectly well I'll never experience them again. Not because childhood doesn't come back, or however the cliché goes. But those days no longer exist. They're destroyed. I don't like getting depressed, I have no time for it. But sometimes I get sad because I realize what I, what all of us, have been robbed of. Because my daughter will never see the things that made me happy. I wish there were names for the guilty parties. But we only have concepts—progress, standard of living, industralization, growth. How can

112

we fight against these? It's hopeless, and we stand alone.

"When I came here from the city, I was happy to have nature all around me. And then I took my first walk— and saw the construction site for the Helios plant. A lot of factories are ruining this area, and I would have put up with them. But this factory was different. It was materialized arrogance, a symbol of thoughtless immoderation, of the rape of nature and the enslavement of man. When I saw that gigantic construction site, the hills cut down on one day and put up again a day later and a mile further down, the meadows that were green on one day and gone the next, I knew what had robbed me and all people of the hot summer days of childhood.

"I had a dreadful anger, and I still have it today. At the plant, not at you. I'm afraid you could convince me that my anger at the plant is groundless, just a thoughtless reaction of my romantic yearning for a time that's lost forever. And I'm glad that you don't try to convince me. I've been talking too much."

Martin Born didn't answer. Anne stood up and bent over him. He was asleep. She placed her hand on his stubbly cheek. In his sleep, he reached for her hand and held it tight. She stood there for a minute, perusing his face. She didn't succeed in forming any opinion on details. If the police had asked her, "Did you see the man?" she would have said, "His face was angular and dark." Then she noticed he was staring at her from half-closed eyes. She wanted to draw her hand away, but Born clutched her wrist. He kissed her timidly, expecting her to stop him at any instant.

In the living room, he bumped against the dining table. He cursed. Anne smiled and said, "Now left. Careful, there's a chair."

He had trouble with the buttons on her blouse. He liked her because she didn't say, "I'll do it."

Her skin was dry and hot. She didn't dig her fingernails into his back. She didn't moan. She kissed him the entire time,

113

responded to every movement, and finally pressed against him, gasping.

Afterwards, they mutely explored their bodies. Born said, "You may not believe me, but I haven't done anything for——"

Anne put her hand on his mouth. He dressed. She brought him to the door, naked He kissed her right breast. "The other's for tomorrow."

"That's how a woman becomes a collaborator," Anne said.

Born kissed her on the forehead. "They'll tar and feather you."

33

Inspector Kramer said into the phone, "We have a clue, Commissioner. A man who fits the description spent two days with a woman in a small rooming house here in List. The landlady says the woman looked like a real lady. Oh well. . . . They left after two days because they didn't like the area. No, they didn't say where they were going, but they probably wanted to stay on the island, says the landlady. We don't have any names; they didn't register. But we do have a description of a car. A red Alfa Romeo sports car. Frankfurt plate. There can't be that many of them. Maybe you could. . . . Thanks. No, I don't think so either. It apparently belonged to the woman, and as long as we don't have her name. . . . I'll call again."

34

Larsen was disappointed when he deposited the newspaper-woman at the Black Eagle. There was still so much to say. She had put him off until tomorrow. Seeing the Helios sign at the crossing, Larsen wondered for an instant whether he shouldn't drive to work. Then he stepped on the gas and stopped after fifteen minutes at a house in Carding the neighboring village south of Grenzheim. It took five minutes for the door to open.

"Peter," said the girl happily. She had sleepy eyes. "No, you didn't wake me. Come on in. Ooh, I'm so happy."

Larsen found her breasts too droopy and her hips too bony. But, to make up for it, she always said, Do anything you like with me.

35

"I didn't want to wake you," said Born. He and Sibylle still slept in the same room. Neither had the courage to put up in the guest room.

Born didn't care whether or not he had awakened Sibylle. She had enough time to sleep during the day, and she made proficient use of that time. The hours between two and four P.M. were taboo for telephone calls. That had been so even years before when they couldn't endure separations of more than half a day without at least telephoning. Sibylle's love of sleep was a riddle to Born. Sleep was a law of nature: the body needed rest to regenerate. A purely functional necessity. Born slept short hours, never more than six, and thoroughly, exactly the amount of sleep that supplies the body with enough energy for the next eighteen hours and with a reserve for any unusual stress, like today.

Sibylle was a sleep prodigy. In the early days of their marriage, Born had watched with astonishment as she went to bed at eight in the evening and often slept through till noon the next day. At first he thought the honeymoon trip—to the Bahamas, as Sibylle wanted—had worn her out. Then he thought she was sick. Diabetics, for instance, sometimes need a great deal of sleep. But she was in perfect health and performed ever new versions of her sleeping skill, which at first amused and finally annoyed him.

And then again, she could be wide awake, get through long nights without a trace of fatigue when she was with a lot of people. Born could remember a three-day New Year's party in the villa of a friend in the south of France. Sibylle had uninterruptedly celebrated, flirted, talked, laughed, organized outings, suggested games, and barely slept. As a reward, she had been elected New Year's Queen before their departure. Born had once spoken with a physician about Sibylle's sleeping mania. The physician had tried to explain that sleep was not just a bodily function but also a psychological matter. Sleep as escape, sleep as regression to the womb. Born had wondered what Sibylle was fleeing and why she wanted to withdraw into an imaginary womb.

"I was still up," said Sibylle.

"Did you eat out?"

"Yes."

"Was it good?"

"Scallopini in white wine, at Mario's."

"Was there a bite to it?"

"What do you mean?"

"That mark on your right shoulder."

"Nonsense. That's from the creases in the sheet. Do you need a nightcap?"

"No."

Sibylle walked naked to the refrigerator. That too was one of the conventions they both observed: Don't hide your body from the other. Earlier, it had made sense because each wanted the other's body. Today it was merely an empty demonstration, nakedness in quotation marks. The first to hide his body would have admitted the truth. Neither wanted this because each was afraid of the consequences. But why, thought Born. Sibylle came back, fleshly, sensuous. Born thought of a vacation in Sylt. With jealousy and pride he had observed herds of men gathering around Sibylle on the nude beach, hiding their erections in the sand.

Sibylle pulled the blanket over her breasts. "Good night," she said. "Do you have to set that stupid clock so early?"

"Move to a hotel," said Born and turned over on his side.

Sibylle stared thoughtfully at his back. This tone was new.

36

EXCERPT FROM THE MANUSCRIPT OF *THE DICTATORSHIP OF THE TECHNOCRATS,* BY ALEXANDER FUCHS

The poet Gottfried Benn divided mankind into monks and soldiers. I divide it into human beings and technocrats. I first encountered the technocratic type in my father. My father is a physician, a surgeon. He operates as much as twelve times a day. He does his examinations on the run. He says: "How's the cirrhosis in 112, nurse?" Or, "How's the duodenitis in 401?"

He talks about cases, not human beings. He is interested not in sufferings, but in the defects of the machines he calls bodies. He prefers complicated cases, for then he can give another paper at the next medical convention. My father says about himself, "I know my job. If you can say that about yourself one day, then you can call yourself a good doctor."

My father belongs to the master race that rules the world. They call themselves Socialists, Liberals, Communists, Conservatives. But under all those masks they are the same: technocrats, members of the techno-lodge, which can be recognized not by the way they shake hands, but by their scorn for humanity. Their guiding principle is: A technocrat is someone who does something for its own sake.

The technocrats are told: Construct a bomb with a maximum explosive force and calculate at what altitude it has to burst in order to have its optimal effect. They construct the bomb. They would never dream of translating these formulations into human speech: Make a bomb and explode it so that as many people as possible will be wiped out.

The technocrats are told: Build a nuclear power station that creates as much current as possible. They do not translate this into human speech: A plant that can kill and cripple thousands of people.

Klaus Fuchs, who gave the Soviet Russians the American atomic secrets he had learned while working on the first atomic bomb at Los Alamos, said, when a few colleagues proposed concealing their knowledge from the military, "You're too late. It's already in the hands of the technicians."

He meant the technocrats, and the result was Hiroshima. The power of the technocrats, the modern high priests, is based on the human search for models that make the world comprehensible and lucid. The ideology of figures and formulae, which is the ideology of technocrats, is the most effective poison. The technocrats say: The world is one-dimensional. The technocrats say: Imagination is harmful. The technocrats say: We have everything under control.

The day will come when they shall lose control of the forces they are playing with. The day will come when the oppressed people will realize that the dictators in the laboratories and at the computers are using the entire world as a field of experimentation and all of humanity as guinea pigs.

That will be the day of Revolution, and it will not be a Revolution of class against class, but a Revolution of human beings against the technocrats.

This day will not come by itself. It will come only through action.

37

At 3:30, Alexander Fuchs awoke. His testicles ached. They were still swollen. He remembered hazily that Sibylle had come by. He had had a confused dream. His father had been in it, Sibylle, his rifle, and a boar. A boar of all things. He tried to fall asleep again, but the pain was too strong.

Fuchs dreamt a lot.

Two dreams recurred regularly.

In one, he went through a bombardment in a city. Sometimes he escaped, drained by total fear, sometimes he died, and the last image before his eyes was the bomb killing him, first tiny, like a bit of steel plopping from the airplane, then bigger and bigger, unfolding its stabilization wings, plunging straight at him.

In the other dream, he lived in a huge highrise. All the people that Fuchs hated also lived in this highrise. Some had familiar faces (his father, Hitler). Most of them he didn't know. But he did know that he hated them. His apartment was very high. The rooms were full of glass cages. The cages had spiders, snakes, flies. Fuchs pressed a button. The cages opened, the creatures were free. They didn't touch him, but streamed and hummed like a restless black river around his

119

body, out through the door, and poured into the building. A short time later, he heard the tenants screaming in panic and agony.

He stood up and fixed coffee. He flung open the windows, but the hot, hazy morning air outside locked in the bad used-up air of his room. Fuchs sat down at the small desk, a present from Sibylle, and drank coffee. He leafed casually through a pile of manuscript pages, shook his head, and gazed at the wrinkled, good-natured face of Bertrand Russell.

He loved him, and the photograph, signed by Russell himself, was the only thing he described as his property. He alone, Alexander Fuchs, knew that Russell was the most important man of the twentieth century. The scientists—Russell was a mathematician and philosopher—called him a dilettante and the politicians regarded him as a dreamer. The scientists based their opinion on Russell's warning that science should not do everything that's possible. There is knowledge for which mankind in its present state is not yet ready. A colleague of Russell's commented on his warning as follows: The old guy is too senile to do research, that's why he wants to prevent us from doing it.

The politicians didn't take Russell seriously because someone who wants to abolish wars, annihilate weapons, and do away with power politics was beyond their grasp.

They had locked him up—a Communist!—when he had called for resistance against atomic armament, and they had laughed at him when he had held his Vietnam Tribunal, declaring America's war in Indochina genocide.

Fuchs loved him. He loved him because the old man had shown him the way. He loved him although he knew that the old man would curse him after what had happened yesterday and today, and was still to come.

He smiled at the old man on the wall. He put a sheet of paper into the typewriter. He held it with his knuckles not his finger tips because of the prints. He wrote:

120

"Today, at one o'clock, a serious accident happened at the Helios Nuclear Power Station, at Grenzheim, during the dedication ceremonies. Two coolant pipes broke. The destruction of the long-distance mast cut the plant off from the electric network. The accident was just barely brought under control by the emergency cooling system, which instantly pumped in water, and by the emergency electric supply. The population of the surrounding communities, the inhabitants of Darmstadt, Frankfurt, Offenbach, Mannheim, Ludwigshafen, Wiesbaden, Mainz, Rüsselsheim, and Worms escaped a catastrophe that would have depopulated at least one of these towns.

"The operators, constructors, and advocates of the atomic station will probably ascribe the fortunate issue of the misfortune to their security system.

"They are mistaken.

"The accident was planned in every last detail, just as it occurred. It was caused by carefully placed plastic bombs. It was an act of sabotage. According to technocrats, acts of sabotage cannot take place in a nuclear power plant.

"The aim of the sabotage act in the Helios atomic station was to demonstrate that the technocrats, obsessed with atomic energy, are lying. That they lie the moment they pronounce the word "safety." The goal is to force our fellow citizens, who are still unsuspecting, to take a drastic look at the deadly threat of atomic energy plants. The aim is to inspire our passive citizens, who therefore think they are helpless, to take immediate action against all nuclear stations, to fight against the technocrats, bureaucrats, and power politicians.

"Two plant employees were killed during the action.

"The men in power will use this to shift attention from the facts. No one should be fooled by this. These men deserve no pity. Anyone who toys mercilessly with the death of hundreds of thousands has earned death a hundred thousand times. There are still too many men like them.

"The men in power will likewise attempt to write off the action at Helios as the deed of 'an insane criminal anarchist.'

"If we were insane, if we were mass murderers like those who accuse us of being so, we would have placed the bombs in such a way as to destroy the entire safety system, and a catastrophe would have been inevitable.

"Yet we are fighting for, not against, the population. We kill, but we only kill those who bar the way for Reason.

"Our action is sand in the oiled gears of the technocrats' world. After the accident, the Helios Nuclear Power Station will lie idle for a year.

"Similar accidents will take place in other atomic plants with our help. We call upon mankind:

"Seize the time. Form ranks! Solidarity! Force the politicians, technocrats, and bureaucrats to stop the atomic insanity. Force them to cut the billions spent on atomic programs. Force them to change the laws. Force them to tear down all the atomic piles. It is one second to high noon."

He didn't find the letter especially impressive. He would rather have written more, about Russell and Hiroshima and his father and the invisible army. A lot more. But the page was full, and there was no room here for personal problems. He addressed the letter to the German Press Agency in Frankfurt.

He put a second sheet in the typewriter.

"Dear Father: I have to tell you once again that my monthly check is no longer enough. Everything is costing more. You are legally obligated to make it possible for me to study in the manner to which I am accustomed. I therefore ask you for the last time. . . ."

38

The telephone jingled at five-thirty. Sibylle was the first to hear it. She tried to ignore it, moaned, rolled over across Born, and picked up. "It's for you," said Sibylle.

"Herr Dr. Born? This is Seume."

It took Born two seconds to shake off his sleep. He strained to sound friendly. "Herr Dr. Seume. You can't come?"

"I can't come," said Seume, the radiologist from the radiobiological institute at the Frankfurt University Hospital. "But that's not what I'm calling you about. The reason I can't come is much more important."

"What is it?"

"I need you here, Dr. Born. As fast as you can humanly make it, Something very screwed up has happened."

"I don't quite understand. . . ."

"It would take too long to explain on the phone. Get into your car and get going. And bring along Herr Larsen if possible.

"Wait a moment," called Born. "An accident at the plant? Is . . . ?"

But Seume had already hung up.

Born tried Zander's extension at the plant and then the guard center No, Larsen wasn't there. Zander was, but he was somewhere in the plant. They were to leave him a note that the night shift needn't wait for the doctor. Of course, Herr Director.

"Goddamn it!" said Born and hung up. "If that Larsen pulled a fast one on us, I'll strangle him."

Sibylle murmured, "Are you leaving?"

"Yes." Born was already on his way to the bathroom.

The doctor's voice had disquieted him. A radiation accident? Impossible. Otherwise he would have been rung up by the people at the plant. But what could it be? Von Neumeyer, his old professor, had been at the University Hospital for six months now, slowly dying of leukemia. Born had visited him a few times. But Dr. Seume wasn't treating Von Neumeyer. He was in a different ward. So it *was* an accident?

At twenty past six, Born was at the Radiobiology Institute. He was drenched with sweat from the heat and the furious drive. He gratefully took the coffee that Dr. Seume's assistant offered him. It was bad coffee, the kind drunk wherever it was meant more for diversion than enjoyment. Seume greeted him, warded off his questions, and took him through a maze of neon-bleached corridors to a room big enough for three beds. But there was only one bed. It stood against the wall, between the window and the door, just its outline visible because the curtains were drawn and only the night light burned.

"Are you awake, Yvonne?" asked Seume.

An incomprehensible answer. Seume touched the light switch. The girl in the bed squinted and shielded her eyes with her arm. She dropped it gradually.

"This is Dr. Born," said Seume. "He wants to help you."

The girl had a narrow, clear face with large, dark eyes and dark skin. The Italian look was enhanced by her smooth, shiny hair, black and heavy. It was carefully cut across her forehead. Her shoulders in the coarse linen nightshirt were bony and frail like those of a bird. She was ten or eleven years old.

She had been crying.

"Yvonne." Seume sat down on the edge of the bed and took her hand. "Are you still sad?"

She nodded mutely.

"Do you have any pains?"

She shook her head.

"Do you want the nurse to bring you something to drink?"

She nodded.

"I'll tell her as soon as I've examined you."

Yvonne pulled the cover up to her chin and stared at Born.

"He won't do anything to you," said Seume. "He's a doctor, too. He'll make you healthy very fast. But he has to find out what's wrong and where you have pains."

Born had stepped over to the bed. From up close he saw that a festering rash covered her lips and was spreading over her cheeks and chin. Seume gently pulled the cover out of Yvonne's hands. With a small, helpless moan, she turned her head aside and put her hands over her eyes. The right hand was bandaged. On the right side of the back of her head, there was a large, white, hairless spot, two inches wide.

Seume pushed Yvonne's nightshirt up. Her body was pallid and skeletal. The ribs and hipbones stuck out, the legs were so thin that the knees looked like bumps.

"She hasn't eaten properly for four weeks."

The right leg was thickly bandaged from the knee to the hip. Seume bent it carefully and gingerly loosened the bandage.

"My God," whispered Born.

From the hip to halfway down the thigh, the outer part of the leg was covered by a blue-black wound. At first glance, it could be taken for a heavy hemmorrhage caused by squeezing or bumping. But Born knew what it was when he saw the colony of bloody points the size of rice grains. They were blossoming on the edges of the injury.

"Petechiae," said Seume and wrapped the bandage around the wound again. "Petechiae also in the vaginal area and in the oral mucous membrane. And on the palm of the right hand." He clipped the bandage. "Here on the thigh, sub- and intra-cutaneous. Open bleeding, though fortunately limited, on the mucous membranes. As you can see, ulcerations on the lips, fortified by herpes viruses."

The doctor took a thin strand of hair next to the bald spot on the back of the head. He held the strand between his thumb and forefinger and pulled slackly. The strand remained in his fingers. It had left the skin of the head without Yvonne's noticing it.

"Epilation," said Seume. He covered Yvonne up again. "Okay. That's it."

Yvonne didn't stir. She hid her head between her hands.

Seume looked up to Born. "Plus fever, nausea, dysentery, insomnia, reduction of the white corpuscles. I think that says enough."

Born nodded. Years ago, he had read the examinations by the Japanese Tsuzuki, and it caused him an anxiety that he soon forgot. After all, those times were past, and they would never come again. Now that he saw what he had known only from reports and statistics, he was shocked. He couldn't speak. He fought the urge to run out of the room. Then he forced discipline upon himself and let his brain write a list of the symptoms that Seume had counted up.

Petechiae were dot-shaped bleedings under or in the skin. They were caused by destruction or weakening of the hair-thin little arteries that supplied the skin with blood. With very powerful petechiae, thousands of blood-clots in the center of the destruction formed a hemorrhage. In the unprotected mucous membranes, the results were open bleeding.

Ulcerations were tiny ulcers, aggravated here by the herpes virus that crawled over the skin and turned them into watery blisters.

Epilation was loss of hair.

Plus nausea and dysentery.

And a lower count of white blood corpuscles.

There was only one disease that showed those symptoms. A young disease, only a few decades old. It doesn't come from God or from the devil or from nature. It's much too cruel for that. It was invented by men. Against men. The first places where it spread its terror were Hiroshima and Nagasaki.

The nurse came into the room.

"Get her something to drink," said Seume. "And give her some sedation. She was awake all night." He made a gesture

126

of injection so as not to frighten Yvonne with the word itself.

The nurse bent over Yvonne and spoke soothingly.

Seume said, "Now you'll sleep, and in a few hours Nurse Susanne will read to you again. Okay?"

Yvonne had turned around and stared at Born with wide eyes. He tried to smile at her. He had water in the corners of his eyes. Yvonne touched the ulcerations on her lips, carefully, hill by hill, crater by crater.

In Seume's office, Born drank a second cup of bad coffee and noticed the shock was waning.

"What do you feel about the matter?" asked Seume.

"Obviously radiation sickness," said Born. "The classic symptoms, just as Tsuzuki described them in the victims of Hiroshima, Nagasaki, and the Bikini fallout. It's not an overall radiation. Otherwise the blood-dots would be distributed over the entire body. But please tell me what it has to do with me."

"It's your fault," said Seume drily.

Born wanted to retort furiously.

The physician raised his hand. "Come along."

Once again through the maze of corridors, then a steel door that said LABORATORY. Three more doors, and they stood in a room divided by a wall of glass and brick. Born knew that the bricks were lead and the glass made of special elements. Behind the wall was a "hot cell," a room in which radioactive material was tested and processed. This was where they prepared the radiation capsules of cobalt bombs used for treating cancer patients. Here they opened the ampules of radioactive iodine and calcium solutions that were injected in order to detect illnesses in the thyroid and the bones.

Born thought, No one said anything about that at the discussion yesterday, but radioactivity doesn't just cause sickness and death. If it's sensibly used, it can also heal and save lives. I should have thought of it.

On the wall screening off the hot cell, there were steel objects looming to a height of ten feet, with thin, silvery white metal rods hanging almost to the floor. There were grips at the end of each rod.

"We really ought to put on our smocks," said Seume. "Oh well."

He took hold of one of the rods. Behind the thick glass pane, two steel claws moved in the hot cell, artificial, electromechanical hands, more sensitive and more precise than human hands. Born admired the skill with which Seume operated the prolonged metallic fingers. He could work them too, if necessary, but he had coordination problems. Even as a child, he had had trouble with his toy steam shovel game. You were supposed to make a small steam shovel, by means of remote electric control, transport as much sand as possible to a box within a specific amount of time. There was a button for moving the crane right, another for moving it left, one to let down the bucket, another to bring it up, one to open it and one to close it. The first time, Born was able to keep the proper sequence. But the second time, he messed it up. His hands weren't independent of one another.

"Okay," said Seume. The claws had reached a small lead box and were gradually lifting the cover. They glided with two metal rings to the table in front of the glass pane. The rings were about one centimeter thick, one centimeter wide, and had a diameter of four centimeters. "There are three more of these things in the box," said Seume. "But these two are enough for you. Do you know where they come from?"

"I haven't a clue," said Born. "If you imagine they're from the Helios plant, you're dead wrong. There is no place where such rings are used."

"They're not rings," said the doctor. "They have traces of being sawed through. They come from a larger component, a pipe for instance."

Born wiped the cold sweat of his hands on his trousers. He looked at the dial of the counter, which indicated the radioactivity of the metal rings. The dial had leaped up the scale.

128

Born said tonelessly, "Valve pipes. Two months ago we replaced a couple of valve pipes. But they were packed away instantly. You know the regulations."

All reactor components coming in contact with radioactive substances, directly in the core, near the uranium, or indirectly through cooling water, steam, or exhaust gases, became radioactive themselves. If they had to be replaced in case of a defect, they were immediately transported to the hot chamber of the reactor. There, depending on the strength of the radiation, they were packed into special sacks, casks, or lead boxes and brought to the storeroom. They were kept there for several months under the most rigorous supervision until the most violent radiation had waned. Then the deadly cargo was freighted to North Germany, near Brunswick, and lowered a few hundred meters into the no longer functioning pits of the Asse Salt Mine. Asse swallowed not only the atomic refuse of Helios, but also the polluted inventory and the burned-up uranium of all German reactors.

"Yes, all your people know the regulations," said Seume. "But whether they observe them is another question."

Martin said sharply, "That's an accusation against myself, Dr. Seume. I am not ready. . . ."

"Keep calm. We've always gotten along very well with one another, Dr. Born. No reason to change that. We both know perfectly well that carelessness is human and perfect control impossible. Why didn't your security head, Herr Larsen, come along?"

"I couldn't get hold of him," said Born. "He's not at home and he didn't leave an address where he could be reached. That's against regulations. But please tell me finally what these damn pipes and that poor little thing in the hospital room have to do with one another."

The doctor, using his remote-control hands, stowed the metal rings back in the lead cases.

"The girl Yvonne has been in the hospital for a week, not here, over in dermatology. The family doctor first thought it

129

was gastric, then some skin disease—a particularly cunning herpes infection or something of the sort. Understandably, especially since the doctors in dermatology thought the same thing. The hemorrhage on the right thigh wasn't so bad, nor were the blood dots. The dermatologists asked the mother and the little girl what she had eaten, where she'd been, what she'd touched, and so on. Nothing came of it. They gave her the usual medicaments and tried radiation, but the symptoms kept getting worse.

"Then it finally dawned on one of the young doctors, Dr. Körber. He had once read something about the Bikini fishermen, the Japanese who had gotten into the ash rain of the H-bomb. They had the same symptoms—petechiae, hair loss, and so on.

"Körber called me, and after half an hour we finally discovered that Yvonne and her mother had taken part four weeks ago in one of your public tours of Helios."

"Whom did you ask?"

"Yvonne of course—and her mother. Don't worry. We're not stupid. We asked in such a way that they didn't get suspicious."

Born was relieved. "But the little girl couldn't possibly have gotten to the sawed-off pipe during the tour. It was in the storeroom, and that's more tightly locked than a bank vault."

Seume said, "The metal pieces weren't in the storeroom. We asked Yvonne if she had found anything during the Helios visit, if she had taken anything along. At first she wouldn't tell us. She was afraid we'd go to the police. You know how kids are. It was only when we'd made it clear that we didn't give a damn whether she'd pick-pocketed everyone in the place, and that we only wanted to find out if she'd been infected by some object, that she helped us."

"Well?"

"At some point during the tour, she went over to the rubbish pile on the grounds. Just like that. She was simply bored. And one of these rings was glowing under the sand. She pulled it out and kept looking, and then she found four more buried somewhat deeper in the sand. She put them in her pocket. She didn't know why. Kids just put a thing in their pockets if it's round and glitters and jingles nicely. At home, she tied the rings on a string and wore it like a necklace. But she didn't like the necklace, or else it was too heavy. At any rate, she put it in her pocket and used it only as a toy or good luck charm. She carried it with her everywhere for three weeks. She even dragged the things along into the hospital. She really became angry when we took them away. I promised her new rings."

"Four weeks," said Born. "And a couple of days in the hospital. But why didn't anyone notice anything, damnit. Even a blind man could see that the girl doesn't have an infection but——"

"You're being unfair." Seume had finished his juggling tricks. He switched off the equipment and walked with Born to the lab door. "You might have seen it, maybe even I. But what is a general practitioner supposed to think when a little girl complains of nausea and a rash? Do you expect that doctor to hit the nail on the head. 'Aha! Radioactivity! Radiation sickness!' "

"Okay," conceded Born. "Not during the early days. But later on, with those petechiae on the thigh, the lesion on the hand, the ulcers on the lips. . . ."

"Not even then," said Seume. They entered his office, and he closed the door. "Naturally, the whole syndrome was peculiar and didn't fit any conventional disease. But the picture of radioactive contamination is not in the consciousness of our physicians. Unless the accompanying circumstances are blatant. If, for instance, one of the workers at your reactor were suffering from hemorrhages and hair loss, then we would obviously have to consider radiation as a possible cause. Above all, independent of any symptoms, we would instantly consult a radiological physician. But who would connect a ten-year-old girl with radiation poisoning?"

Born nodded. "I'm sort of confused. I'm really the last person in the world to reproach others. I ought to thank that young doctor—what was his name?"

"Körber."

"I ought to thank Körber on my hands and knees that he noticed something in time."

"Nearly in time."

Born sprang up and leaned over Seume's desk. "What do you mean? Won't she survive?"

"She'll survive," said Seume. "We don't have any exact data on the kind and intensity of the radiation. We're still computing. But the Japanese experiences with the fishermen of Bikini showed that the body can withstand even larger doses of radiation. In Yvonne, however, the case is somewhat different. The Bikini fishermen were poisoned by fallout, from radioactive particles of dust and ashes. The radiation was distributed over the entire body. With Yvonne, however, the radiation concentrated on a hundred square centimeters on the right thigh—exactly where the metal rings were carried in her pants pocket. The hands got some too, and the parts of the body that she touched. But the leg is worst off."

"How badly?"

"We have to amputate it."

"No!" said Born.

"We can save the right hand. The leg is lost. Furthermore —this is strictly between us—I am going to do a tubal ligation, on my own responsibility. I'm going to sterilize Yvonne."

Born felt tears in his eyes. He stared out the window into the hospital park. A nurse in white was pushing an old man along in a wheelchair. Dust whirled up behind the wheels. It was seven A.M. and already as hot as at noon. Born thought wearily, I'm looking for something. A name. When his brain gradually pushed the name into his consciousness, his body stiffened in rage. Larsen, thought Born. Larsen, when I get my hands on you.

"I know that the sterilization is problematic," said Seume.

"But I'd like to save Yvonne from further misery. Her ovaries are poisoned, it's certain. Perhaps she's sterile anyway by now. But if not, she'll give birth to a child someday, and when she sees her child, she'll lose all hope."

Born nodded. He knew the high percentage of deformed babies born to mothers whose ovaries had been hit by radioactivity.

"We're operating within a week," said Seume. "She's not strong enough yet. But since yesterday, she's been getting a carefully worked out diet and masses of vitamins. We've also given her blood and plasma transfusions. At first we thought we could get the thing on the leg under control with antibiotics. Streptomycin, acromycin, and so on. But after the careful examination. . . ." The doctor shook his head.

"You'll have to report it," said Born.

"That's why I called you. Naturally, also," Seume twisted his face into a bitter smile, "to give you a shock and induce you to find and punish the people responsible for this horrible business. But as to the first point, I can imagine it would be very good to discuss the procedure for reporting it."

Born said, "That little girl in the bed, those eyes and that lesion. I'll never forget them. Never." And then soberly, "If you report the matter through the usual channels, the Board of Health and so on, then it will trickle out to the papers in a couple of hours, and tomorrow we'll have a huge scandal. On the one hand, I would welcome it, although it will definitely cost me my head. Even if West-Elektra didn't want to, they would have to throw me out. The pressure of the public and the politicians would be too great. I wouldn't even be a scapegoat, for I'm partly responsible for what's happened to that girl. You were right, Dr. Seume."

The doctor lifted his hand, fending off the remark.

"No, no," said Born. "I'm responsible. I accepted Larsen as head of safety even though I had reservations. But that makes no difference now. I would welcome a scandal because it would definitely prevent something like this from happening again. It would be a warning. But on the other hand, it would strike a heavy blow against the reactor program. The people would make Yvonne a martyr and march out against atomic energy. I don't believe another reactor would be built for years. This accident is horrible—but it doesn't justify such consequences. After all, it doesn't tell us anything about the safety of reactors. It only says something about human stupidity. My stupidity, for instance."

"What do you suggest?" asked the physician.

"In a couple of hours, the Governor will be here for the dedication of Helios. The Federal Minister of Research will also be here, for the same reason. I'll talk to both of them when the ceremonies are over. They have to decide what's going to be done. They're political opponents, but I assume that in this case they'll concur. They're going to decide that the thing has to be kept secret, no matter what. Thus, no report to the Board of Health. Naturally, exact records have to be made of the entire case. But they will remain under lock and key."

"That's somewhat beyond the pale of the law," said Seume.

"You won't be affected. Both men will speak to you personally. You'll be safe. But of course, it will depend totally on you, whether you care to go along with it. If you insist on following regulations to the letter, then both ministers will have to put up with your decision."

"I agree with you," said Seume, "about the relativity of the means. What has happened to little Yvonne has affected me deeply, and I will do more than my medical duty in seeing that she remains at least to some extent mentally sound. But even if this sounds cynical, we shouldn't act as though this misfortune spells the end of the world. I'll wait for the Governor's telephone call."

"Where does the family live?" asked Born.

"Near Garding. The mother's a widow. Yvonne is her

only child. She's here in the hospital; she's been examined for radioactive damage. Seume wrote the address on a slip of paper. "May I use your phone?" Born asked. The doctor pushed it over to him.

<h1 style="text-align:center">39</h1>

Larsen sleepily answered the phone. Half an hour ago he had left from the meager bosom of the dental assistant and had driven home to rest for a couple of hours before the strenuous opening ceremony. Upon hearing Born's voice, the undertone in that voice, he became wide awake.

"Larsen, drive to the plant immediately. Immediately means the moment I've hung up. You can drive there in your pajamas for all I care. You will take two men from the anti radiation squad, the usual measuring and decontamination instruments, and you will thoroughly check out the apartment of Frau Elisabeth Werbke in Garding." Born dictated the address to Larsen. "I advise you to do it thoroughly, centimeter by centimeter. Especially the room in which there's a child's bed. If you find anything, you will see to it that decontamination work is done."

"But——" Larsen began.

"Is that clear?" asked Born curtly. He didn't wait for an answer. "You will call me at the plant at nine sharp and report. At ten sharp you will personally arrive in my office at Helios."

Larsen's amazement was audible though he didn't say a word. Born pressed the cradle and dialed the number of Helios. He asked for Zander. The man answering was not Zander; he was one of the anti-radiation squad men. Born ordered him to get all the men available and check the entire grounds for radiation, especially the scrap piles. He wanted to know the results at nine.

"How will your people get into the apartment?" asked Seume.

"They have special instruments. Licensed by the police. I have to go now. All I can do is thank you, Doctor. I hope I can return the favor someday. You were damn fair."

"That's true," said Seume. "But only because I know that you deserve fairness."

Born was already in the corridor when he turned around once again. "I don't have to tell you this, but I will anyway just to make sure. Give the little girl everything she needs, no matter what it costs. Get her a few presents to divert her. I can promise you one thing. Yvonne will never have to worry about money, even if I have to pay it myself. A poor comfort, I know. But what else can we do?"

40

On the way to the car, Born stopped in his tracks. He looked at his watch, then he hurried through the patients taking their morning constitutionals. He reached a flat, gray building opposite the radiobiology division. In room 411, a young nurse was sitting on an old man's bed, supporting him while he urinated into a bowl. The nurse spun round indignantly when Martin entered the room. She spilled some of the yellow fluid. Before she could frame her indignation in words, the old man whispered with a radiant face:

"Martin! How wonderful." He didn't wait for the last drop to fall. "Finished, Nurse Irmgard. Couldn't we shorten the morning wash?"

"No," said Nurse Irmgard. She emptied the bowl into a

white container. She dipped a rag into a small bowl of water and began washing the old man's face.

Born sat down. "Nurse Irmgard is right, professor. After a call of nature, before eating. . . ."

Nurse Irmgard punished him with a severe look and narrow lips. It was comical because her face was doll-like, with apple cheeks, button eyes, and a cherry mouth.

With spare strokes she dried the old man's face and genitals and got to her feet. "You mustn't talk too much, Herr Professor," she said. "Remember."

"Naturally, my princess," whispered the professor.

With a reproachful look at Born, the nurse quit the room.

"She does take herself a bit too seriously," said the professor, softly, hoarsely, "But I like to have her about. She's young. It's pleasant feeling, youth. What brings you here at this time of day?"

Martin told him the story of Yvonne. He didn't tell it to get advice. He knew what had to be done. He told the story in order to get rid of the shock, to have a rest, to see the lively clear eyes in the mortally sick face of the old man and to thus gather the strength he would need in the next few days.

Carl Von Neumeyer was one of the great names in German science. He was a physicist. He had worked with Niels Bohr and Enrico Fermi and made a few significant discoveries. In the thirties, he had repeatedly been on suggestion lists for the Nobel Prize but had never succeeded, probably because he was a loner and lacked a lobby of friends to influence the prize committee. In 1935 Von Neumeyer had emigrated to the United States. He was not in danger. On the contrary, the National Socialists had made tempting offers—a free hand and almost unlimited sums for any research projects he liked. But in Munich Von Neumeyer had seen German physics students heckling and beating up German physics professors with Jewish backgrounds. When his best friend was given a teaching prohibition and just barely managed to escape the Gestapo by fleeing to France, Von Neumeyer (he had no family) gave up his institute, his research, his library, his house, and followed him. Together they went to the United States, got teaching jobs—Von Neumeyer at Columbia University, his friend at Harvard. In 1942 they were summoned to Los Alamos, where the best scientists in the Western world were working on the most expensive (until then) research project of all times: the Manhattan Project.

After three years, a gigantic mushroom of smoke in the New Mexico desert announced the success of the brain army. They had invented the atom bomb. Von Neumeyer was one of the few men to speak out against the use of the bomb. After Hiroshima and Nagasaki, he gave up any physics work for ten years. He wrote a few philosophical–political books, one of which—*The Destruction of Reason*—became a classic.

In 1955 he returned to Germany, taking over the chair for theoretical physics at the University of Munich. Martin Born had been his best student and Von Neumeyer was Born's friend, mentor, and someone he could talk with. Their conversation was interrupted after Born's doctorate—Von Neumeyer vainly tried to talk him into pursuing an academic career. But the conversation was resumed later on: Born took advantage of every appointment in Munich to visit Von Neumeyer and talk deep into the night with him over some excellent Chinese tea.

After Von Neumeyer's retirement, Born had found him a villa in the Taunus, a small white villa in a lavish garden with a view of the valley. Von Neumeyer had only managed to enjoy it for two years, writing a sequel to *The Destruction of Reason*. Then the disease of the atomic researchers made him anemic and powerless: leukemia. For the last six months he had been dying, incapable of moving, barely capable of speaking. The doctors gave him two months, four at the most, and Von Neumeyer used to say, "I hope I make it in two, for there are people who need this bed more urgently than I do."

He was dying cheerfully, adjusted. Not fatalistic or surrendering, not resigned—"One can't change it, after all"—but sensibly. "Seventy-five years are really enough—I couldn't endure much more life." After each visit, Born couldn't grasp how a dying man, dying in so much pain, could inspire him with so much courage for life. Von Neumeyer listened to Born's account, his clear eyes open, unblinking, like a hawk.

When Born was done, Von Neumeyer whispered, "You feel guilty, Martin, and that's good. Keep that feeling, but control it. Do not be tortured by it. That would make you weak and confused. And if you want to prevent something like that from happening again, you need a clear head."

"The thing that drives me crazy," said Born, "is that it's so senseless. If it had happened because of a real risk, if we could calculate something like this, then it wouldn't be any less cruel, but it would somehow be understandable for me. I would be prepared. But we have a perfect security system, Professor, a system that excludes the least error. And now along comes an arrogant idiot like Larsen and puts it out of commission."

"He can't have his eyes everywhere," said the professor.

'He can. He must! But that's not it at all. The fault lies with his infantile heroics. You know it: Not wearing an anti-radiation suit in the protected area as a sign of courage. Front fighter Larsen. I can imagine the kind of remarks he made about the security measures when repairs were being done. And I'm convinced that this was how he gradually made the men think there were no radioactive rays or that they were harmless and the protective measures were nothing but a harassment."

The professor said, "There's a bottle of port and a glass on the lowest shelf of my night table. Do you want some too?"

Born shook his head and smiled. He stood up and filled a glass of wine.

"Hide it behind the books," said Von Neumeyer. "If Nurse Irmgard notices, she'll wash me ten times a day as punishment."

Born held the glass to the professor's mouth. He drank in small swallows.

"Marvelous," he said. "To think I can still taste it. There

are things I regret. According to what you tell me about this Larsen, he was born a couple of decades too late. There was an era in which heroes were needed among physicists. Robert Oppenheimer—a man whom I could never stand, incidentally, an able scientist, but a conceited oaf and a dreadful opportunist —Oppenheimer dreamt often enough about the heroic period. He meant the twenties in Göttingen, when Born and Hilbert and Franck and whatever their names trumped one another with discoveries, formulas, and hypotheses. It's comical if you think about it. Göttingen was a really medieval town back then, with turrets, merlons, framework houses, a lot of nature. And it was in this atmosphere that they hatched the most important ideas of the atomic era.

"Yes, that was the age of heroes. I was such a hero too. But unconsciously so. Radioactivity didn't bother us at all, even while we sensed it was dangerous—though we didn't yet realize how dangerous. We only cared about alchemy, the fission of elements, the transformation of one element into another. We were obsessed, despite the warnings of such people as Paul Nernst, an esteemed colleague. He said at the time when it was gradually becoming clear that our earth, and all matter, consisted of atoms, and that these atoms were by no means solid and secure, but were constantly changing, falling apart, insecure candidates.

"Well, Nernst said, 'We're living virtually on an island of gunpowder, and we haven't yet found the igniting match for it, thank goodness.' We all ignored that 'thank goodness' and looked for the match like mad—until we found it.

"When I think back on what quantities of radioactivity we swallowed in our labs! It's a miracle I've only caught my blood cancer now. The Curie disease—the capable Madame was the first to be punished by the rays for discovering them."

"There must have been awful conditions even with the first military reactors that were built for plutonium production," said Born. "Tin walls by way of protection. That was all. It did cost a few lives if I remember correctly."

Von Neumeyer nodded. "A few cases became known, most of them didn't get out. But with the soldiers, it was innocence. For them, only things that crashed were dangerous. Professional blindness! The scientists knew very well they were playing with death. But they kept playing. Precisely from a feeling of heroics, which has also infected your Larsen. I wasn't always free of it myself. We did it, despite all risks, for the same reason a mountain climber starts up the north wall of the Eiger or a racing car driver steps on the gas pedal, even though he senses his car is going to smash up. We atomic scientists stirred up infinite forces of nature, forces that we didn't know, that could destroy us. We wanted to know how far they could be stirred. In Los Alamos, Louis Slotin called it 'tickling the dragon's tail.' Slotin was a semi-genius and a mad dog. Do you know what he used to do?"

Born knew, for Von Neumeyer had told him the story several times. But he didn't say anything and he listened to the barely audible voice of the old man.

"We were computing the energy released by splitting uranium. That was important for the triggering mechanism in the A-bomb, which was made of two hemispheres of uranium, that were supposed to unite only when the bomb was thrown. That was the famous 'critical mass' that set off the chain reaction, the explosion. Naturally, we had to know how much uranium we needed, how great the distance had to be between the two hemispheres, at what speed they had to come together, and so on.

"We couldn't figure it out on paper, so we had to experiment. The most enthusiastic experimenter was Louis Slotin. A mad dog, I tell you. He had fought in the Spanish Civil War —on the Republican side, of course—and he had been thrown out of the Royal Air Force right after the start of the war because he had concealed the fact that he was nearsighted. Nevertheless, he had already gunned down a few German aircraft.

"He was just as reckless with nuclear fission. The construction of the experiment was simple: the two hemispheres were put on a track and slowly pushed towards one another until the critical point, the first sign of chain reaction. When this point was reached, the two hemispheres had to be pulled apart instantly to prevent the chain reaction from reaching its full force and causing a nuclear explosion—a small one, to be sure, but the radiation would have been fatal for the people in the room.

"That was why most of the scientists made the experiment with the protection of a lead wall. Not Slotin. He placed the track with the hemispheres right in the middle of his lab and pushed the uranium with screwdrivers. Screwdrivers! A cough, a sneeze, a tremble of his hand would have been enough to kill him. But the game always worked. Dozens of times. I said to him three or four times, 'Louis, what you're doing is crazy.' I threw all sorts of quotations at him—'Man shouldn't tempt the gods' and similar things—but he laughed and said, 'All you need is nerves, Carl, and that's one thing I have plenty of!' The others also warned him, but gradually everyone got used to it. Because nothing ever happened to him. He just had a natural talent for being relaxed. Until May 21, 1946. I've never forgotten that day."

Born stood up and let the old man sip at the glass of port. "Slotin died?" asked Martin.

"I would have wished him to die on that day. He lived much too long after that.

"On May 21 Slotin and a few colleagues were preparing the triggering mechanism for the atomic bomb that was to be tested over Bikini atoll. After Hiroshima and Nagasaki, nearly all scientists were deathly afraid of, or at least deathly in awe of, the power of atomic energy. Except for Slotin. He calmly kept playing his screwdriver game. But this time he lost. A screwdriver slipped—no one knows why. The two uranium hemispheres closed together, became critical—the chain reaction started lightning-fast, bathing the laboratory in a harsh, bluish light.

"The men were paralyzed. Only Slotin reacted after a couple of seconds. He could have thrown himself down to shield himself against the radiation. But Louis Slotin was simply Louis Slotin—crazy, but courageous. He plunged upon the sphere and plucked it apart with his bare hands. In this way, he saved the lives of his colleagues in the lab. And condemned himself to death. He knew he had too much radiation. He died nine days later. I spoke to physicians who were with him. He screamed for two days and two nights—despite the morphine."

Von Neumeyer fell silent. Then he asked, "Do you have a cigarette, Martin?"

Born lit one for him. "Nurse Irmgard will kill me," he said.

"You can run away. I'm at her mercy." The professor spoke with the cigarette in his mouth. He was too weak to hold it in his hand.

"Slotin was an exemplary type for me. What was more or less there in all of us was concentrated in him: A thirst for knowledge at any price, the will to forge into the heart of nature without caring about the consequences. The passion for discovery is important. Without it, we'd still be in the Stone Age. But the discovery of atomic forces was the point at which the research drive could wipe out, with one fell swoop, all the progress that it had made until then—

"Actually, we should have banned people like Louis Slotin on the day of the first nuclear fission. And people like Oppenheimer, too."

"But it was Oppenheimer who kept pointing out the dangers of atomic research, the dichotomy of scientists between——"

"I know," whispered Von Neumeyer. He gave Born the burnt stub, which Born threw out of the window. "He flaunted this dichotomy when dichotomies were chic. But previously, in the late thirties, there was no man who was more fanatic about constructing an A-bomb—except for the military of course. It was types like Oppenheimer who destroyed the grandest idea in scientific history. If that idea had been realized, the world would look different today. Better. More peaceful. More hopeful."

"What idea?"

"A few scientists, including myself, wanted to form a secret international alliance. Anyone, anywhere in the world, dealing with atomic forces, would become a member and promise not to transmit any research result, any formula, even the least speck of information to military men or politicians. What a dream! Both because of the Slotins and Oppenheimers, and because it was the government that was already financing most of the research."

The professor's voice was barely audible. He lay slack and weary in the pillows. His eyes were fixed on Born.

Born stood up. "I have to let you alone," he said. "You need rest. I'll come back soon."

"Martin," whispered Von Neumeyer. Born stood still. "Thank you. I know I ought to encourage you, especially now when you've got so much trouble. But there's something I have to tell you. Who knows whether I'll live long enough to say it. What I say I mean honestly. It's not the delirium of an old dying man. It's the balance sheet of sixty years' work with atoms and molecules and protons and neutrons and electrons, sixty years of books and laboratories. I tell you: I wish we had never discovered that diabolical thing. I wish God had built a barrier in our brains to block certain kinds of knowledge. I wish he had made us stupid. And I wish he had turned every single one of us super-arrogant and super-curious men into salt—like Lot's wife. But now it's too late."

At the door, Born ran into Nurse Irmgard.

"You've overstrained him," she said sharply and hurried to the professor's bedside.

Born left wordlessly.

41

At six A.M. watchman Rogolski was relieved. Baumann, head of plant protection, also left the glass cabin. Rogolski drove home. Baumann went to Zander's room. He still wasn't there and no one had seen him. Baumann wasn't worried. The plant was big, and Zander may have been dozing in a corner somewhere. That wasn't his problem. Zander was his boss, and Zander's boss, in turn, Larsen, was supposed to worry about him. Not he, Baumann, who was three times removed from the top. He informed the night shift that they didn't have to wait for the physician, then went to the off-duty room and lay down on a cot.

The control officer from the police was coming in three hours to check over the schedule of the dedication ceremonies and to hold a last-minute briefing. Baumann had to be fit for that.

42

"Disgusting!" cursed the mechanic from the maintenance service when he saw the dark spots on the floor in front of the pipes in the reactor building. "They pour their fuckin' paint out and they don't even wipe it away afterwards."

Knowing how the department head, Werner Marcks, reacted to dirt in the reactor dome, the man got hold of a pail, a scrubbing brush, and a rag, and he wiped the spots away. The water turned brownish. If the mechanic had bent over some more, he would have been able to see the shoes of Zander's corpse. But the mechanic had back trouble.

43

Anne Weiss had slept fitfully. The sheet and pillows were drenched with sweat, and her hair stuck to her head. At eight, she awoke Michaela and they showered together—a ceremony they both loved, especially Michaela, who was always astounded at the conspicuous differences between her own body and her mother's. She simply couldn't believe that someday she too would have something as bothersome and soft as breasts and hair between her thighs—"that tickles!" Anne first dried off Michaela, who then rubbed the drops from her mother's back. Michaela took this task very seriously.

The doorbell rang. Anne told Michaela to put something on, then slipped into a bathrobe and opened the door.

At the door stood Mayor Rapp in his best navy blue suit, with a carefully knotted tie and shiny shoes, his hair combed over his mutilated ear.

"Good morning, Frau Weiss. I have to talk to you."

"As you can see, I'm not dressed," said Anne. "Could you please——"

Rapp marched past her into the living room. Anne followed and sat down opposite him in an armchair. Her bathrobe was short. Rapp's eyes kept wandering to her legs. His eyes were watery, the color of bitter gargling fluid.

"To be perfectly frank——" Rapp began.

"You can spare me the rhetoric," said Anne. "What do you want?"

It took Rapp several seconds to find a new way to start. "Many citizens of Grenzheim are of the opinion that you are not behaving the way one would expect an official to behave in every situation."

"What does that mean?"

"You know perfectly well. Your behavior towards Minister of Economy Hühnle. . . ."

"Ahh!" said Anne. "And what about Hühnle's behavior towards me?"

"Minister Hühnle, if you please. The measure is full, Frau Weiss. We've shown a lot of understanding for your pranks up till now, even though we sensed that your teaching profession was considerably restricted by your activities in the Civic Initiative. But now. . . ."

"Prove it," said Anne. "Prove that except in my leisure——"

Rapp interrupted her. "But now our patience is at an end. Incidentally, not just my party friends in the local board, but also many worried parents who have often asked me whether they can entrust their children to such a—shall we say—radical person. I can no longer answer this question with a clear conscience."

"What are you asking of me?"

"Give up your position as spokesman of the Civic Initiative. That would be in your best interests. Haven't you noticed that your association is gradually becoming more and more influenced by radical forces preparing a red brew under the camouflage of democracy? Don't you know that our Ministry of Education is very consistent about the issue of the Radical Law. . . ."

"Forget it," said Anne. "I was elected spokeswoman, and that's what I'll be as long as the Grenzheim citizens entrust me with the job. Anything else?"

Rapp shook his head in a fatherly way. "I would think that over, if I were you. My dear Frau Weiss, you're basically a reasonable young woman. Don't be so so mule-headed, so pigheaded. An attractive woman like you has quite different means of——"

"You heard my answer," said Anne. "Goodday!"

The mayor's cheeks turned spotty red. "One more thing," he said. "I don't want you people to demonstrate today. You will see to it that your friends call off the demonstration. That is an order."

Anne laughed. "The demonstration has been given official permission. Quite legally. And no one will call it off. You can give all the orders you like."

"People will be hurt," said Rapp.

"Since when you do you care about that? Six months ago, after the demonstration, you expressly thanked the police for bashing in the heads of two girls."

Rapp said, "If the demonstration takes place, you won't have a leg to stand on in Grenzheim. I swear!"

Anne crossed her legs and smiled. "You're scared, aren't you, Your Honor? You're scared of the next town elections, and you're scared of Hühnle and Klinger because you can't purge your own village of protesters. It's hard on The Little King, isn't it? Now please leave!"

Rapp may have had no notion of atomic physics, but he now turned into a living example of a chain reaction. He had been shot at, had reached the critical point, and he exploded.

"You dumb bitch!" he shrieked. "You gunmoll! You Communist slut!" He strode over to Anne. She thought he was about to hit her and she raised her hands in front of her face. Rapp hissed, "You're lucky I don't hit women. You're finished, Frau Weiss. You can pack your bags." He hurried out the door.

Michaela came into the room with large, scared eyes. "Why was the man so angry?"

Anne said, "I don't know," and stared at the telephone. She would have liked to call Born. She needed his voice and his security. She thought, He's got more important things to worry about. Aloud, "I'll make breakfast now, honey."

44

At eight-thirty, Born turned into the road to the Helios plant. For the first time he felt neither joy nor pride upon seeing the white dome looming before him in the plain. He thought of Anne's words: That's a monster! He could understand her. He wasn't afraid—things would never go that far. But for the first time he wasn't sure if this energy ball could be as controlled as he had thought. He had put too much trust in other people. He finally had to learn to trust only himself.

Maybe it was useless for him to cudgel his mind about it. It was quite possible that West-Elektra would fire him after the accident with little Yvonne. He didn't care. He would accept it as fair retribution for his sloppiness.

It had gone so fast. He'd worked for years, day and night, personally supervising the tiniest details, recalculating every figure, always doubting. Was that enough? Can't it be a bit better? And one fell swoop had ruined everything. A few pieces of metal, a little girl with sad eyes in a hospital room. It was as if the previous years had never been.

When Born got of the car, he saw men in the yellow suits of the anti-radiation squad at the machine building. He walked over and asked, "Find anything?"

"Nothing. But most of the refuse is way back there, towards the cooling towers. What are we looking for? Is something missing?"

Born shrugged. "Could be. Only a suspicion. Watch out especially for pipes and pieces of pipes. And let me know immediately."

The men walked on to the next pile of refuse. They carried measuring instruments with cables attached to a box that they pulled along on a wagon behind them. The sides of the box consisted of glass-covered, semicircles with thin black dials.

Gerlinde Katz had made a long list of people who'd called since eight A.M. They could wait. He was in no position to argue with the head of the cleaning firm about the quality of Turkish cleaning women or bargain with a wholesaler about the price for the next delivery of diesel oil.

He looked at his appointment calendar. "Kitty Katz," he asked, "could you do me a favor? Take over the meeting with the press agent for me, would you, at nine-thirty? He's going to want to go through the entire procedure once more, and you know it better than I do. Tell him I'm plastered. You have full authority."

"Okay," said Gerlinde Katz.

Born enjoyed the first good coffee of the morning and banged his pencil impatiently on the telephone.

Shortly before nine, Baumann, the head of the anti-radiation squad, arrived. "I'm sorry to bother you, Herr Dr. Born. But the discussion with the police is at nine, and Herr Larsen isn't here yet."

"He's not coming till ten," said Born. "He's doing something else. Zander is to take his place here."

Baumann wondered whether he ought to tell Born that no one had been able to find Zander all night. But then he thought to himself that Zander might get into trouble. And he didn't want that. Zander was a good guy.

"Herr Zander was on night shift," said Baumann.

"Oh that's right, he switched with Larsen. Okay, I'll do it myself. It won't take long. I only have to wait for a phone call. I'll be right down."

Larsen rang at five past nine. Yes, there was radioactivity in the apartment. Yes, they would take care of it. Yes, a wardrobe and a child's bed would be carried off because they were too far-gone. Yes, he'd be at the plant at ten sharp. Of course, the apartment would be sealed off.

After this conversation, Born could barely pay attention in the conference room. The plant protection men, together with the police (fifty officers) and the national guard (a hundred men), and two armored vehicles were going to protect the dedication against interference. Baumann knew his job. And with a police superintendent and a national guard major to support him, nothing could go wrong.

45

Peter Larsen looked tired. He was unshaven, and Born noticed that his beard was dark despite the white-blond hair. His hair stuck to his head as always.

Born told his secretary not to disturb them, and he ordered two cups of coffee.

Larsen repeated his telephone report. He said the child's bed and the wardrobe were being examined and would then be put in the storeroom for radioactive waste.

Then he asked, "Where does the radiation come from? How did you know about it? No one from the plant lives there."

"Later," said Born. "First I have some questions for you. I tried calling you at six this morning. Where were you."

"With a lady friend," said Larsen.

"As head of the supervision department, you really ought to know the regulation that you must always leave a number where you can be reached in case of an emergency."

"I know. But who could guess——"

"Don't play the fool," said Born. "That's why the rule was made. For precisely such cases."

"I'll remember in the future."

"Comforting to know that. You had night shift, didn't you?"

"Yes, but you know about it. I told you at the discussion last night that I traded with Zander."

"Why?"

"Well, the discussion interested me. And I think I made a few contributions that could help the plant——"

"I've already put you in for a purple heart," said Born. "Can you think why I gave you the night shift from Thursday to Friday, from yesterday to today?"

Larsen shook his head.

"I did it," said Born, "because I, as a total security-layman, imagined that if somebody was after Helios, then the day of the official dedication would be the best target time. The Governor is here, the TV is here, foreign journalists are here —all guaranteeing maximum attention. And since I imagined that, I told myself, once again very much as a layman, precisely before and on such a day, the head of security should be personally present. He has to keep a particularly sharp lookout to make sure his people don't sleep. To make sure no outsiders come into the plant. To make sure the men don't get sloppy about anti-radiation measures. That was why you had the night shift."

"But Zander's a good man, and you can't possibly mean that something happened last night?"

"No," said Born. "As far as I know, nothing happened. Not last night. But that makes no difference. Do you believe, Larsen, that a good head of security behaves in this fashion? That the moment he's needed or could be needed, he hands over his responsibility just to appear at a discussion—only because a couple of important people are on the podium, people who have to learn what a genius is wasting away here in the provinces?"

Larsen wanted to retort, but he held back when he saw the expression on Born's face.

"No, Larsen, a good security chief would not do something like that. He would concentrate on his responsibility every second of the way. Furthermore, he would not only make sure that other people followed the rules, he would make sure that he himself didn't violate regulations in even the tiniest way. He would leave a telephone number behind, even if he went to a whorehouse."

"What are you leading up to?" asked Larsen. His cheekbones were burning red and his blue eyes glittered. More than ever he looked like a Boy Scout. Short pants and a broadbrimmed hat would have suited him. "You don't want to make a state affair out of my switching shifts and forgetting to leave a phone number behind! But if you take it that seriously then I swear on a stack of Bibles it won't happen again."

"You don't have to promise. I know it won't happen again." Born leaned back in his chair and gazed out the window. He gazed as far as the concrete wall of the machine building. "You're dismissed, Larsen. Without notice. Clean out your desk and get out. I never want to see you here again."

Larsen was dumbstruck. "You can't do that. You have no grounds."

Born stood up and positioned himself in front of Larsen. "Keep your mouth shut, you elegant pig. No grounds?" he roared. "A ten-year-old girl who's going to wake up one morning next week without her right leg. Isn't that a good reason? A girl who'll have to live as a cripple and can never have children. Isn't that a good reason? A girl who will someday die a tormenting death of leukemia. Isn't that a good reason for throwing out the guilty man?"

"What do I have to do with that?" stammered Larsen.

"The girl's lying in the Frankfurt Radiobiology Institute," said Born, very softly now. "She was here in the plant a few weeks ago, on a tour with her mother. The girl was playing on the ground and she pocketed a few metal pieces to make herself a necklace. A few days later she started vomiting. Her skin itched. Her eyes burned. She became fatally ill.

"The girl didn't know that in this fine, white, clean Helios

153

plant, there was a bastard who didn't watch out when workers threw pieces of a reactor pipe into the refuse. She didn't know that a pig had sneaked in here who would rather be lauded by journalists than do his duty. Get out of here, Larsen. And go and visit the kid. Show her the man to whom she owes her wooden leg, her sterility, and her leukemia."

Larsen sprang up. "You're crazy," he screamed. "You can't hang that on me. If you do, then—then you're involved too. You're just as responsible if what you say is true. If you throw me out, there'll be a stink!"

Born smiled malevolently. "I told you to keep your mouth shut, Larsen. Not just now. If even one word comes out about this, I'll know who's behind it. And then, Larsen, you can look the wide world over for a job, and you won't get one. I'll make sure of that. And not only I. If you want to create a stink, go right ahead. But you'd better swallow cyanide right after. Now get out."

Larsen's sweat was dripping into his shirt collar. "You can't do that to me. There are labor courts. There's still a union."

"Get out," said Born.

Larsen obeyed.

Born called Baumann. "Herr Larsen is unfortunately leaving us. Please go to his room and make sure he packs only his personal belongings. Accompany him out of the plant. Helios is off limits to him from now on, forever. Please inform your men."

46

Inspector Kramer of the Federal Criminal Agency had forgotten his fatigue, as he spoke into the phone: "Hold tight, Commissioner. Henning found the woman's name. It's on the list of the Alfas licensed in Frankfurt. Sibylle Born. But hold tight.

She hasn't lived in Frankfurt for a long time. . . . Yes, to Darmstadt . . . And what does the name Born suggest? . . . Dr. Martin Born is the director of the Helios Nuclear Power Station. Sibylle Born is his wife and she's having or she's had an affair with our number seven, Alexander Fuchs. . . . Yes, I called Born. He doesn't know the name. I'd have been surprised if he had. . . . No, Fuchs isn't registered in Darmstadt. I couldn't get the Born woman on the phone. I'm driving out there right away. . . . How I feel? Lousy. Commissioner, something's in the works. We don't have any proof yet, but I'd rather call off the damn dedication and search the entire plant . . . I know, I know, only if there's no other way. We'll know in an hour. I'll call you back."

47

At a quarter to ten, some thousand demonstrators had gathered at the visitors' areas of Helios and were waiting on either side of the street that led past the parking lots to the gates of the plant. They were waiting for the dedication guests to arrive. Policemen, fortified by national guardsmen, had put up barricades ten paces in front of the high fence surrounding the plant. The gates stood open but were blocked by a wall of uniformed bodies—sweating policemen, who carried their white helmets with plexiglas visors under their arms.

Most of the demonstrators were young. The older citizens hadn't come because they feared for their health in the heat. The thermometer had reached 92 degrees in the shade, and there was no shade around Helios. The closest trees flickered far away in the heat mirage of the asphalt highway. A few demonstrators had put up umbrellas against the sun. Others had fled to the shade of the two TV trucks, and those who had brought signs, held them over their heads horizontally, so that one could scarcely decipher the words: "Be active, not radioactive!" "Put Klinger in the Clink!" "Hühnle's a Hun!" "One million dead at GPA!"

Despite the slogans, the atmosphere was calm and relaxed. People moved indolently like flies gorged on marmalade. A girl in a bright cotton dress walked over to the policemen at the fence and offered them a drink from her thermos. The first two begged off, but the third one accepted with a smile and passed the bottle on.

Born, who was waiting behind the gate, on the Helios grounds, heard the national guard major say to the police superintendent: "Looks like they don't need us here."

"Just wait," said the police superintendent. "In this heat, people are unpredictable. But I hope you're right."

Born discovered Anne nearby in the crowd of white shirts and dresses. He watched in amusement as she and two colleagues, including Achim Berger, tried to make order among the schoolchildren who were holding flags.

As the demonstrators raised their signs and placards, Born saw the motorcade of guests, a serpent of black vehicles, still far away, twisting along from the highway towards the entrance road to the plant. The police at the edge of the road formed a chain, driving back the demonstrators.

The convoy was flanked in front and on the sides by policemen on heavy motorcycles. First came the black Mercedes of the Governor, with Minister of Economy Hühnle sitting in the back. Then the Mercedes of the Minister of Research, with Mayor Rapp. Behind them came the cars of the other guests: members of the federal and state parliaments, directors and board members of West-Elektra and other electric companies, bank directors, ministerial officials who had been involved in the approval procedures for the Helios construction, two representatives of the American firm that had been the prototype for the Helios reactor, politicians and businessmen from abroad, including large numbers from France and interested people from East Germany and the Soviet

156

Union. Finally, there was a motorcade of journalists. When the motor vanguard was within twenty yards of the gates, a wheelchair came out of the crowd. The first motorcyclist could just manage to brake, as did the Governor's chauffeur. His colleague in the next car did not react fast enough and he banged into the Governor's Mercedes without causing any great damage.

The area became dead silent. Only the schoolchildren around Anne were waving their paper flags. A few policemen were about to clear away the wheelchair, the hindrance. But the police superintendent stopped them with a wave of his hand.

All the TV cameras were trained on the wheelchair, and in it sat a man.

His skull was a landscape of rampant scars. Dead crimson flesh quivered over the top half of the head. The flesh was pushed up in rolls and bulges with deep, white furrows. The man didn't have a single hair on his devastated face. No hair on his head, no eyebrows, no lashes, no beard. His nostrils were fringed, his lips bloated and then drawn as though with sewing yarn The man had no ears.

Achim Berger, holding a megaphone, climbed on the roof of a parked automobile. He said:

"This is Yukio Tamura. He is fifty years old. Once, Yukio Tamura did have hair, ears, a smooth skin. Until August 6, 1945, when the Americans dropped a bomb on him and several hundred thousand other people. Yukio Tamura lived in Hiroshima. It was in the morning, at a quarter to eight. People were getting dressed or going to work. Children were gathered in schoolyards on the way to class. People from the surrounding areas had come to Hiroshima to go shopping. Then the atomic bomb exploded at an altitude of 2,000 feet. It may be that some people, especially some of the gentlemen in their shiny cars, would rather forget what happened then. To keep you from forgetting so easily, I would like to give you a description of the event, as formulated by a scientist.

"On that August 6, 1945, the most shameful day in human history, the following happened:

"The heat, pressure, and radiation of the bomb worked at full force. The air was clear and dry, so that the thermal and ionizing radiation could spread unhindered. The force of the pressure waves smashed the houses underneath. Houses struck at an angle or from the side collapsed, burying the inhabitants. Walls, towers, and trees fell over, loose objects shot at bullet speed through the streets, windows burst, showering the people indoors with a hail of glass fragments.

"The people in houses were smothered or crushed, those outdoors were consumed by fire or severely burned, even those as far as two or three miles from the explosion point. The heat ignited wooden buildings, and soon a fire storm raced through the streets, broiling everything alive. The entire city burned for days. Skin was detached from bodies, clothing ripped away by the pressure wave. Because of the burns, or to escape the fire storm, the inhabitants leaped into the arms of the Ota River and hundreds of them drowned. Many suffocated in the smoke, others refused to leave the fire because they wouldn't abandon their families.

"An ash-blackened radioactive rain fell for hours, over the northern and western part of the city. One hundred thousand people died that day in Hiroshima. Many others died years later, after tormenting illness, eaten up by the radioactive poison. Any survivor has survived like Yukio Tamura. He survived as a warning to the entire world, a warning for all of us. Yukio Tamura cannot speak anymore. But he has written down what he calls his lifetime will. It is only three sentences long. You people in your cars, open up your ears. Yukio Tamura tells us: 'Our fate threatens all of mankind. Tell those who are responsible. And pray to God that they listen!'

"We promise you, Yukio Tamura, we shall make sure that the responsible men listen, as they do now. That they listen and finally act. We demand that you abolish the atomic power stations!"

158

Berger climbed down from the roof of the car. Choruses began. A few cars at the end of the serpent began beeping. The driver of the Governor's car lost his nerve. He pressed down on the gas. In the last second two demonstrators managed to shove the wheelchair out of the way. A few demonstrators leaped upon the Governor's Mercedes, kicked the body, and tried to smash the windows. But the lead and the glass were bullet-proof. The demonstrators began to turn over the car.

Born ran towards the tumult. He saw Anne Weiss attempting to take away her children and yelling at the demonstrators: "Stop it! They'll set the police on us!"

Born wanted to fight his way over to her. But he could already hear the trampling of police and national guard boots behind him. Born was pushed aside. Brandishing plastic shields and billy clubs the police crashed into the crowd. Women screamed and men yelled. The water jet rolled out of the gate and spurted into the chaos. A few demonstrators tumbled down. A cameraman was thrown to the ground by a policeman, the camera smashed by boots. After two minutes, the demonstrators fled. They ran down the road or tried to escape from the police across the meadows. A few rolled bloodily over the ground, their hands shielding their heads. The police kept clubbing them.

"Tell them to stop," yelled Born to the police superintendent. The superintendent pretended he hadn't heard.

Born was relieved to see that Anne was leaning, uninjured, against the fence, twenty yards away from him. The schoolchildren were thronging around her. Anne was crying. Two policemen were running towards her.

"Don't!" screamed Born and broke into a run.

The first policemen pushed his club like a phallus into Anne's abdomen, the second struck her on the shoulder full force. They raised their clubs at the same time like tracklayers. But before they could strike again, Born knocked them over. They fell in a heap, and Born grabbed one club. They struggled up and attacked in unison, using their shields like battering

159

rams. Born eluded them and hit one cop with the club, breaking his nose. The other cop banged his shield under Born's chin and pushed him towards the fence. Born tried to kick him, but the policeman grabbed his foot and pulled. Born's head struck the concrete ground. Then suddenly there were three or four men over him, and the pains in his head, his back, his arm, and his genitals united into one stream of pain. Before blacking out, he heard the police superintendent ordering them. "Get back!"

Anne was sitting next to him, stroking his head. Her throat was red and swollen. When Born saw the white closets and the box with the red cross on it, he knew he was in the plant hospital. In front of him stood Hühnle, Baumann, and the police superintendent.

"Are you okay?" asked Born.

"*I* am," said Anne. "But just look in a mirror."

Born preferred not to. His head ached. A bandaid was stuck over his right ear. His left hand was bandaged. It felt larger than his right hand—it was probably sprained. His upper lip seemed heavy and clumsy like a trunk. He preferred not to smile and mumbled, "Anything serious?"

Baumann said, "No. It'll be all right tomorrow. I never thought I'd be using the plant protection squad to save my own boss from the fuzz."

Born said to the police superintendent, "It's my fault too."

The police superintendent said icily, "I shall call my men to account. Are you going to prefer charges?"

Born shook his head. "You ought to send the two boxers to a course on the relativity of means, and on beating up women."

The police superintendent clicked his heels together. "They will be disciplined. Naturally, we will pay for all treatment."

The police superintendent strode stiffly out of the room. Baumann nodded at Born and followed the superintendent.

Hühnle said: "My respects, Herr Dr. Born. I would have done the very same thing. The matter will be followed up, and the police won't be happy about it. I hope you'll be able to go along on the plant tour. Until then."

When he was gone, Anne said, "He can actually be nice." She no longer caressed Born.

Born asked, "Are you really not hurt?"

"No. You came in time."

"Did anything happen to the kids?"

"Luckily not. They were shocked, but they're all right. Achim Berger is taking care of them down the hall."

Anne leaned over him. Her hands closed behind his neck, her tongue explored his teeth, his mouth. He gingerly touched her injuries. Anne wept. She whispered, "You damn fool hero."

48

By the time Born sat down in the first row of chairs in front of the podium, in the shadow of the reactor dome, Governor Klinger was in the middle of his address. Klinger was not a dynamic speaker. As appropriate to a Governor, he spoke quietly, with touches of dialect, inspiring trust like a Pietist preacher, spreading wisdom like a professor of philosophy. Klinger had been both prior to his political career. His manner of speaking fit him like the custom-tailored suit on his slender body. Newspapers friendly to the administration apostrophized him as a "silvery-haired gentleman," opposition newspapers as a "walking champagne ad."

At the last election, he had gained a majority—even though one week before the election his political opponents had dug up a story from the last days of the war that showed

Klinger to be less than a gentleman. In April, 1945, a sixteen-year-old German soldier, only just drafted, had, at the sight of American tanks, thrown away his bazooka and skedaddled. Klinger had the boy brought before a court-martial the same day. He was condemned to death and shot. But that was so long ago it wasn't relevant anymore. Besides, Klinger had brought the state forward quite a space during the eight years of his term in office. He could be confident of having the greatest electoral victory of his career at the elections in three weeks, and that would make his secret goal (according to people who knew him)—the nomination for Federal Chancellor —tangibly near.

"Prosperity," Klinger was saying. "Prosperity is energy. Without energy, our highly industrialized land would be a gigantic ruin. Without energy, the assembly lines would stand still; without energy our cities would die; without energy, our houses would be cold and dark; without energy, there would be neither cars nor trains. The most important form of energy is electricity, the energy of the future. Electricity is not a gift of nature. We must produce it ourselves—with the help of energy made available to us by nature.In the furnaces of the power stations, we burn mineral coal and brown coal, oil and gas, to satisfy the electricity hunger of households and industry day and night, a hunger that grows by eight percent year after year.

"But some day, the furnaces will go out. The fuel reserves of the earth are limited. Oil, still an important source of energy today, will last for another forty or fifty years. Then the tanks under the deserts and oceans will be empty. We have enough coal for two hundred years. But from year to year, it must be hauled up from greater and greater depths, becoming more and more expensive and some day priceless.

The Federal Republic of Germany may be one of the richest industrial nations in the world. But in regard to natural resources, we are beggars. We can remember all too well the time of the oil boycott when our poverty and dependence became drastically obvious to us from one day to the next.

162

"That is the situation. It would be hopeless—if there were not a way out. This way out is known as nuclear energy. And if we do not wish to become a banana republic, if we do not wish to reduce our country to a medieval agrarian status, as though belatedly fulfiling a Morgenthau Plan, then we must go the way of nuclear energy, as rapidly, as decisively, and as carefully as possible."

The guests applauded.

"I am proud," continued Governor Klinger, "that I can say to you that this administration recognized, early on, the signs and demands of the times, earlier than others. Nuclear energy supplies eight percent of the power to our country. Today, with the dedication of the Helios Nuclear Power Station, the greatest atomic power plant in the world, that portion rises past eighteen percent."

Applause.

"In ten years, ladies and gentlemen, half the electricity in this land will come from nuclear energy. This is hardly an exaggerated estimate, as some of our political opponents assert. These data are in our program, and we will follow this program unerringly."

Klinger paused for the clapping.

"There are, of course, critics." Klinger took a sip of water. "Who have other reasons for opposing atomic energy. They claim nuclear energy is dangerous. They claim atomic plants pollute the environment with radioactivity, heat up rivers with hot water, and threaten mankind with catastrophes of inconceivable scope. I do not want to go into these allegations any further; they have been refuted a thousand times. I merely want to state one thing decisively: The overwhelming majority of the population of this state and of this republic favors nuclear energy. This has been confirmed by all polls. The minority who, with its protests, demonstrations, and legal proceedings, is trying to sabotage the construction of nuclear power stations is clearly acting against the vital interests of the majority of our people.

163

"I am convinced that some of the anti-nuclear people are honest and acting in good faith. They are simply misinformed and biased—conditions that lead to emotional reactions. But we cannot risk the economic future of our state merely to accommodate the feelings of a few people who refuse to take off their blinders."

Applause. Born didn't clap because Anne was watching him.

"But, ladies and gentlemen," Klinger's voice became sharp, an effective device after the pleasantly chatty South German flow, "I do believe that these misguided, emotionally confused citizens would be in our ranks today if it were not for agitators who are using the gullibility of others for their own political goals. I do not want to merely drop hints and allusions. I shall call a spade a spade. We have reliable information that behind a few Civic Initiatives against nuclear stations (including the recently popular anti-Helios movement here in Grenzheim), there are forces that have a major interest in weakening the economic and political achievements of the Federal Republic of Germany. These people do not themselves believe a single word about radioactive pollution, about the "greatest possible incident," about environmental destruction, and all the horror fantasies. They do not believe in these things because their trained, highly intelligent minds *know* that all these horror fantasies are bald-faced lies. Yet they incessantly evoke them in order to impede the economic progress of this land. Just look closely at the spokesmen of the so-called Civic Initiatives . . ."

Born looked at Anne, who was standing near the schoolchildren and smiling.

". . . and check how many of them are actually citizens affected by the power station. I can tell you. Very few of them. They are always sent from their central agencies in the large cities of the Federal Republic to wherever agitation promises success.

"These people, ladies and gentlemen, are, for my money,

not fellow citizens and not people with whom one can have a serious discussion. I regard them—and I say it quite openly in front of the cameras and microphones—I regard them as rowdies, as agents, and as the mortal enemies of our democracy."

Great applause. A few hisses from the back rows.

Klinger let the words take effect slowly. Then, very seriously, "Ladies and gentlemen. Today, West-Elektra is taking over the Helios Nuclear Power Station. It is an important day, not only for our country, but also for the men and women who for many years have tirelessly worked on the planning and construction of this plant. It is these people I would like to thank, the workers and engineers, the scientists and laborers, and I would like to call out to them: We are proud of you."

The applause roared, and Minister Hühnle patted Born on the back.

"Helios," said Klinger, "produces two billion watts of current, enough to provide for two cities with a million inhabitants each. It is thus the biggest nuclear reactor in the world. That is a success. But it is also an obligation. Protection of the life and health of the population has priority over any technological achievement. I can assure you that, in constructing Helios, we have fulfilled this commandment—if at all possible —even more rigorously, more precisely, more responsibly than ever before. Instead of a detail being checked ten times, it was checked twenty times. Plans usually revised thirty times were revised sixty times. That is why I can say: Helios is not only the biggest, it is also the safest atomic power plant in the entire world."

Applause. Baumann motioned to Born. He stood up and moved out of the row.

"I think they want you inside," said Baumann. "Telephone."

Entering the building, Born heard the opening sentences of the Governor's concluding tribute.

"The infrastructure of the Grenzheim–Garding area will now have over two thousand jobs. . . ."

49

Inspector Kramer, in a phone booth in the middle of Darmstadt, had shouted over the noise of cars. "The Born woman
says she doesn't know any Alexander Fuchs. But there's also
the maid. The girl undeniably recognized Fuchs in the photo.
He was with Sibylle Born last week. The maid doesn't know
his address, but she does know the street. We'll have him in
half an hour. It smells rotten, Commissioner. He could have
gotten plans of the station from the woman or who knows
what. In any event, I want your permission to search the entire
plant immediately . . . Thanks. . . . Of course, I'll ring up Born
immediately. . . . Yessir, I'll let you know."

50

Kramer had then called Born. After talking to him, Born
thoughtfully hung up. Baumann was standing near him.
Born said, "Take ten men and search the entire plant. The
police say there may be a bomb somewhere. A real one this
time. In case you find anything, have the place cleared immediately. I'd prefer clearing it right away, but as long as
we're not certain. . . ."

Baumann ran out the door. Born called Sibylle. No one
answered.

51

A gray Volkswagen had been parked in front of the next house ever since the inspector's visit. Sibylle wondered whether she ought to try and call Fuchs. She didn't. Maybe they were already monitoring her phone. She put on jeans, a shirt, and knee-high boots. She pulled down the blinds in the bedroom. Maybe the detectives out there in the VW would think she was taking a nap. She walked over to the safe with her little traveling bag. The safe wasn't hidden behind a painting. It was built into the bar, a safe right in the middle of the room.

She counted the cash: barely five thousand marks. She pushed it into her bag.

She left the house through the cellar door, squeezing through the hole in the fence onto the neighbors' property. She walked along the parallel street to the taxi stop. She woke up the cabby, who had fallen asleep in the noon heat, and she had him take her to the Avis office. She dialed Fuchs's number. No answer. She rented a white VW. She drove through Grenzheim in the direction of the Rhine. The ferry was just leaving. She pressed her horn. The ferry inched back and waited. She parked the car at the foot of the Tauberschlag and climbed up the hill. The fir trees crackled. Resin dripped down their slender trunks. Swarms of flies teemed around animal droppings. The flies scattered as Sibylle passed by. The heat weighed on the treetops.

Fuchs was sitting on the bench under the firs on the top of the hill. He was staring through binoculars at the opposite side of the Rhine, where Helios was gleaming white in the sun.

Sibylle said, "I knew you were here. The police asked about you. You've got to go away."

Fuchs ignored her.

52

After the speeches, Born took the guests through the plant. Next to him walked the Governor and the Research Minister, both at the same level, as though following a protocol that didn't exist for this visit. Klinger made cautious jokes, the theme of which was that he, as a man of the humanistic school, didn't know much about natural science, but nevertheless greatly respected the men of action, the technicians and engineers. Born accompanied the visitors directly to the switching center. There, Governor Klinger would press the button that would turn Helios on full speed and send two billion watts through the lines for the first time. Born hoped that the turbines would survive the strain, at least for a few minutes. Then he intended to reduce the performance as soon as the dedication crowd retreated.

At the sight of the control room, the murmuring of the retinue faded. The room was sixty feet long and thirty feet wide. The wall facing the corridor, in the back of the operating personnel, was all of glass. The other walls shone and sparkled with circuit diagrams, measuring instruments, clocks, lights, buttons, TV monitors. The front side, facing the eyes of the personnel, was agleam with the models of the control-rod system, geometrical, checkerboard figures, that precisely indicated where and how far the neutron-absorbing control rods had penetrated between the fuel cells. Computer clocks, whose figures rocked rhythmically like green waves in an aquarium, signaled the neutron flow and the amperage. On the right-hand and left-hand walls, black dials quivered on white backgrounds, controlling the water pumps, valves, and turbine parts. In the middle of the room, there was a control desk, fifty feet long, strewn with buttons, monitors, green and red circuit models, operated by three men in white smocks who worked with concentration, not allowing themselves to be distracted.

"Impressive," said Governor Klinger. "Impressive."

Born led him to the center of the control desk.

"Just show me the proper button," said Klinger. "Otherwise, I may blow up the place."

53

Two men from the protection squad—in frog suits—crept under the pipes in the machine room. Both of them discovered Zander's body at the same moment.

"Keep looking," said one, crawling back to the corridor. "I'll put it through."

The other noticed something gray beneath a pipe. He scuttled over, touched the gray mass, and murmured: "This is insane! Why, that's. . . ."

54

The Governor pressed the button that increased the water circulation through the core and provided more steam—and more current.

A flat bang, very far away. The light went out for a split second. A few dials fluttered. Born thrust aside the Governor and bent over to one of the men at the control desk. "The high-tension light," murmured the man. "A short circuit or something like that."

And then an explosion, dull, very near. The lights flickered, went out, flared up again. Born stared at the water-pressure indicator. It was dropping, just like the pressure in the reactor container. Red lights blinked. "Switch it off!" yelled one of the men at the control desk. The Governor and his retinue stared incredulously at the scene. Only Minister of Economy Hühnle asked calmly, "Is something wrong?"

"Get out!" shouted Born. "Everybody out. Get out!"

55

Inspector Kramer said: "I have to talk to him immediately. It doesn't matter where he is. The plant is in absolute danger. We've found a letter draft that. . . . Then get him, goddamnit, get him!"

Kramer heard the cracking in the telephone line as Gerlinde Katz dialed the control room. Someone picked up, but no one said anything. All Inspector Kramer could hear was the wavy howling of sirens.

He dialed the number of the Federal Criminal Agency. He said, "Too late, boss. Too late."

PART TWO

Experts at this point in time are not able to have a full overview of all the sabotage possibilities in the machinery of nuclear power stations. For that reason, the extent of the protection against such sabotage cannot be precisely determined.

From a report of the
Institute of Reactor Safety
Cologne, Germany

1

EXCERPT FROM: THE PROVISIONAL REPORT ON THE
COMMITTEE FOR INVESTIGATING THE ACCIDENT AT THE
HELIOS NUCLEAR POWER STATION AND ITS CONSEQUENCES
("HELIOS REPORT"):

Preliminary remarks: The sixty members of the committee have unanimously resolved to publish a preliminary result of their activities, now, ten months after the catastrophe, even though the investigation cannot yet be regarded as concluded. The committee and, with it, the administration and all the parties represented in parliament, nevertheless feel that the public has a right to information about the present state of the investigation. We do not exclude the possibility that new data can lead to a different view of various details of the accident. . . .

1a. The first bomb (plastic explosive, combined time and acid fuse, for details, cf. adjoined, pp. 858–875 and tables XXXI–XXXIV), detonated in the fourth square of the annular room at 13:01, instantly killed the employee of the anti-radiation department who had found the bomb, removing it from feedwater pipe 1. Since the explosive device did not detonate directly at the pipe, the effect intended by the bomb planter was reduced. The feedwater conduit, through which about thirty-five percent of the coolant flowed into the reactor core, did not break apart immediately. It was at first only dented in a few places.

As a result of the deformations, several long, deep cracks appeared in the welding seam of the pipe, from which water

173

shot out under a pressure of 70 atmospheres and at a temperature of 190° Celsius (375° Fahrenheit). The effect of these jets of water, some of them as thick as a human arm, was devastating.

Although for obvious reasons—the destruction of the plant, the impossibility of inspecting the grounds—it will never be possible to determine precisely the damage caused by the missilelike jets of water, one can nevertheless suspect that the following parts of the equipment were seriously damaged:

1) part of the ventilation equipment (which ceased functioning throughout the plant a few seconds after the first explosion);

2) part of the live steam conduit;

3) a bridge seventeen feet above the leak in the pipe.

Whether the second anti-radiation man was killed by the explosion or by the weight of a jet of boiling water is undetermined.

For the first phase of the accident, it is clear that: The feedwater conduit, made of steel alloy 22MiMoCr37, proved to be thoroughly resistant, permitting the operating personnel to gain control of the accident, something that would have been problematic if there had been a total break in the pipe, with water streaming out of both ends.

1b. The security system provided for such emergencies responded after about ten seconds. The insertion of the control rods in the core quickly switched off the reactor. The valves in the defective conduit were closed, preventing a further drop of pressure in the coolant circulation. The changeover valves switched the major part of the water meant for Pipe 1 into the three still intact feedwater conduits. Furthermore, the hydraulic accumulators emptied and flooded the core with so-called poisoned water, which interrupted the chain reaction. Six seconds after the accident, the temperature of the fuel rod envelopes had risen from 300° C. to 860° C. (600° F. to 1700° F.). But it did not mount any further after the floods from the hydraulic ac-

174

cumulators. Thus the temperature of 1260° C. (2300° F.), critical for the envelopes, was not reached. The pressure in the security dome kept rising, but with 5 bars it fell below the maximum of 5.69 bars. . . . The temperature in parts of the dome reached 90° C. (195° F.) for two minutes, but then dropped rapidly . . . At this point, the operating personnel seemed to have the accident fully under control. . . .

2

The voices of the visitors echoed from the corridor, above all of them the South German tones of Governor Klinger, who kept repeating, "I demand an explanation. . . . I demand. . . ." His bodyguards, supported by Baumann, pushed him to the elevator. Most of the other guests had to use the stairs.

Born was standing in the control room, staring at the instruments. He hadn't registered Klinger's protests or the wavy howl of the sirens that penetrated the glass room, muted, but distinct. His head felt as though it were padded with cotton. His brain processed only what he saw—the blinking checkerboard; the digital indicators of the neutron flow gauges dancing like waves; the quivering needles and twitching thermometers: water temperature, building pressure, fuel rod heat, turbine rotation, steam production, pressure drop in the coolant system, electric output, pump performance, radioactivity, emergency cooling.

Each bit of data made the picture of events clearer, following upon the dull detonation at feedwater pipe 1. Born knew he was making unnecessary efforts. The computer had long since grasped the situation, and even if his brain had been as fast as the electronic brain, he couldn't do a thing. The automatic system made its programmed decisions and brooked no interference.

But Born didn't think of that. Nor did he think of the man who had planted the bomb or the possible catastrophe. He made his brain work to save himself, to shake off the paralysis attacking him at the explosion, to turn the fear of the unknown into the fear of a surveyable danger. That was Von Neumeyer's guiding principle: Fear means giving up, means acknowledging that the danger is more powerful than oneself. Fear leads to resignation or panic. Both are fatal. But once you've mastered it, you know the danger and you can defend yourself.

One of the three men, who, like Born, had been following the play of instruments motionlessly, suddenly sprang up and banged his flat hand on the glass pane covering the revolution counter for the circulation pumps. "Got it," he grunted contentedly, and Born realized that, ludicrously. The man had just killed a fly.

"What's wrong?"

Born turned around. Minister Hühnle was wiping the sweat from his chin with a plaid handkerchief as it began dripping again on his temples.

"You ought to leave," said Born.

"I'm staying." Hühnle stepped towards Born to emphasize his statement. "I helped build this diabolical thing. What's wrong?"

"Sabotage," said Born. "A bomb in a main coolant pipe. It caused a leak, but the safety system has been functioning—till now at least."

"And . . . ?"

Born turned away. "Leave me alone. Get out or stay, but don't bother me."

He looked at the clock. Ninety seconds had passed since the explosion. A ridiculously short time. In ninety seconds, a good runner can do at least 700 yards. In ninety seconds you could play half a hit parade number. Ninety seconds weren't enough to read out a page of a manuscript. But the reactor, in an accident like this, needed only twice ninety seconds to become a deadly weapon.

Born reached for the phone. He spoke into the mouthpiece: "Delta. And send all available men from anti-radiation to me in the control room." His lips were still swollen, and it was hard for him to talk. But he no longer felt any pain in his hand.

No questions. With the code word, Born had triggered the emergency plan for Helios: evacuation of all employees except for those who were absolutely required; blocking of the entrance road; no one allowed to enter the grounds; measurement actions by the anti-radiation squad at twenty-five precisely marked points in the plant; alarming the central anti-radiation squad in Karlsruhe.

Born dialed the number: "In thirty seconds we'll need the emergency diesels. They're okay, aren't they? Yes, I know one's being repaired, but we can make it with three, that's almost fifteen thousand kilovolt amperes. Turn the after-cooling pumps on, full force. Switch off anything that's dispensable. Be careful that the aggregates aren't——Shit, you know that yourselves."

Hühnle said: "Why is the current——?"

"For the last time," hissed Born. "Shut up!" Then cooly to the three men at the control desk: "The connection to the network is interrupted. The pumps are running on emergency batteries. Now they're adding the emergency diesels. Nothing can be allowed to happen, no overload, no short circuit. If the pumps fail. . . ."

The three men nodded and quickly worked out the division of the measuring instruments they had to watch during the critical phase.

The neon lights flickered, then dimmed. "Switch off the monitors," said Born, "we don't need them."

The five TV screens, on which vague outlines and surfaces from the reactor interior flickered, now went out. The sixth was already dark. The explosion had destroyed its camera. The men held their breaths and watched the instruments hypnotically. Even Hühnle stared at the counters and figures, whose meaning he didn't understand. For seconds, the concentration and tension in the room were so powerful that the control room was like a chapel.

The room suddenly became brighter. Hühnle snorted. One of the men said, "The guys are running." He sounded happy. "And how they're running," said another. The third stated soberly, "Core temperature okay. We've done it."

Born was silent.

Baumann stormed through the door, followed by twelve men in frog suits, who were reeling clumsily. They were dragging four heavy metal trunks. Born opened one and pulled out a frog suit.

"The high tension pylon fell right over," said Baumann. "They must have used a couple of pounds of dynamite. Was the thing inside here a bomb, too?"

Born nodded. "We have to search the pipes in the annular room. If there's one bomb, there might be two or three. We had luck with the first one. We won't be able to take a second one." Born climbed into the frog suit. "This is a volunteer's job. I can't force anyone to come along. The radiation is too high, over one hundred roentgens. The temperature at the explosion point is 62° Celsius. If there really are more bombs, they might explode while we're hunting them or tranporting them away. Who's coming along?"

The twelve men, their visors up over cube-shaped hoods, didn't stir. After five seconds, three stepped forward, Baumann the first.

"I need more," said Born.

He understood the men who had remained standing. They received a good salary and a danger perquisite because they handled radioactive material every day, loading the waste, storing new fuel cells, checking the work rooms endangered by radioactivity. They knew they were at a high risk for cancer and that they might not be able to father children after the age of fifty. But they weren't prepared for a hero's death. They had families, homes, gardens.

Born zipped up his frog suit and tested the fit of the oxygen container. Normally, a man in a suit would use a compressed-air tube for breathing—there were aggregates for that throughout the plant. But in a contaminated room, that was no longer possible.

"Okay," said Born. "We'll try it with four men. That'll take longer, and if there's a bomb ticking away, we'll certainly come too late. But this isn't the army. Get lost, so you won't be blown up."

"Wait!" Hühnle stationed himself foursquare in front of the men. "I know you're not chicken. Otherwise, you wouldn't have a job like this. You're thinking of your wives and kids. That's fine. But just think a bit further. You alone can prevent the catastrophe. If you back out and Helios goes up in the air, then your wives and kids have had it. I have a wife, a daughter, and two sons. I want to see them again—see them healthy, not as atomic corpses. That's why I'm joining the hunt. Hopefully, you've got a frog suit in a large size."

The appeal worked. Most of the men grinned, and began to check their equipment. Two hesitated and then gave in to the majority. Baumann helped Hühnle squeeze into a suit. He explained the functioning of the breathing equipment and the built-in walkie-talkie.

Born pulled on the gloves.

"Uh-uh, doctor," said Hühnle. "You're staying here."

"I've got to lead the hunt," said Born.

"Bullshit! *He* can do that!" Hühnle pointed to Baumann. "He probably knows his way around in there better than you! Isn't that so?"

"I can't expose my men to a risk that I don't take on myself."

Hühnle snorted. "Fine. But you're needed here much more urgently."

Born wanted to protest, but he knew it was unwise. He

could only have tried to stop Hühnle with violence. Further-more, his suggestion was sensible. Born was more useful in the control room than in the reactor dome, especially if another explosion occurred. He climbed out of his frog suit. Baumann stood before the outline of the reactor building, a metal plaque on the oblong wall.

"There are fourteen of us. Four men each are to search the pipe rooms of the first and fourth square. The radiation is highest in the fourth. Who's joining me . . . ? Good. Three men each are to check the second and third squares. Concentrate on the feedwater pipes, emergency cooling lines, and so on. We don't know what kind of fuse the bombs have. If you find one, carry it out as cautiously as possible, through the materials sluices—they can stand more if something goes wrong." Baumann handed Born a walkie-talkie. "Switch on the reception. Anyone who finds something suspicious is to report it directly to you."

The zipper of the frog suit caught at Hühnle's belly, but after some efforts he managed to close it. "The first overweight Martian," he murmured. Before pulling on the gloves, Hühnle shook Born's hand. Born had never liked him, but in this moment Hühnle filled him with endless confidence. He knew that if any bombs were ticking anywhere in the reactor, Hühnle would find them and defuse them with his mere touch. Strange, thought Born, as Hühnle squeezed his hand. He dis-trusted the most perfect technological system. But he instinc-tively attributed superhuman capabilities to a man he hardly knew—because he believed in him.

"Good luck," said Born.

"Hold your ears if it explodes," said Hühnle, stomping off in second place behind Baumann in the fourteen-man group. They headed towards the personnel sluice, looking as though they were about to fly off into outer space. Every other man carried a measuring instrument, a small case attached by cables to a rectangular plate.

Born picked up the telephone receiver. "Inform the bomb squad in Frankfurt," he said.

180

He turned the walkie-talkie on full strength. It hummed. The men were probably in the personnel sluice. His stomach growled. It occurred to him that he hadn't had any real food for twenty-four hours.

3

After driving away the demonstrators, the police and the national guard had re-stationed themselves in front of the plant fence. The Civic Initiative people, after fleeing across meadows and roads, had collected again, some to get their cars, most of them to demonstrate in front of the Governor and other officials as they left.

Before any explosion, Anne Weiss and Achim Berger, together with forty schoolchildren, were sitting in the cool lobby of the administration building. The canteen had distributed cokes, lemonade, and ice cream, and the children were trying to put away as much of the refreshments as possible before having to form a guard of honor for the departing guests. Anne had long since given up warning the children about diarrhea and overeating. She only hoped that the record gluttons wouldn't get sick till they were at home. The children were making so much noise that Anne didn't hear the bomb detonating at the high-tension pylon. She started up when Berger grabbed her arm. He pointed to a window and whispered: "That can't be!'

Anne saw a cloud of dust rising up from between the four steel legs of a pylon, which, a thousand yards away, looked like its own toy model. Then the one side of the fence twisted over the ground and the pylon listed. The two double stays rocked and plunged askew like the yards of a leaking ship. For five or six seconds, the thick high-tension cables kept the pylon in that condition. Then they tore. The pylon snapped, smashed

181

against the earth, the points of its double stays striking first. Between the cloud of dust and smoke, the only thing visible was a tangle of steel girders forty or fifty feet high.

Anne whispered. "I hope there's no one around there. How can a pylon . . . ? That's impossible!"

"A bomb," said Berger. "It's the only explanation."

Three squad cars with blue lights raced along the road to the disaster area.

"If I know the cops, they'll blame it on us."

"The Civic Iniative?" asked Anne, incredulous.

"Sure. With their logic. . . ."

Anne fell silent. The children hadn't noticed the incident. Some were playing tag.

Anne said, "Who could possibly do a thing like that—blow up the lines to an atomic station. If there's a short-circuit in the plant, maybe even a fire. . . ."

The dust over the snapped pylon had wafted away. The high-tension cables had ignited the dry grass, and the ground was burning in many places within a radius of several hundred yards. The police formed a cordon. It was unnecessary. The demonstrators on the parking lot didn't budge. They were surprised, shocked, uncertain. The fire engines zoomed out of the gate.

"Lots of people would do a thing like that," said Berger. "There are enough crazies around. Thomas and his Maoists, for instance.

Anne shook her head. "He'd never do a thing like that."

The sirens began howling. The children became deathly still. A few started crying. The watchmen in the glass booth sprang up, yelled at one another, reacheᴅ for the telephones. Anne said, "Something's happened in the plant."

"Nonsense," said Berger without conviction. "It's because of the thing out there."

"And what does that mean?" Anne pointed to the exit to the reactor dome; men in navy blue suits were hurrying, pushing and gesturing as they left. They were led by plant protection men past the reception and administration buildings to the black limousines on the visitors' parking lot. Anne recognized Governor Klinger, Mayor Rapp, the Research Minister, the American ambassador. She felt her hands trembling. She smiled convulsively and said: "The rats. . . ."

Four men in security uniforms ran into the lobby. One pushed through the children towards Anne and Berger. "You've got to get out of here immediately. Where's your bus?"

"On the grounds," said Berger." Pretty near the fence. But what's wrong?"

"I'll take you," said the security man. "If you don't start now, the road will be choked up."

"First I want to know——"

"Let's go," Anne interrupted curtly. She called the children together, had them form a double line, and hurried them through the door.

Outside, she counted the children again. Employees were pouring out of all the buildings: secretaries in summer dresses, bookkeepers in starched shirts, chemists in white smocks, mechanics in overalls, their jackets over their arms. There was a throng at the gate because the starting convoy of visitors' automobiles was blocking the narrow entrance road. A slender man in glasses was fighting, screaming something incomprehensible, pushing through the crowd, using his attaché case as a weapon. A woman was spewed out of the crush, her head bleeding from an injury. She remained lying on the ground.

A loudspeaker police van drove up to the fence. Out clambered a policeman, holding a megaphone. The company security man said, "They're crazy."

Anne asked, "What are they doing?"

"Evacuating," said the man." The people on the parking lot ought to get going."

"But that's impossible," exclaimed Anne. "It'll be chaos if they all try to leave at the same time. . . ."

"I told you, they're crazy."

"Do something!"

"What can I do? I can't order them around!"

Anne ran up to the loudspeaker van. She grabbed the sleeve of the policeman who was about to raise the megaphone. "If you order them to evacuate, there'll be a panic. Can't you see what's happening at the gate? Wait five minutes till the employees' cars are gone from the lot. And let the bus with the children go first!"

The officer said: "Sorry. My orders. Immediate evacuation of all people in the vicinity of the plant grounds. You'd better worry about the kids." He glanced at the white concrete dome. His face was covered with fear.

"If you make your announcement," said Anne, "not a single child will get out of here. The people will crush one another."

The policeman cleared his throat and raised the megaphone to his mouth. Anne tried to wrest it out of his hand. The policeman shoved her away and spoke. He had learned the words by heart. "Ladies and gentlemen. A technical disturbance has occurred in the plant. Please leave the plant area immediately. Please be disciplined. There is no reason for panic. As of now, the entire area around Federal Highway 44 is declared a restricted area. Anyone not following the evacuation order will be liable to prosecution . . ."

"You idiot!" screamed Anne.

The announcement was like a bomb.

The last car of the visitors' convoy had already passed the plant gate. But the fleeing employees didn't get that far. The parking lot teemed with demonstrators and spectators trying to reach their cars. The roads were choked by vehicles, blowing their horns, striving to get to the street.

"Five hundred cars," said the security man. "A battle feast."

A VW van had plowed its way through the mob, beeping, pushing, its engine howling, until it got within six feet of the street. As it turned into the street, a red Mercedes came zooming from the right, smashing into the van. Metal and glass sprayed about. Behind the two vehicles, others began piling up. A truck tried to get past the obstruction and shoved three waiting cars into one another. Men leaped out of the cars, tore open the truck door, and pulled out the driver. He went under in the mob. The police had retreated unsurely behind the fence, hesitant to interfere. A chopper circled the battlefield, its loudspeaker churning out verbal fragments. Far in front, the first cars escaped the tumult and raced down the road. Suddenly, in the parking lot, flames appeared. Heavy black smoke rose in the air. A scream pierced through the other noise for two seconds.

"Hey, that's someone burning!" said the security man.

The bus stood in the half-shade of a concrete cube. Skulls on the cube's steel doors warned against high tension. Against the chaos in front, the cube seemed to Anne like a stronghold, like an elephant that would carry them through all the hazards of the jungle.

The bus, a '65 Mercedes, seating forty, was as red as a fire engine. The body metal shimmered in places where the paint had peeled off. The roof was made of greenish antiglare glass, smeared on the inside with the soot from countless cigarettes, on the outside with dust and dirty rain. Even in blazing sunshine, the bus was as dim as the tropical house of a botanical garden. The side windows were hung with yellow curtains that hadn't been washed for years. The cloth seats were ragged, and on the backs there were rubber nets for holding food, clothing, or newspapers. The bus belonged to the town. It had been taken over from a private company after it went bankrupt, and the town made it available to schools, officials (for company outings) and the soccer club. A sign next to the center door said: "Pay the driver." The driver was missing. The key was in the ignition.

"We have to wait anyhow," said Berger. "It'll take us at least half an hour to get through the gate." He helped the children up the high metal-covered steps.

"How do you know we can wait that long?"

The security man indicated the film strip on his chest. "No radiation out here. Otherwise, this would be black. But that can change fast."

Anne had spent a great deal of time studying the theoretical course and results of accidents in atomic stations. If something serious had happened—and the panic of the Helios employees seemed to indicate that it had—then the children had to be quickly taken as far from Helios as possible. She surveyed the fence locking her and the children in: Nine feet high, with four rows of barbed wire on the top. Unlike the lower fences screening off individual buildings throughout the grounds, it had no gates.

She asked the security man, "Are there any ditches in the meadows out there?"

He looked at her blankly. "I don't know. Why . . . ? No, there are no ditches for the first two hundred yards. They were filled in during the construction of the plant because the trucks. . . ."

Anne looked around and discovered the police superintendent. He stood on the roof of a car, shouting into his megaphone. Anne ran over to him. She waited till he stopped for breath. "The children have to get out of here. Have the fence torn down at some point. Then the bus can reach the road across the meadows."

The police superintendent gazed at her with obvious repugnance. He didn't like taking orders. Especially from a woman. He shook his head. "You're talking to the wrong man. I can't order the destruction of property. Not without a compelling reason."

"An accident in the plant," cried Anne. "Isn't that a compelling reason?" She pointed at the chaos by the gates. "Are they running away without any reason?"

"Could be," said the police superintendent. "We have no grounds for assuming that anything really dangerous is going on."

Anne wanted to curse him out, but she merely stamped her foot helplessly, furiously, like a child.

"That's a great idea," cried someone behind her. It was the national guard commander. He turned to the police superintendent. "Don't you think?"

"I have already explained to the lady. . . ."

The major grabbed Anne's arm. "C'mon. I'll send over a couple of men with cutting pliers."

Five minutes later, the pliers and an armored car of the national guard had smashed a breach in the fence almost twenty feet wide. "The driver has got to watch out," said the major. "He has to drive directly to the road. He mustn't brake even if the bus shakes slightly. The ground is soft here. If the bus gets stuck, it won't get out again."

"We don't have a driver," said Anne.

"That's all right," said Berger. "I can drive it."

The major looked doubtful. "I can give you one of my men."

"No," said Berger firmly. "You need every man here. I can manage."

Anne had never seen Berger drive a bus, but she knew it was no use arguing with him. She walked through the bus once more, talking calmly to the children, telling them they'd soon be home.

Berger squeezed into the high driver's seat behind the large, almost horizontal steering wheel and started the heavy diesel engine.

Anne touched Berger's shoulder. "So long. Be careful. Get them home safely." She paused. "I have to take care of something."

"Be reasonable." Berger grabbed her wrist. "You can't go back into the plant."

Anne waited till his grip loosened, then she sprang out the door. "I'm not reasonable. I'll follow you as soon as possible."

"What about Michaela?" cried Berger.

Anne didn't hear him.

At the administration building, the entrance door, controlled by a light barrier, was shut—but only the metal frame was still standing, so she could step through unhindered. During their flight, the Helios employees had smashed the glass panes. The lobby was empty. Here, the howling of the sirens was ear splitting. On the wall, there was a board that said "Work Organization"—the white cards were scattered on the floor tiles. Next to the board hung a diagram of the Helios plant. Anne's location was marked by a red dot. She looked for the control room. She found a triangle that said: "Control Equipment and Operations Building." She noted the location and walked through the administration building to the back exit. It was open.

She walked to the left, past the reactor dome, crossed beneath a glass-covered bridge between two concrete hulks, and climbed up a stairway. At the door, she hesitated and then turned left. There was no one in the long hallway. The desks in the rooms on either side of the corridor were empty. White summer coats were still hanging in some of the wardrobes. Lights blinked everywhere on the walls. When Anne passed the small sirens located every thirty feet, she had to hold her ears because the strident howling cut through her eardrums. In a mezzanine, she tripped over a crumpled frog suit. One more stairway, sixty feet of hallways, then she stood in front of a long glass wall. Born had his back to her, just like the three men at the control desk. They were staring at a black walkie-talkie.

4

"Nothing," rattled out of the loudspeaker. The frequencies weren't enough for Hühnle's voice volume. "We've searched half the rooms. Could he have planted his bombs further in? Directly by the compressed-air containers maybe?"

188

"Very unlikely," said Born. "During operations, that means for the past twelve months, no one gets through the concrete shields. The radiation's too high. If there *are* any more bombs, they must be outside."

"We'll keep hunting," said Hühnle. "How are your emergency diesels doing?"

"They're doing great," said Born.

"I'll stay on the air," said Hühnle.

Born heard Hühnle giving the men instructions, then the dull clanging of metal being knocked, Hühnle's sighs as he bent down and crept between the pipes.

"The used-air equipment," said Hühnle. "I'm checking the individual ribs. Nothing. Nothing. Nothing again."

Hühnle's voice put Born at ease, and, he thought, probably Hühnle himself.

"Wait a minute," said Hühnle. "Square two calling." Pause. Born bit his lower lip.

"Nothing," said Hühnle. "I'm now standing by. . . . Damnit!"

"What is it," cried Born.

"A black case," said Hühnle. "Between two coil springs under a 12-inch pipe without any sign on it. It's about one yard from a round steel plate that says A Roman three. I think it's a bomb. What do you think?"

Born feverishly studied the building diagram. "Could be. How big is the case?"

"About thirty inches by fifteen. I'll pull it out."

Hühnle snorted. "It's hot in here, and very damp. I'd like to know what kind of a fuse the thing has. If it's a time fuse, we may be in luck. If it's an acid fuse, which can be set off by shaking, then we need more than luck. . . . I've got the case in front of me here on the floor. I'm opening both snap locks. . . . Careful, very careful. These damn gloves, you can't feel anything. I'm opening the cover, very slowly. I hope there's no wire in there."

Born held his breath. He thought he could hear Hühnle's pulse beat. Then there was a boom in the loudspeaker.

189

The boom was Hühnle's laughter. "The bomb," he huffed, "the bomb consists of three screwdrivers, two wrenches, two, no, three, pipe wrenches. It's a tool box."

Born took a deep breath. Hühnle said, "I'll keep on. Did you hide a few more Easter eggs for me?'

Born didn't answer. Half the pipe room surface had already been searched. In ten minutes he would know there was no danger threatening in the reactor dome. He was confident. Maybe because the experience with the tool box had used up his tension. He wondered how he ought to organize the repairs of the destroyed pipe. First the radiation had to wear out. Only the measurements and analyses of the radioactivity could tell how long that would take. Then the decontamination troop could get into action, supported by the anti-radiation people from Karlsruhe. At the same time the technicians would check the damages in the core. Assuming a few fuel rods were bent, Born began computing the number of days the reactor would be out.

The loudspeaker cracked. Born threw down the pencil and thought, I'm not normal. Fourteen men are risking their lives in there, and I'm acting as if the whole thing were just a troublesome operations disturbance.

Hühnle's voice: "We'll be through soon. Put a beer on ice for me. I could jump out of my armor when I think of a bottle of Pils."

Born registered Anne's fragrance before she touched him. He pulled her over with his left arm.

"What happened?" whispered Anne.

"Just an accident till now," said Born.

Hühnle's voice: "The first and second square are done. I think I must have lost twenty pounds in this sauna suit. My doctor'll be delirious."

"Hühnle?" asked Anne.

Born nodded. "How did you get in here?"

"After the alarm, there was total chaos. The people were killing one another. The entrance isn't being guarded anymore."

"And the children?"

"Berger's driving them to safety. What are you looking for in there?" Anne pointed at the TV screens.

"Bombs. You have to leave."

"I'm staying till I know you're out of danger."

Hühnle's voice, soft and earnest. "In front of me on a pipe, which I can see from an angle of about 45 degrees from below, there is a grayish brown mass. It's about an inch and a half thick and measures about eight by twelve inches. There might be more of them, I can't quite tell. It's a bomb. I'm crawling over to it. I'm starting to detach it from the pipe. It's not working. I'm removing my gloves. One corner's off. . . ." A long silence. Then: "Baumann's with me now. He's holding his hands under the thing so that it won't detonate on the floor when it drops."

Hühnle coughed. "Baumann's got the bomb in his hand I can't see any fuse or cables. They're probably in the dough. We're crawling under the pipes back to the corridor." Hühnle snuffed. "We're on the stairs leading to materials sluice 2. I'm going in front of Baumann so that he can tread softly."

Born followed the path of the two men on the reactor diagram. Baumann had made the right decision. The way to materials sluice 1 was shorter, but it led right past bundles of pipes, including two emergency coolant pipes. Instead, Baumann now had to pass a relay room and a valves and fittings room. They were shielded by thick steel doors, but. . . .

Hühnle said, "We've just about made it."

The explosion seemed to blow up the walkie-talkie. The antenna trembled. Born ran his hand absentmindedly over the black grid of the loudspeaker. Black oblique lines shot across the TV screens. At almost the same instant, the images on all of them flared up, shivered, and went out.

Anne pressed her face on Born's arm.

"Relay room 3-A," said one of the men at the control desk. His voice was hoarse. "An emergency diesel went out. The emergency cooling pumps are falling off. . . ."

"We have two more diesels," yelled Born. "That's enough for the emergency pumps. Are all the other power consumers off?"

"Not here," said the man. He hastily clicked various switches back and forth. "The air conditioning's on again. The feedwater pumps in the dead pipes too. . . . The explosion's screwed up the programming."

"Dead," cried another man. "Short circuit on emergency conductor rails five and six. There's only one diesel left. That'll never hold. We've got to——"

The control room blacked out. Only the battery-driven emergency lighting and the instruments gleamed bluishly.

A voice from the walkie-talkie: "Bertram of anti-radiation. I can see the explosion area from the work bridge. There are shreds of frog suits everywhere. The door to the relay room flew thirty feet away. Water's pouring into the relay room. I think the fittings room also got something. Where are the firemen, goddamnit. . . ."

"It's over," said one of the men at the control desk. "We'll never get rid of the short circuit."

Still, he and his colleagues kept working, as though possessed, at the switches, buttons, and levers, tensely studying the reactions of the indicators. They didn't react.

One man asserted soberly, "All the cooling pumps are at zero . . . The steam charge is rising . . . The fuel rod envelopes have reached 900° Celsius . . . They're at 90° below maximum. . . . The first one's are bursting. . . ."

Born counted the seconds the way he had, as a child, counted the time between a flash of lightning and a burst of thunder: Twenty-one, twenty-two. . . . At thirty-nine, he asked, "Anything moving?"

No one answered.

Born dropped into a chair. His sprained wrist was thudding painfully. Anne knelt next to him, her hair and her face shimmering blue in the neon light. She looked at him expectantly. Born shook his head. He couldn't do anything more.

Now the reactor was in charge. The time of the great purge had begun, and any resistance was useless. The lights, numbers, and dials were merely putting on an electronic show. The instruments were no longer in control. They helplessly registered anarchy and agony The control room, the brains of Helios, was in a deathly fever.

Born remembered a passage from Dostoyevsky's *The Idiot*. He had read it ten or fifteen years ago and forgotten most of it, except for the descriptions of Prince Myshkin's epileptic fits. They were announced by tiny waves of a feeling of happiness, interrupted and toned down by feelings of deep horror, of fear at the verge of the abyss. However, the pleasure rose, spread, and swelled. And finally, when the pleasure could barely be endured, and the body twisted, the joy flooded over all dams, and tore the mind along in irresistible torrents into a paradise, in which death and life, pleasure and pain, could no longer be told apart.

Born reached for the walkie-talkie. "Come out! Let it burn. Be sure that everyone leaves the plant, even the police and national guard. They'll get new orders en route. I'm sounding the catastrophe alarm in Grenzheim and Frankfurt."

Born turned to the three men at the desk. "Get going!" The men silently took their jackets from the backs of their chairs.

Born reached for a yellow telephone in a small niche under the control desk. He held the receiver ten seconds, then said: "This is beyond belief. We have a hot line to the Grenzheim town hall, and no one's picking up." He pressed a blue button. He waited. "What do you mean Frankfurt authorities? This is a direct emergency line to the Ministry of Economy. Fine, but hurry up. . . ."

He turned to Anne. "Just like my nightmares. A hot line for emergencies, and no one at the other end."

He screamed into the telephone. "The Ministry of Economy, goddamnit . . . Finally. This is Born, Helios Nuclear Power Station. . . . Get me the assistant. . . . Okay, then the deputy. . . . Born, Helios Nuclear Power Station. We've had an accident. You've got to——What? Of course I know the Minister of Economy's here . . . Why don't I tell him? Because he's dead. . . . You're not all there, man. Every second can. . . . Asshole!"

Born threw the receiver on the cradle. "He thinks I'm joking." Born leafed around in a red-bound telephone directory and pressed four buttons. "I need car telephone 7–0–3. That's the Governor's number. It's urgent. Thank you."

He touched Anne. "You have to go. Take my car. Don't stay in Grenzheim. Get as far away as possible from Helios. Use the side roads. After the alarm, the main arteries will be——"

"What about you?"

"I'm staying."

"But you can't do anything more."

Born looked at the instruments. A few were dead, a few out of control—leaping, twitching, circling. But most of them were functioning, carefully showing the progressive destruction in the core. The oscillogram of the turbine vibrations, fine blue and red lines on a checkered strip of paper, breaking off in a curve valley, reminded Born of delicate Japanese ink drawings of mountainous landscapes.

"I *can* do something. I can help. I can observe the fire in the reactor. I can say when the uranium melts and the radiation is freed. I can calculate what direction it spreads in. Between this room and the reactor there are concrete walls many feet thick. They'll protect me for quite a while."

"Then they'll protect me too."

"And Michaela? Do you want to leave her alone when Grenzheim is evacuated?"

Anne kissed him. "Give me the car keys."

Born said. "A blue Mercedes. When you leave the reception building, it's fifty yards to the right.

Anne walked over to the door, a bluish shadow, ghostly, with radiant hair and dark eye sockets.

"It makes no sense my crying or talking about what might

194

have been. I'll picture how my life would have been with a man I loved and hardly knew. Do you remember what I said last night about the plant? It scared me from the very beginning. I instantly knew it would bring me unhappiness. I thought it would destroy me. Now it's destroying you. And that's the same thing."

Born smiled. "I'll be out of here, Anne. I promise you."

The telephone jingled. Born switched on the loudspeaker. "Your radio call to the Governor."

Anne walked slowly down the corridor. Then she thought of Michaela and began running.

5

The Governor said, "Those miserable fanatics, Herr Dr. Born. I hope you've managed to get the better of them with the forces of the law. I intend to call a special session of the state parliament and urgently recommend legal sanctions for such shameful outrages."

"Herr Klinger," said Born. "The plant has been sabotaged. Two bombs exploded in the reactor. You have to put the catastrophe defense plan into action."

"But that's impossible." Klinger laughed uncertainly. "When we drove away, Herr Dr. Born, the big pylon on the left of the road had toppled over. I understand that this led to a minor technical irregularity, which was why you had to interrupt the dedication ceremonies, for safety's sake. But I cannot imagine——"

"The reactor is out of control," said Born. "There was another bomb. Do you understand me, Herr Klinger? Helios is destroyed. In another hour, or even half an hour, it will start spewing inconceivably powerful radioactive rays. The sur-

195

rounding towns and villages have to be evacuated. Do I make myself clear?"

For a few seconds Born could hear only the noise of the driving car from the loudspeaker.

"If your indications are incorrect, Herr Dr. Born," said Klinger, "if this action turns out to be unnecessary and exaggerated, prompted by poor information and thoughtless reaction, then you shall bear the consequences. They shall match the importance of the procedures. Do you realize what consequences such a false alarm could have on the general public?"

"If you keep talking," said Born, "soon there won't be any public. Do you really believe I've made this up? We've got the greatest possible incident, and it's going to be even greater than we ever assumed."

"Then do something!" screamed Klinger. "Why are you sitting there? What do you want from me? I'm no technologist. I'm a humanist. I don't know a thing about technology. Please repair your damn reactor, instead of staging a tragedy. Who was it who was so full of hubris as to pledge the total security of the reactor? Keep your word now! Prove yourself! Hic Rhodus, hic salta!"

Klinger's voice was hysterical, an octave higher than normal.

"Herr Klinger," said Born calmly. "This conversation is being recorded. At some point, it's going to serve as evidence. At some point, the seconds will be counted and the decisions investigated. And if you don't listen to me now, you will be condemned, if not by a court then by the victims on your conscience."

"Very well," said Klinger, wearily. "I'll start the catastrophe defense plan. In fifteen minutes you will hear from me, from the ministry."

6

EXCERPT FROM THE HELIOS REPORT:

1c. The Helios operating crew was faced with the problem of keeping the afterheat in the reactor core under control, i.e., to cool it sufficiently.

(Note on the term "afterheat": In a reactor quick-action closure, performed by inserting control rods and by poisoning of the coolant, the chain reaction is interrupted, but the energy production in the fuel rods continues. It produces afterheat, which is so great that without constant cooling, i.e., without a steady renewal of the water evaporating in the core, the fuel envelopes and the fuel itself can melt.)

Since the reactor itself produced no more current and since it could not feed itself from the network because of the destruction of the high-tension lines, the emergency diesel aggregates had to run the cooling pumps by way of generators.

At the time of the accident, one aggregate was being repaired. The three functioning aggregates together produced over 14,000 kilovolt amperes, enough to supply electricity to all the necessary equipment. The diesel aggregates were switched on without any problems. . . .

1e. The second explosion inside the reactor building, approximately one and a half times as large as the first (cf. appendix, pp. 858–875), took place at 13:15 P.M., killing, either directly or by means of flying metal pieces, two of the fourteen members of the voluntary squad looking for further explosive devices in the middle annular room of the reactor dome. The victims were Minister of Economy Eberhard Hühnle (for an apprecia-

197

tion of the minister's achievement, see "Documents on the Provisional Report, etc.", pp. 114–145) and head of plant protection Ernst Baumann. The explosion destroyed or damaged the following equipment:

1. Relay room IIIa;
2. The fittings room;
3. Materials sluice 2;
4. Two geiger counters (AED-sextuple monitor equipment)

1g. The damage mentioned under point 1 in 1e. triggered the catastrophe. The pressure of the explosion or the weight of the concrete and metal parts destroyed parts of relay room IIIa, which contained important electrical equipment. The connection to a generator of an emergency diesel aggregate was interrupted, so that now only two diesels were providing current for the emergency cooling pumps. This alone would not have been so fateful, because two aggregates would have been sufficient for the energy required.

But because of the explosion, several contacts of the programming went out in the relay room. These contacts switch off all the plant's not absolutely necessary power users when power is cut off and the emergency diesels are turned on. The result was that many of the power users isolated from the grid when the switch-off occurred, for instance pumps, condensers, air conditioning, etc., suddenly began drawing on the grid again. Within a few seconds, this caused a short circuit, which blocked off the entire power supply. The emergency cooling pumps stopped, the reactor core could no longer be cooled sufficiently. . . .

2.a. The accident ran according to the following reconstructed schedule:

Time (in seconds)   Event

0   The emergency diesel stopped working.

198

10	The emergency cooling pumps stopped working.
15	The water level in the reactor sank. Brief, powerful development of steam.
25	Temperature of the fuel rod envelopes reached 1,100° Celsius (2,000° Fahrenheit). The first fuel rod envelopes burst.
40	Over half of all the envelopes in the core burst.
60	The temperature of the envelopes rose to over 2,000° Celsius (3,600° Fahrenheit). The first uranium fuel pellets fell out of the burst envelopes into the reactor.
100	The melted envelope material reacted with the water still present ("metal water reaction"). Several explosions occurred.
250	The uranium began melting at temperatures of over 2,800° Celsius (5,100° Fahrenheit).

PART THREE

Catastrophe: a brutal and massive disproportion between the aggressive forces (of any sort) and the survival possibilities of the victims as well as the means of helping and fighting (against injuries and damage) that people can deploy against this aggressive force within the shortest possible time.

R. Favre.
French expert on civilian defense

1

"But Herr Andree!" said the secretary to the Federal Chancellor.

She was indignant, not because the state secretary in the Federal Chancellory, Eckart Andree had sprawled in the chair and put his feet—in red and white checkered socks—on the huge mahogany desk, but because the chair and desk were in the chancellor's office and were meant exclusively for his feet and seat.

Andree grinned. The secretary smiled in spite of herself. She knew—and understood—that Andree's grin was seductive. But at fifty-eight, she was out of the danger zone.

"It's cozier here than in my place," said Andree. "And it's so nice and cool. In my office, the sun's beating mercilessly. Anyway, I have to look through his files."

The secretary knew that Andree was in no way obligated to go through the papers on the chancellor's desk. On the contrary. Most of the files and letters landed on his own desk first, so that he could sort out the unimportant ones. On the chancellor's desk, there were only the documents personally meant for the chancellor—and some came directly from other ministries and agencies without Andree's involvement.

"We've got to relieve him of work," said Andree. "During the election campaign, he never gets to do anything."

You think knowledge is power, thought the secretary. She had been working with politicians for thirty years. She had known all the types in the "for-the-benefit-of-the-people" business (the expression stemmed from her first boss, a head of the state party), and within a few days she could fit any newcomer

203

into his type category. She had known Andree for six years, and despite his skyrocketing career, she put him under the heading of "young man" in her unwritten private file. She was convinced he would never really make the leap into the "solid handworker" or "charismatic politician" category. He did have something of a background. A first-class training in national economy, ambition, and a taste for power. But he lacked the most important qualities: he had no patience, he couldn't hold his tongue, and he had no sense of diplomacy with people. In other words, he knew nothing about politics.

Anything Andree got involved in had to go quickly: discussions, decisions, careers. He couldn't wait. Slow-witted people, cautious weighing, red tape—they all made him furious. Fury loosened his tongue. "Congratulations," he had once said to an older member of his party, who, without any special qualifications, had become Housing Minister in the new cabinet, "Congratulations on the successful close of a shitty career."

He was no more reserved in public. When displeased, he would unabashedly comment, "idiocy," "stupid," "bullshit," applying these epithets equally to fellow party members or opposition politicians.

Andree never meant anything personally—he called his insults "my spontaneous reactions to badly resolved issues." But the targets always took them personally. Andree barely had a friend in the party. The officials had hated him since he had suggested abolishing some of their privileges and had responded "impossible" to the topic of "shorter working hours": "Impossible. Our pencil pushers might then be awakened by 1:30 P.M." Only his own staff, mostly young people he had chosen from the university, stuck to him—and the Federal Chancellor, his teacher and mentor, the only person for whom Andree showed absolute loyalty. But that didn't mean he didn't often criticize him.

"Okay," said the secretary with a sigh. "Make yourself at home. What can I bring you? A Coke?"

Ever since his guest professorship at Harvard, Andree had had a weakness for Cokes.

Andree pushed back the chair and stood up. "Thanks, you're a doll. But I've got to get back. Briefings!"

He got into his shoes without bending over. Andree was of medium height and stocky. His tapered shirt tensed over his chest (he was a fanatic swimmer) and over his belly (he drank Grand Marnier in his Cokes). His white slacks were too snug. His jacket, thrown over his shoulder, had wide lapels. He had displayed this modish style since his marriage to a twenty-five-year-old Italian journalist a year earlier—her first, his second. Andree had close-cropped gray hair, a crooked nose, and crooked white teeth, which he wouldn't have fixed because they gave his face a "bold, predatory expression," as the gossip columnist of a tabloid had once written. He was the kind of man who, by noon, looked as if he hadn't shaved that morning —and, the secretary decided once again, on him it looked good.

"I'll take these along," said Andree, wedging three red files under his arm. "I swear I'll bring them back personally."

"But don't wait till next year!" The buzzing of the telephone summoned her to the adjacent room.

Andree passed through an empty room. The tenant, an assistant to the chancellor, was on vacation. Andree came out in the hall and ten steps later he entered the small conference room next to his office. Despite the blinds and the roaring air conditioner, the conference room was blazing hot. The three men at the round teakwood table had unbuttoned their shirts down to their navels. "For all I care, you can run around naked in this heat," Andree had told his staff. But they weren't sure he meant it. They were cooling their hands on misty glasses filled with tinkling ice cubes.

"Hi!" said Andree and threw his jacket on the lowest bookshelf on the oblong wall. He sat down and opened a bottle of Coke. Poppe, the third man in the press office, pushed the ice bucket over to him. Andree ignored the tongs and grabbed the ice cubes with his bare hand. "Where's Zernowski?"

"He sent his excuses. He's evaluating the new computer forecasts," said Meyer-Schönwald, the assistant to the campaign head. His fine appearance had originally misled Andree into underestimating his excellent organizing talent.

"What's the score?"

"Not so good," said Meyer-Schönwald. "Thirty-six for us, forty-four for them, six for the liberals."

"But that's the cleaning woman oracle," said Kern, Andree's assistant, now working for the party's ad agency, which had thought up the campaign for the state elections. He was referring to a polling service whose prognoses were often so unreliable that experts joked: They interview their cleaning women and call it a representative survey.

Andree took a sip of Coke. "What can we do in the next three weeks to change it?"

Kern said, "It'll change when the TV commercials and the ad campaign have some effect. But that'll take a while."

"I wouldn't count on it," said Andree. "They're shitty."

"Which?" asked Kern, piqued. "The commercials or the ads?"

"Both. But that's spilled milk. Can't be saved. And maybe I'm wrong. Miracles happen all the time."

"The chancellor has to do more," said Poppe. "Our candidate can't do anything against Klinger. But the chancellor can run rings around Klinger."

"The surveys prove it," said Meyer-Schönwald. "Whenever the chancellor speaks, we're much better off."

"Whoa, gang!" said Andree. "The man's booked up till kingdom come. Besides he's got to do some governing now and then. I can't do everything for him."

The men grinned.

"That's true," said Poppe. "But still, you've got to try to get a few dates free for campaign speeches."

"The others have to get into it, too," said Meyer-Schönwald. Some of them are taking things too damn easy.

Bernhard for instance." Bernhard Weigel was Minister of Justice. "He's popular, he was once mayor of Frankfurt. And what's he doing? Vacationing in Sweden. He won't be back till next week and he'll be making fifteen speeches. That just won't do."

"I've gotta kick Bernhard's ass a little," said Andree. "Do you know where his wife's vacationing?"

"In Sweden too, so far as I know," said Meyer-Schönwald.

"In Stockholm," said Andree. "With the kids. Bernhard's a couple of hundred miles away, on a skerry island. All alone. He wants to think. I'm not quite sure why he needs that French girl to help him think. But don't pass it on. He'll be here on Monday. That's definite. What about Simmering?"

"I'd like to build up Reichelt a bit," said Poppe. Reichelt was running for the job of Minister of Economy. "He really cornered Hühnle on that TV panel last Wednesday."

Andree noted. "He's a good man, I agree. I'll take care of him. Maybe we can send him out directly against Hühnle, about that nuclear plant. Not about the principle *per se*, of course, but about the location and the tricks in the approval procedure, and so on."

"That's dangerous," said Poppe. "We've got the same problems in Lower Saxony—and *we're* the ones who picked the location there."

"That's a good point," said Andree. "But if *we* start, we'll have the advantage. Let's wait and see what happens at the dedication. It's today, isn't it?"

Poppe nodded.

"They wanted to demonstrate. If there's trouble, we can put in a pitch about moderation, conversation between citizens and the state, and so on."

The telephone rang. Andree picked up. "Governor Klinger," said his secretary. "Urgent."

2

14a. The catastrophe defense plan, worked out four years ago (reckoned from the day of the accident) by the Ministry of the Interior, and presented to the institutions involved, was commenced at 13:31 at the behest of Governor Klinger, who was in his official automobile en route to Frankfurt. An examination of the telephone records has revealed a difference of nine minutes between Plant Director Born's notification of the Prime Minister (13:21 P.M.) and the first telephone call by the Federal Chancellory to police headquarters or the Ministry of the Interior. The delay, probably costing human lives, cannot be explained by technical defects. Since Governor Klinger died of a heart attack just a few weeks after the Helios accident, before the investigating committee came upon the time gap, we can only make conjectures, to which, however, we ascribe a high likelihood.

The Klinger/Born telephone conversation at 13:21 reveals that the Prime Minister was not immediately convinced of the earnestness of the situation, and that he considered the plant director's reaction exaggerated. The Governor was known as a statesman who carefully weighed all his decisions and never decided upon an important issue without first consulting experts and colleagues. Since, at 13:21, he had no other information about the extent of the accident than what he was told by the plant director, whom he barely knew, he must have struggled with himself for a long time, trying to decide whether to initiate, at one man's urging, the vast scope of measures projected in the catastrophe defense plan. He would with certainty have accelerated his decision had he had knowledge of the eyewitness account of the Minister of Economy, Hühnle, who, however, had been tragically killed ten minutes earlier.

On the other hand, it must be regarded as a correct estimation of the situation by the Governor that he put the catastrophe defense plan into action in just a few minutes. It must therefore be counted as pure speculation that commentators described the Governor's resignation a week after the Helios accident and even his death as the result of a "personal feeling of guilt."

It can be established that Governor Klinger acted as any responsible statesman would have acted in his place. It cannot be contested that other types of politicians might have reached a faster decision and thus saved more human lives. But at that point no one could have known whether a fast decision might not be hasty, thereby endangering human life. . . .

Finally, we must point out the speech given by the Federal Chancellor at the state funeral of the Governor: "In the instant of danger he, like any responsible representative of the people, forgot the political opposition and knew only one goal: to protect the people against damage. When I took over the leadership of the catastrophe action, which he so excellently organized in just a few minutes, we spoke no word about political jurisdiction. Tacitly, both of us knew that this was not the time for federalistic fighting, that there was only one thing to do: act. The exemplary action of the Governor during the first few hours after the accident, plus the news of dreadful events and ever more dangers, planted the seeds of a premature death in a man who had just barely recuperated from a serious illness."

14b. In its investigation of the chronological course of the catastrophe, the committee came upon a second time gap. Before notifying the Governor, the plant director tried to reach the Ministry of Economy in Frankfurt and the mayor's office in the town of Grenzheim by way of direct lines that had been established for such an emergency. The responsible assistant at the ministry was accompanying Governor Klinger back from Helios. Because of his absence, he had allowed his secretary to leave earlier than usual and neglected to delegate some one to take over the direct line.

The employees at the mayor's office in Grenzheim, since they were not participating in the dedication ceremonies, had the afternoon off after 13:00. Since the janitor began his shift only at 14:00, any communication was impossible for the plant director. This mistake caused a loss of at least six minutes.

3

"Andree."

"This is the Secretariat of the Governor in Frankfurt. The Governor is calling the Federal Chancellor."

"Okay, kid," said Andree. "Put him through."

The line crackled. Then, Klinger's voice: "Who is there, please?"

"Andree. State secretary."

"Of course, Herr Andree, we've met, though infrequently. I would like to speak to the Federal Chancellor. . . ."

"Impossible. He's out. Tell me, and I'll pass it on to him when he checks in by phone tonight. Of course only if it's not a personal matter. If, for instance, you want to excuse yourself for that remark you made at Giessen about the chancellor being the faith healer of the nation. . . ."

"This is no time for jokes, Herr State Secretary," said Klinger. "It is a matter of extraordinary urgency, a matter in which, moreover, only the truly responsible men can now be involved. Otherwise, the implications——"

"So you don't want to tell me anything."

"Can we reach the Federal Chancellor's deputy, the foreign minister?"

"He's out campaigning too," said Andree. "I'm sure your crew's on the road, too."

"Well," Klinger hesitated, "I have no other choice. I ask you, however, to register the fact that in this moment I, as Governor of a federal state, am not fulfilling any duty, but rather notifying you voluntarily in order to avert possible damages to the people."

"Lemme guess," said Andree. He looked at the three men at the table, pointed to the receiver and made a crazy sign.

"Herr State Secretary," interrupted Klinger. "I hereby inform you that at the Helios Nuclear Power Station in Grenzheim, there has been an accident probably due to sabotage. I have just set off the catastrophe defense plan projected for such cases."

"When did the accident happen?"

Poppe was just telling Meyer-Schönwald a Klinger anecdote, something about a mulatto girl in Paris. Andree raised his hand, and Poppe broke off. He saw that Andree was suddenly listening seriously.

"Well, I assume about half an hour ago," said Klinger.

"You assume?" asked Andree. "Governor, I must inform the chancellor about it. So please be exact! Every detail can be important. What kind of sabotage? A bomb? Several? How serious is the damage?"

"It must have been a bomb," said Klinger. "Perhaps even several. I haven't had a report about the exact damages yet from Dr. Born, the director of the nuclear plant. However, he is of the opinion that radioactive matter has been released."

Andree covered the receiver and said to Meyer-Schönwald: "Go to my office and get me Dr. Born at the Helios Nuclear Power Station on the phone." And to Kern: "You get the chancellor. He's giving a speech in Wetzlar." He asked Klinger, "What are the most important points of the catastrophe plan?"

"Defense plan," Klinger corrected him. "One moment please, my papers. . . . Okay. First, the Ministry of Economy, which has jurisdiction over the reactor, will be—I mean was—notified, then the police headquarters, the regular and voluntary fire departments in the surrounding villages and towns, the Technical Auxiliary as well as——"

"Herr Klinger," snapped Andree, "it doesn't matter now who's got jurisdiction over what. I asked you what we should do. Where are there blockades? Who should put them up?"

Klinger said, "How dare you, Herr State Secretary. I do not owe you any information whatsoever. . . ."

"All right." Andree cramped his hand around the receiver. The knuckles stood out white. "*Please* give me the information, Governor."

"Yes, blockades are projected, and namely— one moment —three blockade circuits, each with Helios as its center. The first with a one-mile radius, the second with a four-mile radius, the third with a twelve-mile radius. All inhabitants are first evacuated from the four-mile radius. Decontamination stations are erected at the borders of the one-mile and four-mile circuits. Twelve anti-radiation troops with vehicles and helicopters measure the radioactivity at one hundred and ten determined points. . . ."

"And what do you want to do with the couple of men from the police and fire departments?" asked Andree.

"Well," said Klinger, "they *are* supported by voluntary helpers, after all."

Andree didn't notice he was screaming. "You can't put up a blockade circuit with a few hundred nozzle holders and village constables. You might as well let the people march through right away."

"That's not permitted," said Klinger. "As you may know, radioactively contaminated people are a hazard to their healthy fellow citizens. That is why people coming from the potentially contaminated area must be examined, decontaminated, and, if need be, isolated."

212

"That's precisely why I'm asking, Governor. The inhabitants of the blockaded areas near the reactor are going to try to reach safety as fast as they can, and they won't give a shit about those decontamination stations. You need the army, the national guard, maybe even the Americans— —"

"I am going to lodge a complaint against you," said Klinger. "But to put your mind at ease: For two minutes now, the announcement that was worked out in case of a catastrophe has been sent out over the radio and television, asking the inhabitants of the endangered regions not to leave their homes."

"What did you say?!"

"I was clear enough. For two minutes now——"

"For God's sake," roared Andree. "You tell the people that a nuclear plant's exploded, and you expect them to sit in their houses like good little children? Get on the telephone and cancel the announcement! Immediately!"

"I will not take orders from you," said Klinger.

"Do it," said Andree, quite calm suddenly. "Do it, or you'll be guilty of mass murder. Where's the operations center?"

"The catastrophe operations headquarters is at the police headquarters here in Frankfurt. I have assumed leadership."

"Congratulations," said Andree. "I'll be there in half an hour." He hung up before Klinger could protest.

"Dr. Born," called Meyer-Schönwald from Andree's office.

"Coming," Andree leaped up. At the door, he said to Poppe, "Tell the flight people to prepare the jet."

"The federal president's using it now."

Andree cursed.

"Then get me a chopper."

"The Alouette?"

"I might as well walk. The new one, that SA contraption, which can do 160."

"South Aviation 341," said Meyer-Schönwald, who knew about technical things. "Hopefully, it's free."

Andree picked up the receiver. "Call the Defense Ministry and the national guard. They are to keep units on the alert for catastrophe action in the Darmstadt/Worms area. Keep the lines open. Orders will come in a few minutes."

The three men threw themselves on the free telephones. Andree pulled over a pad. "Dr. Born?"

4

RECORDING OF THE ANNOUNCEMENT MADE AT INTERVALS OF TWO MINUTES ON JULY 31, AS OF 13:33 OVER THE FOLLOWING SYSTEMS: ARD TELEVISION, SECOND GERMAN TELEVISION CHANNEL, HESSIAN RADIO NETWORK, SOUTHWEST RADIO NETWORK, SAARLAND RADIO NETWORK.

Important announcement of the Catastrophe Operations Headquarters to the population in and around Grenzheim, Garding, Bergstrasse, and Darmstadt. A nuclear accident has taken place at the Helios Nuclear Power Station. For the protection of your health, the population is asked to remain indoors and shut all doors and windows. Switch off all ventilation and air conditioning in order to prevent contaminating your body, your clothing, and your residential and business space.

Lock up domestic animals immediately in your homes or stables. Do not go out of doors for the moment. If you have been outside, remove your upper clothing and your shoes and leave them outside your buildings. Cleanse all uncovered parts of the body with soap. Put on only clothing and shoes that were in your homes. For the time being, eat nothing if possible, or else only from cans, jars, bottles, or other dust-free packages that were in your home. Avoid all fresh fruit and vegetables picked after yesterday, drink no fresh milk or water from wells. Feed your domestic animals only fodder or feed stored in your house, barn, or stable. Before watering cattle, be sure to rinse the buckets or the automatic watering equipment thoroughly.

For safety's sake we recommend the population residing near the affected areas to remain indoors. They are warned against moving outside the areas of their towns or villages. Drivers of vehicles are asked to avoid the above-mentioned areas in the region of Southern Hessia, Rhine-Essen, and South Baden. The following roads have been blocked for traffic between towns and villages: Federal highways E 4 and A 81 between Gross-Gerau and Weiterstadt in the north, and Mannheim and Heidelberg in the south. Likewise, federal highways. . . .

River traffic on the Rhine, both upstream and downstream, is closed from river kilometer 444 3 (above the commercial port of Worms) to river kilometer 475 (near Biebesheim). Fellow citizens: Please remain calm and sensible. If it should turn out to be necessary to evacuate certain areas, you will be notified in time. Even then, do not leave the areas in question in your own vehicles. Please wait for the buses and trucks sent in by the catastrophe headquarters or for the announcement of the gathering points at which to reach these vehicles. We appeal to the discipline and sense of responsibility of all citizens. You will receive further information shortly.

5

The parking lot in front of the Helios plant looked like the aftermath of a low-level bombing attack. Anne steered Born's blue Mercedes carefully around burnt-out car wrecks, torn clothing, demonstration signs, police helmets, and shoes. The police and the national guard had retreated. They had removed the people who had been injured or killed during the panic at the gate and in the parking lot.

The fire to the left of the entrance road, set off by the destroyed high-tension wires, had turned the grass into black ashes, and it was now burning near the federal highway, where bushes and trees blazed into the sky like Van Gogh's cypresses.

After five hundred yards, Anne stopped and looked back. Over the quivering asphalt, Helios glowed in the noonday sun. The dome loomed white and perfect in the blue air. Nothing indicated that it was being eaten away on the inside. It was beautiful, like a consumptive maiden in a nineteenth-century novel, blossoming in her hour of death and pretending recovery to her hand-holding lover.

Anne shaded her eyes. Black smoke swarmed from the exhaust chimney, which usually never excreted more than a barely visible light mist.

The radio announcement came as Anne turned left onto the B 44. The inhabitants of the three-house villages visible from Helios didn't need the warning. They had heard about the accident twenty minutes earlier from the fleeing Helios employees. They had already escaped or were loading their belongings into their cars.

Two and a half miles before Grenzheim, at the entrances of the side roads from larger villages, the traffic became heavier. Passenger cars, trucks, tractors, threshers, motorcycles, scooters all pushed recklessly into the crossing, all steering towards Grenzheim in the northeast, where they intended to reach the highway.

Two miles before Grenzheim, the jam started.

The drivers were honking. From somewhere a policeman bobbed up and waved his arms. The drivers kept on honking. The police leaned in through Anne's open window: "A dairy truck's turned over up front. It's blocking the road. We'll never get it out without a crane. You'd better walk."

Anne steered the Mercedes to the bank. Upon climbing

out, she discovered the red bus. It was working along on the opposite lane, past the standing cars, its right-hand tires almost in the roadside ditch. Anne motioned. The middle door of the bus hissed open. Anne grabbed the handle, ran alongside for ten paces, and then leaped on the first step of the footboard. A dozen hands of children clumsily seized her shoulders and upper arms. She dropped upon the rippling metal floor and pulled herself up on a metal pole, gasping, ten seconds later. She pulled herself forwards, using the backs of seats as supports, and finally sank exhausted into the codriver's seat.

Berger was staring at the road. His glasses were misty. Beads of sweat hung in his moustache. His hands embraced the wheel. The veins on the backs of his hands stuck out.

"Why are you driving back?" asked Anne.

"The road's clogged up."

"We can walk with the kids. It's only half an hour on foot."

"Do you know whether we have that much time? Besides, the kids can't stay in Grenzheim. How can we get them away without a bus?"

"The police'll have vehicles ready."

Berger threw the wheel to the left, preventing the bus from skidding into the ditch. "The Police? They don't even know what's really going on. Where are they gonna get cars for a couple of thousand people?"

"What do you intend to do?"

"I'll follow the country road along the Böttger farm. We'll come out at the Grenzheim graveyard, near the church. You can get Michaela from the kindergarten. Then we'll figure out what to do next."

Anne stared at the Barbie doll dangling from the mirror. She smiled at the children, who were convulsively trying to hold on to their seats. "We'll never get across the creek."

"We've got to try it. We can always walk if we have to."

Berger drove onto the Böttger farm. It was deserted.

"They've gone," said Anne.

217

"Or else they're in the fields." Berger drove past the stables and then through a fence onto a narrow path running across fields of forage. Berger could only use the left side of the lane. At the right, the wheels dug into the soft, dry soil. Periodically the engine howled as the wheels got caught.

One child began crying. Anne wanted to stand up and comfort him, but the bus jerked and rocked so vehemently that she was thrown back into her seat.

When she heard the rattling, she at first thought there was something wrong with the engine. Then she saw the green helicopter, flying only ten yards above the fields. She could make out the pilot and another man in the plexiglas cockpit. Shreds of the announcement being broadcast through the loudspeaker wafted through the howling of the bus motor: "Nuclear accident. . . . calm and sensible. . . . information shortly. . . ."

The chopper, shaking like a buzzard, held over a group of farmhands. Hay whirled up. The farmhands clambered on to a tractor. It rumbled across a rye field.

The bus drove through a grove of pines. Branches crunched against the sides and wiped and squeaked across the glass roof. Berger stopped at the edge of the grove. In front of them flowed the creek, edged by high reeds. They got out.

Anne turned around. "We've got company."

Five or six drivers had seen Berger turn into the country road and had followed the bus. They leaped out of their cars and ran towards Berger and Anne. Berger paid no attention.

He walked to the creek. After two months of heat, it was only a thick, green drain. Berger stepped upon the bridge, which was thirteen feet wide and made of slanted wooden planks. A few planks looked rotten. One was missing in the center of the bridge. A hand-painted sign in front of the bridge said: USE PERMITTED ONLY BY PEDESTRIANS AND AT YOUR OWN RISK.

One of the car drivers, a robust, bald-headed man, said, "Let us across first. You'll never make it with the bus."

218

Berger turned to Anne. "Bring the kids across the bridge." To the bald head: "You may not make it with your car, either. That's why I'd rather try first."

"You can't," said the bald head. "If the bridge collapses. . . ."

"We'll see." Anne and the children had reached the other side of the bridge.

"Wait a minute," said the bald head and grabbed Berger's shirt. "You'd better make room for us. If you don't, you'll be sorry." The other drivers nodded.

Berger knocked the bald-headed man into the reeds. He rolled down the bank and splashed into the bed of the creek. While the other drivers stared at him, Berger leaped into the bus and turned on the engine. The drivers sprang in front of the bus, waving their arms. Berger stepped on the gas. The men leaped in all directions.

By the time he reached the bridge, Berger was going at twenty-five miles an hour. The steering wheel wrenched at his hands. When the front wheels hit the first wooden boards, Berger saw the bridge arching in front of him. A wooden board slid into the creek. In the middle of the bridge, the left front wheel sank down. Berger held his foot on the gas. The planks clattered. When the front wheels were almost at the end of the bridge, which was now carrying five and a half tons, the first quarter of the bridge broke away. The stays twisted out of the earth in the bank. The bus slid forward. Berger smashed into the gas pedal. The front wheels grabbed solid ground again, but the bus seemed to stand still. The planks that hurled up by the back wheels struck the bus. Berger saw Anne bring her hand to her mouth in horror. Then the back wheels took hold for seconds, catapulting the bus forward. Soil dashed across the bank. And while the rest of the bridge plunged into the creek, Berger halted the bus next to the children.

Anne had the children climb back in. The men on the other bank were yelling furiously. A stone banged into the chassis close to Anne's head.

When they were driving again, Anne touched Berger's sweat-drenched arm. "That wasn't fair."

Berger said, "I've got a bad conscience."

Sirens began howling all around them.

6

"Finally someone who knows his business," thought Born as he listened to Andree's precise questions. While answering, he kept observing the still-functioning instruments.

"Three bombs. The first destroyed our connection to the electric grid, the second destroyed a cooling pipe, the third a relay room. Short-circuit in the emergency diesels. Kaput! The core has no water."

"What's happening now?" asked Andree.

"The core's melting. The liquid uranium's dripping on the floor of the pressure container and devouring it."

"Can't the concrete foundation of the reactor dome hold out against the uranium?"

"No. The uranium's like a hot iron on a cube of butter. The lava will melt through the foundation and ooze into the earth. According to my calculations, in about thirty or forty minutes. The radioactive radiation will be released by then at the latest."

"How strong will it be?"

"I don't know," said Born. "I can only estimate. Maybe twenty percent of the nuclear radiation, maybe more. It depends on how much radiation is braked by the ground and the concrete. The most dangerous things are the lightlike gamma and neutron rays. They'll contaminate a radius of over one mile in fractions of a second. They'll kill anyone out of doors."

"So it makes no sense putting up the first blockade at one mile?"

"It's too late," said Born. "You'll need your people much more urgently at the four-mile circuit. You've got to get all the refugees through before the radiation cloud reaches them."

"Cloud?"

"In less than an hour, Helios will be a radiation focal point. It's smoking even if you don't see the smoke. Radioactive gases and radioactive particles will climb up and compound with the passing masses of air into a radiation cloud. Moreover, the neutron and gamma rays will infect every drop of water and every other substance within reach with radioactivity."

"So what we're dealing with is an exhaust cloud, like in an accident in a sulphur factor?"

"With one difference," said Born. "The radiation cloud is invisible. We have to locate it with instruments. Get all the meteorologists and radiation experts that you can dig up. Get airplanes, choppers, and anti-radiation suits ready for them. They have to observe the radioactivity released on the earth and in the air. Beforehand, I need an exact weather report as fast as possible—temperature, air pressure, humidity, wind speed, wind direction, forecasts for the next few hours."

"Right away," said Andree. "The catastrophe operations center is at police headquarters in Frankfurt. I'll fly over. Switch to a standing line. Then you can reach me any time and vice versa."

"One more thing," said Born. "An anti-radiation train is en route here from Karlsruhe. Make it turn around. It can't save anything in Helios. But it's got decontamination stations."

"What about you?" asked Andree. "I can send you a chopper."

"It'll be needed elsewhere," said Born. "And I'm needed here."

7

"But if Klinger thinks he can settle this on a state level. . . ." The chancellor's voice was drowned out by a calliope playing in three-quarter time, the yelling of children, and the shrill voices of barkers trying to outshout one another.

"Klinger isn't all there," said Andree. "He just doesn't understand what's happening. The thing is too big for him. He's closing his eyes and imagining it's all a village fire department drill. . . . I spoke to Born. If we're lucky, we'll just escape with a catastrophe. If not, it's the end of the world."

The line crackled and went dead for two seconds.

"A state of emergency then," said the chancellor. "That'll be grist for the Constitution Court."

"If we don't hurry, there won't *be* any Constitution Court." said Andree.

"Okay. Take all the necessary steps. Call the crisis staff together."

"They're already notified. We only reached six people, but the fewer we have, the better."

"It is essential for the Defense and Interior ministers to be present," said the chancellor.

"The Defense Minister's coming along in my chopper. The Minister of the Interior is en route from Wiesbaden to Frankfurt."

"I'll be at the center in half an hour. And, Eckart. . . ."

"Yes?"

"You've got all powers. Use them cautiously. No rash decisions."

"Of course."

Andree hung up. His office was teeming with the heads

of agencies, assistants, and secretaries who could still be reached in the various ministries despite the parliamentary vacation, despite the fact that it was Friday, despite the time of day, 1:45 P.M. It was the silent reserve holding ground during the summer months of Bonn.

"State of emergency," said Andree. "It's starting. Everyone takes over a telephone call. The return calls go over my extension."

Meyer-Schönwald pushed through the throng and attached a map of southwest Germany on the wall. "I couldn't find a better one."

Andree stood near the map. "This is Helios. This is the four-mile barrier circuit. Klinger is trying to put this circuit up with police and firemen, but they're not enough of course. So. Call up the Defense Ministry. Army units with choppers, tanks and ABC equipment to beef up the circuit. Focal points: roads and highways. That's where we'll have the most trouble. Call up the Ministry of the Interior. National guard units with the same orders are to start marching. They're to work things out with the army units so that they won't overlap. The circuit is divided into four sectors. The command in each sector is to be taken by the senior officer of the first unit reaching the place. Local fire inspectors, village policemen, officials have nothing to say. If they get pushy, kick them out.

"Furthermore, decontamination stations will be put up at five points on the edge of the blockade. Anyone leaving the restricted area will be examined there for radioactive contamination and, if necessary, isolated and treated. The five points are: In the northwest, federal highway B9, south of Alsheim. In the northeast, B44 north of Grenzheim. In the southeast, B47 west of Lorsch and B44 south of Bürstadt. And in the southwest, B9, north of Worms.

"The anti-radiation center in Karlsruhe is now sending choppers and trucks, transport decontamination stations or provisional tents to those places. They need help from the Technical Auxiliary—personnel, geiger counters, decontamination equipment, and so on. The Red Cross has to send as many doctors and nurses as possible to the checkpoints. The German Red Cross has a state of emergency plan. It is in effect as of now.

"The next call is to the Americans in Frankfurt. They are to send out their ABC war experts with equipment. Of special importance are the helicopters equipped with geiger counters. The watch over the radioactive cloud is to be organized by the Meteorological Institute in Frankfurt. The Americans are to contact it immediately. The same request for help is to go to the French.

"The air space over the entire Federal Republic of Germany is closed as of now. Departing and landing permission only for those flights involved in catastrophe operations. Everything clear?"

Someone asked, "What about the police in the other federal states?"

"The state governments are now being informed by the Federal Chancellor," said Andree. "Their auxiliary troops are under the army and the national guard. Until a crisis staff is constituted in Frankfurt, I'm in charge of operations. You can inform all departments that any orders from Klinger and his consorts are invalid if I don't expressly confirm them."

The room had emptied. Andree said to Meyer-Schöwald: "You've got the most important job. The——"

The telephone rang. Andree pressed the loudspeaker button. "Brigadier-General Carter in Frankfurt. He doesn't believe——"

"Put him through," said Andree.

"Are you people nuts?"

Andree switched to English with an almost imperceptible German accent. "No one is nuts. Your information is correct. We need your help. I speak in the name of the chancellor."

"Okay," said General Carter. "But if you're trying to bullshit me——"

"Go to the police headquarters in Frankfurt. In thirty

minutes, the chancellor will speak from there with your president."

"You'd better be right," said Carter and hung up.

"The evacuation," said Andree to Meyer-Schönwald. "You've got to do it from here. There's nothing much to be done in the four-mile circuit, but——"

"Why not?"

"Klinger had the brilliant idea of telling people about the Helios accident via radio and TV. He also asked them politely to remain in their homes. Which means that at this moment all the inhabitants in the Helios area are fleeing towards all points of the compass in their automobiles and the roads are clogged up. If the checkpoints are at the arterial roads, the jams'll get even worse, especially when the contaminated people arrive."

Andree looked at his watch. "According to Born's reckonings, the first wave of radiation is due in about twenty minutes. A sensible evacuation is thus possible only as of the four-mile blockade. It has to concentrate on this ring here: Outer border Pfungstadt, the north from Mannheim, Worms, Alzey. The evacuation is to go from inside to outside. The principle: As few private cars as possible, to prevent any traffic jams. Instead, gathering points, from which the population will be brought to safety in buses, trucks, and so forth. The gathering points are indicated in Klinger's so-called catastrophe defense plan. But naturally, he doesn't have enough cars. Find out where the gathering points are and dig up some vehicles—army, national guard, riot police, private vehicle companies. Defense Minister Krüger is sending an experienced sergeant. You'll work with him."

"Where are we to evacuate them to? And how far?"

"Twenty-five miles. No farther. Otherwise, it'll take too long before the cars can get the next batch. And we can't strain the urban concentration centers. General directions east and west."

"How many people live in the evacuation zone?"

225

"Oh God," groaned Andree, "how should I know? 200,000, 300,000. Don't calculate. Start!"

"One last question," said Meyer-Schönwald. "Should we use the radio network?"

"No. I've ordered a total news blackout. If the Frankfurt population finds out there's been more than a minor mechanical accident down there, then all hell will break loose. They'll notice it soon enough, anyway."

Meyer-Schönwald walked into the next room. At the door he said, "We'll never make it."

"I'm hard of hearing," said Andree.

Poppe called from the conference room:"Krüger's waiting by the chopper. Klinger's assistant is on the line."

Andree stood up and pulled on his jacket. "He can go to hell. Transmit all important calls over the radio center to the chopper. I'll ring you by Frankfurt at the latest."

8

Alexander Fuchs waited for the heavy trucks from the Karlsruhe anti-radiation center. In case of accident, according to all plans, they would arrive immediately to help out the plant personnel. The trucks didn't come. Fuchs waited for the fire engines that in case of accident would come racing to Helios from all the towns and villages in the area. The fire engines didn't come. The plant was deserted. Car wrecks were smoking on the parking lot. Black smoke was pouring from the exhaust chimney.

Fuchs didn't hear Sibylle.

Sibylle said, "Honestly, a silly goose. How romantic it was. Experienced woman meets attractive young man. Young man lets himself be seduced. Experienced woman can't get enough

226

of him. And I believed everything. I didn't notice what an ice-cold bastard you are. I thought you wanted me because I've still got a passable body. But I could just as well have been a fat cow or a cripple in a wheelchair, and you would have grabbed me. I was the director's wife. I was useful to you. I could get hold of blueprints for you. I could reveal names to you. I hope you're happy now. You've got what you wanted. You don't need me anymore. Here—kick me."

The sirens began screaming, from all directions, tortured, pained, uncoordinated, inspiring horror rather than warning. Church bells hammered loudly among the sirens.

At that instant, Fuchs knew his action had failed. He had done something wrong. He had overestimated the resistance capacity of technology and the technocrats. He had annihilated them. No tears for them. But what about the innocents who were endangered now—the people he had wanted to save with his Helios warning signal? Two technocrats had died by his hand because the higher law of humanity required it. For Fuchs, they had been nothing more than door locks for a burglar: nuisances.

But now the sirens and bells were playing a tune that made his hair stand on edge, his teeth chatter, a melody announcing danger, fear, and torturous death—now he knew. He was a murderer. He, Alexander Fuchs, an unknown soldier in the army of humanity, was a butcher. No, thought Fuchs, that's not the way it is. That's wrong. I did it for *you*. It's for your good. You've got to believe me.

"Maybe I'm mistaken," said Sibylle. "No one is that good an actor. Or maybe it was like a marriage of convenience—love coming with time?"

But how will they talk about me, thought Fuchs. They'll say: A lunatic hungry for fame, ready to do anything to get it. The papers will make me headline news: The mass murderer of Helios. They'll put me in the same category as the madmen who wanted to make history with annihilation. If everyone sees what I've done, no one will realize what my intention was. He thought of Bertrand Russell's kind, wrinkled face. I've brought shame on you. You're going to thrust me aside.

That heat. And that woman next to him who wouldn't stop calling his name. His head. Were these the diabolical rays already? Was the devil's white egg down there bursting already? Fuchs hurled the binoculars at the Helios dome. Thirty feet below, they bounced on a rock and burst into pieces. Fuchs sank to his knees and wept.

Sibylle pulled his head to her breast. Running her hands through his thick hair, she whispered, "Don't worry, Sasha, I'm here with you."

Fuchs stammered incomprehensible words. His face was white. His eyes were blank. His hands twitched.

Sibylle froze. This wasn't a hot summer's day in green vineyards. This was an ice-cold moonlit night in the bluish Arctic. Her body was paralyzed and dying. Could one love a man without realizing that the man one loved didn't exist? Could one sleep for months with a man without recognizing that he was insane?

Now that she knew, she recalled words and scenes that should have made the truth clear to her. Alexander, running through the streets aimlessly for hours at a time. Alexander, prophesying the end of the world. Alexander, hinting at secrets he couldn't reveal to anyone. All these had been signs that she in her blindness had failed to decipher.

Never the least doubt. And why should there have been? There was the other Alexander: Alexander, whose eyes shone when he saw her. Alexander, whose mouth caressed her, whose slender body twisted around her.

And even though he was alien to her, she still felt something of that Alexander as she pressed him to her and dabbed tears from his cheeks.

He was sick. He had murdered and destroyed because he was sick. And the awareness of his deed had made him even sicker. He was helpless. She couldn't leave him alone.

She glanced over at the white dome of Helios. Was Martin down there? Was he dead? Had he escaped? She thought: You calculated everything, you perfectionist. You had a computer at hand for every random chance. And all at once a dissatisfied woman meets a crazy fanatic, and destroys your perfectionism. Sibylle hoped that Martin was alive. She knew he was alive. Whatever happened in the plant, he would manage to overcome it.

Fuchs moaned. "Okay," said Sibylle.

Fuchs needed help. She wondered whether to hand him over to the police. She saw the cold official face of the inspector who had questioned her a few hours ago. The police would treat Fuchs like a criminal, not like a sick man. They would torture and destroy him. She had to get Fuchs to a hospital, a sanatorium. Wagner. Dr. Wagner. He was the man she could turn to.

She stood up and helped Fuchs to his feet. "We've got to get back to Darmstadt, Sasha. You're ill. You've got a temperature. I know a doctor who can help you."

They stumbled down the hill between fragrant pine trees.

"They hate me," said Fuchs. "But I did it because I love them. Do you understand?"

"Naturally."

"I computed everything, honestly."

"I believe you."

"Everything. For weeks and weeks."

"Come on." Sibylle pulled Fuchs into the car.

"I could have put the bomb directly on the biological barrier. The explosive force would have been strong enough to. . . . You can read about in the manual. . . . But I put it six feet away. . . ."

Sibylle opened the door on the passenger's side and pushed Fuchs on the seat. She stared at the bag on the back seat and felt tears coming to her eyes. She and Fuchs didn't need the money anymore.

When she started the engine, Fuchs opened the door.

"I wanna die."

"Don't you love me at all?"

"They despise me. They hate me. They don't realize that it was only for them. . . ." He looked at her. "And you despise me too," he yelled.

"You're ill, Sasha, you need a doctor, Sasha, come on, Sasha."

"You think I'm crazy, don't you. Get the fuck out of here. Leave me alone. You haven't the foggiest idea. You're playing the cool lady, and you're nothing but a slut."

He tried to climb out.

"There's only one way to get them to understand you," said Sibylle. "You've got to explain it to them. And you can only do that if you come along with me. The police are hunting you. They'll find you if you stay here."

"So what! That's what you want. Then you'll be rid of me. I want it too. Then I can talk. I'll convince them that——"

"Be reasonable. The police only want your confession. They don't care about explanations. They'll turn the words around in your mouth."

Fuchs sank down in the seat. He bent over to Sibylle and kissed her. "Forgive me. You're right. I need time. Peace and quiet to think. Oh yes. I'll find the words that will shake them up. . . . My testament. . . . And then they can do to me what they like."

En route to Worms, a helicopter rattled close over the car. The loudspeaker was saying something, but Sibylle only understood the word "evacuation." She eyed Fuchs from the side. He was smiling. Sibylle was afraid.

230

9

The 600-HP turbine drove the blue and white SA 341 at a slight angle (the tail being higher than the glass cockpit) at over 170 miles per hour at an altitude of over 3,000 feet. Defense Minister Krüger was absorbed in assembly plans. Andree was tugging at his earphones. His sweat-drenched hair stuck over his ears. He asked the pilot: "How much longer?"

The pilot held up two fingers. Twenty minutes.

Shortly before Koblenz came the weather report. The meteorologist apologized for the delay: They had first had to gather precise data.

Andree requested a connection with Born from the radio center. The connection was poor. Andree shouted: "The uranium. How far is the uranium along?"

Born shouted back, but Andree could barely understand him. "It's already melted through the pressure container. It's eating through the foundation now. . . . Maybe ten more minutes, then. . . ."

"What do you say to the weather report?"

"What?"

"Wea-ther re-port?"

"I haven't gotten it."

"Those assholes," yelled Andree. "What the fuck are they doing? They ought to inform you first. Okay, are you getting this down? The Institute of Meteorology and so on. Readings for the Grenzheim area and so on. Air temperature on the ground: 32 degrees Celsius (90 degrees Fahrenheit). Humidity: sixty-two percent. Air pressure: 1,020 millibars, with a slightly falling tendency. West-southwest wind: two meters per second, almost a lull. The wind will quicken in two hours. Clouds forming around the Rhine. Valid until three P.M. One addition: In the Frankfurt/Mannheim area, there's been a definite inversion since this morning at ten. In downtown Frankfurt, at one P.M., they registered 45 carbon monoxide concentrations of 55 milligrams for every cubic meter of air. The sulphur dioxide concentration is 1.0 milligrams per cubic meter. Both are considerably above the admissible limits. . . . Is that good or bad news?"

"In our situation, there can only be bad news," said Born. "With an inversion, the warm air can't rise over the surface of the earth. The radiation cloud forming over Helios can't divide and disperse. It will float densely over the ground—a mobile radioactive source, annihilating all living things within a radius of 500 or 1,000 yards. On the other hand, we know in what direction the cloud will be drifting and its motion will be slow. If the wind doesn't quicken, then in one hour the front of the radioactive cloud will——"

Born broke off. Andree shouted: "Born? Are you still on?"

After fifteen seconds, Born said, "Two explosions. Cracks in the wall. Part of the dome probably collapsed. We're getting there."

"Did it hit you?"

"No," said Born. "As long as the concrete walls stand, nothing will happen to me, unless the whole thing blows up because of some detonating-gas explosion. In one hour, the cloud will reach Grenzheim in the northeast and continue towards Aschaffenburg. The evacuation should concentrate on that area. Not exclusively, of course. The wind can shift. Are the anti-radiation choppers on the way?"

"If not, then God have mercy on their souls," said Andree.

"They've got to hem in the cloud. Determine everything precisely, the length, breadth, height. Report any change in direction."

"Okay," said Andree. "But what about you? You've

got to get out of there. You can't do anything more. I'll have——"

Born laughed. "You haven't been listening. The radiation is free. I'm sitting in the safest vault in the world—screened from millions of roentgens of radioactivity. No one in the world could get in here, Andree."

"And no one could get out," murmured Andree. He waited till the radio center had put through the new connection, and said: "Sector I, Northeast, has priority in the evacuation."

"Hey," said the Defense Minister. "We're flying south."

"Southeast," said Andree. "I want to see the damn thing before it's totally gone."

They crossed the Rhine near Rüdesheim and left the northern spur of the Palatine Mountains behind.

"Alzey," yelled the pilot and pointed to the right. Then they saw the Rhine again in the distance. The pilot reduced speed. Helios. Tiny at a distance. Toylike. Harmless.

"Why can't we fly nearer?" asked Andree.

The pilot shook his head. "Because of the radiation, I'd have to go to over 1,300 feet. That's impossible without oxygen masks. Besides, I have no desire to see the egg."

"Then let's go to Frankfurt," said Andree. He glanced back at Helios vanishing in the midst.

10

RECORDING OF THE RADIO CONVERSATION BETWEEN THE METEOROLOGICAL AIRCRAFT D-LACO, THE CONTROL TOWER OF THE RHEIN-MAIN AIRPORT, AND THE METEOROLOGICAL CENTER (JULY 31, 14:29–14:31.):

Pilot: I have the scene in sight. Altitude 10,000 feet.

Observer: We're directly over the plant now. Radiation zero. Are you getting the reports?

Center: Perfectly.

Observer: It's moving. The dome is moving. It's leaning towards the south. A lot of smoke. I don't recognize anything.

Pilot: I'm descending to 8,000 feet.

Tower: Your altitude should not be under 10,000 feet. Do you read me?

Observer to pilot: Why are they carrying on like that. The radiation isn't very high yet. Go down.

Center: Remain at 10,000 feet. You might fly into a radiation concentration.

Observer: Okay, okay. Now I can see clearer. The dome has sagged down on the south side, but it's still standing. There's a fire next to the dome. Not very big yet.

Tower: Climb to 10,000 feet. Please read back.

Center: Go up, you idiots.

Observer: The pilot's blacked out. Hey, let me at it. Shit, I feel so sick. I. . . .

Tower : You're losing altitude. Have you got radio trouble?

Center: Hello. We can't read you. Hello.

Tower: You're out of radar coverage. . . . you're out of radar coverage. . . .

11

The office excursion was a success. The director said it himself. The office was just the right size for an excursion. Everyone knew everyone else, you didn't have to introduce yourself and hem and haw to people from other departments. They had left

Darmstadt at nine in the morning. They were off to the Oden Woods, but then, said the manager, they would go by way of Grenzheim for lunch. There was a restaurant right in the vicinity, where you could get a delicious but inexpensive roast venison. They had drunk some Asbach wine before, then red wine and beer, then something for the digestion. The director had said: "After a meal you've got to rest or at most take a stroll." Seeing that the director wanted to take a stroll, most of the group had opted to go along.

After ten minutes they had discovered a small birch forest with a dredged-out lake in the middle, hardly larger than a swimming pool. The director had stripped down to his underpants and jumped into the water. The bookkeepers had followed him. The older secretaries had remained seated. The young ones, wearing transparent panties and with wobbling breasts, had capered about on the jelly, had turned around, so that the head clerks wouldn't miss anything, and then they had dived into the water in sportly dives.

The director, his wreath of hair still wet, lay behind grass and bushes now, remote from his talking, laughing, drinking employees. He was on top of a secretary. He knew he shouldn't do it. She'd expect favors. She might even blackmail him. But she was young, warm, tanned. And the sun was hot, the birches were fragrant, the fish splashing in the water, the wine pulsing in his veins.

The girl writhed and emitted sighs that the director had long missed in his wife. He felt slender, powerful, animal, and gave off small grunts while increasing the tempo. Then the tense face of the girl swam before him. His skin turned cold. He slackened. The arms on which he was propped to hold his belly over the young body buckled. The director threw up. He crashed on the girl like a rock. She tried to roll him off, but realized she had no strength left. The director gasped, grabbed his head, and rolled over slowly.

The girl had vomit on her body. She was throwing up venison, peaches, and red wine. She crawled towards her colleagues. She didn't crawl any faster than the bugs fleeing before her. Her sphincter muscles opened, and she left a trail of stool, urine, and blood. Her skin burned, her eyes teared, her stomach convulsed in spasms that shook her entire body. At the edge of the clearing, she pushed the grass aside with one hand and whispered, tormented by fits of choking: "Help, help."

No one could hear her. The manager was lying with his upper body in the water, mechanically scooping up water over his head. The assistant head of the bookkeeping department was wallowing on the ground, pressing her hands to her stomach. A few people were crouching apathetically on the ground, having vomited everything out and still retching.

The girl wanted to stand up, but a new burst of vomiting flung her to the ground. She gasped for air. She had no strength left to open her mouth. Gall dripped from the corners. The girl felt insects crawling over her naked body. She stared at the sky. Near the sun, tiny aircraft were circling. The girl shut her eyes.

12

EXCERPT FROM THE HELIOS REPORT:

17d. As of today we have not managed to estimate even approximately the intensity of radiation released by the emergence of the molten mass from the shielding concrete dome. Within split seconds, a radius of two kilometers (over one mile) was contaminated by permeating gamma and neutron rays, i.e., before the cloud containing the major part of the radiation had even moved more than a hundred yards from the radiation source in the reactor foundation. The cloud, in turn, emitted both gamma and neutron rays as well as alpha and beta rays, directly and in the form of radiation-induced hot particles. . . . None of the approximately one thousand people out of doors within a one-mile radius at the time of the release of radioactivity survived. It was the neutron- and gamma-ray dose of the first few seconds that had the deadly effect. The estimates by experts of this out-of-door dose lie between 15,000 and 50,000 roentgens. Seven hundred roentgens make survival unlikely. . . .

17e. The radiation cloud forming immediately upon the emergence of the molten mass from the reactor dome (the cloud constituted itself out of many small clouds drifting across the contaminated area) likewise emitted a far-reaching direct radiation (about 1,000 yards) and also contained radioactive particles (dust, water, gases). Because of the wind conditions, these particles were at first largely concentrated within the area of the cloud. Nevertheless, some of them spread faster than the cloud itself, and many people touched and breathed radioactive air or else drank and ate ionized liquid and food during the first hour. . . .

The cloud contained approximately 200 radiating isotopes, of which the most effective are: Plutonium-239 (most endangered organ: the lung), iodine-131 (most endangered organ: the thyroid), strontium-90 (most endangered organ: bones), krypton-85, radon, cesium-137, phosphorus-32, yttrium-90, xenon-141, carbon-11, carbon-14, niobium-94, barium-133. . . .

17f. The high radiation intensity near the plant and within the radius of the radioactive cloud can be determined by citing Rayevsky's thesis of the 3.5-day effect. Rayevsky established that laboratory animals irradiated with 1,000 to 15,000 roentgens throughout their bodies all died at the same time within 3.5 days, whether they received a dose of 1,000 or 15,000 roentgens. Immediate death ensued only after 50,000 roentgens. Since many victims of the Helios rays died within hours and presumably even minutes after absorbing the radioactivity, the intensity of the radiation must have reached or exceeded the limit of 50,000 roentgens at some points. . . .

The early symptoms of the radiation sickness, fatal within just a few minutes, resembled those of the non-fatal illnesses: nausea, vomiting, diarrhea, which can be seen as a reaction of the autonomic nervous system being destroyed. . . .

13

The helicopter landed on the area near the police headquarters. Two young policeman were waiting at a respectful distance, tightly holding onto their caps, which were blowing in the rotor wind.

Andree and Krüger hurried towards them, bending. The policemen led them through a side entrance to the elevator.

"The operation leaders are on the tenth floor," said one of the policemen. "They can take over the communication equipment of the traffic headquarters up there."

All this jargon they teach the rookies today, thought Andree. He asked, "Is the chancellor here yet?"

"He just came a minute ago."

The corridor was stacked with files cleared from the shelves of the adjoining rooms to make space for plans, ordnance survey maps, radios, and television sets. Men with teletype messages in their hands rushed past them unheedingly.

The traffic headquarters was located behind a frosted-glass door. It was a gigantic room, at least 300 yards square. The two oblong walls were covered with monitors. Andree couldn't tell what images they were showing. Control desks ran along the walls. The men and women at the control desks were telephoning. They spoke loudly, and since all were talking simultaneously, some had already begun yelling. The wall facing the door consisted of a map of Frankfurt, on which red and green lights were glowing. Two teletypes were rattling in a corner. To the right, in front of the enormous window revealing the panorama of the city roasting in the sun, there stood a long conference table. The shelves piled on top of one another next to the table showed that it had only just been put up there.

At the table, Andree recognized Federal Minister of the Interior Klein, Minister of Research Gerner, Lützkow, the head of the opposition party, Grolmann, the head of the party in office, a national guard general, an army general. The two generals were studying a map of Germany.

In front of the table stood the chancellor and Governor Klinger. Behind Klinger there were faces that Andree couldn't place: State ministers? A police superintendent? Assistants?

He walked towards the group. The air was hot and misty.

Klinger's high, hysterical voice: "Our legal measures suffice perfectly to deal with this difficult situation. Which does not mean that I do not welcome your advice."

All he has to do now is throw back his curls, thought Andree. He would have kicked Klinger aside, thrown him out. Klinger's protest was merely a rearguard action. Everyone could tell he was relieved to give up the responsibility. But he stuck to appearances. And wasted valuable time.

Andree admired the chancellor's composure. The crude, bony, sweat-glistening face with tiny eyes remained calm. The chancellor said:

"Governor. The consequences of the Helios accident involve and endanger our whole country. For that reason we ought to forget about arguing over federalistic jurisdiction issues. . . ."

Klinger still didn't give up: "I do hope you realize that the state of emergency, Article three, Paragraph two, in our state constitution gives me exclusive authority in the event of a catastrophe. And I certainly feel able——"

"Yessir." That was the Frankfurt police superintendent. "After all, laws aren't made just to be ignored at the first opportunity."

Andree pulled the police superintendent along. He nodded to the chancellor. "C'mon. Just tell me what you've already been doing."

The superintendent wanted to protest. But when he saw the expression on Andree's face, he gave his report.

The chancellor said, "We don't need any legal wrangling. I've already declared a federal state of emergency, Governor, and I am taking over as of now the leadership of the catastrophe operations center.

Klinger shrugged in surrender. "You must know what you are doing." He sat down at the conference table and pushed together a few imaginary crumbs on the table top. He hated this man. A parvenu. A refugee. A dubious sort.

The chancellor asked Andree, who was operating on a Coke bottle with a pair of scissors, (there was no bottle opener): "How is the situation?"

"As good as nothing has happened here," said Andree. "Police and fire department. That's all. The police superintendent has just inadvertently told us that a local fire chief, upon hearing the action orders, replied: "Fight an atomic accident with our equipment? That's like fighting a four-alarm blaze with a fire swatter."

The bottle cap sprang off. Some of the cola foamed upon the table. Andree took a sip.

He briefly described the measures he had taken. "In the chopper, I sent out orders to get all the threads to run together here: evacuation, decontamination, observation of the radioactive cloud, reception camps, emergency hospitals."

The two generals leaped up almost at once and grabbed telephones that their aides-de-camp handed them.

"It's functioning," said Andree.

"What can I do?" asked the chancellor.

"In the next few minutes, you have to answer calls from people who still believe that the state of emergency is a mistake. I also consider it advisable for you to inform the governments of the neighboring countries, and the President of the United States because we want to use his men. Or do you still wish to wait?"

The chancellor gave a shadow of a smile. "I've already asked for the lines. In five minutes, the conference call will begin. My question was about the ongoing evacuation."

Andree made a gesture of apology. "We can only hope that it's working without too much trouble. The next weak point will be at the decontamination station at Grenzheim. The cloud will reach it in forty minutes. All refugees have to pass the checkpoint by then."

"Why can't we manage that?"

"First of all, there's a traffic jam, according to the latest reports. Secondly, there are only four decontamination stations so far, and——"

"Why not more?"

"We only have twelve altogether so far. And they're not even in the right places yet. If you count about thirty seconds for decontaminating each person—and the direct radiation has probably reached a couple of hundred people by now—then in one hour you can process four hundred and eighty people at the outside. And we haven't even got an hour."

A man shouted: "Chancellor for the president of the German Red Cross. Extension four."

"I'll be right back," said the chancellor.

"I'll be in the chopper." Andree pulled his jacket back on. "I'll inform you directly about the state of the evacuation."

14

RECORD OF THE FIRST INTERNATIONAL CONFERENCE CALL
AFTER THE ACCIDENT AT THE HELIOS NUCLEAR POWER
STATION.

Participants: The President of the United States (USA), the
Chairman of the Communist Party of the Soviet Union (SU),
the French Prime Minister (F), the British Prime Minister
(GB), the President of the State Council ⌐f the German Democratic Republic (GDR); the heads of state of Belgium, Luxemburg, the Netherlands, Denmark, Sweden, Norway, Cze,
choslovakia, Austria, Switzerland, Italy, Poland; the
Chancellor of the Federal Republic of Germany (D):

D: Gentleman, I have decided upon this unusual step because I have to inform you of something with previously unpar-
alleled, perhaps major, consequences. About eighty minutes
ago, at the two-thousand-megawatt atomic power plant Helios,
about fifty kilometers southwest of Frankfurt, an act of sabotage caused an accident that has gotten out of control. The
highly radioactive uranium fuel has fully or partly melted
through the safety barriers and released radiation, which is
moving northeast in the form of a cloud. At this time, it is only
a few kilometers from Helios.

In the present state of the weather, the cloud is drifting
at a rate of seven kilometers, or about four miles, per hour
towards Aschaffenburg, the Rhoen, and the border of the
GDR. In the event that the wind conditions change, other
countries might also be endangered, especially if upwinds break
up the radioactive cloud and spread it over wide areas.

GDR: I hereby protest sharply. For five years now the government of the GDR has been warning about irresponsible adventures with giant reactors. Now the chickens are coming home to roost.

GB: Have you caught the perpetrator or the terrorist group?

D: We know who the perpetrator is, but he is still at large. As far as we know, the act was not politically motivated, but merely an insane deed by one person.

USA: What do you need to fight the catastrophe?

D: Thank you, Mr. President. We need experienced anti-radiation personnel and anti-radiation equipment, particularly decontamination stations.

F: Are there any casualties yet?

D: We have no exact figures.

SU: What are you doing about it?

D: We are evacuating.

GDR: And hoping that the radioactive cloud will quickly vanish from your country.

D: That is an unfair insinuation.

GB: I believe that Great Britain is the only country that has experienced a similar situation—in October, 1967, with a windscale reactor. The wind drove the radioactive cloud out over the Irish Sea. . . .

GDR: Central Europe is not an island. Before the cloud reaches the sea—you most likely mean the Baltic Sea, Herr Prime Minister, it will cross densely populated areas. GDR areas. . . .

USA: You'll have enough time to protest. We have to act now. I propose that all countries not immediately endangered start sending personnel and matériel immediately. The Federal Chancellor will keep us up to date.

SU: I agree. We are all threatened. Our nations must cope with this together.

15

The red bus halted at the exit to Grenzheim. "Get Michaela," said Berger. "I'll wait here."

"I'll try and find the parents, too," said Anne. "They must be worried about their children."

"That makes no sense. We mustn't lose any time. We have a greater chance of getting through if we stick together."

The kindergarten was located at Kilian Square across from the Black Eagle restaurant. Anne had a slow time of it. The narrow streets were choked with cars. Anyone owning a truck, the butcher or the grocer, for example, had loaded it with furniture, TV sets, washing machines, and trunks, which had been packed so hastily that shirt sleeves and trouser legs were dangling from them.

A few policemen tried to clear the road, but to no avail. Anne wondered why it was impossible to evacuate a village of six thousand without such chaos. She asked a policeman, "Didn't Mayor Rapp give you any instructions?"

The policeman grinned wearily. "Rapp? When he heard about the accident, he dashed over to his villa. He has to get his Persian carpets to safety."

"Who's giving you orders?"

"The checkpoint station up there on the arterial road. But they've got enough to do with that decont——well, you know, that radioactive cleaning place. They're totally blocked up."

Anne ran to the kindergarten. Its windows were painted over with laughing suns, ships with swelling sails, and comical heads. The place was empty.

"The little tots are on an outing," said a groaning voice. It was an old woman in a wheelchair. She was in the care of the kindergarten teachers. "They wanted to go swimming."

The old woman's head rocked as though mounted on a spring.

On the outer roads, it was the same as at the center of town: cars loaded with children, animals, furniture.

Anne kept running. In her home, she fell exhausted into an armchair. She looked at the terrace where she had been sitting with Born the night before. She saw a dress on the back of a chair. Michaela hadn't wanted to put it on that morning. Michaela loved jeans. Anne changed out of her torn, sweaty blouse and skirt into a polo shirt and slacks. She took all the cash from the desk drawer and got the bicycle from the garage.

She pedaled along the small, filthy river. It smelled of scent materials—the perfume factory three miles upstream. Among the trees, she saw the tank and soldiers. She recalled old war movies. Sirens, low-flying bomber attacks.

She biked past the zoo, the pride of Grenzheim. The animals—a camel, a monkey, a couple of goats, three flamingoes, countless guinea pigs—were calm. They had never heard of the doughty geese on the Capitol who had once warned the Romans of the attack of the barbaric Celts.

At the next rise, Anne leaped off the bike and pushed it along as she jogged. She listened for the shouts of children in the direction of the swimming pool. She heard nothing.

Reaching the top, gasping, Anne saw the children. Two lay twisted in a pool of blood in the middle of the road. The blood shone darkly in the sun. One hung with outspread arms in the fork of a hazelnut bush. The others sat at the edge of the road, pale, paralyzed, sobbing.

Michaela sat among them.

Anne enclosed her in her arms.

Michaela stammered: "The car. . . . the car. . . ."

The car was a blue Opel Admiral. It had smashed against a tree trunk, squeezed up to its windshield. Anne recognized the face of the teacher under the car. She was dead

Something moved in the car. The door opened slowly. A

man fell out, rolled over the ground, stood up. Mayor Rapp. His face bloody. He felt himself, legs, ribs, head. He stumbled towards Anne.

"I didn't see them," he said. "They suddenly appeared before me. I couldn't turn. Please believe me."

Anne was examining the children. Two had arm injuries.

"I was driving slowly," said Mayor Rapp. "But they were walking in the middle of the street."

Anne said to the children, "Don't be afraid. Come with me."

She picked up Michaela. The children followed her. Rapp stared at his car. He shrugged his shoulders and ran after Anne and the children.

"Where are you going? Don't you know the radioactive cloud is coming towards Grenzheim?"

Anne said, "Don't cry, Michaela. Everything's going to be all right."

Rapp said, "I've lost everything. Twenty years of work down the drain. That goddamn nuclear plant. If only I hadn't brought that goddamn nuclear plant here."

Berger helped the children into the bus. Anne made sure that the two injured ones got seats.

Rapp said, "Take me along."

Anne turned to Berger. "He ran down and killed four people. That's how anxious he was to get away."

Rapp, one foot on the entrance step, cried, "I couldn't help it. I explained it to you. I couldn't help it." His face was twisted with fear. His sliced-up ear shone scarlet.

Berger pressed the button that closed the doors. Rapp pulled his leg back just in time. "Get the hell away," Berger shouted.

Rapp beat his fists on the metal and yelled, "I can help you. You'll never get through the blockades. I'm the mayor. I've got an ID card." Berger looked at Anne. She nodded. Berger opened the door.

Rapp threw himself into the bus.

246

"I knew you'd be reasonable. Hurry up. The cloud must be very near already."

Anne said, "Don't talk so much. Help me to bandage the children."

Obediently, Rapp aided her in putting on the makeshift bandages. He touched her arm. "You're a capable woman. I always knew it."

Anne shoved his arm away.

Rapp rubbed his hand.

Berger shouted, "We're at the end of the traffic jam. You're needed, Herr Mayor."

16

Born had pulled on an anti-radiation uniform. He didn't believe it would help much, but he wanted to take every precaution, hold out as long as possible. He didn't ask himself why. The men out there, fighting the catastrophe, didn't need him anymore. And whether he lived another two minutes or two hours or two days didn't matter. This was no fire. You couldn't hope that the rescuers would finally come if you only avoided the flames long enough. For Born, there was no more hope. And yet: He wanted to live.

He didn't know how high the radiation was in the control room. The instruments no longer reacted. Either the batteries were empty or the shocks had ruined the sensitive measuring equipment. The film strip that every plant employee wore on his lapel would have been useful now. Born had lost his during the fight at the demonstration.

The alarm sirens had fallen silent. The stillness in the room was interrupted at minute-long intervals by dull explosions from the reactor dome. Now one hundred and eighty tons of glowing uranium were pouring through its foundation into the open. Born wondered what molten uranium looked like. He knew that crude uranium was gray and processed uranium yellowish, which was why it was called "yellow cake." The melting uranium was probably the color of lead, like the water of a lake shortly before an evening storm.

The slanted top of the control desk was covered with closely written slips of paper.

Numbers. A few scrawls on a three-by-three-inch scrap of paper were enough to describe the total annihilation. The scientists had built models. They were all very lucid, they were all phony. But people prefer an imperfect picture of reality to a perfection that can only be described abstractly in figures. In this model of an atom, spherical electrons gravitated around proton bundles that looked like bunches of grapes. Neutrons whirred like medieval flint bullets against nuclear shells, which burst apart like shrapnel—images, fantasies, mock-ups. Even horror films were more obvious about dangers. The frog-legged creatures from other planets, the armored monsters from black lagoons, King Kong on the World Trade Center: They all inspired dread in a visual form, they all symbolized a collective fear that no one could escape.

But the energy from atoms remained invisible. It killed silently. It attacked without lightning, flames, or thunder. It planted its tiny explosives in bones, blood, tissue, the body unable to defend itself. It was the perfect murderer: efficient and anonymous.

17

The helicopter flew low over the Frankfurt–Darmstadt highway. The lanes towards Darmstadt were choked. At Weiterstadt, the police had put up a roadblock for the south-bound traffic.

Andree telephoned the operations center: "You've got to free all lanes for the evacuation transports to the north. Haven't you stopped the traffic by the Frankfurt entrance to the highway?"

The police superintendent replied: "Naturally. But it will take a while. This is vacation season, and it's Friday afternoon. All the Darmstadt commuters are driving home now. We're rerouting them to side roads."

Andree shook his head impatiently.

They flew over Darmstadt. For a moment, Andree thought about what would happen if the cloud deviated just a few milles off its calculated course. He pushed back the thought.

The pilot brought the helicopter up to 6,000 feet. The mountain highway lay to the left. The summer landscape shone in the afternoon light: villages, churchtowers, castles, forests, fields, lakes, creeks. The countryside showed its luxuriant nature. In a few hours, it would be poisoned. The villages would decay. For years or decades, no human being would be allowed to enter the contaminated zone.

They crossed the bright ribbon of Highway 10. Traffic tie-ups here too, but the gaudy stream of vehicles was moving, flowing from the right lane into twisting roads that made it head back north.

Six miles away, the white dome of Helios loomed from the green plain.

"Lower," Andree shouted to the pilot.

Five thousand people weren't many. Five thousand people represented a meager crowd for a soccer game. Five thousand people were easily lost on the surface of the olympic stadiums in Munich or Berlin.

But five thousand people squeezed together into a few square yards, jammed between cars—that was a fearfully huge mob. All of them seemed to look up as the chopper swept over their heads. Thousands of faces on the highway, on the fields. The crowd poured out of the first red-shingled houses of Grenzheim, puffed out on both sides of the street like a balloon, and narrowed down in front of the stone bridge leading across the tiny Alzach River, narrowed down into a human trickle oozing across the bridge and through the green and white gates that were guarded by soldiers. There was also a long cordon of soldiers flanking the river. The chain was fortified by tanks.

Beyond the bridge the center of the checkpoint was composed of six cars with red crosses shining on their roofs. The cars were surrounded by white and yellow tents. A few yards away stood four green army trucks adorned with antennas. In front of the lined-up trucks, at an angle, stood a blue MAN truck, with a steel scaffolding of TV cameras and antennas on top. To the left and right of the highway there were twelve rows of buses and trucks—an army of colors: green and gray vans of the federal army and the national guard, blue and green police vehicles, red and yellow German railroad and post office vehicles, white ambulances of the Red Cross and auxiliary organizations.

In front of the tents, people were scurrying to the vehicles. At brief intervals, packed buses and trucks left the front row and drove in columns in a northerly direction on Highway 44, towards Biebesheim. The vehicles returned empty.

Orderlies were pushing a litter into a bell helicopter. Andree's SA 341 landed after the other had left. Andree sprang out before the runners touched down. He ran to the blue MAN with the antenna construction. Inside, two policeman were handling telephones and radios. A gray-haired man in an army major's uniform spoke into a walkie-talkie. "I know it's a hard thing, but the highway has to be cleared first."

He nodded when Andree introduced himself, and he said, "A bus and a truck, accident, a mile from here. Six dead, some injured. The orderlies first want to take away the injured, but I've got to give the rescue vehicles priority so that the evacuation won't be held up."

Andree asked, "Where are you transmitting the TV pictures?"

"Directly to the Frankfurt operations headquarters."

"Do the other checkpoints have a TV connection?"

"Only Worms. Cars like this are rare." The major knocked on the chrome of the truck.

"What's the situation like at the other control points?"

The major handed Andree a teletype. "Hot off the ticker. Here's the map."

The message read: "The four-mile blockade is up. Traffic jams at all decontamination stations. All roads within the area are blocked by private cars. Sector 1: in great danger."

"That's us," said the major. "All the others have enough time to check the people for radioactive contamination. But we've got to lift the blockade soon. The cloud'll be here in twenty or twenty-five minutes."

"Why can't the checking be done faster?"

"Don't ask me," answered the major. "Ask the medics over there. They'll tell you. We can't work any faster. Every sixth person standing on the bridge is already greatly contaminated. The later arrivals have an even greater percentage, about twenty or thirty percent more. From minute to minute, the decontamination is taking longer. I'm amazed that the people have such an angelic patience."

"You mean rather than storming the bridge?"

251

The major nodded.

"Do you have enough men to hold them back?"

"Three hundred soldiers and six tanks," said the major. "Theoretically, that's enough."

"Theoretically?"

"I know my men. Pioneers. First-class soldiers. Courageous. Obedient. Decent. They'll volunteer for the most difficult tasks. There's only one thing they won't do: they won't shoot at unarmed, scared, helpless people."

Andree gazed at the refugees thronging the blockades. Behind the fences, they were checked with geiger counters by anti-radiation experts in yellow astronaut uniforms. The procedure reminded Andree of B-grade detective movies in which ingenious safe crackers with an arsenal of special instruments are poised at tenfold secured steel doors, listening, lighting, X-raying, following, getting the right combination with an unerring stroke.

The anti-radiation experts worked with four different types of equipment: Some were box shaped, some like hairdriers or vacuum cleaners, some like portable search lights. Andree knew them all. Two years ago, at a hearing entitled, "The Safety of Atomic Energy," they had been demonstrated at the Federal Parliament building. Afterwards, Andree and the Research Minister had played radiation detectives, properly done up in frog suits, laughing, a big joke.

The ionization counters measured the ionized particles bursting from the gamma rays released from the atomic shell. The proportional counters indicated the energy of the radiation. The Geiger-Müller counters crunched—the electric tension produced by radioactivity. The scintillation counters flashed: they contained zinc sulphite, which lit up in response to radiation.

Those refugees who had a dangerous dose of radiation had to undress and stuff their clothing into plastic sacks. About two hundred naked people waited in front of the four decontamination tents of yellow plastic. Their arms hung down stiffly—the anti-radiation men had advised them not to touch their heads or mouths to keep the radioactivity from getting into the body.

Andree thought: That's what the ramps must have looked like at Auschwitz. People fit for work into the camp; the old, the sick, the children into the gas chambers.

Yet people were being saved here.

The naked people were embarrassed. A pregnant woman held her belly like a burden that wasn't part of her body. An old woman with scraggy thighs that looked as if they'd been nailed to her hips was weeping unabashedly because she had been forced to give up her handbag. A young man and a young girl with a lovely, slender body stood next to one another, arm in arm. A cripple sat piggyback on an attendant. Children wept.

The decontamination stations in the yellow plastic tents contained barely anything but soap and showers, which gave out a mixture of warm water and special cleansers. Andree knew that experts had divergent opinions about the effectiveness of decontamination. Some said that up to a certain dose it was child's play, no more difficult than delousing. Others, however, maintained that soap and water would eliminate only the grossest radioactive substances but were useless against the internal contamination, the radioactive particles inhaled or swallowed.

By way of precaution, the decontaminated, badly dressed refugees had to take iodine tablets as well.

Iodine tablets had also been mentioned at the hearing.

"Do they work?" a parliament member had asked a doctor.

"Placebos sometimes work too," the doctor had replied.

A fat man in shorts collapsed en route to the buses. Two orderlies pulled him aside, pounded his chest, listened to him and shook their heads.

The major said, "They're dropping like flies out there in front of the bridge too."

Andree studied the map. "Where does the crossroad begin?"

"Here in Grenzheim." The major pointed at the houses. "Six hundred feet, then to the right."

"It passes into Highway 9, right?"

"After five miles, south of the Alsheim checkpoint."

"Why don't we send the people waiting here to Alsheim? The cloud isn't heading that way. There's enough time to——"

The major was offended. "I've already thought of it. But we won't get the vehicles through. Just look at the road—car after car, all abandoned. A wall of tin."

"Tanks," said Andree.

The major looked at Andree. He banged his fist against his palm. He sat down in front of the radio. He pulled a switch. A high, piping tone. Then an observer in a tank tuned in.

"The three rescue tanks are to go to the bridge," said the major. "On the other side of the river. Clear the road until the next road crossing it. Then clear the crossroad."

The major spoke into his walkie-talkie: "Get thirty vehicles ready for crossing the bridge. The road is to be cleared. Load up the vehicles, then to the right till Highway 9. Two men are to escort every vehicle. . . . A hundred men across the bridge. Get the people off the road. Tell them they'll all be transported. No reason for panic."

Andree climbed up a ladder through a hatch in the roof. He saw tanks far away, plunging headlong into the flat river bed and shooting up again on the other bank. At thirty miles an hour they raced towards the highway, sending up a swirl of dust and grass. On the bridge, soldiers pushed back the waiting people. They pulled aside a roadblock. Five buses with rattling diesels were standing in readiness.

The tanks plowed into the three adjacent rows of wedged-in cars, pushing them into the roadside ditches like freshly fallen snow. Metal crunched, glass shattered, horns set off by short circuiting honked. A few cars started burning.

254

The column of buses and trucks crept along on the cleared road just behind the tanks. As they drove, refugees clambered in through the doors, into the backs, assisted by soldiers and orderlies, all wearing frog suits.

"Thanks," said the major next to Andree. "I would have ——"

Andree waved his hand. "It's just a temporary solution anyway. We can't manage them all by the time the cloud arrives."

A policeman called from the foot of the ladder: "Headquarters for Andree."

Andree slid down the ladder. The major followed him.

"The first figures on the radioactive cloud are in," said a meteorologist, whose name Andree didn't catch. Andree motioned the major to listen in. The major pulled on earphones.

"The radioactive cloud is now one decimal nine miles wide. Its altitude diameter varies between six hundred and twelve hundred feet. Its distance from the ground is zero to one thousand feet. At zero decimal six miles from the rim of the cloud, the direct radiation out in the open is as high as two hundred roentgens. This is a temporary figure, because we don't yet have the results in from all the measuring points. The cloud front has reached the village of Bergen and it's advancing towards Grenzheim at the rate of six to seven and a half feet per second. The next plotting will be taken in ten minutes. Over."

The major pulled off the earphones. "We don't even have twenty minutes."

"What are your orders for this event?"

"I have none. In five minutes, I'm lifting the blockade so that the people can reach safety."

Andree stared at the throng, which, despite the people being freighted off in buses and trucks, was not shrinking.

"And why are you putting on that big performance with the tanks?"

"Herr State Secretary," said the major, "I'm following

255

orders as long as they make sense. My orders are to prevent radioactive people from getting through the blockade unchecked. Clearing the road was a possibility for carrying out those orders. . . ."

"And a few minutes later you simply forget the orders and turn them upside down?"

"If humaneness——"

"Get me operations headquarters in Frankfurt," said Andree to the policeman at the telephone.

Ten seconds later, the call was put through. Andree asked for the Federal Chancellor.

"Do you have Grenzheim on your TV tube?"

"We've been watching your tank actions."

"You know the cloud's going to be in Grenzheim in less than twenty minutes?"

"Yes, we hope that by then all the people——"

"It's hopeless," said Andree. "Three thousand unchecked people will still be waiting when the first radiation hits them."

"What do you suggest?"

"There are two possibilities," Andree said. "First, we remove the blockade and bring the people to safety without any radiation check. Or rather, we let them reach safety on their own, because we don't have enough vehicles, and the tanks have destroyed only a portion of the private autos."

"I believe," said the chancellor, "there is no other possibility."

The major nodded.

"I know what you mean," said Andree. "A spontaneous, humane decision. But this decision will ruin all the work of the past few hours. We might as well stop all this evacuation nonsense."

"I don't understand."

"You understand me very well. And don't think it's easy for me to put it into words. Our rescue system depends on isolating the contaminated people from the healthy ones. If we let the three thousand people still waiting here in Grenzheim pass unchecked into uncontaminated areas—people of whom twenty or thirty percent have had contact with radiation—then we'll suddenly have thousands of new radioactive sources all over the place, in Frankfurt, Mainz, Koblenz, wherever they flee. If we still regard our system as sensible, we have to prevent the waiting people from breaking through the blockades, and we have to use any means possible to stop them. Or else we have to surrender unconditionally to the catastrophe."

The chancellor didn't answer. After a long pause, he said: "Do you really want to leave these people, these tired, sick, exhausted people, behind and at the mercy of the radiation cloud? Do you want to condemn them to death in cold blood?"

"No," said Andree. "I don't want to, and neither do you, neither does the major next to me here. But we have to. If we save three thousand now, we'll be endangering thirty thousand others. Even humanity requires a relativity of means."

The major stared at Andree. The corners of his mouth had gone up in scorn.

"I would not like to make this decision alone," said the Chancellor. "The crisis staff has listened in on our conversation and is now going to vote."

Silence.

After thirty seconds, the chancellor's voice: "Major, these are the orders of the crisis staff. Evacuate as many people as possible up till the last minute. Then blow up the bridge and make all roads and streets leading from the danger zone impassable. Retreat with your personnel and equipment to the next receiving station at the twelve-mile blockade. Use your weapons only if your men are in danger. Anyone attempting to escape the cloud on foot should not be hindered."

"Not necessary," murmured the major. "The cloud'll get them all. Women, children, old people, and then the heat. . . ."

He grabbed the walkie-talkie and gave his orders.

Andree eyed the throng on the other side of the bridge, glanced at his watch, and said: "Twelve more minutes."

18

Berger stopped the red bus behind the last cars of the jam, which was blocking streets and crossings. All the cars were empty. The people were trying to get to the checkpoint at the bridge by foot.

The children climbed out and crowded around Anne. "Take us to the checkpoint," said Berger. "Show your ID. If not, I'll hand over a killer of children to the police." Mayor Rapp nodded eagerly.

The group got underway, Berger and Rapp at the head, Anne bringing up the rear, carrying an exhausted four-year-old girl on her arm. Michaela walked close by her side.

Kilian Square had been turned into a hospital. Hundreds of people sat and lay on the tiles, the asphalt, the ground, amid trunks, clothing, and baby carriages, or else they lay twisted on benches under lime trees.

The noise of coughing and choking people vied with all other sounds—the squawling of children, the sobbing of mothers, calls for missing family members. An acrid vapor mixed with the stench of burning: Smoke was pouring from the attic of Black Eagle. In the wild flight, somebody had forgotten to turn off a gas flame or electric plate. No one bothered about the fire.

Anne did not see any familiar faces. These people must have arrived only a few minutes before from the vicinity of the plant. They were ill. Instinctively, Berger led the children in a wide arc around the miserable camp.

Anne wanted to help, to run over to the boy who was rolling on the ground and spewing up blood, to ease the pain of the woman who was pressing her husband's pale head to her bosom, taking great care not to injure him with the sharp diamond brooch pinned to her blouse. She had put it on not to adorn herself, but because, like the necklace on her throat and the rings on her fingers, it was wealth, acquired and kept for such emergencies.

Anne knew she couldn't help. These people had fled too late, had been caught by the death rays that were now destroying their bodies.

Unsuspectingly, they passed on the poison. The mother, in between gastric convulsions that brought tears to her eyes, comforted her child, rubbing the fatal substance into his skin. The girl who desperately threw herself upon her boyfriend, whose weakness had paralyzed his feet, was caressing flesh that radiated disease.

Behind Kilian Square stood the first waiting people, the last of the human throng pushing towards the bridge, centimeter by centimeter. Anne couldn't see the bridge, which was cut off by heads and bodies. She knew it was where the helicopter was rising.

Berger and Rapp, pushing, shoving, and elbowing, brought the group some fifty yards forward. Rapp kept calling: "I am the mayor. I have to get to the station to help you all. Please let me through."

At first the people let themselves be pushed aside without resisting. Waiting in the blazing sun had made them apathetic. But when they saw that it was a short, fear-driven civilian who was pushing his way up, they protested.

A beefy young man with a blond crewcut stomped in front of Rapp and held him at arm's length. He said in his broad Hessian dialect, "You'll wait like everyone else. And now get to the back of the line."

Rapp's trembling hands fumbled for his wallet, pulled it out of his crumpled jacket, and flashed his ID card. The beefy man grabbed Rapp's wallet, stuffed the card back in without reading it, and shoved the wallet back into Rapp's jacket. He grabbed Rapp by the shoulders and spun him around.

259

Rapp shouted, "I'm the mayor. You'll pay for this."

He discovered a policeman in the throng. He was holding a walkie-talkie. Rapp pushed through the crowd and gasped, "Get us out of here. Get us to the station. We've got to bring forty children to safety. They're wounded and——"

Again he presented his ID card. The policeman studied it, eyed Berger, Anne, and the children. He handed back the card. "Sorry. I can't help you. Even if I wanted to, no one could get through here. You've got to be patient. It won't take forever."

Rapp's laughter switched into a screeching. "Forever! The rays are coming towards Grenzheim, and we'll all be atomic corpses if we're not out of here."

There was a deathly silence.

The policeman hissed, "Are you out of your mind?"

The beefy young man tore Rapp around: "Are you crazy? How do you know?"

"I'm the mayor!" said Rapp.

The man turned to the policeman. "Is what he's saying true? Are the rays coming here?"

The police didn't answer. Then he hastily murmured inaudibly into his walkie-talkie.

"Did you hear?" called the man. "The bastards at the bridge are holding us up even though they know that the atomic rays are coming."

The crowd became restless. Calls shot out: "Finish up. . . . break through . . . storm the bridge. . . ."

The policeman wanted to say something but two men struck him to the ground. A chopper roared over the heads of the crowd. "There is an acute danger that the bridge may collapse. The evacuation is interrupted until the construction has been strengthened. Please maintain discipline. . . ."

The crowd surged forward. "Get out of the way," screamed Berger. "They'll trample us to death."

Anne fought her way to the side of the crowd, protecting the children with her body. Two or three children were swept into the human torrent and washed away. Behind her, Anne heard Mayor Rapp gasping. She fell against a fence. She lifted the children across it. Berger took them on the other side.

Rapp was the last to roll over the barrier, which the crowd was raging past.

"We've got to get back to the bus," Rapp panted. "I know another road."

Anne was talking to the children. She saw they couldn't take it much longer. But she was relieved to note that none of them showed signs of radiation poisoning. As yet.

They stumbled through gardens, over fences, across back yards until they reached the place where they had left the bus.

The bus glowed inside like an incubator. Anne made sure the weakest children lay down on the floor. Berger was gone. A short time later he clambered in through the door, his arms laden with bottles of water. "From the store," he said. "It wasn't locked."

Anne gave some water to the children and cooled their hot, sweaty faces.

Berger asked, "Why don't we drive west to Highway 9?" Rapp, knowing nothing about Andree's tank operation, shook his head. "It's choked up. We'll drive east, on the old road to the gravel pit. It crosses the federal highway and continues on to a bridge across the Alzach. After that, we'll soon be on the speedway."

Berger started the engine. "But the bridge is closed."

"It's always closed. It's broken down. No one knows the entrance road any more." He grinned complacently. "Except for me, of course. I have some property there."

They had trouble crossing Highway 44. Berger and Rapp had to shove a few cars aside. The road to the bridge was a barely visible trail in a pine plantation. But the bus tires had sufficient grip on the ground, which was interlaced with roots.

In front of the bridge, a medieval ruin of mossy stone, stood a few abandoned vehicles, tractors, threshers, rickety trucks.

Soldiers stood on the bridge.

Behind the bridge stood a tank. It was a crouching leopard, its cannon aimed at the red bus.

The soldier signaled them to halt.

Berger and Rapp climbed out and walked towards the bridge.

"Don't come any closer," called a junior officer. "You can't pass here. "The next decontamination station is in Grenzheim, a mile. . . ."

"I know," said Rapp. He pulled out his ID card. He had kept it in readiness in a side pocket of his jacket. "I am the mayor of Grenzheim. I have a special assignment. I am supposed to bring these children," he made a motion towards the bus with his head, "out of the radiation zone."

He threw his card towards the officer. The card fell on the ground. The officer didn't touch it.

"Cut the monkey business," he said. "I'm not keen on getting any radiation. Drive to the decontamination station at Grenz——"

Rapp's half ear turned scarlet. He roared: "You pigheaded bastard! Did you understand what I said? I have a special assignment. The Governor personally——"

"Never heard of him," said the officer. "If you have any special wishes, you can ask the major."

"Where's the major?"

"In Grenzheim."

Rapp took a few strides towards the bridge. The officer raised his machine pistol. Rapp whispered: "I'll be glad to put in a good word for you with the Governor."

The officer said, "The more time you waste here, the less chance you'll have of getting to Grenzheim before the radiation cloud. This bridge is being blown up in two minutes."

Anne stood next to Rapp, Michaela at her side, and asked the officer: "What kind of a human being are you?"

"I'm carrying out orders."

"I've heard that before," said Anne. "You're just doing

your duty, right? Why don't you just tell your soldiers to shoot us? Maybe you still have time to dig a mass grave. And don't forget to pull the gold from our teeth when we're dead."

The officer grinned uncomfortably. "It's no use getting excited. If you hurry, no one has to die. Drive back."

Mayor Rapp was fumbling with his pants. When his hand came out again, it held a pistol with an angular barrel. Rapp wrested Michaela over to himself and pressed the pistol against her temple. Anne grabbed Michaela's arm. Rapp kicked her in the knees so that she collapsed on the ground, whimpering.

"Okay," said Rapp. He walked slowly backwards towards the bus.

"Clear the bridge. C'mon. Tell your men to move back, Have the tank turn around."

The officer signaled to his men.

"I have seven bullets," said Rapp, with one leg in the bus, "That's seven kids. And don't imagine I'm fooling. I'd rather spend my life in prison than die of radiation exposure."

Berger helped Anne to her feet.

"You two are coming along," said Rapp. "Get moving."

Anne, leaning on Berger, hobbled back to the bus.

Rapp sat down on the codriver's seat with Michaela. "All the children get back." Anne hesitated. "You too. Nothing will happen to your daughter if you're sensible."

Anne smiled at Michaela. Michaela wiped away her tears and didn't smile back.

Berger steered the bus towards the bridge. Rapp cowered in the seat so that he wouldn't be seen from the outside. The bridge was arched. The bus rose, sank, was on the other side. Rapp poked Berger.

"Tell them I'll kill the kids if they try to follow us."

Berger lowered the window and relayed the message.

The officer retorted, "We'll get you anyhow."

"It wasn't my idea," said Berger and saw that the officer didn't believe him.

After two miles, they reached a country road. Rapp let

Michaela go. She ran over to Anne and wept on her shoulder.

Rapp said, "Instead of gratitude, just contribute something to your favorite charity. And now let's go to Griesheim."

Anne stared at him.

Rapp grinned. "You don't really believe I would have shot your daughter?"

"I certainly do," said Anne. "I certainly do."

19

The soldiers had cleared the bridge near Grenzheim. At the decontamination tents, some twenty or thirty people were standing naked in the sun. They didn't know that they were the last to escape radioactive death.

Since the conversation with the Federal Chancellor, the major hadn't spoken another word to Andree. He ignored him. He said into his walkie-talkie: "Detonation in seven minutes." Andree glanced at the throng beyond the bridge. He noticed he could distinguish individual faces, which seemed to be looking at him—the sun-tanned girl in the bikini, the white-haired man in the dark suit, the children on the shoulders of their fathers. He walked over to the chopper. Soldiers, policemen, and orderlies were taking down the tents. They didn't touch the sacks of radioactive clothing.

Andree felt as if he'd been brought back to half a millennium ago. The plague was coming. Horses and coaches were racing out of the town gates. The healthy were fleeing. The sick remained behind. Those who were thought to be ill were being driven away with sticks. Burning heaps of corpses in front of the town. And everywhere, the doctors and monks in ghostly beaked masks that gave off incense.

The men in the frog suits did not let themselves be irritated by the major's impatient shouts. They did what they had to according to plan and at a precisely calculated speed, as they had practiced a thousand times: "Once the work with contamination hazards is terminated, the persons performing the work should remove their protective uniforms without the help of other people. This removal must be practiced in order to prevent transferring the contamination from the protective clothing to the hands, face, and underwear. Climb carefully out of the anti-radiation suit and let it slide down upon a loose plastic sheet without touching the outside of the suit. The respirometer should be put down off to the side. Now take the plastic sheet by its four corners, lift it up with the suit, and deposit it in the plastic sack. . . ."

The anti-radiation people had finally also stowed away the aqualungs, which had pumped oxygen into their frog suits. They vanished into a six-wheeled truck with a Karlsruhe license plate.

The siren of the command car began howling.

"Let's go," said Andree.

The chopper rose high in the air.

At almost the same time there was a roar from the engines of the police cars and ambulances, the trucks and buses. At a fast clip, but very skillfully, without interfering with one another, they formed into a column and tooled up the northward road.

The tanks swept along both sides of the road across the fields, in a fog of dust, flattening hedges and saplings.

The men in anti-radiation uniforms who had been holding back the crowd on the bridge waded across the river and sprang into waiting jeeps.

And then Andree heard the scream that ate through the whirring and rattling of the helicopter. It flared like a forest fire, ignited more screams, until a single, swelling scream of despair, rage, and hatred filled the air.

Before the crowd could start moving, the bridge collapsed, puffing up in a cloud of dust. A dull bang reached the chopper.

Below, the jeeps were racing away.

The front rows of refugees stumbled across the river, crawled up the bank, and ran away from the invisible death. A few dragged heavy suitcases as they ran. Fear made them oblivious to the weight.

The cars not damaged by the tanks moved out of the jam. They hurtled along the river bank, seeking a place to cross. There was none.

The helicopter rose to 4,000, then 5,000 feet. The people became tinier. They seemed to linger where they were, becoming a dark spot on a green background, a part of the landscape.

Andree gave them ten more minutes.

The chopper had reached 13,000 feet. And now Andree saw the radiation cloud for the first time. He saw it not as a compact formation, a swelling mass of water and dust. Below him there was nothing but a fine haze, scarcely dimming the view of towns, rivers, roads, and fields. But he did see its outlines. They were marked by twelve or more dark points: helicopters at intervals of 1,500 feet. They had flown as near to the edges of the cloud as the radiation permitted, and they stood there motionless, beaming their measuring data back to Frankfurt.

Andree, panting in the thin air, tied the dark points together on a piece of paper, like stars into a constellation.

He drew a stinger to indicate Helios. A body swollen and fringed on one side, smooth and even on the other, stretching to the rooftops of Grenzheim. And two curving, atrophied pincers embracing Grenzheim.

The radiation cloud looked like a scorpion.

266

20

At 4:05 P.M., two air force officers evaluated the photos of the catastrophe zone around the Helios plant. The photos had been taken by a reconnaissance plane from an altitude of 40,000 feet. The enlargements showed the burning plant, the car wrecks on the parking lot, the toppled pylon. The two officers didn't need a magnifying glass to see the motionless figures in rye fields, lakes, lying next to bicycles, on tractors. On a bright, sandy road, the bodies were so twisted and scattered that from above they looked like Chinese ideograms. On the meadows, there were dead cows, hills with black and white spots. The observers struggled over one picture until it hit them: It was a swarm of birds that appeared to be plunging directly towards the Helios plant.

The shots of the Grenzheim checkpoint were not hard to interpret. When they put together the scenes, which had been taken at five-second intervals over an eight-minute period, the sequence told a story. First a mass moved in quadratic formation like a Greek phanlanx in a northeasterly direction across roads and fields. Then the order broke up, left back individual people, then groups. On the last pictures, there were only two dozen figures pushing along.

"I've been looking for the damn thing the whole time," said one of the officers. "But all you can see of it are corpses."

21

Since leaving the Taubenschlag hill, Fuchs hadn't spoken a word. He had turned the radio on full blast. There was no mention of an accident at the Helios nuclear plant. Yet the helicopters, circling the streets in low flights, droned announcements about it from their loudspeakers. The radio program consisted only of traffic indications—a list of closed roads and highways and traffic control stations.

Fuchs listened attentively. Sibylle sensed that he had overcome his shock and shaken off his helplessness. She sensed that he was regaining the peculiar strength that had fascinated her for such a long time. She had to shield herself against surrendering to that strength again. She warned herself: He is not innocent. He is not an idealist. He is not a genius. He is crazy. It's his fanaticism that makes him appear so strong. It's his fanaticism that forces me to find his face so earnest and beautiful and Christlike and to regard his every word as intelligent and redeeming and to consider him more valuable than the rest of mankind.

She thought: Don't forget that he used you.

The villages they drove through were deserted.

Fuchs switched off the radio. "Stop the car."

"Why?"

"Stop the car." His voice was quiet and sharp.

Sibylle stopped.

"Turn around."

She turned and drove a few hundred yards.

"To the right."

She turned into a cobblestone road.

"You really thought it out," said Fuchs. "There's a checkpoint at Alsheim. Who are they looking for? Goodday, gentlemen, here is your saboteur. You almost pulled it over on me."

"But Sasha, I was the one who talked you into not going to the police."

Fuchs guffawed. "I never had that idea. You want to get rid of me. You want to turn me over to the cops. You're scared. Scared."

"Where do you want to go?" asked Sibylle calmly.

"To Darmstadt. I have to go to my apartment. But we'll find a road that isn't being watched. The radio didn't say anything about this one here."

They drove past a sparkling lake. In a black boat a fisherman was casting out his line with regular swings.

They dipped into green forest shadows. A wooden barrier blocked the road.

A fire engine was parked beyond the barrier. Two men in yellow anti-radiation suits were leaning on the hood. Whistles and distorted word fragments from a radio came out of the cab.

"Get away from here," said Fuchs, cringing in his seat.

Sibylle did a U-turn. The two men made no attempt to stop them.

"We're gonna walk," said Fuchs. "Through the woods. They can't be everywhere."

"They're not looking for you," said Sibylle. "This has to do with Helios."

Fuchs smirked. "You're really very cunning. But you won't catch me. Get out. We've gone far enough."

He pulled Sibylle out of the auto.

"Go by yourself," she said.

He smiled. "So that you can sic them on me? C'mon!" He pushed her forwards.

After a hundred yards, he shoved her behind a tree. In front of them ran a narrow path, edged by bushes and shrubs. Beyond the bushes Sibylle saw the khaki body of a tank.

Fuchs giggled. "All of Pharaoh's armies."

They sneaked towards the left, under cover of the trees,

until they reached the path. Vineyards loomed beyond the path, but between the path and the first grapes there was a strip of meadow thirty yards wide, fenced in by low barbed wire.

"You first," said Fuchs.

"They'll shoot."

Fuchs nodded. For an instant Sibylle thought he would give up, take her in his arms, surrender to her.

Fuchs said, "Maybe they'll hit me. Then you'll make it. If they don't hit you first."

He pushed her on to the path. Sibylle stumbled, fell, crept to the barbed wire, wound her way underneath it, and ran towards the vineyard.

A shout from the right: "Stop! Stop or I'll shoot!"

Sibylle kept running. She heard Fuchs behind her, he shouted something at her. A rapid-fire gun banged drily. Sibylle threw herself down between the dense vines. She turned around. Fuchs raced across the meadow, ducking his head. Next to Sibylle's head, green grapes burst, showering her with juice. Fuchs glided next to her.

"Keep going."

They hurried across the rocky ground. The soldiers weren't following.

Five minutes later, they were running along the rails of a one-track railroad line. Ten minutes later, they reached a white village railroad station. In front of it, farm families were crowding around buses, which expelled black diesel clouds.

A man in gray uniform trousers asked Fuchs distrustfully: "Are you coming from the south?"

"From the west," said Fuchs. "We were going to Rhein-dürkheim, but they wouldn't let us through. Then our car stalled. What's going on anyway?"

The man pointed to a green bus. "You can take this bus. It's going to Mainz."

They joined the line of waiting people. Sibylle saw that the ground around Fuchs's right foot was getting wet. Blood.

270

When she tried to bend over, he grabbed her wrist so hard that she let out a soft cry.

"Careful," called the bus driver, massive and cheerful in his short-sleeved holiday shirt, "the box is closing up."

The doors shut. Sibylle was pressed tight against Fuchs's body. He put an arm around her. A peasant woman smirked and winked at Sibylle.

22

EXCERPT FROM THE HELIOS REPORT:

22c. Despite time-consuming misunderstandings, especially in the communication between state authorities (for example, in the Rhineland/Palatine Ministry of the Interior, which had been asked for help, the code word "sunshine" for the catastrophe defense plan was not known, which led to protracted requests for more detailed information), sufficient transportation had been set up by shortly before 14:30 at the four-mile barrier, which was mainly closed off by military and paramilitary units, so that a speedy evacuation could have commenced. However, this turned out to be impossible because at all five checkpoints the roads were blocked by private vehicles for many miles.

The reason for this development (cf., 22d) was obviously something that had been foreseen in the catastrophe defense plan and automatically carried out, namely, the notification of various radio networks. As of 13:33 radio and television networks began to broadcast the emergency announcement, which had previously been kept in a sealed envelope. Even though the announcement (which, after being broadcast twice, was taken off the air at the prompting of State Secretary Eckart

Andree) expressly admonished the population to remain calm and warned them against any movement outside their homes, most of the inhabitants of the blockaded zone tried to flee the real or presumed danger area in private vehicles.

Since then it has been asked whether the catastrophe defense plan could not have foreseen the tragic consequences of the radio announcement.

The investigating committee can only reply to this question with a clear affirmative.

At a panel discussion in Hanover on atomic energy and the environment, on February 3 of last year (just six months before the catastrophe), the Hamburg psychologist Dr. Georg Bèrlitt made the following contribution, which is quoted verbatim below:

Question: Herr Dr. Berlitt, if the fear of the atom bomb, or let's say in general, the fear of radioactivity is so deeply rooted in the population, as your investigations have shown, wouldn't the only possible public reaction after an accident be naked panic? And aren't, then, all so-called catastrophe defense plans not worth the paper they're printed on because one cannot make plans with people who are panicstricken, i.e., who don't know what they're doing?

Dr. Berlitt: I fully agree with you. The measures necessary after a reactor accident, especially the evacuation, would have to be carried out in a brief time and only with an extraordinarily disciplined population. To prevent a traffic jam the people affected must forego using their private cars when fleeing. They simply have to wait for the evacuation vehicles at the gathering points. But now I ask you: If you live two miles from a reactor, and you hear on the radio that it's spreading deadly radiation—would you sit and wait until someone calls for you? One doesn't have to be a psychologist—whereby I don't mean to say that psychologists generally know much about human behavior; they merely earn their living by acting as if they did. [laughter.] You don't have to be a psychologist to predict the

272

reaction in ninety percent of the cases: The people won't wait They'll jump into their cars and drive like hell to get away from the invisible death.

Question: Then why is this radio announcement part of the catastrophe defense plan? (Followed by reading of the announcement).

Dr. Berlitt: Because politicians know even less about the human psyche than psychologists. During the past five years, I've worked as a police psychologist in two different states, and in both of them I pointed out to the responsible ministers and police superintendents that in an emergency such an information policy would wipe out any possible rescue measures. I've never gotten any reaction other than the well-known formula: "We will think your suggestions over and take them into account in our planning."

Question: What alternative do you propose?

Dr. Berlitt: You know my fundamental alternative· We should not build any atomic reactors, at least not in the present stage of technological development. But if people do build them and take the risk of an accident upon themselves, they should then pursue a cautious information policy in the event of an accident, in order to prevent high-density areas of hundreds of thousands or millions of people from turning into battlefields of suicidal lemmings. . . .

(The letters containing Dr. Berlitt's suggestions have been submitted to the investigating committee.)

22d.   In the twelve-mile zone, more vehicles were involved in the panicky flight than in the four-mile zone. But it was only in this latter zone—and here in the northeast, at the Grenzheim checkpoint—that the flight had catastrophic consequences. At the edge of the twelve-mile zone, the forces of order had a relatively large amount of time (especially in the south and the west) to break up the traffic jams. Furthermore, at this point thorough decontamination controls were unnecessary since only a handful of the refugees had been closer than

273

four miles from the Helios reactor and thus could not have been affected by the radiation cloud. The victims between the four-mile and twelve-mile circuits died as the result of traffic accidents.

In Grenzheim, on the other hand, the situation was critical for three reasons:

a) Grenzheim was the most densely populated village in the closed zone;

b) Grenzheim was seriously endangered by the drifting radiation cloud;

c) At the checkpoint there were already numerous more or less strongly contaminated people who had to be treated in the decontamination tents.

Thus, when the cloud front was about a mile from Grenzheim, the crisis staff was forced to make a difficult decision, which was explained in the following way by the Federal Chancellor in his Message to the Nation, telecast on August 4 of the past year:

"We were confronted with a problem that was no longer a matter of life and death; it was a problem concerning solely —and please do not consider me cynical—the number of fatal casualties. Many of you, my dear fellow citizens, will recall a similar situation, although one hardly comparable in scope: namely, the murderous assault by anarchists on the German embassy in Stockholm. At the time, the responsible men in power fully realized that the anarchists had killed hostages and would kill further hostages if their demands were not fulfilled. They demanded the relase of the most dangerous anarchists from custody and imprisonment.

"If these demands had been met, the released anarchists would most certainly have continued their bomb attacks, their bank robberies, and their capture of hostages. They would have endangered the lives of dozens if not hundreds of people. Thus the alternative for that crisis staff was: The rescue of a few and the endangerment of many— or the rescue of many and the endangerment of few. You know what decision the responsible men reached, and you know that their decision was greeted by wide approval in the population.

"Naturally, the conditions of the Grenzheim tragedy were totally different. But in principle, we were faced with the identical situation, a dreadful situation that the Greek tragedians called *aporia*—no way out. No matter how one might act, one would transgress a law, in this case, the law of humanity.

"You, my dear fellow citizens, know the course of events. They have already become part of history, a historical phase whose consequences we feel and our children and children's children will continue to feel.

"I can no more defend our decision than I could defend any other decision that might have been made. Forgive us, as I hope that the Highest Judge of History will one day forgive us. . . ."

22e. During the dramatic events at the Grenzheim checkpoint, the evacuation in the three reamining sectors proceded speedily (although near Bürstadt there was a confrontation between the population and the forces of order, resulting in the loss of thirteen lives). Likewise, the northern and northeastern part of the twelve-mile circuit area was cleared up to the suburbs of Darmstadt without any major incidents. In Mainz and Wiesbaden as well as Ludwigshafen and Mannheim, isolating stations were put up for radiation cases. Physicians from throughout the Federal Republic of Germany joined the already present medical personnel. . . .

23

Andree's helicopter circled at 700 feet over the mountain road, a mile in front of the radiation cloud. The scorpion had pushed its body over Grenzheim and was crawling towards the mountains. Andree wished it would move faster—away from Darmstadt, away from Frankfurt, Mannheim, Ludwigshafen, away from the millions of people who, squeezed into street canyons, paralyzed by their great number, would not be able to flee if the cloud were to turn towards them.

But that did not seem to be its intention. We're lucky thought Andree, damn lucky. Although he could still see the desperate, screaming refugees at the blown-up bridge near Grenzheim, he was not ashamed of his relief.

The light wind drove the cloud steadily in an east-by-northeasterly direction. It was now three miles wide and six miles long. Its northern flank was rubbing four miles south of Darmstadt. Radioactive clouds were still forming over the burning Helios plant and joining the big cloud. A few minutes ago the measuring technicians had said that the radiation intensity was waning at the end of the cloud. Since the uranium from the reactor core was melting deeper and deeper into the earth, the earth was already screening off part of the radiation.

The cloud still lay close over the ground because inversion weather had prevented the lower air strata from rising.

It would remain that way until it reached Siberia, a meteorologist had stated. The cloud was blazing a deadly trail, he said, but we would still be ahead with the evacuation. It could then spread out over the steppes without wreaking havoc.

Wishful thinking. Soon, somewhere over the mountains, upcurrents would grab the cloud and pull it high. The radioactivity would be distributed in the atmosphere and then sink to the ground after hours, days, months—as fallout and rainout, dust and rain.

The strength of the radiation would be diminished, thinned in the air and scattered over wide areas. But even then it would be strong enough to kill and cripple people. The number depended on where the wisps of cloud would rain down, over the sea, on sparsely populated land, or on a metro-

276

polis. And where it descended—that was up to the wind and the temperature.

But even if the worst were to happen, Andree knew, the number of victims would be much smaller than if the wind had blown from a different direction . . .

Andree was freezing despite the lined jacket the pilot had given him. He looked down. The roads were empty. The evacuation had gone without a hitch here—loudspeaker announcements, gathering points to which people had driven in their private cars, transportation in trains, buses, trucks.

He looked up to where the cockpits of helicopters were blinking as they marked off the cloud front.

"To Darmstadt," said Andree into the microphone. "They're having trouble with the vehicle reinforcements. Some mayor is flexing his muscles."

The pilot lifted the chopper to 2,500 feet. They flew near a measuring helicopter. The pilot greeted with his thumb. "Sea Stallion," he said. "A great machine. Does 200. Built by Sikorsky for the Leathernecks."

Andree radioed the operations headquarters in Frankfurt. The voices in the loudspeaker did not come from Frankfurt. Nevertheless, Andree listened in. Beads of sweat formed on his upper lip. The voices said:

"I'm losing contact. Don't fly too far south."

"Okay." Pause. "I've been holding this position for five minutes. We're not one inch too far south."

"That can't be. The radiation is definitely reduced. I'll calculate again." Pause.

"One of us is making a mistake. Not me. My data work out."

"My instruments are correct too. Maybe we're both right. Maybe the southern front of the cloud is moving away from us, couldn't that be?" Pause.

"I'm an idiot. Calling headquarters Frankfurt. Hello, headquarters Frankfurt. . . ." The voice gave position reports. Andree wasn't listening. He only heard the last sentence: "The wind has turned. It's coming from the south-southeast." The voice drawled out the last syllable. "The cloud is drifting into map square B1 and D2."

Andree didn't need a map to realize what new direction the cloud was taking. The scorpion was now crawling towards the north. Towards Darmstadt. And towards Frankfurt.

23

EXCERPT FROM THE DECLARATION OF THE CRISIS STAFF ON JULY 31, AT 16:30 BROADCAST OVER ALL WEST GERMAN RADIO NETWORKS:

The forces of rescue and order have brought the accident under control. There is no reason for further concern.

Nevertheless, please keep your radios turned on so that you may be informed of measures possibly necessary for your protection. In such an event, please follow the directions of the assigned personnel accurately. Avoid all travel and stay within your homes.

The borders of the Federal Republic of West Germany are closed for all incoming and outgoing travel.

In case of symptoms such as nausea and vomiting, consult a physician immediately.

We repeat: There is no reason for further concern. The forces of rescue and order have brought the accident under control.

24

The windows in the room of the catastrophe headquarters on the tenth floor of the Frankfurt Police Headquarters could not be opened.

The architect had planned them that way so that the air conditioning would not be interfered with. Yet the ventilators and filters waged a hopeless struggle against the hot, smokey, used-up air. More than a hundred people were in the room. The noise was ear splitting: telephones, radios, teletypes, a Babel of voices. Two mechanics in blue overalls were drilling the wall to find a defective telephone line.

The men around the conference table didn't notice the heat and hubbub. They stared at a TV monitor, which was gradually flickering and crystallizing into a clear image: the Helios dome, very small (shot from great altitude), wreathed in blue-black smoke.

Even as the Federal Chancellor spoke, the eyes of the men kept straying for seconds at a time to the miniature view of the death source.

"The worst danger is over," said the chancellor. "The cloud is drifting east-northeast and will spare Frankfurt." He stepped over to a map of West Germany occupying the entire wall.

"In the evacuation, we have hitherto been concentrating on the areas lying in the direction of the wind. Naturally, we will also clear these areas here," he pointed to Darmstadt, Mainz, Mannheim, Ludwigshafen, "until we have a free circle of twenty-five miles around the plant."

"Will that be enough?" asked Krüger, Minister of Defense.

"According to the meteorologists and radiobiologists, yes. The radiation released into the air by the uranium at Helios is weakening."

"But now it's poisoning the ground water," said Research Minister Gerner.

The chancellor nodded. "And the Rhine too. The towns have been warned not to drink any water. Supplying them will be a problem now. But we can worry about that once the radioactive cloud has finally vanished in the atmosphere. . . ."

". . . and rains radioactivity upon all Europe," completed Gerner.

"This will cost us quite a bit," said Lützkow, the head of the opposition party. "Money and prestige." Lützkow was the foreign minister in the shadow cabinet. The chancellor had assigned him the task of informing all endangered countries about the various stages of the catastrophe.

"Is someone reproaching us?" asked the chancellor.

Lützkow said: "Not directly yet. But the French——"

"We don't have time for speculations," the chancellor broke in. "The fact is: All countries are showing solidarity. The Americans are helping with soldiers, doctors, and vehicles for the evacuation. An hour ago, a Hercules left New York for Frankfurt with radiation experts, frog suits, decontamination stations, and special medicaments. The Netherlands, Sweden, France—everyone's helping. Even the Soviet Union."

"Only the East Zone isn't," said Lützkow. He used this term, as he had once explained, "because it's too complicated saying 'GDR' with the quotation marks.""They've announced a protest note condemning the Federal Republic for the negligent assault on the health of the population of the German Democratic Republic. They're refusing to help at all."

"Can't blame them," said Grolmann, the head of the government party. "They'll need their stuff themselves if the cloud doesn't go the way the weathermen say it will and ends up in the GDR instead."

The Federal Chancellor addressed the Defense Minister: "In case that happens, there must not be any bureaucratic difficulties. I am going to instruct our people that GDR planes can enter our air space and that army and police units can cross the border. Endangered Germans from there can be evacuated into West German territory without any formalities."

Krüger took a deep breath.

"This offer," the chancellor went on, "is not tied to any conditions. It will stand even if East Berlin refuses to grant us the same rights."

"But our defenses," said Krüger. "NATO. . . . You just can't——"

"I can. And please don't tell me that the GDR will take advantage of this opportunity to conquer the Federal Republic. I'm waiting ten more minutes. If the radioactive cloud hasn't broken up by then, I'm notifying the GDR state council president."

Now Lützkow too wanted to protest. The chancellor waved him off.

"This offer is an important document. It shows our will to protect other nations against any damage from the catastrophe triggered in our country."

"In our country," said Lützkow. "But maybe some Commie brought this on our heads."

"Don't make a fool of yourself. We don't know anything yet about the perpetrator."

Defense Minister Krüger stood up. "I'm notifying the Commander-in-Chief of NATO in West Europe."

Governor Klinger had followed the discussion silently. He was the only one at the table who had neither removed his jacket nor loosened his tie. He turned his gold Parker ballpoint in his fingers and said: "That is the self-surrender of our state." Before anyone could reply to this concluding verdict, the telephone buzzed next to the chancellor. The loudspeaker was switched on full volume, so that all the members of the crisis staff could hear Andree's voice, which drowned out the noise of the operations headquarters and the helicopter turbines. The voice said: "The wind has shifted. The cloud's moving towards Darmstadt and Frankfurt. It will reach Darmstadt within one hour at the latest."

That same instant, a meteorologist dashed into the room and ran over to the conference table, pushing aside anyone who stood in his way.

The chancellor nodded at him and pointed at the telephone.

Andree said: "Darmstadt and Frankfurt must be evacuated instantly."

Klinger began to laugh. He was pallid. His silvery hair stood on the back of his neck. His eyes bulged, squeezed by the swollen bags beneath them. "Evacuate Darmstadt and Frankfurt! What a calm word, gentlemen! And what a nugatory word in the face of the cosmic disaster! Go ahead! Evacuate Darmstadt! Evacuate Frankfurt! Emulate the daughters of Danaos who wanted to scoop up water in porous jugs!"

Klinger collapsed in his chair. His head sank to the side. Minister of the Interior Klein and the police superintendent grabbed Klinger under his arms and carried him out the room.

"He didn't express himself very clearly," said Research Minister Gerner. "But he's right. We'll never do it."

The chancellor asked the German army general at the other end of the table: "Can we evacuate Darmstadt in one hour?"

The general sorted out his maps of Germany and German cities: "One hundred and forty-two thousand inhabitants on about seven thousand hectares. In the south, twenty to thirty thousand already evacuated. With conventional means, a short-notice evacuation is impossible. Gathering points on the arterial roads, vehicles for transporting the people—we'll get at best fifteen hundred people per minute out of the city."

"What do you suggest?" asked the Chancellor.

"Every man for himself," said the general, hinting at a smile. "All the inhabitants walk out of town, towards west and east."

"What about the old people, invalids, little children?"

"Vehicles," said the general. "As long as it's possible. And then. . . ." He shrugged his shoulders.

Krüger, who had just informed the NATO Commander-in-Chief that the Federal Republic would open its borders to the GDR, said: "That may work in Darmstadt. But in Frankfurt? Have you ever seen fifty or sixty thousand people leaving a stadium after a soccer game? In Frankfurt there would be seven hundred thousand or more people on their feet. Seven hundred thousand scared people on narrow streets and roads. Seven hundred thousand who wouldn't know where to flee. . . ."

"Panic then," said the Federal Chancellor.

The Defense Minister nodded. "Panic and a total blockade. Grenzheim multiplied by a thousand."

Andree's voice: "We have no choice. With an evacuation, people at least have a chance."

"Are we all agreed?" asked the chancellor. "Evacuation."

The men nodded.

Andree said: "A duet please."

Only the chancellor understood the formula both men used when desiring a tête-à-tête. He walked into an adjoining room, where a young man was operating an old calculating machine. The chancellor wondered what he was computing: Deaths, injured people, wind speeds, distances? He waited till the phone rang, and he picked up.

"In three or four hours the cloud will be in Frankfurt," said Andree. "Move headquarters to Bonn."

"I'll send Klein and Gerner."

"Fly with them," said Andree. "It may not even be three hours. If the wind grows stronger. . . ."

"I said I'll send Klein and Gerner. . . ."

"You're just as stubborn as Born. He too would rather——"

"Would rather what?"

For a couple of seconds, Andree's voice was drowned out by the rattling of the chopper. "You know! He's playing captain on a sinking ship. I respect this attitude, but if he had allowed himself to be pulled out a couple of hours ago, nothing would have changed. With him, it has some sort of meaning, even though I don't quite understand it. He's feeling guilty. He probably thinks he could have prevented the accident. But it's different with you. You're head of the government. You're responsible for the nation. . . ."

". . . . and I'm supposed to hop a chopper and go off while the nation dies? No, Eckart. You really understand nothing, nothing about Born and nothing about me. But that's all right. Come back. We need you here."

When he came back to the operations headquarters, the police superintendent's seat was empty. "He copped out," grinned his party friend Grolmann.

The chancellor said: "Klein and Gerner will fly to Bonn and organize a substitute headquarters. I can't prevent any of you from vanishing like the police superintendent as long as there's still time."

Minister of the Interior Klein and Research Minister Gerner left the room. The other men didn't move. The chancellor thanked them with a nod of his head.

25

One Sunday afternoon, when she was about six or seven, Anne had seen *The Wizard of Oz*. Dorothy had ended up in the fairyland of Oz, desperately looking for the Wizard, who was the only one who could get her back to her farm in Kansas. As she searches, she is pursued by the Wicked Witch of the West who wants to kill Dorothy for her ruby slippers. The witch catches Dorothy and locks her up in her castle. She puts down an hour glass: When all the sand has run down, Dorothy must die. The scene, with the camera panning back and forth between the hour glass and the girl's face, was something Anne had never been able to forget. Not because of the impact of the images, but because at that moment all the children in the movie house were screaming and crying with fear, sympathy, and unbearable suspense, which intensified the horror of the scene.

Almost all the children in the bus were crying, even the three nine-year-olds, the oldest, who until then had fought back their tears. While Berger steered the bus towards Gries-heim (all the entrances to the federal highway were closed) and Rapp cowered wordlessly in the codriver's seat (he had given up justifying himself when Berger and Anne refused to answer), Anne walked down the aisle, trying to calm the children. But most of them wouldn't be comforted. They had gone through too much in the past few hours—the chaos on the Helios parking lot, the flight to Grenzheim, the people dying on Kilian Square, the panic, Rapp's threat to shoot Michaela. Anne couldn't soften their shock. She was only the teacher. The children needed someone to hold them in their arms, to tell them it was only a bad dream, a gruesome movie. They were weeping and screaming for their parents.

Anne wondered how many children would never see their mothers and fathers again because they had lost their lives somewhere behind the cloud of dust whirled up by the bus— lost their lives in accidents, in the panic at Grenzheim, in the radiation. And she thought with horror of the time when the parents of the two children trampled in the mob at Grenzheim would ask: "Where is our daughter? Where is our son?"

She caressed Michaela, who was also weeping, but more out of solidarity. Anne noticed that her daughter was ashamed of being the only one to have her mother here, protecting her. Rather than exploiting this advantage, she withdrew from Anne's hand.

Rapp said, "We're almost in Griesheim. You are to do the following: I'm getting out and taking your daughter along. I'm passing through the barrier with her. Then we're taking a bus to Frankfurt. I'll release her at the Frankfurt Main Terminal. That's where you can get her. If you call the police, Michaela dies."

"Stop this nonsense," said Anne. "You can go without Michaela. We won't say anything to the police. They've got more important things to do, heaven knows, than worry about hit-and-run drivers."

Rapp smirked cunningly. "You're talking sensibly, Frau Weiss. But I know you. You don't like me. You never did like me. And after the business with the kids and your daughter. . . . You'll never let me escape. But my dear child, escaping is the only thing that can save anyone now. Far, far away, before this goddamn country is totally poisoned."

Rapp seized Michaela's arm and pulled her towards the front door.

Half a mile before the Griesheim checkpoint at the edge of the twelve-mile circuit, a man in a yellow frog suit motioned the red bus over to the side of the road. "You'll have to stop here. The cars are standing in front there, in four columns. Go to the station on foot and get on line."

Berger pressed the button opening the doors. The doors opened with a hiss. Rapp held on tight to Michaela. "Take your time coming with the children," he said to Anne. He held the pistol in his right trouser pocket and climbed backwards out of the bus.

Michaela suddenly screamed: "I don' wanna! I don' wanna!" She wrenched free and fell forwards into the bus.

Rapp, one foot on the steps, one on the ground, was surprised. After two seconds, he pulled out his gun and pointed it at Michaela.

"Tell her she's got to come."

Anne nodded mutely and opened her mouth.

Berger's hand barely moved as he pressed the button closing the automatic doors. Rapp tried to fall back, but he was too slow. The door caught his right hand. The pistol wavered. Rapp fired when he thought he was aiming at Berger. The bullet shot through the window, leaving a clean hole. Berger grabbed Rapp's hand and pressed it to the side. Rapp screamed when it broke. By now the anti-radiation man had grabbed him from behind and was pulling him out. Rapp didn't put up a struggle. He murmured: "You can't do that. I'm the mayor. You can't do that. I'm the mayor."

Two policemen led him away.

Anne and Berger took the children to the blockade. Here in Griesheim, the police and the soldiers had managed to prevent any chaos. There were, of course, crushed heaps of metal smoking by the roadside, and a few bodies, superficially covered with cloth, blankets, and pieces of clothing. But the people were waiting, patient and disciplined, in ten lines, which were speedily moving through the gates. Perhaps they were so calm because they thought that the giant cloud drifting northeast was not endangering them. Perhaps, after the strenuous flight, they were too tired to rebel.

For the first time, Anne had the feeling that she and Berger and the children had been through the worst. For the first time, she was certain they would survive.

Three orderlies—they too, as well as the physicians, nurses, policemen, and soldiers, wore protective clothing—led the children past the waiting line.

Technicians with geiger counters felt over their bodies. When it was Anne's turn, she stared transfixed at the counter scale. The technician said: "Not much, but you ought to shower and change your clothes."

Anne stepped into a head-high cabin made of plastic. A figure in a yellow uniform explained the cleansing and showering formalities. One minute later Anne, dried by a warm stream of air, was standing in the sunlight again. An orderly pointed to a red house, a school now serving as a makeshift hospital. A nurse gave her clothing, not new, but guaranteed to be free of radiation.

Anne looked at herself briefly in the door glass and thought: I look like Mother Courage.

She heard the children's voices in the next room.

Berger, wearing a checkered shirt and baggy linen pants, was talking to the doctor. He turned to Anne, who was peering out for Michaela among the children and then waved upon discovering her. Berger said: "All the children have to go to the Frankfurt Clinic. Only two of them are hurt, but they've all gotten a shock. We're leaving in five minutes."

Anne nodded, then turned to the doctor. "Who's in charge of all these actions?"

"Here in Griesheim, a police inspector. He gets his orders from Frankfurt, from the crisis staff. . . ."

"Can I telephone there?"

The doctor looked at her in amazement. "You can try. The inspector's down that corridor, second room on the left."

The police inspector had red eyes and a bandaid on his cheek. The bandaid was so big that it must have been covering more than a razor cut, maybe a boil.

He said Anne could not call the crisis staff. Besides, there was no one named Born on the staff.

Anne said, "He's the director of Helios."

The policeman was stirring a cup of instant coffee, from which no steam was rising.

"Please," said Anne. "I only want to know if he's still alive."

The inspector telephoned. He hung up.

"Dr. Born is still at the power plant. He is in contact with the operations headquarters. He's alive."

"Thank you," said Anne. She walked back down the hall. The walls were hung with children's drawings, suns, kites, horses, ships.

Berger and the children were no longer there. Anne went outside. Her tears blurred the teeming cars and people. A horn honked. Children were waving. She walked towards the bus. This one was green.

26

Helios burned, and Martin Born was dying. For a few minutes, a powerful pressure had been crushing his head. His ears buzzed. His hands were ice cold. Something was wrong with his circulation. Rays, lack of oxygen—he made no great effort to analyze it.

Even though dull explosions shook the room at one-minute intervals—the room that had once been the control station, the brains of the plant—the cracks in the wall hadn't grown. Born sat at the end of the long control desk. The telephone receiver lay before him. For fifteen minutes now, the loudspeaker had only been releasing the hum of the line, interrupted by the crackling of the relays, which sounded like disengaged springs.

Born played with the gaudy buttons and switches on the desk. He remembered the first great disappointment of his life. When he was six or seven, his parents had given him a construction set. His parents were convinced he had a practical mind. He'll build bridges some day, his father used to say. His father would have much preferred being an engineer rather than a mechanic. The box said: The Little Engineer. And Born had put the structure and the crane and the lights together in two days. But when he pressed the button that was supposed to start everything, nothing moved. He had looked for the mistake for two days. He didn't find it. The toy store refused to exchange the set. His father had then thrown the crane and the set out the window and not spoken to his son for a week.

They ought to call, thought Born, touching the phone. He felt superfluous. The Frankfurt people didn't need him anymore. They now had their experts on the spot and were totally occupied with the evacuation. He envied Andree. The man's composure impressed him. Andree could act, could make, revise, and put through decisions; he had no time to think.

Born felt sick. So it *is* radiation, he thought.

Was he guilty? Could someone draw up an accusation: "Martin Born, age thirty-six, Doctor of Physics, is accused of the murder of ten or twenty or a hundred thousand people"? He would never know how many victims there were.

It was possible. It was possible to blame the catastrophe completely on him. It might not be fair, but it couldn't be refuted.

While preaching safety religion to others self-righteously, he himself had transgressed it.

At the decisive moment, he had been inattentive and weak willed. If he hadn't accepted Peter Larsen as head of safety, if he had held his ground against the head of the board who wanted to launch his protegé, if he had at least done the right thing after the first evidence of Larsen's incapacity, then last night the plant would have been protected by a head of safety who knew his job.

A better man than Larsen would not have stuck a doddering old man into the watchman's cabin.

Rogolski's statement, which Born had learned about a half hour ago, left no doubt that the saboteur had used Werner Marcks's ID card to get into the plant. Now experts were examining the signatures in the book, which an alert safety man had taken along on his flight.

A better man than Larsen would have been at the plant that evening, rather than showing off at some silly public discussion.

A better man than Larsen would have noticed the absence of an employee like Zander immediately.

A better man than Larsen would have used the two-man patrols on the eve of the dedication not only throughout the grounds, but also in the buildings.

A better man than Larsen would have prevented the sabotage.

And a better man than Born would have made sure that an idiot like Larsen would never be entrusted with such a crucial job.

If he had not stayed with Anne Weiss after the discussion, but instead driven to the plant to check out Larsen. If, after visiting little Yvonne, he had called off the dedication ceremonies and had the plant thoroughly searched for any radioactive waste, so thoroughly that they would have found the bombs. . . .

And Sibylle. Was she really having an affair with the saboteur? It seemed so absurd. He would never have imagined it. And he didn't believe it. He thought the suspicion was the result of hectic investigations in which everyone was initially suspected.

He knew his wife. A rich, good-looking man with a lot of time and, as Sibylle put it, "standing" in society— that was the sort of man he expected her to get. But apolitical, uninterested, luxury-loving Sibylle as the accomplice of a mad bomber? Impossible.

"Herr Dr. Born? Born, can you hear me."

Andree had to shout three times before Born registered his voice.

Born tried to answer. A coughing fit shook him. When the black circles waned before his eyes, he said. "I hear you. Bad news."

"Worse," said Andree.

"I can't make you out so well. Where are you?"

"In a chopper on the way to Frankfurt."

"I thought you'd forgotten me. Is the evacuation working?"

"Yes," said Andree.

"And the cloud?"

"The cloud's moving towards Darmstadt and Frankfurt."

"Cut the bullshit," said Born after a pause. "With a west-southwesterly wind, it'll pass far from Darmstadt, not to mention Frankfurt."

"That was ten minutes ago. The wind has shifted. It's coming from the south now."

"How far has the cloud front drifted to the east?"

"About four miles east of the E4."

"Into the Oden Forest. The upwind has to have driven the damn thing up."

"No," said Andree.

"Is Darmstadt being evacuated."

"We're just doing it."

"How much time is left?"

"Not even one hour."

"And Frankfurt?" asked Born after a pause.

"We're doing our best," said Andree, "and that's not good enough. According to the weathermen, the cloud will be over Frankfurt in four hours—if the wind remains that weak. In four hours, a few hundred thousand people will still be in town."

"The wind can shift again. The inversion can stop, and the cloud will move up into the atmosphere."

"It doesn't look that way."

"So there's no hope."

"No hope. Unless you know someone who can spirit away radioactive clouds."

"I lost his phone number," said Born.

"Do you go to church?" asked Andree. He didn't want to ask 'Do you believe in God?'

"No."

"Neither do I. Otherwise, I would say the weirdest prayer of all time: God, send me a giant bellows." Andree guffawed. "I'm starting to envy old Klinger."

"Why?"

"He had a heart attack. They brought him to the hospital. He's totally off his rocker ever since the news came that the cloud was moving towards Frankfurt. He was supposedly talking off the wall and then he went out like a light. He's lucky."

"You're the last person in the world to reproach himself," said Born.

Andree's voice turned sharp. "Herr Dr. Born, I know you're cultivating a guilt complex. I can imagine what the inside of your head looks like. A thousand people warned about the dangers of nuclear energy, and with a perfectly good conscience you replied that an accident was highly improbable. One chance in a million, one in ten million, something like that, wasn't it? And now you're telling yoursef: If I had only listened to the warnings. If I had only been more critical. And so on. You know what, Born? There's nothing anyone can do against sabotage. You can believe me. I've been banging my head against the wall long enough about security problems. There is no perfect security. If a lunatic wants to bump off the Federal Chancellor, he'll bump him off, even if the chancellor's inside an army of bodyguards. And if someone wants to blow a nuclear station to kingdom come, he'll do it in the end. That's something we have to live with."

"Or die with," said Born.

Andree didn't hear it. "*I* ought to go off my rocker, Born. *I* ought to reproach myself. You weren't in Grenzheim. A couple of thousand people condemned to death, and now it turns out it was all for nothing. I can still see the people before me, the way they——"

"Andree." Born's voice sounded tired and hoarse. "There was that airplane."

"What airplane?"

"The observation machine that crashed near Helios."

"They went down too far and got radiation. Two casualties."

"How deep?"

"Why are you so interested?

"I'll explain if you can get me the altitude of the plane at the moment the radio connection broke off."

"Okay. In two minutes."

Born's hands had become stiff. They could barely hold the

pencil. His chin was wet. He wiped it with his left hand, which was inside an anti-radiation glove. When he pulled his hand back, the glove was bloody. Brownish-red bits of vomit fell between Born's thighs. His ears were roaring.

"Born? Here are the data. The plane was at first circling at over 10,000 feet above Helios. . . ."

"Right above it?"

"No, some 1,500 feet to the southwest, above the grain fields. Then the machine went down to about 8,000 feet, and then it happened."

"Funny, isn't it," said Born. "Compare that with the cloud data. The cloud at that time had an altitude diameter of at most 1,300 and was at best 1,000 feet from the ground. So the outer edge was at most 2,300 feet high. Figure about 3,300 feet for the radius of the fatal radiation, and you come to a dangerous distance of 5,600. Yet the plane was flying at an altitude of 8,000 feet."

"Then the cloud data was wrong."

"No," said Born. "It was by and large correct. But the few choppers and planes couldn't measure every square inch of the cloud."

"What's it mean?"

"It means that parts of the cloud had risen higher in the air than the great mass. The upwind over the grain fields drove it beyond the inversion limit."

"Parts," said Andree. "What good is that?"

"It's in the manual for glider pilots, Andree: sandy areas, grain fields, towns. There's always an upwind over areas like that."

"But it's much too weak," said Andree. "It won't help if bits of the cloud drift six or seven hundred feet higher than the rest."

"No, that won't help."

"Then what's the use of all this figuring?"

Born choked and threw up. "Sorry," he said. "You were praying for a bellows before, Andree. We don't have a bellows.

But we do have another way of blasting the cloud into the air. An upwind."

"I don't understand."

"We can create a gigantic current of hot air, which will drive up and disperse the cloud."

"I still don't understand."

"Set fire to Darmstadt, Andree."

After five seconds, Andree said, "That's the most sensible, crazy idea I've ever heard."

"In medicine, this is known as homeopathy," said Born. "Fighting madness with madness."

"I'll inform the chancellor right away. Do you believe we really have a chance? Born? Born?"

Born was too weak to answer. What does chance mean, he thought, spitting blood. We have to do something. As long as we do something, we still have a chance.

27

"You can't be serious," said the chancellor. The men at the table nodded in agreement. The head of the opposition party, Lützkow, made a crazy sign.

Andree's voice: "Of course. Born's right. It's simple physics. Hamburg, July 1943, the fire storm after the bombing attack. Ashes and dust were driven so high by the hot air that they didn't fall down again until they were out over the Baltic Sea. The radiation cloud is drifting straight across Darmstadt. If Darmstadt burns, the cloud will be blown into the atmosphere. We can save the population of Frankfurt, There's no other way."

The chancellor said, "I'll notify you as soon as we've reached a decision."

"We don't have much time," said Andree. The loud-speaker crackled.

Before the chancellor could ask the men anything, Lütz-kow said, "Total nonsense. We can't cover Darmstadt with kerosene and then bomb it! Hasn't enough been destroyed? And there are still people in the city, the old, the sick——"

The chancellor interrupted him. "It's no use discussing it until we know whether destroying Darmstadt will have the intended effect."

He reached for the phone. They could all hear. "Dr. Born has made a suggestion——"

"I know about it. State Secretary Andree just informed me and asked about the prospects of success."

"And what do you as a meteorologist say?"

"It's possible that at least part of the cloud will mount into the atmosphere. But no one can guarantee that."

The chancellor hung up. He turned to the men of the crisis staff: "Krüger?"

"We have to use any possibility of saving Frankfurt," replied the Defense Minister. "If the bombing has a fifty-fifty chance of success, we should do it. I would even be in favor of it, if the chances were one in a hundred."

Lützkow said, "But there are still people in Darmstadt!"

"How many?" asked Grolmann, the head of the government party. "And how many will die in Frankfurt?"

The chancellor nodded. "Human lives against human lives. That seems to be the only kind of decision permitted to us today. First Grenzheim. Now Darmstadt. When would the bombardment have to start?"

Krüger said, "At the latest, in forty minutes."

"Are all the people out of the city?"

"The healthy ones. Anyone who can't walk himself and has no one to take care of him has to wait for the special transports, and they're taking their own sweet time. And even then there'll be people they'll forget—old people, children at home alone. . . ."

The chancellor was silent. He reached for the phone. "State Secretary Andree, please. Yes, radio."

Andree came in.

"I hereby order," said the chancellor, "that squadrons of fighter bombers set fire to Darmstadt. Target time in exactly forty minutes. The Defense Minister will ask the Allied air forces to assist us. Where are you now?"

"Five minutes from Frankfurt Airport."

"We'll need to use civil aircraft too, Eckart. You take over the operations organization of that. You'll need some diplomacy, Eckart. We can't ask any crew to take that danger upon themselves."

"I know. It'll work."

Lützkow stared at the chancellor with pallid eyes and said: "No one will ever forgive us for this."

28

Evacuation Convoy II from Pfungstadt crossed under the federal highway (no traffic, but there were abandoned cars on the lanes) and turned into the Heidelberg Road, which led directly to Darmstadt. The column consisted of four buses (one bore the owner's sign: "Georg Gröhner—Makes travel finer"), three trucks (one an army vehicle), three ambulances with room for eight patients apiece, and a national guard tank (officially called a "special protected car"), and five jeeps. Evacuation Convoy II was assigned to bring people from Darmstadt's hospitals and old-age homes. They were escorted by twenty German and American soldiers armed with machine pistols.

At the outskirts of Darmstadt, the streets were empty. It was only at the Lincoln Settlement, shortly before the bicycle racing track, that the convoy met buses and trucks with people thronging in front of their doors and loading entrances.

The column turned into Landskron-Strasse and stopped. The soldiers jumped out of the jeeps. The first car in the convoy, a shabby Mercedes bus, was blocked by an enormous moving truck with a trailer. The man driving the truck kept sparking the engine every few seconds, as though he wanted to ram into the bus. An army lieutenant demonstratively lowered his machine pistol and tried talking to the man. He climbed on the running board. The man in the moving truck was scraggly, his arms were scrawny, hardly thicker than the spokes of the steering wheel that he was hugging. His hollow cheeks and pointed chin were unshaven. He wore nickel-framed glasses. Only his voice was virile and deep. He shouted: "You won't get it. You won't get it. I didn't slave for ten years so that you could smash it up."

The lieutenant's answer was lost in the howl of the motor. He leaned over to a soldier. Yes, they had wanted to confiscate the vehicle for the evacuation. The guy had simply zoomed away.

The truck was vibrating so powerfully that the lieutenant naα to hold on to the door handle with both hands. A soldier slinked around the truck to surprise the man from the other side.

The man shouted: "You could do it under Hitler or Ulbricht. But not here, not with me. I'm a free man, and I don't give a shit about your state of emergency. Get the hell out of the way."

The lieutenant said something like: "Please be reasonable. . . . You're breaking the law. . . ."

The man spat, just barely missing the lieutenant's head. The soldier who had stepped on the running board on the other side attempted to open the door. It was locked. He hammered on the window with the butt of his machine pistol. Since he had to hold on with one hand, his banging had no

298

force. The window remained intact. The man inside stared incredulously at the soldier as though unable to grasp that someone was smashing against his truck.

Then he went berserk.

He appeared to be laughing. His right hand dropped from the wheel. The gear locked like a rusty railroad switch. The diesel engine howled. The man switched gears. The truck leaped forward. The officer and the soldier were hurled to either side. Two other soldiers raised their machine pistols and fired at the driver's door. The truck smashed its left front fender into the Mercedes bus, veered to the left, banged against a hydrant, and its hood shot into the window of a grocery store. The driver's cabin tore huge chunks out of the brick wall and was smashed flat. The trailer whirled, leaned, and remained stuck in that position, the broad side looming over a car parked in the street.

The soldiers didn't check to see whether the scrawny man was still alive. They climbed into the jeeps. The bus was barely damaged. The convoy started off again. A few minutes later, they passed a gate that was guarded by gilded lions and they stopped in front of a gray, ivy-covered building.

"Saint Jesus Hospital," said the staff physician who gave orders to the convoy. "First station."

The head physician of the hospital, an old man with a moustache, gold-rimmed spectacles, and a vest open over his belly, was already waiting. "We still have thirty-seven patients here. They are in the receiving room. Ten of them really shouldn't be moved, stomach cancer, gallbladder, only just operated on."

Orderlies carried the patients into the vehicles. All the patients had cards strung around their necks, with their names, addresses, diseases, and treatments and medications scrawled on them.

An orderly carefully placed an old man next to the stone steps when he noticed he was dead.

A young woman, her arm in a sling, cried: "My husband wanted to visit me today, for the first time. Where's he going to find me?"

The head doctor said, "Okay. You have them all."

The staff physician said, "Aren't you taking anything along? No records, nothing?"

"This is my hospital," said the doctor and smiled. "I've had it for twenty-five years, even though it really belongs to the church. I wouldn't want to abandon it."

He climbed up the stairs with tired paces.

The closer the convoy came to the inner city, the denser the throngs in the streets. The scene recalled the time of the aerial attacks during World War II. Some of the older refugees had probably run through the streets during the destruction of Darmstadt in 1944 exactly as they were doing now, with children on their arms and carrying tiny suitcases of valuables and clothing.

Shortly before Prinz Emils Garden, the column was stopped by a young soldier. He shouted to the lieutenant. "There are looters in the department store over there. Ten people. They're loading refrigerators and God knows what else into trucks. They're armed. One of our men is dead."

The lieutenant spoke into his walkie-talkie: "Five men into the department store. The soldier'll show you the way. No warning shots."

The soldiers stormed into the building, holding their machine guns ready.

A couple of minutes later, there were dry shots. Two grenades went off.

Fifty yards from the column, two young men leaped into a truck. A few soldiers wanted to go after them. The lieutenant held them back. "Forget it. They won't get very far."

Evacuation Convoy II drove through a side street where two houses were burning. On an iron fence, two dead children hung like a pair of lost gloves that a polite finder has put up.

The people dashing by paid no heed, as though they were used to living among corpses.

The convoy stopped in the shade of two gigantic elm trees in front of an old age home. The young woman from the hospital, sitting in a bus, said to a nurse, "Frankly, why are we going to all this trouble with the old people? They've got to die anyway soon. The longer we wait here, the more dangerous it'll get for us."

The people in the old age home were unaware. A few were strolling through the park in the afternoon sun, which was taking on a leaden tinge in the rising vapor. A few were drinking coffee on the terrace. Some were asleep or were up in their rooms. The head of the home, a woman with severe, mummy-like features, folded her arms and stood in the path of the soldiers, doctors, orderlies, and nurses on the stairway.

"Evacuation? Are you out of your minds? Do you have a certificate from the church board? I shall complain to the bishop. You have no right. . . ."

The staff physician explained the situation while the orderlies hurried into the building. The old woman wouldn't listen. "Sir, I most decisively protest against your actions."

The old people on the terrace, thankful for the excitement and ready to put up a fight, had rallied around their director. The orderlies led them to the vehicles with gentle force.

The staff physician asked, "Where's your file? We need it for identification purposes."

The woman wouldn't answer. The physician realized she was trying to read his lips. She was deaf and refused to admit it. He ordered a soldier to get the file.

After thirty seconds, the soldier was standing in the office. On the peeling walls there was a globe of the world with a cross planted upon it and a wooden board that said, in Gothic letters: "Blessed are the poor in spirit, for theirs is the kingdom of heaven."

The filing cases stood on the cracked desk. He took them and started back.

Walking through the somber corridor, he heard a whimpering. At first he saw no one, then he doubled back a few steps and discovered an old woman squeezing against the wall behind the broom closet, gazing at him fearfully. When he took her by the hand, she allowed herself to be led trembling from her hiding place. She explained she didn't want to leave the home without Lori. When asked who Lori was, she said it was a dachshund, and it was asleep in a basket in room 208.

The soldier brought the woman to a bus and promised to get Lori.

He pushed past the sobbing, screaming, struggling old people, who were being propelled down the stairs by orderlies and nurses. One orderly grinned at the soldier. "One of the old farts yelled 'Auschwitz,' and now they all think we're carrying them off to the gas chambers." The old people dragged along whatever they had been able to grab in their panic—a bouquet, a family photo, an embroidered pillow, a fox stole.

In room 208, there was a dog basket. In the basket sat a dachshund. He was as fat as a pig. The soldier heaved him up and carried him to the bus.

The old woman beamed: "Lori, my Lori!"

Just as she was about to lift the dog upon her lap, an orderly said: "No animals." He grabbed the dog by the scruff of its neck and threw it out the door. Three men had to hold the old woman fast until an injection calmed her down.

After the old age home was evacuated, there was no room left in the vehicles. In the buses, the people sat and stood like sardines. The buses were hot and smelly. The bodies of the children, old people, and patients were reacting to fear. The backs of trucks were filled with stretchers, hopping and sliding over every bump in the road. The patients screamed.

In front of the city hospitals people were sitting and hobbling. They looked relieved when they caught sight of the convoy. The vehicles didn't halt. The patients threatened with their fists and crutches. The staff physician shouted, "There are trucks coming for you right away." He was lying.

The convoy drove past upheaved cars, plundered shops, corpses in the gutter, empty streetcars, trampled valises, deserted fire engines.

Shortly before a railroad bridge crossing the road towards the west, the convoy caught up with the mass of the human trek fleeing from Darmstadt. The people scarcely heeded the vehicles and moved aside automatically.

29

"Soldiers!" Fuchs pulled Sibylle into the shadow of the entrance to his building. After three minutes, the soldiers came back out of the house. They pushed a weeping woman and two children along. "It's true," one soldier implored the woman. "You've got to believe me. You have to leave the city. That's government orders."

"They're looking for me," said Fuchs, "but they won't find me. They're too stupid."

He yanked Sibylle into the house. They climbed up the stairs. All the apartment doors were open. It was still.

"No one's looking for you," said Sibylle. "They're evacuating the city. Can't you understand that! We're in danger here. Darmstadt is probably threatened by the radiation. Let's get out of here, Alexander!"

Fuchs whirled around. "You're always talking about us, but you only mean yourself."

"You're hurt! Your foot's still bleeding. You need a doctor."

"Don't start that again," said Fuchs. "I can't stand your mealy-mouthed tirades anymore."

"Then let me go."

Fuchs laughed. "Oh no! In sickness and in health! You can leave me when my justification is finished. Then you can put the police onto me. Then you can get your revenge."

"I don't want any revenge."

"Oh c'mon! Do you think I wasn't observing you on the way from Mainz? Do you think I didn't notice you wondering whether to tell the doctor who I was? This is Alexander Fuchs, the mass murderer!"

He was right. A doctor had taken them along. Fuchs had told him they were Red Cross helpers, and the doctor had seen no reason to doubt it. Aside from orderlies, only lunatics would voluntarily enter the catastrophe zone. Sibylle had wondered whether to tell the doctor that the perpetrator was sitting next to him. She hadn't dared. She knew Fuchs would kill the man.

"Come on now," said Fuchs. He stood on the landing in front of the door to his apartment. What was he planning? He would write down what he called his justification. And then? Would he let her go then? Certainly not. She was unimportant to him, a nuisance, a threat. Would he kill her? She studied his face. Oh yes, he would kill her.

She climbed two steps. He clutched her wrist. When he turned to the door, she stamped on his bleeding foot with all her might. He loosened his grip in pain and surprise. Sibylle tore free and ran down the steps. Fuchs ran after her. He didn't scream. He didn't pant. The only thing she could hear were his fast hobbling steps.

He almost caught up with her at the entrance door. Sibylle shrieked. Fuchs tripped and crashed down the three stone steps leading to the sidewalk.

Sibylle halted. Fuchs was bleeding from an abrasion on his head. His right leg underneath the knees was sticking out at an unnatural angle.

"Sibylle," whispered Fuchs. "Sibylle."

She walked back three steps. He smiled at her. "I really loved you," he said. "I didn't want to use you. It just worked

304

out that way. Please help me, Sibylle. Help me. I have to get up to my books. I have to write. I have to explain. Please."

Sibylle bent over him and caressed his hair. He grabbed her hand. Gingerly this time, gently, as in the past. Sibylle drew away, saying, "Poor Sasha."

She walked off. At the corner, she looked back. From the distance, Fuchs seemed like a crippled alligator as he tried to pull his body up the stoop with his arms.

30

Andree had the reputation of being immune to stress. He had once endured three successive night sessions of the Common Market in Brussels without any trouble. After the fourteen-hour mammoth conference on security questions in Geneva, he had been as fit as at the beginning. Two months ago, he had spent thirty-six hours negotiating with some skyjackers and still knew what was going on when the exhausted ministers were so nervous they were considering measures which fortunately never leaked out to the public. Now Andree felt drained as never before in his life, and he had to struggle against a powerful desire to sleep.

The streets that the chopper hummed over en route to the airport were black with people and vehicles. According to the latest information, there were, in fact, individual clashes between the populace and the police and army units—people put up a struggle against giving away their cars for the evacuation or being driven out of their homes without being permitted to take along at least a small suitcase.

But there were still no signs of panic. Andree assumed that the absolute news blackout on the Helios events was functioning. The accident was known to the populace of

Frankfurt from the initial radio reports (which had been so devastating in Grenzheim) and through the press announcement by the crisis staff. But no one as yet knew that Frankfurt lay directly in the trail of the radiation cloud and was threatened with annihilation. Furthermore, the Helios reactor was located over thirty miles from the center of Frankfurt—a halfway safe distance for all who knew little about the movement and speed of radioactivity.

At last, beyond the trees, the control tower of Frankfurt Airport loomed in the air. The sky was empty as during a controllers' strike. The few aircraft that landed were bringing physicians, auxiliary personnel, and equipment. These were instantly loaded into helicopters and transported to the operations points along the edge of the evacuation zone.

As the SA 341 touched down, a TWA Boeing 707 was starting. Well, well, thought Andree. The Americans aren't taking any chances. They're taking army families to safety.

The airport director was waiting for him in a green jeep at the next hangar. Andree ran over to him, bowed. For a time, he had tried to shake the habit of ducking the rotor blades (they whirled ten feet over the ground and couldn't possibly guillotine him), but finally he had yielded to instinct. He clambered into the jeep. The airport director drove it himself. He curved, sure of what he was doing, in between the planes. He said, "I don't know what you're planning, but I've asked all the available crews and managers to assemble in clearance building A. I hope my people have left some space. You'll soon see what I mean."

He drove past the tail of a Jumbo jet and halted. Andree saw what the director meant. Clearance building A had turned into an army camp. Vacationers who had had already donned their straw hats for Mallorca, businessmen, English tourists, a couple of dozen Japanese, school classes, Turkish and Greek laborers with tightly bound and bursting cardboard boxes— they had occupied every square inch of the hall. Their delegates fought their way up to the counters to shout their questions to a uniformed stewardess who answered with a shrug. The hall was hot, as though built on fire. The snack bar was shut. The head waiter was encircled by fifty people waving paper money and demanding something to drink. He tried to withdraw slowly, while yelling: "There are no more drinks. We're sold out. Don't you understand? Sold out. The beer's gone. Understand?"

The announcement board behind every flight number said: Delayed.

Andree followed the director, gingerly climbing over valises, children, and sandwich packages. Around the information stand, which was strewn with black and yellow signs, airport employees had drawn a ring. Andree estimated that something like a hundred pilots and fifty representatives of the air companies had come. The director clambered onto a rickety tubular-steel table. He asked Andree to come up and stand next to him. Andree hesitated, then was relieved to see that the table could hold both of them.

"Can't we do anything with the people?" asked Andree, pointing to the throng. They probably had smelled out some air catastrophe. None of them seemed to have heard about the Helios accident.

"I don't have enough men to kick them out," said the director. "You'll have to put up with them."

He introduced Andree and let him speak.

Andree said in English: "I am speaking in the name of the government of the Federal Republic of Germany. We need your help. The Helios atomic reactor has been sabotaged. A highly concentrated radioactive cloud, measuring about three by seven miles, is drifting towards Darmstadt and Frankfurt."

Some of the passengers in the hall screamed. Andree heard a woman's voice: "Let me through. I've got to get to my kids."

The pilots remained calm. Andree continued. "The only way of stopping a mass death is to make the cloud rise into the atmosphere. Since inversion weather is now prevailing, the cloud will not rise by itself. The Federal Chancellor has therefore ordered the German air force, with the support of NATO, to bomb Darmstadt in thirty minutes. The bombing will produce a fire storm that will blast the cloud upwards, if we're lucky. To make Darmstadt burn quickly, we have to first soak the town with kerosene. We need all passenger machines that are equipped with an automatic outlet for fuel."

The pilots and managers talked excitedly, chaotically. A young man, blond, rosy-cheeked, with the Pan Am button on his lapel, had the loudest voice, "That's suicide."

"Why?" asked Andree. "So far as I know, airplanes doing an emergency landing or any dangerous landing first let out fuel without blowing up."

"That's different. In an emergency landing, it's the lesser of two evils. If the gas pipes break during the crash landing, you can prevent the fuel from igniting on burning parts. But it's still a big risk."

"You've got to decide for yourselves," said Andree, "whether a few million human lives are worth this risk. I can't force any of you to join us. I could, of course, confiscate your machines—even though it's illegal. But by the time the substitute crews from the air force arrived, it would be much too late. I'm totally dependent on you, on your resoluteness, your courage, your solidarity."

The air company managers were discussing the situation together. Finally, one of the representatives of the Soviet Aeroflot called, "I can't decide right away. I have to inform my superiors in Moscow."

"And your bosses will have to ask their bosses, and so on, and we'll have the answer next week. You've got to decide now, this very minute."

"And who'll pay if something happens? Who'll replace the machines? Who'll provide for the families of the pilots?"

"I have full authority from the Federal Chancellor to guarantee damages to an unlimited extent."

Andree noticed that some of the older pilots were already nodding to him imperceptibly. They were used to exceptional situations. They could mentally switch as fast as lightning from routine things to maximum performances—even risky ones—if they were convinced of the necessity.

"I cannot take responsibility for an agreement," said the Pan Am man stiltedly.

A pilot, black hair, bony face, shouted: "Bullshit! You're not risking your asses, so stay out of this. I'm flying. Anyone else, raise your hands."

No pilot's hand stayed down.

"Thank you," said Andree. "And don't worry. None of you is getting a medal. I'll protect you from that."

The pilots grinned.

"The fueled machines are to take off first. On the double. How long until the empty ones are fueled?"

"We can pump four thousand liters a minute with the dispenser hydrants," said the director. "We've got——"

"Great," said Andree. "Pump through all the tubes for fifteen minutes. All the machines that have at least one liter of kerosene more than they need for the round trip are to take off. The operation will be directed from the tower."

The pilots turned to go.

"One second." Andree wiped the sweat from his forehead. "First of all: Keep your crews as small as possible. You know why yourselves. Secondly: It may be that you'll find people left in the city. That shouldn't get in your way."

Andree and the airport director drove to the tower. The controllers, in shirt sleeves, were sitting in front of monitors and lit-up radar screens. Three sentences were enough to instruct them. Andree, through binoculars, watched the airfield. The first planes were already rolling. The voices of the controllers mixed into a noise carpet.

"Expedite taxiing and take-off. . . . Remember you don't have to fly a traffic pattern . . . weather report . . . proceed along the highway . . . climb on track to 15,000 feet . . . take-off clearance. . . ."

Then the machines rose into the air. At brief intervals, they climbed into the reddish-blue late afternoon sky: Jumbo jets, Caravelles, Concordes, an old Vickers Viscount of the New Zealand Airways, an Aeroflot Tupolev with narrow, angular wings, numerous Boeing 727's and 737's, a half-dozen BAC-Super 111's, two compact DC 9's, two slender DC 8's, two Ilyushins of Czechoslovakian Airways, four BEA Tridents.

"Over fifty machines," said the airport director. "They'll circle the town in squadrons. The town area is very small, about three by four miles. If the jets fly across it in a straight line, they won't have enough time to deliver the fuel and they'll have to come back. That'll be a waste of minutes.

"How much kerosene do the largest planes have in their tanks?"

"Over a hundred and ninety thousand liters."

"Thirty seconds to go," said one of the controllers. And then: "Oh my God! He's flying too low. . . . Climb up to 15,000 feet. . . . watch out for radiation. . . . Oh boy. He finally heard it."

Andree pointed to a radar screen.

"What are those dots? Passenger planes?"

"No," said the director. "Those are attack bombers, a Phantom squadron of the German Air Force. They're waiting for the 'steersman's' orders."

"Steersman?"

"That's what pilots call the head officer who controls the attack bombers from the operational HQ and gives them the attack order."

"*Attack.* That sounds just great," said Andree.

"Do you know Darmstadt?" asked the airport director.

"Not really."

"I was born there. It was a beautiful city."

310

31

EXCERPT FROM THE NOTES OF THE SECOND INTERNATIONAL
CONFERENCE CALL AFTER THE ACCIDENT AT THE HELIOS
NUCLEAR POWER STATION

Participants: The heads of states of all European countries,
with the exception of Albania; the President of the United
States of America: the head of state of the Soviet Union.

Germany: I must contradict the French Prime Minister.
Even if we don't take this desperate measure—bombing Darmstadt—the radioactive cloud, under the present weather conditions, will rise in two or three hours anyway and spread out in
a northerly direction, for hundreds of kilometers. Thus there
can be no possibility of our endangering other countries in
order to save our population or the inhabitants of Frankfurt.

GDR: We insist on an international investigating committee for checking your information and, in case it doesn't con-
form to the facts, bringing you to account.

USA: We can talk about commissions when we have survived this catastrophe. We now know that during the next few
days and weeks we have to reckon with radioactive fallout and
radioactive rainout. I therefore propose that we let the Federal
Chancellor return to his difficult job and that we confer in the
next thirty minutes as to how we can best help one another.
So far as I am informed, a few countries have as good as no
anti-radiation experts or equipment. These countries would
best be served with a mobile anti-radiation commando, for
which the Soviet Union, France, Great Britain, and the United
States will supply personnel and equipment. I am thinking of
some five hundred men. . . .

32

INSCRIPTION ON THE SUN CLOCK OF THE WEDDING TOWER IN
DARMSTADT

The day passes across my face, the night it gropes slowly by,
and day and night are a balance, and night and day are one.
And the shadowy writing circles forever. Lifelong you stand in
the darkened game, until the game's meaning strikes you: the
time has come, you are at your goal.

33

Eric Shaw, captain in the U.S. Air Force, had never bombed
a city. He hadn't been to Vietnam, and during the training
courses and homings in Texas and New Mexico he had
dropped bombs and rockets only on wooden villages and mock-
up tanks.

Upon getting the orders to attack Darmstadt, he, like his
buddies, figured it was a joke. Some colonel must have flipped
out, thought it was 1944. But the order was perfectly correct,
and it came from the German chancellor himself, not from the
Air Force.

"We're gonna do a Brothers Mongolfiere number," said
the squadron leader. "We're supposed to produce hot air to
make that damn cloud float up like a balloon."

Shaw kept his Starfighter F-104 G at four hundred miles

312

an hour. He looked to the right. The Starfighter next to him seemed to be pasted to the tip of his wing. Perfect formation flight. One minute to go.

The squadron commander's voice bellowed out of the earphones.

"No lower than 8,000 feet. If you get anywhere near the radiation cloud, you've had it. Dump your bombs, shoot your rockets, and then get back home." Shaw corrected his altitude. Thirty seconds to go. Below, the suburban houses cropped up, interrupted by meadows and woods. Then railroad tracks, lawns. Those lawns everywhere in the town, thought Shaw. How are they supposed to burn?

Zero hour. High-rises, towers, bridges, 2,000-foot nose dive. Shaw released the two 454-kilogram bombs and the 907-kilogram bomb at the same time. The Starfighter almost gave a sigh of relief. Then Shaw pressed the button that sent out the two Sidewinder rockets. He pulled the machine up and around. Below him, fire and smoke. The northern sky glittered. There must have been at least two hundred machines, Phantoms, Mirages, Lightnings, Harriers, Fiats, Cessnas, Sabres. Shaw watched wave upon wave plunging towards the city.

When the fighter planes had turned, the bombers came. They weren't numerous, scarcely more than a dozen, just American B-52's. But the stream of bombs they spewed out didn't seem to run dry. The reeling black points hurtled like rain showers upon the city.

And the city burned. The kerosene, thought Shaw. The civilians had done a good job. The city was unrecognizable under the smoke cloud. When Shaw flew over the northern outskirts, oiltanks were exploding, sending black fumes into the air. If there are any people down there, thought Shaw, they don't have to worry anymore about any atomic death.

34

The boy was six, the girl four. The boy didn't like his sister. His sister waited until he had built a town with houses, streets, and trees for his cars. Then she destroyed the town with her feet. When he hit her, she ran screaming to their father. The father slapped the boy and cut off his pocket money for two weeks. His sister sat there, smiling sweetly. Now they were at the same point again. The town was nearly finished. The pride and joy was the new skyscraper, which bore a Shell conch on top. The Shell gleamed when you pressed a button. The boy also put a couple of small sandbags on the ramp of the warehouse. Then he started the blue delivery truck. His back door could be clapped up on an axle, just like a real one.

He knew what would come next. His sister threw her colored pencils on the drawing book and looked at him. She stretched our her left foot, and a boulevard tree toppled over. The boy didn't say anything. He thought, She's gonna be surprised. She thinks I'm scared of father. But father's on a trip, and he won't be here for three weeks. And mother isn't so strict. She won't hit me. At least not so badly. And she's always so tired when she comes back from shopping. If only those sirens would stop. He knew there was a siren drill twice a year. But it never lasted this long. They were howling for half an hour already. Luckily, you couldn't hear them so clearly up here on the eighth floor. He would have liked to see what was going on below. But mother had locked them in because his stupid sister had run out on the terrace last time.

His sister had already knocked over three more trees and was about to topple the Shell building. The boy warned her. She wouldn't listen. When the skyscraper collapsed, with the

314

Shell sign breaking off, the boy made a dash for his sister. He beat her up as though there were no parents in the world, no punishments. He paid her back everything. The dirty pig deserved it. She could tell on him, but first, she'd get what was coming to her.

When his sister cried, the boy stopped. Suddenly he felt sorry for her. Had he hurt her? He touched her gingerly, but she slapped his hand away. He said he hadn't meant it. After all, it was her fault, she was always destroying everything.

His sister sobbed.

He heard the rumbling in the sky. The whole building seemed to shake. The boy ran to the window and climbed on a chair. Planes! Jumbos! And then jet fighters. The heavens were filled with jet fighters. What a sight! His sister climbed up next to him on the chair and clutched his arm.

Suddenly the roof of the house facing them was no longer there. The boy screamed because the window pane splintered in his face. He and his sister ran to the bedroom. They jumped into bed and pulled the blanket over their heads and wept. The boy caressed his sister. He thought, I'll never hit you again, never again, but please, dear God, make the noise stop.

35

Alexander Fuchs crawled into his room, pulled himself up to his desk with a moan, reached for Bertrand Russell's picture, and pressed his face against the old man's countenance behind glass. Help me, he thought.

He foraged through the desk drawer. The manuscript pages of his book *The Dictatorship of the Technocrats* were gone. The bookcase was empty. Russell's works, Von

Neumeyer's *The Destruction of Reason,* Taylor's *The Suicide Program,* the reports of the Club of Rome—just bright spots on dusty wood. The police had even carried off his typewriter, his notebook, letters, the tape recorder.

They had him in their hands now. They would read, they would see that he was struggling on the side of Truth—and they would destroy all the evidence so as to pillory him as a mass murderer. He knew them, the technocrats. They feared the hatred of the population because they knew they were guilty. And that was why they would portray him, Alexander Fuchs, to the people as an object of hatred. He's the one who killed your children, mothers, and fathers. Stone him. They would do everything to prevent people from knowing and punishing their true enemies.

Fuchs laid his head on his arms and sobbed furiously and without tears. His leg hurt. The ache numbed his brains. He mustn't black out now. He mustn't give up. He had to leave something behind in case he died, in case they killed him when they found him. A testament. The Testament of Alexander Fuchs.

He heard the droning of the motors. He crawled to the window.

A silvery troop of giant birds was circling over the town. Something splashed on the street. Fuchs felt a pungent smell in his nose, a smell he knew from airports. A machine dissolved into a harsh ball of fire. The wreckage parts tumbled to the earth.

Other, small aircraft appeared in the sky, very high and in a disciplined formation. Bombs fell, first small, plumping from the tails like stool, then bigger and bigger, pointing straight at him as though they could see.

Fuchs laughed. He pressed Russell's picture to his chest and laughed. They knew he was here. And they were so afraid of him that they had started a war because of him, a war with all the annihilation weapons that technocrats could muster. So that he, Alexander Fuchs, so that his words and his Truth would be wiped out—they were laying an entire city in ruins. How stupid they were. How unteachable. How technocratic. How often they had tried to wipe out ideas by killing people. Yet always, from the ashes of the corpses, the Idea had arisen again, larger, mightier, more indestructible than ever before.

That's what would happen this time as well.

Fuchs saw the first bombs and rockets exploding. They were still far off. He sat down at the desk and wrote:

"I, Alexander Fuchs, am innocent. . . ."

He crossed out the sentence and recommenced:

"I, Alexander Fuchs, am not responsible. . . ."

He crossed out the sentence and recommenced:

"I, Alexander Fuchs, hereby declare that my responsibility for the Helios misfortune. . . ."

He gave up. Words couldn't explain. People had to have faith.

"You must believe," screamed Fuchs and crept out the door. "You must feel it. You must. . . ."

He rolled himself down the steps. He felt no pain. He eyed his twisted leg, the bone sticking out of the trousers like things that had nothing to do with him, like the garbage cans on the corner, the burning automobile on the other side of the street.

He crept outdoors, lay down on his back, pulled himself halfway up and screamed: "Here I am! Don't you see me?! Here I am! Come and kill me! Come and burn the Truth!"

A hundred yards away, a rocket set fire to a gas station.

"You missed!" shouted Fuchs and crawled towards the fire. When he reached the middle of the street, a bomb changed the asphalt into a sea of flames.

36

By the time Andree finished his second Coke, the center of Darmstadt was aflame. The image on the monitors in the airport tower, radioed back by observation planes from over 36,000 feet altitude, was meaningless to someone like Andree not trained to read it. He didn't even know what to do with the dots on the radar screens that sometimes signified an airplane and sometimes nothing. But on the other hand, he could hear the observation reports to the center: "Railroad repair plant burning. . . . Center of town burning. . . . *Wilhelminenenplatz* burning. . . . Orangerie burning. . . . Tank storages burning. . . ."

Every sentence marked off the progress of the destruction. The individual flame focuses, nourished by hundreds of thousands of gallons of fuel, had joined in a gigantic conflagration, that soon covered twenty square kilometers. Any gap was filled within seconds by rockets and napalm bombs.

"The operation is over," said the airport director.

"Let's hope it worked. If not, then you can look up the chancellor and the entire crisis staff and myself in future history books under C. C for 'criminals'. "

The director said, "The evaluators have determined that at the first bombardment there were still a thousand or eleven hundred people left in the town. It is not impossible for most of them to have saved themselves. Of course, that doesn't include the people inside buildings."

Andree caught himself about to say, Thank God there weren't more. He held his tongue and thought: What insanity. That quickly you become used to horror and destruction. That quickly you accept the inconceivable as a reality. A thousand

318

fatal casualties in an accident, a flood or an earthquake or a hurricane, that spelled a catastrophe in the ordered, controlled, civilized world, a catastrophe shaking an entire nation. But when the catastrophe itself became the world order, then we'd be lucky if the disaster didn't rage with its full force. Then the victims wouldn't be mourned. Then we would be relieved about those who might have been struck but were spared. The catastrophe reckoned with percentages, stated the casualty quota of death. And what were a thousand deaths against a risk of one or two million?

"Industry area burning. . . . Castle burning. . . . Pfungstadt burning. . . ."

The airport director pushed a note towards Andree. "These are the provisional losses in the kerosene action. The figures might change because some of the missing machines could have landed in other airports."

Andree read: A Boeing 747 with a two-man crew: Explosion over Darmstadt. A Caravelle 12 with a two-man crew and a Vickers Viscount with a two-man crew collided while trying to land in Frankfurt. A Boeing 707 with a two-man crew during an emergency landing attempt on Federal Highway 81. Missing: a Boeing 747; a BAC 111; a Convair 990 A. . . ."

Corpse statistics, thought Andree. Counting dead people. That'll be our main job during the next few weeks. A thousand people have burned over there to fuel the sacrificial fire that's supposed to drive away the deadly radiation. Old people in tiny apartments, invalids, drunks, kids.

"Are the measuring choppers in the air?" he asked.

"For five minutes already," said the airport director.

"Why aren't those assholes moving?" Andree didn't expect any answer to his question. The longer the observers in their helicopters held up their reports, the longer he could hope. Was the whole thing just a senseless deed of desperation, the idea of a sick man dying at Helios? Was the cloud still drifting towards Frankfurt?

Andree stationed himself behind one of the controllers

and studied the screen. "Where are the choppers?"

The controller pointed his forefinger at white dots on a spotted background.

The teletype rattled. The director waited until the blue strip of paper almost touched the floor. He tore it off and brought it to Andree. He smiled.

Andree read it. He said. "Connect me to Born."

The man at the telephone handed Andree the receiver. "Herr Dr. Born? Born!"

Andree could only hear the humming in the line. He shouted: "Born! Goddamn it! Get on the line." He hung up.

A report came from an observation airplane: "The Helios dome and two adjoining buildings have collapsed. . . . Hardly any flames. . . ."

Andree reached for the phone. He asked for the operations HQ in Frankfurt. The chancellor answered.

"We've done it!" said Andree. "The cloud's dissolving. Frankfurt is saved!"

"Have you reached Born?" asked the chancellor.

"Born is dead," said Andree.

The chancellor was silent. After a pause he said: "Klein called from Bonn. The new operations HQ is set up. Take over there yourself. I'm staying here till Frankfurt's evacuated. There's no acute danger anymore, but the scientists believe that the radiation will rise considerably through fallout in the next twenty-four hours."

"I'll take off immediately. Damnit! It was absolutely unnecessary for him to stay in the plant."

"I already told you once, Eckart, you don't understand us. You're right, but you don't understand us."

Andree walked across the taxi strip to the helicopter. The SA 341 was being checked by anti-radiation people. One stopped Andree. "Were you flying in this?"

Andree nodded.

"Then go to the radiation examination in front of Hall B. This bird's as radioactive as three pounds of uranium."

320

So much for me, thought Andree. Now it's gotten me too. He wondered whether he would manage to call his wife.

In front of the hall stood an anti-radiation man in his yellow uniform. He was waving his geiger counter. To Andree he seemed like an executioner. The geiger counter crackled. Andree licked the sweat from his upper lip.

The anti-radiation man grinned. "What do you want from me? It's only a few milliroentgens. . . ."

Andree grinned back and walked towards the tower to dig up a new chopper.

37

Four nurses were waiting for the children's bus in front of Frankfurt University Hospital. "You'll only stay here for a couple of hours," said a nurse. "Frankfurt has to be evacuated. The hospital patients are being taken to Cologne." Anne kissed Michaela. "Go along with the others. Achim will watch out for you. I'll be right back."

"Where are you going?" asked Berger.

"To the operations HQ. Maybe I can reach Martin—— I mean, Born."

Berger rubbed his nose. "Good luck."

Anne entered the foyer of the high building. A young policeman with a submachine gun stopped her.

"I've got to go the operations HQ," said Anne. "I have to speak to my husband. I am the wife of Dr. Born, the director of Helios." Anne didn't feel she was lying.

"Do you have any identification on you?"

"I had to leave everything behind during the flight."

The policeman telephoned. He shook his head. "Sorry, no

way. You've got to wait a couple of minutes, then one of the men will come down——"

Anne saw that one of the four elevator doors was closing. She ran over and squeezed through the crack. The three men in the elevator eyed her in astonishment.

"Where's the operations HQ?" asked Anne.

"On the tenth floor," said one of the men. "It's already been pressed."

When Anne got out of the elevator, she peered about and then walked towards the big frosted-glass door at the end of the corridor. She paused. She thought, What can I say to him?

Three men walked towards her, pale, drained, their shirts sweated through. The man in the middle was the Federal Chancellor. Anne leaned against the wall. The chancellor was saying to the smaller man to his right, "He wouldn't have stood for any help. It was his decision. We have to respect it. Let's hope he didn't suffer."

"Did you know him?" asked the smaller man.

"Yes," said the chancellor. "I never saw him, but I knew him. I knew Born as well as myself."

Anne walked down the stairs, holding tight to the banister. On the fifth floor, she was apprehended by a policeman.

One hour later, Anne asked about Michaela in the hospital. The head nurse said impatiently, "We're up to our ears in work. I can't worry about every patient."

The hospital was overflowing. Anne wound her way in between the beds and stretchers in the halls. She opened every door and gazed at the apathetic faces in the beds. Michaela wasn't on the first floor.

On the second floor, a furious doctor chased her out of the room in which there were four oxygen tents.

On the third floor, she stopped a nurse who was hurrying to the stairway with a box of ampules.

"The children from Griesheim? Please. Where are they?"

Before the nurse could answer, Anne heard Michaela's voice. She ran past two doors.

There were six beds in the room. The children in the beds

were gurgling and laughing. Two of the children were pressing their lips tightly as they laughed. Their bodies were squeezed into bandages that only revealed parts of their head, and every movement hurt them. Standing on a chair in front of the children, Michaela was making faces with the help of both her hands.

Noticing Anne, she took her finger out of her mouth and smiled. "The doctor said I'm all right." Michaela put her head in Anne's hand. "Don't go away again."

Anne saw Berger standing at the window. She saw only the back of his sweat-drenched white jacket. She took Michaela in her arms and went over to him. Berger gave her a questioning look. Anne shook her head. The sun was setting, but there, where the sky normally glowed around this time, above the rooftops in the west, it was only slightly tinged. In the south, where Darmstandt had been, where Darmstadt was burning, the sky glowed a gloomy crimson. Anne thought she could feel the heat of the burning on her face, and so intensively that it brought tears to her eyes. She cooled her forehead on the window glass.

Berger felt for her hand. Anne let him hold it. With the falling twilight, the glow in the south became brighter.

38

EXCERPT FROM THE REPORT OF THE HELIOS COMMISSION:

34c. The conflagration in Darmstadt drove most of the gases and hot particles several miles up into the atmosphere. Since, towards 20:00, the inversion weather came to an end and the wind reached storm levels between 4 and 6, the radioactive radiation was distributed over large areas. . . .

Over the entire Northern Hemisphere, a rise in radioactivity was registered within two weeks. We may assume that even during the next few years, radioactivity released by the Helios accident will reach the earth through rainout and fall-out. . . .

The most vehement radiation, just hours after the bombing of Darmstadt, was in the Federal Republic north of the Rhine/Main line, Belgium, the Netherlands, Denmark, the GDR, and Poland.

At over a thousand measuring points, one month after the catastrophe, radiation of 150 roentgens and more was registered. Immediately after the catastrophe, the radiation at those places must have reached over 1,000 roentgens.

35a. MATERIAL DAMAGE

The material damage caused by the Helios catastrophe, even taking into account only the territory of the Federal Republic, has not yet been estimated even approximately. The kinds of damage are as follows:

The annihilation of the city of Darmstadt and its entire industry. Annihilation of all the animals, cattle, forests, agricultural surfaces, etc., in an area of 2,000 square kilometers.

The cessation of all agricultural and industrial output in an area of 11,000 square kilometers (main points: Grenzheim/ Darmstadt, Frankfurt, Giessen/Marburg, Kassel/Hanover) for at least two years.

A medium- or long-term evacuation of the above-listed areas, including the large cities. Frankfurt, for twelve months, and Hanover, for three months, should only be entered by selected volunteers for maintaining the necessary functions (gas, water, electricity, fire fighting).

Destruction of private and public property during the evacuation.

Contamination of the ground water in all the radioactive areas, especially along the Rhine.

Closing of the Rhine as a shipping route until further notice.

Closing of federal highways and roads throughout the evacuated areas.

Loss of production because of personal injuries.

35c. PERSONAL INJURIES

1. UNTIL THE DAY OF THE INVESTIGATION

From July 31, of the past year, the day of the catastrophe, until the day of this investigation, May 5, of this year, 22,487 people in the Federal Republic of Germany have died as a result of the Helios accident.

Of these, 4,201 people died, probably without the effect of radioactivity, during the evacuation of the Helios area or during the bombardment of Darmstadt.

18,286 people succumbed to radiation sickness.

9,560 people are still missing.

(Note: Since many areas in which victims are presumed to be cannot be entered (including the major part of Darmstadt), a final count of victims will not be possible for years.

In other countries 2,345 people have died as a result of the Helios accident: 1,013 in the GDR, 502 in Belgium, 223 in the Netherlands, 176 in Denmark, others in Norway, etc.

2. LONG-TERM PERSONAL INJURIES

The number of victims of the Helios catastrophe will be increased by long-term injuries during the coming years and decades. Thus, on April 30, of this year, some 158,000 patients, suffering direct or indirect consequences of the radiation sickness, were being treated in West German hospitals or by West German physicians.

According to the estimates of medical experts, at least fifteen percent of these people will die from the resulting injuries during the next five years, twenty percent during the next ten years.

The number of leukemia cases and other radioactivity-caused forms of cancer (affecting the thyroid and lungs) will increase by at least 400 percent during the next ten years.

Furthermore, miscarriages and deformed babies can be

expected to increase by 250 percent. (The investigations since September of last year have confirmed these estimates.)

36e. THE RADIATION SICKNESS

Aside from the cases in which people were exposed to radiation doses of 15,000 to 50,000 roentgens (presence in the one-mile radius of Helios during the emergence of the molten mass; presence in the direct vicinity of the radiation cloud), the radiation sickness proceeded according to the pattern observed by the Japanese Sassa and Tsuzuki after the atomic bomb explosion at Hiroshima.

First stage (one to ten days):

Symptoms: Nausea, vomiting, diarrhea, fatigue, change in hemogram.

Symptoms sometimes commenced as quickly as three minutes after radioactive contamination. Typically, however, they appeared only after several hours.

The symptoms vanished in some patients on the third day, returning, however, more critically on the seventh or eighth day. About thirty percent of the Helios victims died during the first stage.

Second stage (eleventh day till the sixth week):

Symptoms: Blood dots in the skin and mucous membranes, vomiting of blood, nose bleeds, blood in urine, vaginal bleeding, blood in stool, loss of hair, pneumonia, abscesses, trench mouth, gangrenous tonsilitis, reduction of white and red blood corpuscles.

Some forty percent of the Helios victims died during the first half of the second stage.

Third stage (sixth week to third month):

Symptoms: General improvement, normalizing of the hemogram, but frequent organic dysfunctioning, abscesses.

Some twenty percent of the Helios victims died during the third stage.

Fourth stage (following the third and fourth months):

Gradual recovery with great vulnerability for infections.

326

(Note: "Recovery" indicates overcoming the radiation sickness, but not its long-term effects, such as leukemia, sterility, etc.)

At this time, 8,000 scientists from all over the world are studying radiation sickness and its treatment in the Federal Republic. . . .

40

After the judicial inquiry concerning her involvement in the Helios accident had been cancelled (lack of evidence), Sybille Born opened an antique shop in Munich. Born's insurance coverage had been very good. She now lives alone and drinks a great deal. She fears that she has suffered from radiation near Helios. Every morning she checks her body inch by inch. She will commit suicide the minute she notices the first trace of the sickness.

Peter Larsen, the ex-security chief at Helios, is in the nuclear business again. Thanks to certain connections and the fact that Born's notes on him had been destroyed, he is assistant to the director of a big German nuclear power plant.

Born's secretary, Gerlinde Katz, who was one of the last employees to leave the burning Helios, is missing and presumed dead.

Anne Weiss and Achim Berger are married, with the approval of Michaela. They will have no children.